DANCING *with the* TIGER

DANCING *with the* TIGER

LILI WRIGHT

A MARIAN WOOD BOOK
Published by G. P. Putnam's Sons
an imprint of Penguin Random House
New York

A MARIAN WOOD BOOK
Published by G. P. Putnam's Sons
Publishers Since 1838
An imprint of Penguin Random House LLC
375 Hudson Street
New York, New York 10014

ISBN 978-0-399-17517-6

Printed in the United States of America
1   3   5   7   9   10   8   6   4   2

Book design by Lauren Kolm

For John Bahoric,
who brought me to Mexico,
and for Laila, Sara, and Mercedes,
who made me want to stay

Even in the slums of Mexico City,
pieces of the fallen Aztec Empire keep showing up.

—Craig Childs, *Finders Keepers*

PROLOGUE

The looter dug into the cave with
the fervent touch of a lover. Cranked on meth, he shuddered as he dug,
cursing a lilting lullaby to women and smack. His body smelled. He
noticed, then dismissed it, the way he noticed and dismissed the wet in
the air, his cut knuckles, the dust and sweat that covered his skin like fur.
Lesser men would have whimpered about their knees, their aching backs.
Little pussies. But tweaked, he could work for hours without losing his
cool or quitting from hunger or succumbing to the roar of Aztec ghosts.
Everything that mattered in life was buried, covered up, lost, afraid to
show its true face. Few people had the courage or imagination to dig.

Christopher Maddox was far from home, an American in Mexico,
a college dropout kneeling in the dirt, a holy man. You could find religion anywhere. Two days before, his trowel had hit the leading edge of
an urn or crown, a relic worth enough cash, he hoped, to float him all

the way to Guatemala, where drugs were cheaper than mangoes, where women greeted you with warm tortillas and a goat. *Gua-te-ma-la.* All those soft syllables, adding up to nothing but a hammock and a song. The looter. That's what he called himself. Alter ego, doppelgänger, shadow in the moonlight—the hero of a story that began when a humble man from Divide, Colorado, dug up a treasure that saved his life.

His headlamp slipped. He righted it. Sweat froze in electric beads, a crown circling his forehead. A lot could go wrong underground. *Apocalypse. Asphyxiation. Popocatépetl. The cave that caves in.* Any minute, *pinches federales* could pounce. He picked up his wasted toothbrush and scrubbed, watched stones reveal themselves like a stripper. Sex humped his brain. He dug past time and he dug past death. His skin itched from nerves, the tickle of bugs, the spook of the dark, the thrill of the find.

A shadow caught his eye. Against the cave wall, a figure, a vision: his mother's weathered face flickered across the fissured rocks. Her spotted hand reached for him, trying to yank him back from the abyss. The looter's chest cracked with this new agony. He grabbed his pick, stabbed the ground, not caring what he broke. He just wanted his due. Now. *Ahora. Dá-me-lo.*

An angel sighed. The devil bit his lip. The relic fell loose, five hundred years of Aztec history tumbled into his busted hands. The looter rolled on his heels, giddy, cooing, *Sweet baby Jesus,* because he was no longer in the cave alone. A face stared up at him, a turquoise mask with only one eye.

Into Mexico City he burst, dancing on the points of a star. As his cab roared down Reforma, he rocked the mask in his lap, coddling its splintered face, a mad galaxy of green and blue. Its mouth was a grimace of shell teeth, fully intact. Across its forehead coiled two snakes. One eye was missing. The other had no opening. A mask made for the dead.

He wanted to howl. He wanted to salsa into the snooty antiquities shops in the Zona Rosa, toe-tap into the anthropology museum and see the officials' shock when they realized a penniless gringo had uncovered a national treasure. But more than admiration, more than money or love, he needed a fix.

The cab dropped him at the safe house. Scary fucking place. A compound for *cholos* and bangers, a vault for drug money, a graveyard for the damned, who were chopped into salad and dumped in mass graves, fetid in the wind. They called it a safe house, but no one there was safe. At the gate, the looter flashed his signature cell phone, his only possession of value. Reyes paid the bills. He needed to reach his people 24/7. At the front door, Feo, the human beer can, flexed his gym muscles. Alfonso peered over his shoulder, on tiptoes, in sneakers. Guy was so tatted he didn't need clothes. The word scrawled over his lip formed an illegible mustache.

The looter held out the mask.

Feo turned it over, sneered, offered a grand.

The looter shook his head, disgusted. "I need ten times that."

"You dig. We decide what it's worth."

Fury rose inside him. Stupid, greedy *mensos*. Like his work had no value. History had no value. Nothing had value but their next drug run to the border. He wanted to speak to someone with an IQ.

"Let me talk to Reyes."

Feo grinned. "No one talks to Reyes. No one even *sees* Reyes."

This was true. In three years, the looter had never met the man.

The drug lord was constantly moving, every day a new location, a new face. Mazatlán penthouse. Juárez sewer. A man of a million disguises: grifter, hipster, attorney general. Rumor had it his real face resembled an old man's testicle. Behind his back, people called him that—El Pelotas. Half his right ear was missing. Reyes was high up, a *patrón* who considered himself cultured, collected antiquities by the pound, adored gallery openings and pink champagne. He'd turn up in a *rancho*, toss gold rings to children. Like a magician, he could make men disappear, saw a woman in half.

"Tell Reyes I have something. Tell him this is worth his time."

Feo smirked, eager to watch this debacle unfold. "Oh, *well then*, come in." He swung open the door to an entryway with a circular staircase. "I'll tell the *patrón* his favorite caveman needs to see him right away. Make yourself comfortable. Have a drink."

The looter stood in the gloom with Alfonso. In the next room, a couple of shitty couches faced the world's largest TV. The looter held the mask over his groin, studied the fractured bulletproof windows. The bullets had come from inside.

Alfonso lit a cigarette, blew smoke. "You're a real idiot."

"Regálame un tabaco, compa."

Alfonso threw him a pack and a lighter. "The dying man's last request."

Everyone here smiled and nobody meant it. Footsteps on the stairs. Two sets. The first figure stopped on the landing, left hand on the banister, right in his pocket, gripping a pistol. Reyes was a small man, bow-legged, froglike, his wide chest panting. He wore narrow black sweatpants and a golden poncho. A straw hat streaming with pink ribbons covered most of his face. Some indigenous concoction. The looter was curious about the ear, but lowered his eyes, bit his cheek.

"You wanted to see me?" Reyes's voice was steady and cold.

The looter did some kind of bow, held out the mask. He was proud of his Spanish, knew how to lace it up nice. Humble and flowery. "*Patrón, con todo respeto,* I bring you a magnificent treasure today. It took me two days to remove from a cave."

No response. *No one talks to Reyes. No one even* sees *Reyes.* The looter's throat tightened. He realized his mistake. "This mask is five hundred years old," he went on. "It belongs in a museum. CNN, *National Geographic*—totally viral. It was made to turn a powerful man into a god."

Reyes stared at him like his face was on fire.

The looter tried again, more direct. He was losing his voice, his pants, his bowels. He needed the cash, the rock. He jerked his head, fought to gain control, lifted his chin. "It's worth twenty grand easy, but I'll take ten. Today."

Reyes made no eye contact. At first, the looter thought he'd garbled his Spanish, then he understood a more humiliating truth: Reyes dismissed him as an idiot addict making shit up. A pit of anger caught in his chest. He might do something stupid.

His thigh shook in his jeans. A clock ticked, or maybe his heart.

Reyes threw down a wad of pesos. The bundle lay there, a dead animal no one wanted to touch. Alfonso stepped forward, took the mask. The looter knelt before the money, knew better than to count.

Reyes growled, "Now bring me another."

PART ONE

I've worn a mask most of my life. Most people do. As a little girl, I covered my face with my hands, figuring if I couldn't see my father, he couldn't see me. When this didn't work, I hid behind Halloween masks: clowns and witches and Ronald McDonald. Years later, when I went to Mexico, I understood just how far a mask can take you. In the dusty streets, villagers turned themselves into jaguars, hyenas, the devil himself. For years, I thought wearing a mask was a way to start over, become someone new. Now I know better.

—Anna Ramsey, from her
unfinished memoir, 2012

one | ANNA

She wore black, the color of nuns
and witches, the color of the loneliest corners of outer space, where
gravity prevents all light from escaping, the name given to boxes tucked
into airplanes, the ones that explain the disaster. She chose green earrings to match her eyes, a bra that accentuated her cleavage. The strappy
sandals she fastened around her ankles gave her the three-inch rise she
needed to look him in the eye.

She drove to the Metropolitan Museum of Art, found a garage, let
a valet park her car. The air was so cold she could see her breath.

"I won't be long," Anna told the boy, slipping him a few bucks. "Put
me near the exit."

The reception was already under way. Beneath a cathedral ceiling,
svelte guests murmured small talk and gossip. Gay men in tight pants
and tangerine neckties. Pale nymphs in taffeta miniskirts or cowgirl

braids or Clark Kent glasses, trying to prove they could be beautiful no matter how badly they dressed. Grandes dames, donors, scions of Rockefellers and Guggenheims, women with names like Tooty and Olive, their thinning hair shellacked into gladiator helmets, their spotted wrists weighed down with bangles. The Velvet Underground sang, *"I'll be your mirror."*

Anna plucked champagne from a passing tray, ran her hand down her dress. Her engagement ring caught the light. Familiar faces drifted past. Artists. Celebrities. Critics. A man who had pressed her to sleep with him. She'd told him she didn't do that anymore. She was with David. Monogamous, a virtue that sounded like a disease.

The champagne hit her hard. Anna hadn't eaten since that morning's sugar doughnut. She finished her flute, took another, set off to find David, strolling past Campbell's soup cans, Marilyn, tawdry black-and-white films from the Factory. Everything cheap and loud and repeating itself.

She found him holding court in the Damien Hirst room, schmoozing next to a shark suspended in formaldehyde. Looking into his eyes, she felt nothing. Their three years together, a collapsible hat. Instead of slapping him or sobbing, she dug down deep and pulled up her love, let it radiate across her face. She revealed her whole self, perhaps for the first time. Only hours before, she would have done anything to make him happy.

David acknowledged her with a playful mouth. His circle opened to let her join.

Black, the color of mourning.

Black, the color you could never take back.

"Anna," he said. "You look . . ."

She swept into his arms and pressed her lips over his. Not a cordial peck of recognition or reunion, but a full-body embrace, bare arms wrapped around his head, fingers playing his short hairs, breasts flattening his lapels, pelvis teasing his hips, yes, there. He stiffened, embarrassed, surprised, but then drew her close. Anna put everything she had into the kiss, three years of affection and trust, three years of plans for tomorrow, and the day after that, three years of fucking monogamy. Her warm tongue made the transfer from her mouth to his as her hand entered his breast pocket.

Black, the color of sex.

Black, the color that fire leaves behind.

She let him go. David's forehead creased with confusion. His lips puckered as his long fingers reached into his mouth and withdrew the offending object. Curious guests leaned in; their gleaming faces filled with prurient delight to see the unflappable David Flackston, a curator of modern art at the Met, open his mouth and remove a diamond ring. Even more curious was his new pocket square—a beige pair of ladies' panties.

two | THE GARDENER

When the papershop girl announced
that her family was moving to Veracruz, Hugo felt his blood drain from
his body. He asked *When?* and Lola said *Two weeks* and Hugo said *How
long have you known?* Lola said *They told me yesterday.* Hugo paced the
paper shop, slamming his fist on the counter because she was leaving
him and because in Veracruz every man would see what he'd seen and
smell what he'd smelled and what was now his alone might be stolen by
any man looking for stationery.

Like a good fire, their love affair began with paper. Hugo was writing his cousin in Texas and needed the kind of skin-thin stationery that
makes even the firmest intention seem like a dream. He'd stopped in a
papelería and the girl behind the counter smiled. His stomach tightened. She wore a yellow dress with white bunting, all schoolgirl and
fresh daisy. Her fingerless lace gloves fastened with a snap. The first

customer paid for his pens, the second did his copying. The door jingled shut, leaving the two of them, Hugo and the girl, surrounded by pencils and compasses and pens with invisible ink.

"How can I help you?" she said.

Hugo unrolled his lust, crimson as a Persian rug. The girl twirled her hair, toying with him, promising good service if only he asked. In his mind's eye, Hugo touched her as gently as his nature allowed, tracing his fingertips over her thigh. He was a gardener, a man used to cultivating difficult flowers. His adoration pleased her, he could tell. It pleased her to know he found her irresistible, a pastry in the bakeshop, too pretty to eat. He was a man. Perhaps this alone justified why he wanted the girl in the yellow dress, why he did not ask her age. If she was old enough to work in the *papelería*, she was old enough to handle money and men. Hugo said exactly what he was thinking: "I came here to buy stationery, but then I saw you."

He thought of his wife. Her face came to him in a hard chip of light, an accusation so stark he turned away. Afterward, he did not think of his wife again. Not when he flattered the girl, not when he ran his finger along the underside of her arm. Not the next day, when he brought her yellow dahlias. Or the next, when he led her to the back room, slid his hand between her legs, and discovered the papershop girl went to work every day damp and hungry.

Each afternoon, Hugo returned. He swiped the girl's earbuds, listened to the rhythm of Romeo Santos, then made an indecent proposal of his own. He kissed her ear, combed her hair with his fingers, tattooed her skin with chalk. When a customer called for help ("Is anyone here?"), he pressed a ruler against her throat. After the door slammed, the girl laughed, licked his palm. His desire burned like the end of a match. He wanted to take her youth. He wanted to build her a pyramid that reached the sun. He wanted to put her in a cage and feed her guava and plant his seed inside her every day. He wanted this child to make him a child who would outlive them both. When she took him in her mouth, she called him Papi. She was not really a child. She had breasts, hair. Her lace gloves matched her underwear. She was old enough that he couldn't help her with homework. He shoved her math book across the counter, lifted her dress, slipped inside her, whispering, "Little schoolgirl. This is what I know."

But now she was leaving him. His knuckles bled in the creases. He'd seen men punch walls and now understood the satisfaction. He wound up again.

"*Basta,*" the girl cried, pulling his arm. "I have something to give you."

She dragged him to the back of the store. Hugo collapsed in a chair. The girl nuzzled into his lap, pushed a package toward him. He pulled the ribbon, determined to be gentle, to rouse his best self. A book of Aztec history. He saw she was proud of this adult gift, and he wondered whether she had given him the book because he spoke Nahuatl, the language of the Mexica, his ancestors, one of the original Aztec peoples, or whether she was sending him a message that she would go to university one day, become more than a shopgirl, pregnant at twenty, delivering child upon child, living in a two-room house spiked with metal supports for a second story that would never be built. He flipped the pages—Acamapichtli, Aztec warriors and priests—feeling weak before these brave men. Lola stroked his head, coddling his grief. His hurt hand grasped the hem of her dress.

She read aloud. "*The practice of human sacrifice was fundamental to* the Aztecs' faith. Thousands of men, women, and children were killed each year in hopes of appeasing the willful gods and keeping the fragile universe in balance. On holy days, priests in black robes led victims—warrior, prisoner, slave, or maiden—up the Great Temple and carved out their beating hearts with a flint knife."

Lola noosed her arms around his neck: "If you were sacrificed, how long would your heart beat for me?"

"Forever, my yellow schoolgirl."

Satisfied, the girl seesawed in his lap, blew in his ear, kept reading: "The sacrifice was cooked and eaten, invigorating the living with fresh energy from the dead. Priests hung the skulls on a rack and wore the flayed skins during sacred ceremonies. The morning after the slaughter, the sun rose, proof of the ritual's efficacy. The sky at dawn turned pink, a reminder of the human blood spilled in homage to the deities."

She smiled, flirty, happy. "What sacrifice would you make for our love?"

"I would offer you my heart on a gold plate, and when you ate me, I would live inside you forever."

The girl dropped a flip-flop, wiggled her sparkling toes. "It's like Jesus. The Son of God died for our sins. Now in Communion, we take his body and blood."

"Like love." Hugo peeked beneath her blouse. "I spill my blood for you."

Something inside the girl snapped.

"What blood?" she sneered. "What sacrifice? You come here, spill yourself, and go home to your fat wife and chickens. If you love me, leave your ugly wife and marry me. Punish my father, who watches me through the door when I undress."

Hugo grabbed her chin. "That is a lie. Your father is a lawyer."

"My father is a lawyer who peeks through a crack in the door."

"I will kill him and steal you away."

"You would not dare."

Hugo slapped her. She clutched her cheek, but did not cry. The coldness of her stare stopped his pulse. He buried his face in her breasts, breathed the air she warmed. *She has watched too many telenovelas. She is playing a part.*

"Your father never touched you," he said.

"His desires keep him awake at night. He stalks the hallway like a lynx."

Hugo felt himself slipping backward, losing purchase. He did not want to marry the girl or harm her father. He liked things as they were, the yellow afternoons lined up like books on a shelf. He even loved the paper shop: the smell of ink, the bright pens and notebooks under glass. The shop made him feel like a boy again, only with the bonus of sex, the missing delight every boy senses is his reward if he ever manages to grow up.

"Give me time," he pleaded. "I will arrange things."

But he did not arrange things. Every day, he went home and dug in his flowerbeds and ate food like a hollow man. When his wife asked what was wrong, he said nothing was wrong, and his wife made him tea from plants in the yard and sought advice from a witch doctor, who mixed a love potion that she sprayed in his socks.

three | THE LOOTER

The looter locked himself in the safe-house john, unfolded the money Reyes had thrown him. Two thousand dollars. An insult. A pittance. Degrading to man and mask. To the living and the dead. The looter lifted the window shade, watched night descend. Across Mexico City, mothers fixed dinner. Fathers fell into their armchairs like kings. Children wrote down wrong answers in pencil. Every day ended in darkness.

He lit his last rock.

The rush punctured his psyche, sandblasted his heart, filled him with a glow he could never replicate or describe but, if forced to name, he would have called love. He fell to his knees, pressed his cheek on the cool toilet seat, dreaming a hundred ways to get even with Reyes: rattlesnakes, lead paint, toxic prostitutes. The looter snickered, wishing he had company in his head. A square dance of partners. But it was all high talk. You didn't get even with a drug lord. You got dead.

Who the fuck wears a hat with pink ribbons?

There was one real hitch to his bliss. He was out of crank. Most days, he was one thing or its opposite: In a cave or out. Rich or broke. High or wishing he were more so. This conformed to the Maddox Principle of Opposing Equilibrium, a little theory he'd coined that went like this: His shady life in Mexico was exterior stuff, surface, cover of the book, not the book. What mattered long-term was a man's inside, his core, his heart, mind, soul, *being.* If his insides stayed true, the outside could indulge in sybaritic delights: women, crack, looting. In fact, it would be irresponsible not to. *Because there was time.* Time for hedonism and excess. Time *later* to settle down. Reform. Rise from the ashes for a second act. A third. Wisdom was the rare province offered to those who'd tried everything once.

The faucet dripped. He listened.

He wanted the mask back, but by now Feo had photographed it, logged it in the books. The looter tried to forget the scraps he'd been thrown, but when he closed his eyes, the death mask grinned, ten million bits of turquoise glued onto the shattered face of a man. Its lone eye taunted: *Who the fuck are you? A man or a dog?*

He thought back to high school, how he and his buddies used to cliff jump at Eleven Mile Reservoir. They'd pound a six, staring down two stories of rock at the freezing water, gathering their nerve, until one of them chanted their call-to-arms. *"Dogs, would you live forever?"*

A strip of light shone under the bathroom door. Timeline. Tightrope. Arrow. The looter studied it until he made up his mind.

_____

He snuck out of the safe house, riding an ice skate of adrenaline. Ten minutes later, he reached the orange juice stand. Pico was just a kid but reliable. He wore an Astros baseball cap and a gold cross. His face was round as a plate and just as empty. Pimples. Baby fat. Another *güey* who didn't belong to anyone. Where was his mother? The looter paid cash for his goodies, but didn't know the Spanish word for the last item on his Christmas list. He laid his cheek on paired hands, an angel pantomiming sleep.

Pico laughed. "You have a date tonight?"

The looter cupped his palms. "Big tits."

"Give me a minute. Mind the shop."

Pico popped into a *miscelánea,* returned beaming, brown bag in hand. "Hold on a minute." He cut an orange, squeezed it. Pico always made his clients fresh juice, like he wanted to be sure all his junkies got their vitamin C. Or maybe with pulp under his nails, he appeared legit to the cops, to his *abuela.* He handed over the juice and the bag.

"Hey, some free advice," Pico said. "Take a shower and you won't have to drug her."

The looter gave a wolfy grin. "Hey, more free advice. Ask the pharmacist for medicine to clean up your face."

"Cabrón," Pico swore, but he was smiling, pleased someone had bothered to notice his messed-up complexion.

"Hey, Pico."

"What?"

The looter bowed. Blood rushed to his face. He almost fell over, but righted himself. Harold Lloyd, hanging on a clock. *Safety Last.* He was Everyman. He was Nobody with a capital N.

"Vaya con Dios." He meant this as a joke and he meant this sincerely.

"¿Dios?" Pico chucked the orange peels in the garbage. "We sold God to the Americans with Texas."

"We sold him to the Chinese."

Pico shrugged. Mexicans didn't want to hear about American hardship.

The looter limped down the block, hips stiff from the cave. The limp was new but suited him, a pirate disguise. His hands left sweat stains on the bag. He'd take a bump in the first alley he found. Now always trumped later. The juice made him nervous. Maybe Reyes had poisoned the oranges.

He turned the corner, threw the fucking cup against a wall. The juice dripped down the stucco, a new sun exploding.

That night, he crashed in the safe house. Not that he could sleep. Spirits circled the compound like ghosts, all those dead men—fuckups and cowards, assassins and cons. Who missed them? Who loved them? Who cared enough to sort the arms from the legs? Inside Pico's goodie bag, ten white bullets. It was hard to have confidence in things so small. He stuffed them in his hip pocket. Crafty as Cortés, he set out to explore.

The safe house was a place to flop, store dope, hide stolen cars. From the outside, the place passed for normal: three stories, four-car garage, security wall, grass tough as matches. Inside, the mood was tense, men jacked on coke and paranoia. The first-floor storage rooms were kept under constant surveillance. Normally, the guards huddled on the ground, texting, but tonight the merry threesome played poker: Feo, Alfonso, and some other fool. When the looter strolled up, the men lowered their cards. AK-47s hung from their chests like guitars. Each was working a six of Tecate. A drained liter of Cuervo lay tossed to the side.

"*Señor arqueólogo,*" Feo called out, his face puffy and red, "fetch us more tequila." He lifted his gun halfheartedly.

The looter thought of five things to say, but instead asked, "*¿Dónde?*"

Feo gestured with his gun. "In the basement. Go, faggot. Earn your keep."

The looter found the light switch, headed down the dim stairs, bracing for corpses, but there was just a bunch of yard stuff, barbed wire, dog food, bottles of bleach. A case of tequila sat next to the hot-water heater. He unscrewed a bottle, dropped in Pico's pills, hula dancing them until they dissolved. He didn't budge for a good minute, got stuck there, thinking how most hard things in life were easy, most easy things hard. Then, moving again, he cinched the cap, took the stairs up, two at a time.

"*Caballeros.* Let me break the seal for you." He twisted the bottle open with a maître d's flourish, took a pretend swig.

Feo glared. "He's drinking before us. What kind of service is that?"

Alfonso curled his tatted lip. "Shoot him."

Feo snuggled his gun into the looter's rib cage. It rested there, a thing that could go off. Saliva clogged the looter's dry throat. You couldn't argue with stupidity. You had to wait it out.

The third guy grabbed the bottle, drank, wiped his mouth. "If you shoot him, I'm not cleaning it up. You can explain to Reyes what happened to his precious digger. If not, it's your turn."

Feo stared at the punk. He had a new enemy. He shifted his gun to face the third man. He wouldn't pop him, but if the gun went off, the bullet wouldn't be wasted.

"Play your cards," Feo snarled. "Pass me the bottle."

The looter evaporated, locked himself in the john to wait. He stared at the lonely faucet, the grout, the feminine curves of the pedestal sink, put a name to what he'd committed to: He was risking his life to screw over Reyes. That, or he was finally standing up for himself.

A half hour later, he tiptoed back to the hall. The guards lay splayed, heavy with sleep. He tapped Feo's thick shoulder. Nothing. The looter entered the first storage room, switched on his headlamp. Bricks of marijuana were piled knee-high. Without warning, the third guard lifted his head. The looter flattened into a shadow, closed his eyes. He could die here or he could not die here. The precariousness of the moment brought fresh understanding. Fuck Guatemala. He needed to go home. Make amends. Pay his mother back the three grand he'd stolen. Buy her a new microwave. Rub her fallen arches.

He willed the guard to drop back asleep. As if by command, the man collapsed, curling into a comma, a messy hunk of punctuation, silent again.

The looter's hands trembled as he opened the second door. The room was a wreck of duffel bags, helmets, and guns. His fingers played over shelving crammed with relics—pots, urns, magical flutes, pieces he'd sold to Reyes months ago lay stacked without order or care. A take-out fried chicken container rested on a hammered gold mask. A bully stick balanced on a Mayan urn. Reyes claimed he was an art collector, but he needed Gonzáles to tell his head from his ass.

On the bottom shelf, a familiar blue face glared up at him. *Motherfucker, get me out of here.*

The looter lifted the mask, already calculating his next move. He'd send Gonzáles a photo, have the asshole dealer find a buyer with deep pockets. No need to mention this hiccup with Reyes. Just tell Gonzáles that Reyes had passed on it.

Mask so nice he'd sell it twice.

Floating out of the vault room, he murmured a cradlesong to the junkies and hit men. *Sleep, little babies. Sleep, beautiful boys.* Even the worst men looked innocent when they slept. Their faces were the masks they'd wear when they died. Their own faces, at peace.

Gliding into the perfumed night of Mexico City, the looter whispered, *"Col-or-a-do."* The death mask grinned in his satchel.

four | ANNA

Anna drove fast. Windows open despite the cold. Bare trees, stone walls, classic rock on the radio. Every song reminded her of slow dancing in somebody's basement. She was not loved. She was not lovable. Both were her fault.

The plan was to go home and see her father in Connecticut. Away from the city, she'd regroup, the polite euphemism for figuring out what the hell to do next. She'd have to tell her father she'd changed her mind and needed the money after all. Find out when it was coming, and how much. She'd leave David, move out. Cancel the wedding. Cancel the honeymoon. No moon. No honey. What an idiot she'd been to become so dependent, a fat tick on a dog.

She sipped Jose Cuervo from a dirty coffee cup. Its vomitlike after-taste coated her nostrils. Exhaustion blanketed her cheekbones. She'd hardly slept. After her exquisite departure in her black-cat dress, she'd spent the night on her yoga friend Harmonica's futon, working a bottle of chardonnay, weeping, checking her phone for messages, wondering if David was devastated or relieved. How had she missed the signs? There was that night, post-Chinese, when he'd said: *I don't feel close to you.* She'd been sitting right next to him and joked: *How much closer can I get?* Apparently, his new assistant, Clarissa, got really close. Apparently, *many* women enjoyed getting close to David's video camera. Who did he think he was—Andy Warhol?

She should have skipped the nap. She'd always hated naps, the way they sucked the life out of you, but she'd wanted to be fresh for David's opening, ready to put on a brave face. If "schadenfreude" was the word for taking pleasure in another's pain, what was the word for resenting a loved one's success? Pettiness. No, treason. Of course, she hoped David's show would light up the art world. She wanted that for him, but even more, she wanted that for herself—and her father.

The guest room had been spotless when Anna slipped into the sheets. Monogrammed. DOF. David Oliver Flackston. A present from his mother. The narrowness of the single bed comforted her, like she was a visitor in her own life. An hour later, she woke, stretched her legs, fished up something soft buried at the foot of the bed. Tan and lacy, a mouse of silk. *This was not her underwear.* These beige, nude, sand, camel, fawn, biscuit, buff, ecru bikini panties with peekaboo lace on either hip could have belonged to David's skinny younger sister, only he didn't have one. A guest, perhaps. *What guest?* It was the kind of skimpy underwear Anna wore when she slept with men she barely knew. Underwear she wore before David.

Into his closet she stalked, swatting hanging shirts, digging through drawers, looking for what? A business card? More lingerie? Who walks out of an apartment without underwear?

David's laptop sat close-lipped on his desk. Anna opened the top drawer, where a dozen typed passwords had been taped for safekeeping. Google user name: *DFlackston*. Password: *Plastic*. She had never done this before.

His in-box was bland, a million urgent e-mails about the opening. The "Personal" file had notes from his mother. The "Taxes" file? Dry stuff. "Insurance?" *Insurance!* Why, lookie here. E-mails from Clarissa. With attachments. Two more clicks and Anna saw Clarissa. Young, fit, gymnastically inclined Clarissa, wearing no underwear at all. There were other files. Other women. A regular art collection.

At the stoplight by Swifty's, Anna sloshed herself more tequila. She ate a pickled egg she'd fished from a glass jar at the packy. Protein. Hydration. If she ate little enough and drank a whole lot more, she might slip through a keyhole into a new world. What was the etiquette for recalling 150 "Save the Date" cards? Or did bad news trickle down the street on its own, like sewer water after a downpour?

Strip-mall traffic. Hardee's. Subway. Red light. Anna checked her face in the mirror. Time for an extreme makeover. Forget being the devoted fiancée, the risotto maker and Pilates babe, the recycler who separates trash. Bring on the old Anna. Drinker–smoker–lovable slut. If a misogynist was a man who hated women, what was a woman who hated men?

Smart.

At the market, she bought groceries. All her father ate was cheese and peanuts left over from Christmas. She'd fix him lunch. Five food groups. Cloth napkin. Steering up his pea-pebble driveway, Anna felt her head was about to explode. The dilapidated house, another failure. Warped porch. Cracked paint. Sad bushes. How could someone devoted to art let his home deteriorate this way? A layer of snow lined the house and the yard, as if nature thought it best to cover the whole mess with a dropcloth. When he sold the collection, she'd insist on a paint job.

She popped a mint, slammed the car door, crossed the frozen yard. What would she tell him? Her father had introduced her to David. They'd met at a fund-raiser. David had hidden his disdain for masks. Her father had hidden his disdain for Warhol. Soon enough, they had Anna in common.

She reached the porch, grabbed the banister. A heavy emptiness filled her torso and shoulders, making it hard to stand straight. Posture. Her mother had been big on that. Her mother. Anna looked across the field. She could see the pine tree from here.

Anna knocked, pushed open the front door.

Her father sat in his usual plaid chair. Although Daniel Ramsey saw virtually no one, the collector still dressed with care, as if at any moment he might receive a museum official or give a university talk. Pleated pants. Collared shirt. His favorite goofy explorer's vest, a multi-pocketed khaki affair that made Anna cringe.

He rose, his worn face brightening. He was always happy to see her, which made her feel guilty. She should stop by more often. "What a nice surprise."

Anna hugged him, smelled his breath. Force of habit. After her mother's death, her father drank with the same gusto he applied to acquisitions. His collection of Mexican masks was reputably the largest in the country. His drinking had been equally epic. It took a fender bender to persuade him to go to treatment, which he grudgingly attended, though Anna still worried. She dropped the groceries in the kitchen, went to the living room couch. She had planned to tell him everything, but now the bad news stuck in her throat.

"How was the opening?" he asked, sitting back down. "I could have gone, you know."

Anna was always steering her father away from the proverbial punch bowl. "Full of Warhol wannabes. You would have hated it." She scanned the living room. The walls were riddled with tiny holes, as if from a shooting spree, the only clue that dozens of masks once hung there. Anna sat down, forced out the words. "You remember how I said I didn't need my share of the money, that you should invest it? Well, I might need it after all."

Her father rubbed his jaw, not meeting her eyes.

"Have they signed yet?" Anna asked. "You never give me updates."

He stared out the window into the cold. "There's been a little hitch." He rallied a halfhearted smile. "Let me put it this way: There's good news and bad news."

Anna sat up, wary now. "What bad news?"

"I'll let you read it for yourself." He hobbled to his desk, handed her a letter from the Metropolitan. Anna skimmed the opening paragraph of pleasantries and then read: *"Regretfully, the Museum must suspend negotiations regarding the purchase of the Ramsey mask collection due to worrisome inconsistencies and inaccuracies in its documentation. Any information about the provenance of the masks, particularly receipts of sales, would help our investigation. Specifically, we have concerns about the masks attributed to Emilio Luna and Ricardo Rodríguez. There appears to be adulteration, antiquing, and artificial rusting. We are also unsure about the veracity of your book* Dancing with the Tiger, *where the same worrisome misinformation is presented as fact."*

Anna's mouth went dry. "What worrisome misinformation?"

"There's a second sheet with an inventory."

"After taking wood and paint samples, our curatorial team has con-

firmed the Centurion mask in the collection, reproduced on page 37 of the book, is not turn-of-the-century, as claimed. It appears to have been carved within the past decade. Contrary to claims made on page 122, Grasshopper masks were never danced in a town called Santa Catarina. There are nine Santa Catarinas in Mexico, but none holds a 'Harvest Dance.' These masks appear to be purely decorative, likely carved for commercial sale."

Anna skimmed ahead. Not only was the Met backing out of the sale, it had trashed *Dancing with the Tiger*, the book Anna had helped write. For decades, her father had dreamt of publishing the first definitive guide to Mexican masks, but he never would have finished if Anna hadn't quit her editorial job and stepped in to help. Since then, she had subsisted on fact-checking gigs—and David.

Anna flopped back in the couch. "I can't believe it."

"They will have a field day with this online when it breaks."

"When it breaks?" It hadn't occurred to Anna the disgrace would be public. Who would hire a fact-checker who couldn't get her own book right?

Her father grimaced. "It's a juicy little story for the bloggers. Some will accuse us of fraud. Others will be nice and say we're incompetent."

Anna's shame twisted into anger. "You know more about Mexican masks than anyone in the country."

"Anyone can be fooled."

"You were drinking."

"You would blame global warming on my drinking. That's over. I'm as dry as that plant."

The plant, an ivy, was near death. Anna checked the letter's date. January 5, 2012. "This was sent a month ago. Did you ever respond? They're asking for documentation. Don't you have something?"

"My journals, but nothing official enough to please them." He set down his glass with a frown. "Why should I make their case? Let them send a nice art history docent into the jungle to verify things. Do they think I buy these masks at gift shops?" He hiked his voice into a falsetto. *"Excuse me, Mr. Carver. Do you gift wrap? Oh, and I'd like an itemized receipt with that."*

"It's my fault. I should have gone down there. You expect forgeries in fine art or antiquities, but folk art?"

"The art of forgery is as old as art itself. It's not your fault. The book was my responsibility."

He shifted the crank so the footrest of his recliner rose, then crossed his hands over his belly and closed his eyes, as if something had been decided.

"I need that money," Anna said. "*You* need that money. That's your retirement." His calm infuriated her. "You don't seem that upset."

"I was irate, but not anymore."

"They could be wrong. *You* know the carvers, they don't."

"I suspect what they say is true. But you're forgetting the good news."

"What good news?" Anna nearly spat. She had lost her fiancé and a family fortune in less than twenty-four hours.

"Yesterday I got the most remarkable e-mail from Mexico."

He lowered his footrest, passed her his laptop. On the screen was a turquoise mosaic mask with blockish white teeth. One eye was missing. She noted these basics without enthusiasm.

"Nice mask." She couldn't have cared less.

"Magnificent mask. Sixteenth-century. Aztec. Just dug up in Mexico City. It's for sale. Lorenzo Gonzáles is brokering the deal—"

"Who found it?"

Her father shifted in his chair. "A twigger."

"A what?"

"A twigger. A tweaked digger. A meth addict. An American."

"How would an American twigger even get to Mexico?"

"He took a bus, I imagine."

Anna rolled her eyes. Other daughters weren't doing this.

Her father nibbled the end of his glasses. "He's a rather *famous* twigger in some circles."

"Famous for what?"

"A soft touch. A keen eye. He's not an archaeologist, but he's made significant finds. He's lucky. Got a sixth sense." Her father swelled with avuncular pride, whether for himself or this digger Anna couldn't tell. "The drugs help, of course. He's driven. Always needs more money, more dope. Terribly sad, but what can you do?"

"Send him to rehab."

"I am not his mother."

"Or father—"

"These twiggers work like camels, go days without eating." Her father leaned into his story, voice warming. "Hoover sites, don't leave a scrap. And this one is the best. Here. I am forwarding you Gonzáles's e-mail."

"How much?"

"Ten grand."

Anna groaned.

He finished his drink, whatever it was. Everything he drank looked like water. "This is a pre-Columbian funerary mask. Five hundred years old. A collector's dream, and I have first crack at it. I'm flying to Oaxaca tomorrow to meet Gonzáles. He'll oversee the sale. He gave me his word—"

"How much does that cost?"

"Two-grand commission, and worth every penny. Gonzáles directed the anthropology museum in Oaxaca. Now he's a premier dealer in pre-Columbian art. Top of the line. Whatever he says about a piece—"

"I know. I spoke with him on the phone multiple times. That's the good news? Another mask?"

He ignored her tone. "I wired Gonzáles a deposit. We have an exclusive until Wednesday. I pay the looter directly when I see him. Cash in hand." He pointed to his bedroom, where presumably the money was waiting. "Of course, it would be easier to fly directly to Mexico City, but Gonzáles insists in meeting first in Oaxaca. What can you do?"

Outside, sodden snow had sunk into gray banks. *The average dream lasts about twenty minutes,* a fact Anna had read somewhere, remembered. She had a knack for that: getting little things right and big things wrong. Their book sat on the coffee table. Anna gave it a shove. "Let's face it, the Met isn't buying, and no mask is going to change that. There's not going to be a big 'Daniel Ramsey' in gold letters over the door."

Her father straightened, indignant. Anna knew what was coming.

"This is not about me," he said icily. "The Met is the largest museum in the United States. Four hundred galleries. More than fifty galleries of Asian art, seventy-two galleries of European painting. Guess how many rooms are dedicated to art of the Americas? Three. It's an embarrassment, and they know it. The Met is an encyclopedic museum with many pages missing. *Some people,* apparently, are invisible. The art of *some* countries doesn't matter."

"Dad, I know." She had heard this rant a million times. "They are *still* not going design a gallery for one mask."

"They will for this one. For this one mask, the Rose White Ramsey

Gallery will open with a black-tie reception and international press. Our book will be reissued with proper clarifications. The mask will be featured on postcards and T-shirts. This twigger is a fine digger, a connoisseur of controlled substances, I am sure, but no art historian." He was practically levitating. "This is not some two-bit relic he's dug up. It's *Montezuma's funerary mask.*"

This new absurdity took Anna a moment to absorb. Her father's eyes gleamed. He believed this. He wanted her to believe it. He was drunk. Dry drunk, whatever that meant.

"*The* Montezuma?" she said at last. "There's no such thing." Even as she dismissed this, she remembered reading rumors she'd discounted as apocryphal. Like the Loch Ness monster and the blood-sucking *chupacabra*. "And you believe in this mask because some drug addict sent you an e-mail."

"Gonzáles sent the e-mail. He trusts his digger implicitly."

"Gonzáles," Anna scoffed. "I don't trust any of them. And even if it's true, how are you going to smuggle it over the border? In your boxers?"

"I am done playing fair."

"What's that supposed to mean?"

"Gonzáles will give the mask a legal provenance, say it was part of 'an old European collection.' Prior to 1970. Prior to UNESCO. Another fee, but so be it."

"So he's a liar, too. I thought he was a respected—"

"To accomplish a greater good. He wants *me* to have the mask for the Ramsey Collection. If I don't buy it, Malone will. Then no one will see it but his housekeeper and her feather duster. Or Reyes will use it as a doorstop."

Thomas Malone was her father's friendly rival, a man Anna had never met but loathed anyway. Malone was younger, richer, and lived in Oaxaca, all sources of envy. Óscar Reyes Carrillo was a Mexican drug lord, whom her father knew only by reputation, from hushed conversations in art circles.

"Or . . ." her father continued, "it will be put in a Mexican museum and stolen within the year."

"It's not that bad."

"You know how much a Mexican museum guard earns? Two-fifty a week. You think he's not corruptible?"

"So we'll steal the mask first? That's the American spirit."

"We are not *stealing* anything." Her father's face reddened. "Current cultural property law ignores the essential role the collector plays. *We* are the ones who safeguard art. We hold it and preserve and protect it from scoundrels. What did Hernán Cortés do when Montezuma gave him gold goblets? *He melted them down.* Furthermore, you forget, the gallery is not in my name. It's the *Rose White Ramsey* Gallery. It was your mother's money. My work, but her money. She loved those masks as much as I did."

Love. It justified anything. It was why he drank. Why he collected. Why he had never remarried. Her father had never recovered from her mother's sudden death. Well, neither had Anna. She was only ten, a girl, *a little girl who'd grown up without a mother.* She resented her father's epic descriptions of his loss. By magnifying his sorrows, he diminished her right to her own.

"Mom didn't love masks." Anna's voice was flat, lifeless. "She loved you. She loved Mexico."

Her father's hands pulsed. "Any great achievement requires commitment and dedication. Your mother understood that."

"You never even buried her." Anna stared into the bedroom. "Always another excuse. *Oh, my knees. My back. There's this mask I want to buy. . . .* She wanted to be in Mexico."

Her father picked up his drink. Anna eyed it suspiciously. They had entered new terrain. She wasn't sure what he'd do or say.

"Ashes," he snorted. "A silly romantic idea she wrote in her journal and now you hold me to it. Your mother's gone. Nothing I do will change that. But this death mask could bring the Ramsey Collection back to life."

Anna grabbed the laptop, marched to the kitchen. Hit Google.

"Go ahead," her father called from his chair. "Look it up. Read the history. There's a mask drawing in the Codex Mendoza that's an exact match. Snakes across the forehead, the warts. Turquoise and jade were more valuable than gold because green stones offered protection in the underworld. The *sitio* makes perfect sense. A half mile north of the Templo Mayor. Montezuma would have been buried in secret. Mexico City is a graveyard. The government has no idea what's underground. The entire city should be excavated, but there's no money. Who do you favor? The living or the dead? The present or the past? . . . Are you reading?"

"I'm reading."

"Go to the British Museum. They have the largest collection of mosaic—"

"I'm there."

Anna cinched her hair into a ponytail. "Montezuma the Second died in 1520. He was either stabbed by the Spanish or stoned by his own people for trying to placate Cortés. His death was unexpected. He was fifty-three. His body was thrown in the river. No mention of a mask. No, wait, his servants rescued and cremated him. . . . *It was customary for royalty to be buried with masks to ensure their safe travel in the afterlife, but no one has ever found Montezuma's funereal mask. Collectors have been looking for centuries. . . .* Blah, blah. *Holy grail.* Please. *Such a treasure would be priceless.*"

Anna studied the fridge. It was empty, but you couldn't tell that from the outside. "What's the going rate for priceless? For the Mexican Tutankhamen?"

Her father coughed up something nasty. He did that a lot. It was getting worse. "Crass comparison. The truth is, I don't know. Six million. That's a wild guess. No less than that certainly. I'd give you the money. You'd be free. Your children would be free."

Anna didn't care about her children. She cared about David. A sordid daydream was forming.

Her father read her mind. "I'd like to see David's face at the next curators' meeting when he hears the news. I don't think he fully appreciates what we do."

Anna would like to see that face, too.

Her father coughed again. He was in no shape to travel. His knees were bad. His Spanish was never great. He forgot to fill the bird feeder, pay bills. He was a weak man with large passions or a large man with weak passions. She should have forgiven him by now. She was trying.

"This is the last mask." His voice barely reached her. "The last mask will save the rest. Your mother deserves this."

"Give me a minute. I'm still reading."

But she wasn't reading. She'd drifted into her father's bedroom. On the bureau, she found a bank envelope filled with crisp hundred-dollar bills. She pocketed it, removed her mother's urn and journal from the closet. The urn was Mexican *talavera*, blue and white, sealed with a cork. She brought the urn, journal, and envelope into the kitchen, set them on the breakfast table. Now what?

Her father was still talking, his voice subdued, almost contrite. "I won't do it, if you're really opposed. I don't want to fight about it. Tell me what you think. I trust your opinion."

That hurt. It hurt because he meant it. He was relying on her judgment now. This natural transference should have pleased Anna, but instead it filled her with a strange loneliness. She went to the sink, got herself a glass of water. Her eyes were dry. Her stomach hurt. Her mother had washed dishes in this sink. She'd worn rubber gloves. She propped avocado seeds on toothpicks, waited for roots to grow.

"Dad, where *are* your masks?"

"In the basement. The Met shipped them back. Forty-two boxes."

She heard the pain in his voice. Her father had been so strong since he quit drinking, but how much disappointment could he take?

Anna squeezed the bridge of her nose. She wanted to feel lucky, a woman capable of finding love and treasure, but it was February and the trees had no leaves and her father wanted to go back to Mexico, where her mother had died, and maybe he didn't care if he died there, too. He loved her but considered documenting Mexican art a higher purpose, his calling, and maybe it was. She was too old to play the needy child, but it was hard to argue away this hollow feeling.

"What are you doing in there?" he called out.

"Making you lunch." She had another thought. "Did this twigger find an urn with the mask? Or was it sitting there all by itself?"

"I heard nothing about an urn."

Anna peeled off bacon and dropped it in a frying pan. The heavy smell of grease made her woozy with nostalgia. She and David cooked bacon every Sunday and made love and read the paper as the morning light grew stronger.

She wiped her father's counters with a warm sponge. Outside, three crows flew across the pallid sky. An omen of death. A loaf of white bread lay open on the counter. Another omen of death. Everything was an omen of death, if you thought about it long enough. Expiration dates. The freezer. The broom. The dustpan. The recyclables. Save the date.

Only plastic lived forever. Plastic was happy.

When the bacon was crispy, she made a sandwich, piled on mini carrots, a multivitamin garnish, set the plate on her father's side table.

"Forget about Mexico," Anna said, not meeting his eyes. "The death mask is just another lie."

She left before he could argue, muttering that she had to run out. And she did run out, with the journal, the urn, and the envelope.

five | THE GARDENER

It was nearly midnight and Hugo
knelt in his flowerbed planting dahlias, thinking of the papershop girl.
Lightning bugs circled the yard. Cryptic warnings. Across the valley,
fireworks exploded, light but no noise. Dogs howled with longing.
Every tuber he planted was her. Over and over, he covered her round
hips with dirt and patted her behind with his trowel so she would stay
put, grow, flower before him, as she did every afternoon.

It was easy to love two women, but impossible to leave one for
another.

He and Soledad had built their lives together. Each object in their
home had a story, a familiar weight. They had boiled beans in the bean
pot, drawn the curtains to make love, washed their feet in a bucket.

"*¿Tú vienes?*" Soledad appeared in the doorway, a shadow in a robe.
Her hair hung loose around her shoulders.

"Soon," he called back. "I have another row to plant."

"You are excessive in everything . . ."

Hugo banged his lover's rump, blew the dirt for luck. "I am the man you married."

"What was I thinking?"

He shook his trowel at the stars. "You should have married Him."

"Who?"

"God. Imagine the house. A villa in Huatulco."

Soledad smiled wryly. "God lives in Cancún."

"With all the tourists?"

"God would banish the tourists and have the warm water all to Himself."

"Then why hasn't He done it?"

"He is waiting for me."

Hugo threw a pebble at the screen door.

Soledad jumped. "You're in a bad mood."

"It's my mood. Let me have it."

A minute of quiet, then an accusation: "You are just pretending to plant dahlias."

Hugo dropped his trowel, impressed. "Pretending?"

"You say you are planting dahlias, but that is not what you are really doing."

"What am I really doing?"

"I don't know, but if I knew, I would make you stop."

"Stop trying to be clever." His wife was not a beautiful woman— her younger sister Sonia was lovelier but forever dissatisfied—still, in this light, she glowed with warmth and comfort, a gift of the moon.

"Come to bed," she told him. "You have work tomorrow."

"I am working hard now, extra jobs."

Hugo did not tell his wife that the drug lord Óscar Reyes Carrillo had offered him a hundred times his normal pay to make a pick-up in Tepito. He and Pedro, together. If the job was done right, more work would follow. Hugo knew that Reyes sought him out because he worked for Thomas Malone, and someday Reyes would exploit this connection, but Hugo planned to be long gone before that day arrived.

"We are close," he said. "Are you ready?"

"I've been practicing English."

"We are going to ditch the *gringo de mierda*."

Soledad hurried across the yard, glancing behind at the chapel. The red light was on, as it always was late at night. *"Shhhhhhhh."*

Hugo shooed her worries with his trowel. "He can't hear."

Soledad pulled him. "Come to bed. *Ya basta*."

"Leave me alone, woman!"

"You are shivering."

She ran inside, returned with a blanket, draped it over his shoulders. Though he was grateful, he did not thank her. His fingers were stiff. His calf muscles ached. He was burying his lover. His wife did not appreciate this sacrifice. He dared not point it out.

"What color will the flowers be?" Soledad was crouching, whispering into his neck. Her breath smelled like chamomile and honey.

"Yellow."

"Yellow and what?"

"All yellow."

She flinched, then wrapped her arms around him, the way a mother wraps a naked child in a towel after a bath. He let himself be held. When she spoke, she chose her words with care. "If all the flowers are yellow, our garden will be the most beautiful in Oaxaca. Tell me again how close we are."

He pulled her into his lap, listened to the frogs sing about rain. "Halfway. Maybe more. We can stay with my cousin in Texas." The sureness of this one fact made all the suppositions surrounding it seem possible. "We will leave on a warm night, ride the bus with a picnic of *tortas* and fruit, cross the river on a raft. Jaime will fix us a mattress on his floor. We will sleep without worries on borrowed white sheets. In the morning, I will earn our first dollar. We will press it in a book and give it to our children when they go to university and become doctors and lawyers who take their families on vacation in Cancún, where God has a time share."

He tugged her waist. "The Virgin will watch over us."

The same fairy tale was told all over the valley. Hugo tilted his head, watched the stars, but could not imagine God, or even God's mother, looking down on him with anything like love. Somewhere, the papershop girl was curled in her sheets, one pretty foot curved into the arc of the other, lace gloves paired on her desk. His wife's hair pressed against his throat. All he could see was darkness.

six | THE HOUSEKEEPER

"Santísima Virgen, mother of us all, it's Soledad again. I know it's late, but I cannot sleep. Hugo says we will leave soon for *el otro lado*. I am scared, *Virgencita*. I should be happy, but I don't want to live with Hugo's cousin in Texas. Jaime snorts all day, with his clogged sinuses, and Alicia lets cats eat from her plate. These relatives do not love us. They do not want us to sleep on their floor. I tell Hugo I want to go with him so he will not leave me behind. Men who go to the North by themselves are seduced by American sluts who lift weights in gyms with their boy bodies, and when the men return home they don't love their wives or their country anymore. I am learning English. *Hallo. How are you? My name iz Soledad.* Are the days nicer in the United States? They say so. I hate Sam's Club, *Virgencita*. There is one in Oaxaca, as you know. Towers of cereals and jam and televisions touch the ceiling. I am ready to live in

a box and eat from a box and drive in a box and shop in a box, but how will I get pregnant without Señora Magda's rose water? The last time there was so much blood I thought I was dying. Even chubby Leticia is pregnant again. After we make love, I lie in bed and imagine my womb is a garden. Sometimes I want to stand naked in a field and shout at God. Shake my fist. How do you get His attention? I worry Hugo keeps another woman. He doesn't smell right and he looks guilty when I hold him. Make me strong, blessed Virgin. You see how confused I am. My thoughts are dirty laundry in a basket. Sometimes I listen outside Señor Thomas's chapel. Maybe the sounds I hear are nothing, a movie or a dream, but the big house vibrates with bad feeling. I pray none of its sickness touches us."

seven | ANNA

Anna drove past barren fields,
pole barns, and warehouses. February outside. February inside. The
trees were skeletons against the dun sky.

She could drive back to David.

She could drive back to her dad.

She could drive west until she reached the desert and lie under a
tree.

Instead, she forced down a sick cocktail and ranted to the radio.
I travel the world and the seven seas. Everybody's looking for something.
Outside Norwalk, she stopped at a discount cigarette shack. They only
sold cartons. She bought 199 more cigarettes than she needed.

Driving, smoking, she inventoried all the ways she hated David.
She hated his face. His intense blue eyes, wide forehead, the way his
thin lips conveyed simpering confidence. How he pushed food around

his plate when it wasn't up to snuff. She hated his elite art friends with their judgments of worth and good taste. His inability to relax—always fidgeting a crossword or a German dictionary, his ambition brooding like bad weather. How dare he assume his own handsomeness with such smug regard? She hated his bulletproof résumé. He'd never scooped an ice cream cone. Never bagged groceries. His first internship in high school was at the Guggenheim. Paid.

But she had fallen in love with him. It was true. She could pinpoint the moment. He had been leaning against a wall at a party, holding a beer by its neck, eyeing her, glib. Was that the word? Charming? Consuming her. Talking Warhol. "He said he didn't have to *explain* his art. It was all right there. On the surface."

Could hate replace love in an instant? No, it could not. Hate had not replaced love. She now loved him *and* hated him. F. Scott Fitzgerald said the ability to hold two opposing emotions while still functioning was a sign of intelligence. That made her a fucking genius. Except she wasn't functioning. She was drinking Cuervo. She was ripping her thumbs, wiping the blood on her boots.

By evening, she was back in Brooklyn. Harmonica was spending the weekend at an ashram in Vegas. The Post-it on the fridge read: *Center. Stretch. Olive Leaf Extract 2X a day. xoxoxo.* Anna filled the tub, propped the urn next to the herbal shampoo. Wineglass in hand, she sank low in the water, tried to picture her mother's face, the shape of her fingers on the piano, her knees. Her parents had met at an auction. Her mother had kept the books for an architectural salvage shop, pricing corbels and Tiffany lamps. It wasn't much of a stretch to move from antiques to masks, to fall in love with a man who collected. Would her mother have chased a death mask? Of course she would have. She had. She had risked her life to help Anna's father, and that was why she was dead.

When the bath water cooled, Anna got out and dried herself, put on a dress, no underwear, set the urn next to her computer. Photographs of the Warhol opening had been posted online. David posing with the director of the Met. David posing with a woman posing as Edie Sedgwick. David posing with Clarissa. Clarissa was younger than Anna, shorter, perky, enormous teeth. David looked happy, relieved.

Maybe she had never been right for him. David with his Ivy League degrees, Nantucket summers, his imported peppered crackers. Her previous boyfriend had given her a sweater for her birthday. David gave her a nineteenth-century etching of Aphrodite. Yes, he came from money, but he worked hard, appraising, appreciating, in a way that made Anna go limp when he was admiring her. She was happy to be swept out of her mediocrity, to join the art world of the little black dress. True, her father was an art collector. But without an art degree or museum pedigree, Daniel Ramsey was a scrappy amateur, acting from the gut, which Anna both admired and distrusted.

She took down their book from Harmonica's shelf, slumped on the couch. The masks were as familiar as friends: the glaring Moor, the lewd *negrito* from Tabasco, the *chivo* mask with real horns. Anna's favorite was the plainest: a concave slab of wood painted pine green, beak for a nose, two square eyes about the size of Scrabble tiles, and a ragged slash of a mouth, frozen in a worried intake of breath. What this bird or person, this bird person, wanted most of all, it seemed, was to fly away.

Grief rose inside her. Now she was combing through her mother's ashes, sifting the gravel as if she might find something precious inside.

A last note. Her mother's voice. Anna opened her journal, found the diary entry she'd read many times, a series of Juan Rulfo passages that her mother had copied down in Spanish. Back in high school, Anna had snuck a translation of them inside the journal for safekeeping. She liked to read the Spanish for the sound, the English for meaning.

"I've finished *Pedro Páramo*, the Juan Rulfo novel. Beautiful but spooky. The narrator's dying mother makes him promise to visit Comala, the village where she was born. *'There you'll find the place I love most in the world. The place where I grew thin from dreaming. My village, rising from the plain. Shaded with trees and leaves like a piggy bank filled with memories. You'll see why a person would want to live there forever.'* But when the son goes back to Comala, he finds nothing but ghosts! I want to be buried in Oaxaca. There is so much color here, so much life. The dead don't die. They linger."

Her mother's ashes had sat in a closet for two decades, but for the first time, Anna acknowledged a sad truth: If she didn't bring her mother to Oaxaca, no one else would.

The apartment was dark, except for a strip of light shining under the bathroom door. Timeline. Tightrope. Arrow. Anna studied it until she made up her mind.

She opened her father's e-mail and copied the rendezvous address into Google Maps—15 Jardineros was in Tepito, one of the worst neighborhoods in Mexico City. Switching to Images, Anna skimmed through photographs of market stalls, police in riot gear, tough men with tattoos scrawled on their foreheads, like graffiti drawn with a Sharpie.

She'd fly to Oaxaca, then take an overnight bus to Mexico City, though the State Department discouraged night travel of any kind. *The following items are recommended for extended road trips: cellular telephone with charger; maps and a GPS; a spare tire; first aid kit; fire*

extinguisher; jumper cables; flares/reflectors; and an emergency tool kit.
The list made Anna laugh. As if objects could protect you from people.
As if precaution could protect you from tragedy.

Feeling light, almost gleeful, she set out enough clothes for a week,
combat boots, red lipstick, her little black dress. She packed a pocket
Spanish–English dictionary, a headlamp, and earplugs. She packed a
Swiss Army knife. She packed Tums. The worse the trip sounded, the
better she felt. She was proving something, but wasn't sure what. *Who
needs a honeymoon when you could go to Tepito?*

She was betting on her father. She was betting on herself.

She would buy Montezuma's death mask, the last mask that would
save the rest.

And David? Forever after, the Ramsey Collection would live on in
the Met's permanent collection, while in three months, David's precious
Warhol show would be shipped off to Pittsburgh or Tampa, then disassembled, scattered, forgotten. At the Met, every so often, he'd have to
walk through the Ramsey gallery, be forced to remember what he'd
thrown away. *Who* he'd thrown away. *Her.*

Tepito. Wikipedia claimed the barrio got its name because nervous
policemen would tell their buddies, *If there's danger, I'll whistle.*

I whistle for you. *Te pito.* Tepito.

Anna repeated the word in a whisper. She was going to Tepito,
where no one would save her if she put her lips together. She typed an
e-mail to her father, knowing he wouldn't read it until morning.

Stay home. I've gone to Mexico. I'll bring you back the mask.

eight | THE LOOTER

The looter dreamt it was raining and woke up curled around a fountain in Chapultepec Park, a cop's boot pressed to his nose. *"Váyase andando, patrón."* The cop whapped him twice with his bully stick. *Get going, boss.* The looter sat up, stretched his stiff legs. Bile circulated in his stomach, a toilet of acid. He thought about toast, the normalness of two buttery squares, but wasn't sure they'd sit well. Something better might be found in his satchel. He remembered the mask, panicked that he'd been robbed, but old blue-face peered out, all grimace and attitude.

Buenos días, amigo. What the fuck is for breakfast?

Pico's stash was also safe. Ditto the remains of Reyes's payout and his phone, which had two new texts. First, Gonzáles: Found buyer. Tuesday 4 pm Tres Perros Feroces, 15 Jardineros. Wait there. $10,000.

He blinked, counted the zeroes.

The second text, Reyes. Three words. Consider yourself dead.

The disparity was too much for the Maddox Theory to reconcile. The looter downed one of everything in Pico's bag that didn't require a needle or pipe. He stared into the bushes. The spaces between the bushes. Reyes could be anywhere. He could be selling pretzels. He could be running for president. The looter took off, careful not to leave footprints. He stuck to the shade, where he left no shadow. A scrawny African was selling stuff on a blanket. The looter bought a baseball cap that said I ♥ D.F., the Distrito Federal. Mexico City. The guy was hawking shades, too, but had only three pairs left.

"That's all you got?"

"More later," the vendor answered. "This now."

The looter brought a pair of "this now." The cap. The glasses. He was working his way to invisible. The shrooms kicked in. The grass fluttered. The sky was a blue balloon. The carousel spat out white horses. He shoved his hands in his pockets, anchoring himself to the ground, and thought: *I am a wanted man.*

nine | ANNA

Anna got off the airport bus in Oaxaca and did her best not to look lost. Head pounding nasty jazz, she clutched her backpack and the box containing her mother's urn and waited for the driver to unload the cargo hold. She felt disoriented and exhausted from the multiple flights, the sudden heat, the Spanish, the hassle maneuvering the ashes through security—out of urn, into plastic container, through scanner, back into urn, *carefully* back into carry-on. When the bus driver finally produced her suitcase, she marched out of the station, hoping for an air of efficiency and resolve. Discarded snack bags, mango sticks, and cashew wrappers clung to the curb. The smell of roasting corn hung in the air, mixing with wisps of cigarette smoke. Round women sat on benches like salt and pepper shakers. Hungry men paced. Strangers brushed past Anna, almost touching. A thin guy selling roasted peanuts tracked her movements like a gambler with a bet on a filly. His eyes followed her shifting breasts, a gesture she considered doubly pathetic given that she was so flat-chested. *"Güerita,"* little blonde one, he taunted. Anna sped up. The fact that she wasn't sure where she was going did not hamper her enthusiasm for getting there fast. Besides, she needed a drink.

The taxi wove through the ugly outskirts of the city, past cement factories, tire shops, empty lots of scrap metal. Small fires burned in forlorn fields and barbecue pits. It seemed incredible the mecca for Mexican folk art lay inside this clot of debris. Oaxaca. Population: 250,000. Altitude: 5,100 feet. Chief industries: Mining, manufacturing, and tourism. Visitors flocked to Oaxaca for its mild climate and colorful colonial buildings, for its hot peppers and weak peso. They came to tour Monte Albán, a pre-Columbian archaeological site, former capital of the Zapotec. They came to buy *artesanía*—tin mirrors, painted gourds, fantastical carved wooden creatures called *alebrijes*. Homely girls came to nibble *torta de la soltera*, a yellow cake, which if eaten every Sunday ensured a timely marriage.

The cabdriver thumped his horn—*"Pendejo."* Anna relaxed, a wave of optimism surging through her. Aggressive cabdrivers made her feel invincible, confirming her theory that misfortune seldom struck people in motion. She tapped out three aspirin, swallowed them dry. She'd fact-checked a piece on hangovers once. Ancient Romans prescribed a breakfast of sheep lungs and owl eggs. Assyrians ground up bird beaks and tree sap. She could use some fucking sap.

She straightened, rallied her Spanish. When traveling, she liked to chat up taxi drivers, waitresses, clerks. Men sometimes misconstrued her openness for promiscuity, but this was a risk she was willing to take. In her experience, fleeting connections were easier and often more satisfying than intimacy.

"*Disculpe, señor.* Which direction are the towns where they carve masks?"

The cabdriver shifted lanes, watched her in the rearview mirror, then pointed west. "San Juan del Monte, Santa María, the others, are half an hour up the ridge. You can buy masks directly from the carvers."

"And *torta de la soltera?*"

"Panadería El Alba, near the *zócalo.* Why? You are in the market for a husband?"

"No," Anna said. "Only cake."

They passed a church, a paper shop, a chicken joint called Pollo Loco Loco. Anna touched the urn. It seemed amazing that her mother's remains lay inside, reduced to an object she could carry with one hand.

"Another question," Anna leaned forward. "In your opinion, what is the most beautiful place in Oaxaca?"

"Monte Albán is very popular with visitors."

Anna hid her disappointment. She'd been hoping for a secret place, not a guidebook four-star attraction. The driver swept his hand across the horizon. "From the top, you can see the whole valley. Go in the morning, before it gets too hot. How long are you staying in Oaxaca?"

Anna sank into the ripped seat cushion. "I don't know exactly. *Depende . . .*"

She let this word trail off. She had noticed this custom. Mexicans understood implicitly that the fulfillment of every commitment depended on a host of factors too personal, intricate, or uncertain to catalogue. It was enough to say *"Depende"*—a one-word euphemism for all the contingencies and obstacles that stood between the speaker and happiness.

The cab swung into the old part of the city, jostling under soaring jacarandas, past a chamber of commerce billboard of a grinning devil mask: OAXACA, SHOW US YOUR TRUE FACE. The driver slammed the brakes at a red light. Radio voices from other cars filtered through the window. DJs blabbing about contests. A mural painted on the side of a motorcycle shop depicted a life-size skeleton dressed in a hooker's silk robe and spike heels. The skeleton was whipping two thugs who knelt before her like penitent dogs. Anna held up her phone, took a picture.

"What's that mural about?"

"That's Santa Muerte. Saint Death."

"Yes, I know, but what's she doing?"

The driver accelerated with a frustrated exhale. "She is the patron saint of gangs and drug dealers. The mural is a joke. A fantasy. Santa Muerte will rid Mexico of the *narcos* by giving them a child's spanking."

More than sixty thousand people had died since Calderón declared his War on Drugs in 2006. In the newspapers every day—killings, dismemberments, mass graves. In the most besieged areas, people were so desperate that vigilante groups had taken up patrols. *Autodefensas.* Anna checked her door lock, though she wasn't much worried about drug lords. They were distant, an abstraction. The people most likely to hurt you were the ones you knew best.

"What do you think would work?" she asked.

The driver sliced the air with his hand. "Clean house. New president. New government. New police. Start all over with honorable people. But that is never going to happen. The corruption is complete, from beggar to priest. How many honest people do you know?"

"Fewer every day." Anna checked her phone. Nothing from David.

She found her water bottle, drank, drizzled warm drops down her cleavage. "Some people seem good but are actually bad," she said. Good people. Bad people. She sounded like a comic book. To add a bit of nuance, she said, "Sometimes good people do bad things. And . . ." She had no idea how to say "the other way around." She fudged with: "And the opposite. It's confusing, no?"

"You need a *brújula*."

"What's that?"

The driver illustrated a compass needle with his finger.

Anna gave a short laugh. "Sounds like '*bruja*.'" A *bruja* was a witch. "You need a *brújula* to tell who is a *bruja*."

The driver exclaimed, *"Eso mero."*

"But I still don't understand," Anna pressed. "Why do *narcotraficantes* pray to Santa Muerte?"

The driver threw his hands up—both, before lowering his left back to the wheel. "They see her as their mother, their saint. Maybe the Angel of Death is a comfort if your life is a wreck. They want her power. Her protection. She's the new Virgin of Guadalupe. Sometimes it's better to be a bad girl than a good one."

The driver's eyes locked with Anna's in the rearview mirror. With a single glance, Anna agreed with his statement and declined his offer. The driver settled back down with a huff and a grumble. "When old religions don't work anymore, people make up new ones."

The hotel lobby was air-conditioned, but not enough to do any good. A large woman sat sprawled in a fake-leather love seat, buttocks overtaking the space designed for a suitor. Anna set down her suitcase, pack, and box, fanned her hangover. This was her second attempt to secure lodging. The hotel where she thought she'd made a reservation had no record of an Anna Ramsey. The owner apologized, but had no vacancy. Most hotels were full at this late date, she'd said, but there might still be a room at the Puesta del Sol. Anna knew better than to ask why.

The young clerk turned from his soap opera. He was an effeminate man, gold hoop earring, Peter Pan collar, polka-dotted hairband. She was surprised that such a songbird could exist in this macho society without being crushed, his bones snapped in the fist of a punk or a priest. The clerk pressed his boyish face into the day.

His Spanish was soft, like flannel. "How can I help you?"

"Necesito una habitación para una persona."

Mariposa. Gay man. *La terraza.* The terrace. *Hay una mujer gorda sobre un sofá.* There is a fat woman on a sofa. Spanish vocabulary emerged from her subconscious, like old lovers who appeared in disjointed dreams. Some days, Anna couldn't remember whether she'd slept with a man or only dreamt she had. Some days, she wasn't sure it mattered.

"We have one available."

"Do the rooms have desks?"

The clerk nodded.

"Is it quiet?"

The clerk tipped his hand. "We have a room facing the garden. It has a desk and an old typewriter."

"Ice?"

"There is a machine in the kitchen." The clerk scrutinized her. Women weren't supposed to care about ice. Women were supposed to care about full-length mirrors, sewing kits, the hours of Mass.

Anna smiled. "How much would you charge for a week?"

The clerk looked dubious, as though this question didn't come up much and if she'd been his friend he would have advised against it. With a pompom-topped pen, he punched numbers into a calculator. His mouth thinned. Money did this to the nicest people.

"Thirty-five hundred pesos."

Anna playacted her disappointment. The usual dance. "That's a little expensive. I am a student."

The clerk looked away. He'd heard this lie before. Anna remembered the single most important word in Spanish: *descuento*.

"Is there a discount for longer stays?"

The clerk fluttered, a blizzard of helplessness. "There is no discount this time of year. *It's high season*. My boss would murder me."

Anna squinted into the blinding sun, momentarily unable to remember the time of year. Time had little traction in Mexico. The air smelled like smoke. The mangoes were two weeks from ripening. The peso was tumbling against the dollar. The governor was a bully. The teachers were on strike. The police chief in Juárez had been gunned down without a single witness. It was Mexico. Any year, any day, was high season when Americans inquired.

"It's Carnival?" she said, hoping to God it wasn't.

"It starts the end of next week." The clerk slid gloss over his lips. "Each *pueblo* has a celebration. Parades and parties. Fireworks. People dress in wild costumes and dance in the streets. You should stay. You like to dance?"

The question startled her. She had been thinking about money and masks and whether the man she was meeting in Tepito would be carrying a gun. On TV, a blonde woman in a tight dress wept. Maybe her fiancé was sleeping with Clarissa, too. The clerk's face pinched with concern. It seemed the right moment to press harder.

"Would you take twenty-eight hundred?"

Anna found the clerk's eyes, forcing him to turn her down at close range. He shrugged, as if to say, *Money only matters to little people.* He slid her the register. Anna printed her name, nationality, had to ask him the date. She signed her name in large letters. She needed to take up more space in the world now that she was alone.

"Why is the hotel called the Puesta del Sol?" After saving seven hundred pesos, Anna was ready to be friends. "Can you see the sunset from here?" She glanced over her shoulder, as if the sun might be hiding in the utility closet.

The clerk picked up a nail file. "*Hombre,* if you could see the sunset, the rooms would cost more than twenty-five dollars. In Mexico, the sun only sets for the rich."

Wrought-iron furniture. Bedraggled geraniums. A waterless fountain, a cherub with a broken wing. The hotel's patio was pretty in the same way Anna liked to think she was pretty: enough that she didn't have to try too hard, enough that if she *had* tried hard, she would be very pretty, and knowing this was reassuring enough that she seldom bothered to try.

The guidebook had described the Puesta del Sol as "spartan," but Anna opened her door to decrepit. The bed was a crushed cereal box. The stucco had cracked into spiderwebs. A cross stood sentry over the door. A faded poster of the Pyramid of the Sun had buckled in its plastic frame, as if attacked by the deity it worshipped. The air smelled like cinnamon and dust.

Anna chained the door and, finding no safe, stuffed the urn, the journal, and the envelope in the back of the closet and covered them with her coat. A manual typewriter sat on the desk. She rolled in a sheet of paper and typed, ANNA IS HERE, then added: WITH HER MOTHER. She fell back on the bed, exhausted. Overhead, the ceiling fan shimmied, as if it might decapitate her in her sleep. She rose, poured a duty-free shot of tequila, downed it, felt her mouth turn golden and swampy. She got up to pee. The bathroom smelled like cherry aerosol. A disposable razor lay on the tiles. A faint hairball covered the drain. It was hard to imagine getting clean in such a place. More likely, you'd wind up dirty in some new way.

She showered. Under a thin stream of scalding water, she lifted her breasts into cleavage. She liked her small breasts. She could maneuver. She could run. Departures were her forte, though she had planned to stay with David for a lifetime. Perhaps this seedy hotel was the apt setting for an exorcism. Invite a tall, dark stranger from the *zócalo* back for sex in this rancid shower. He'd speak no English. She'd forget her verbs. They'd parse body language. Hard and wet. She wondered if she still had the nerve for such exploits. She'd like to think she was young enough to be daring, and mature enough to know better.

Anna dried herself with a stiff towel, slapped her cheeks for color, pulled on a dress, then emptied her backpack, refilling it with a notebook, pen, water, Swiss Army knife, dictionary, key. This reduction felt good. She reviewed the next twenty-four hours: meet Lorenzo Gonzáles, take the overnight bus to Mexico City, get a cab to Tepito, buy the mask, be back in Oaxaca, margarita in hand, by tomorrow evening.

Then she'd bury her mother.

Anna sat on the bed, momentarily overwhelmed. The cross glared like a hex. Back in New York, David was screwing Clarissa with the lovely underwear. She was poring over press coverage, tweeting his Twitter, feeding his ego, feeding his face. She'd fix puttanesca. Blow his job.

Anna counted her money. Two grand for Gonzáles in one envelope. Given that her father had already wired the looter two grand, she owed the digger only eight. She put that in a second envelope. An extra two grand remained. Her father's travel money. A slush fund for masks. She slid the bills into her wallet. The money felt filthy and sensual. Like David. She checked her phone again. No calls. No texts. Sadness pressed the roof of her mouth, singed her nostrils, rose into her eyelids. She fought back. She would fight back. She poured half a shot, downed it. Revenge was a dish best served cold. Well, forget about it. This was Mexico. The journey to purchase the greatest pre-Columbian archaeological find of the modern era began with a single step. Anna got up, wobbled. On the threshold, she lowered her shades.

At the cupid fountain, she dragged her hand along the frayed edge where the concrete had crumbled. The baby's plump face was serene, his innocence made ironic by amputation. An angel with one wing was headed in one direction. The only question was how fast.

ten | THE CARVER

Emilio Luna rose from bed and felt, though his furrowed hands attested otherwise, that he was still a young man. The mask carver made coffee, padded onto the concrete patio of his home in San Juan del Monte, a hill town outside Oaxaca. His tools lay strewn in yesterday's wood chips. The air smelled like cedar. He bent to touch his toes, came close, reached toward the sky, came close, hiked his pants, sat down on his tree stump, propping a pillow behind his back. He picked a chunk of wood, then measured the customary thirty centimeters and saw he had a problem.

This piece of wood was too small; still, he didn't want to waste it. He turned it over, waiting for a solution to appear. He sketched his idea on cardboard. He drew human lips and eyes round as coins, with bulging, transfixed pupils. With a machete, Emilio Luna sliced off the bark, roughing out the form. Resting the mask in his groin, he worked pick and mallet until a countenance emerged. Next step, sanding. Juanito, the boy with Tourette's, his usual helper, was not around. The boy's mother was sick and Juanito had to care for his sisters. The carver had forgotten the mess of sanding, how dust settled in your socks and ears. The boy deserved a raise.

His wife appeared. He didn't look up.

"*Voy al mercado,*" she said. I'm going to the market.

"*Sí.*"

"What's wrong with the tiger? It's different."

"Yes, I know." His tone was more scornful than he meant it to be. "I am an artist. I don't have to do it the same way every time." He had on occasion argued exactly the reverse.

His wife frowned. "I took money from the pillow."

He nodded, pretending not to notice she wanted his attention.

"I'll be back."

Only after his wife had turned did Emilio Luna look at her: her wide hips, bowed legs, apron ties. How had he married such an old woman? As a young man, he had imagined married life would be as peaceful as a Sunday picnic, where he would lie in the shade of a eucalyptus tree while a sweet girl soothed him with kisses that tasted like apples.

Of course, his wife would return. Where else could she go?

Emilio Luna painted spots on the tiger's face, which gave the animal a crazed expression, then shellacked the mask and propped it to dry. Tired, he fell into the hammock, listened to the birds.

An hour later, he awoke. The mask was dry. He punctured two holes and tied the mask over his face. He didn't usually try on his masks, but this one was different. Thin shafts of light entered from each side. He grabbed a pair of sweatpants off the drying line and draped them over his head, knotting the legs under his chin. For Carnival, dancers bundled their heads with scarves, but the effect was the same. Darkness. Claustrophobia. His rising panic reminded him of the one time he'd put his head underwater.

The carver paced the terrace, picking up speed and adrenaline. He breathed in what he exhaled. Animal in, animal out. With a broom, he whacked the hanging laundry. His wife's enormous bra fell to the ground, and he hooked the strap and helicoptered it around his head until it soared into his neighbor's front yard. Emilio Luna whooped and chased the cat past the woodpile until the animal leapt over the wall to safety. He stabbed the bushes, jousted the unsuspecting hammock until he caught sight of a wicker chair sitting defenseless in the sun. He bludgeoned the innocent straight through its straw heart.

Everything stopped. Quiet in an instant.

Dizzy and depleted, the carver ripped off his mask and fell into the injured chair, waking from a dream he was already forgetting. The cat inched back, wound crazy eights around his legs. Emilio Luna buried his fingers deep in its fur. *Dumb animal, so quick to forgive.*

Maybe this new tiger mask had a strange power, or maybe he was just a light-headed old man on a warm day. He could make no sense of his feelings but was certain of this: When his wife asked how her bra had ended up in the neighbor's yard, Emilio Luna would blame the cat.

"Buenas tardes, Emilio Luna."

The carver looked over cautiously. Good news seldom came unannounced. Sure enough, a drunk man was leaning on his gate. The *borracho* was short, sallow, unshaven. His faded pink T-shirt was streaked with gray stains. A half-empty Corona swung from his meaty hand. The man seemed pleased, enjoying a private joke.

Emilio Luna was about to tell the stranger to move along, when he spoke in a clear voice: "Why do you not greet me today, my friend?"

The carver recognized the mashed-up features and laughed. "Ah, *patrón*. That's a good one."

It was rare to see Reyes in the village, but the drug lord showed up once a season, a reminder or warning, and bought a dozen masks with crisp bills. Emilio Luna didn't like to sell his art to the detestable El Pelotas—it was like promising your sweet daughter to a pedophile—but what choice did he have? The carver had his pride, but he also had a belly—and a wife, a cat, a donkey, a half-dozen children, and too many grandchildren to remember their names. Every man, woman, and child came to Emilio Luna with a hand open wide.

He stood, wiped his callused hands clean. Compromise was its own sort of courage.

"*Buenas tardes, patrón,* come in." He beckoned his guest with a smile and a lie. "It gives me much happiness to see you in our village today. I have finished a mask that is perfect for you."

eleven | ANNA

A muscular housekeeper with a string of earrings led Anna in to see Lorenzo Gonzáles. The dealer was an enormous man, whose faint goatee struggled to cover his flabby jowls. He was nearly bald and his skin looked anemic against his white guayabera shirt. Dusty books and withered plants cluttered his office. A chessboard rested on a precarious pile of paper. He was playing against himself, winning and losing. The only sign of modernity was a calendar of Garfield, grinning with pointy teeth.

Gonzáles offered Anna a warm, pudgy hand. "It is a pleasure to meet you after our phone conversations." His English was perfect. "Please sit down, Miss Ramsey. Your father is coming." He glanced past her.

"No, he's not here."

"He's coming later."

Anna shook her head.

"He sent you to Mexico alone."

"I sent myself."

"You do not collect masks."

Anna hated when young people turned basic statements of fact into questions, hiking their voices at the end of sentences, even when confirming their names, but Lorenzo Gonzáles had the equally annoying habit of doing the reverse.

"I'm here to collect the mask, but I am not a collector."

The dealer leaned back, looking concerned. "How is your father? The Centurion affair was a terrible shock."

"You heard?"

"I heard."

"Everyone here heard?"

"Everyone." He sniffed. "It is a small circle. Collectors, scholars, dealers, curators."

Anna hadn't realized the full extent to which she had been the last to know. "All the people he cares about."

Gonzáles shrugged. "But your father has not given up. This is a good thing. He has faith in this new mask."

"He has faith because *you* have faith."

"I never make promises until I hold a piece in my hands, but I wanted him to have the first chance to see it. I try to keep my clients happy."

"You trust this looter?"

"Trust . . ." Gonzáles's smile rose and fell. "Understand. I deal art. I collect art. I read. I write." He gestured to his bookcases. "I know scholars from universities, museums, foundations. I know billionaires and princes. I also know gang members, looters, smugglers. I am not afraid of either world. Both need me. With a stroke of the pen, I can make a fake legitimate or a legitimate fake."

He stopped to consider her. "You have great faith in your father."

Her faith—or lack of it—was none of his business. She changed the subject. "I'm planning to take the overnight bus to Mexico City," she said, hoping he would offer her a ride.

"I would take you, but I must make a stop in Puebla first, so we will meet at the direction, sorry, the address, tomorrow. Take a cab from the bus station. Your father should have come. Tepito is no place for a woman alone."

Nothing egged Anna on more than the insinuation she wasn't up to a task. Gonzáles seemed to sense this. "Four o'clock," she said. "I'll be there. I'll bring half the money and pay the rest later, after I see the mask."

The dealer shook his head. "There is no later with people like this. If you do not bring the full amount, he will sell it to someone else. Such people lack patience. You can imagine why."

"But it's not safe to carry—"

"If you want safe, go to the Zona Rosa and pay a hundred times as much. The mask is affordable because your father is buying it *first*. Naturally, there are risks." Gonzáles sat back, making room for his stomach. "Bring me the mask after, and I will make a full report for you."

"Haven't you already—?"

"The mask must be professionally authenticated and its value assessed. You can't do that from a photograph. Without documents, you have nothing but a stolen mask."

"Stolen?"

"Unauthenticated. Without provenance. A lost shell on the beach. It cannot be legitimately bought or sold. The mask needs a history. I will give it one." He tapped his pen on the desk. "You work for a living, Miss Ramsey. Besides the book."

"I'm a fact-checker."

"I don't understand."

"I check information before it goes to print. Make sure everything is accurate."

"But your own book was full—"

"One's own mistakes are the hardest to see."

"How true . . . A fact-checker." The dealer practiced the expression. "The truth is seldom popular. So you are always honest—with family, friends, relationships."

"I used to tell the truth," Anna said. "Now I just keep quiet."

The dealer was quiet himself for a moment, then said, "Your father wants revenge."

"Redemption."

"You travel to Mexico, to Tepito, for him."

"I have my own reasons."

"Professional."

"Professional and personal."

"What personal reasons could a fact-checker have to want an Aztec death mask?"

It was his first genuine question, one Anna had no intention of answering.

She waited out the silence. Gonzáles looked uncomfortable, then rallied a smile. "Well, that settles everything, except, of course, my commission."

"Shouldn't we wait and see if everything goes smoothly tomorrow?"

Gonzáles pretended to actually consider this. "I think not . . . No, I'm afraid that's not how these transactions work . . . Not that I don't trust you, but we've just met. I forwarded your deposit to our friend, as promised."

Anna debated whether to argue, but thought better of it. She reached into her backpack and handed him two grand. The dealer fanned the bills and smiled.

Anna's phone rang as she walked back to the *zócalo*.

"You went, didn't you?"

"I did."

"You have the money, I trust."

Anna was proud of her moxie, but her father sounded more worried than pleased. She told him she had the money. Had he noticed the urn was missing? Apparently not. She wouldn't bring it up.

"You shouldn't have gone," he said. The springs in his chair whined as he sat. Anna listened for ice cubes. "I was going to go."

She found some shady steps across from a toy shop and a *papelería*. "You're not much of a traveler these days," she said. "It's better I went."

"Nonsense. I'll meet you in Mexico City tomorrow."

"Don't worry. I've got it covered. I'll call when I have the mask."

"Where are you staying?"

"The Puesta del Sol, but—"

"See if they have another room. I'll go back to Oaxaca with you after. Or do you have two beds? That would save a few bucks—"

"I repeat: *Do not come to Mexico.*" He'd probably already packed his explorer's vest with bug spray and batteries. "By the time you get here, I'll have the mask. Then I'm taking a vacation for a week. Buying folk art. Getting a tan. Everything's set. I'm meeting Gonzáles tomorrow in Tepito."

"Tepito?"

Anna smiled. "That was the address. Google Maps. Click, click." She couldn't help herself.

"Have the twigger come to his office instead. It's safer."

"The twigger has an office?"

"Gonzáles's office."

"Gonzáles doesn't have an office in Mexico City."

"He probably does. The guy has a finger in every pie." Her father still sounded put out. "If I'd known you were going to take off like that, I wouldn't have told you. Your mother would never forgive me."

Her father did this a lot. Extrapolate what Rose would have wanted or done or thought. Anna softened her tone, told him she was happy to do this for him, for the family. "Mom would have done the same. She often did."

His chair squeaked. He'd gotten up, was walking somewhere.

"You're not going into the kitchen for ice, are you?"

Her father said he was not.

"I mean it. No ice."

"If you must know, I need to take a piss. I am walking to the bathroom, so when we hang up, I'll be eight steps closer."

"No cocktail to soothe your nerves. No father's little helper."

They spoke about his drinking with code words and black humor. Daniel Ramsey had never been a mean drunk, more a sentimental bore, weepy and apologetic, praising his late wife, building her into a saint. *Your mother understood me. She was the only one.* Anna had quit listening. She wanted to remember her mother in her own way, just as she wanted to forget her father's worst days, like the morning she'd found him passed out in his chair, sodden with pee.

"I've been sober two years now," he said, irritation lining his voice. "Don't worry. We'll celebrate the mask of a lifetime with sparkling water and low-fat Triscuits." His tone switched to concern. "Call me when you have the mask."

Anna promised to text.

He sighed with this new burden.

"I showed you, remember? It's easy." She explained it again.

Before they hung up, her father told her he loved her. Anna said the same back. They didn't usually say this. Instead of comforting, the words reminded Anna how far she was from home.

Outside the *papelería*, a pretty girl twirled her hair. She had perfect skin. Anna tried to imagine being sixteen, innocent still, wearing a yellow dress in the sunlight, waiting for adult life to begin.

Water. Coffee. A margarita. Anna needed three drinks to get where she wanted to go. She was gathering momentum, smoothing the ragged edges left from turbulence and translation, bracing herself for the night bus to Tepito.

Her café seat afforded a full panorama of the *zócalo*. She could see how her parents had been so completely seduced. Rose gardens encircled the bandstand. Older gentlemen on wrought-iron benches flexed their newspapers. A shoe shiner beckoned on bended knee. *Zócalo*, the word rolled off the tongue like music. One table over, a Mexican family chattered over Cokes. No doubt they mistook her for a tourist, a woman fretting about the exchange rate, the safety of ice cubes. How could

DANCING WITH THE TIGER

they know she'd traveled all over Mexico as a girl, riding cheap buses with her father, snoring elfin women tipping, tipping into her lap.

A motorcycle pulled up and parked. Its driver scanned the café, chose the table next to Anna's and sat down. He was tall for a Mexican, his features strong but irregular, a jumble of spare parts. With jeans and a frayed T-shirt, he carried himself with a bohemian nonchalance Anna coveted and resented. An elastic cinched his chin-length hair. He looked distracted, as if his body had arrived a few minutes ahead of his thoughts.

There is your tall, dark stranger. Now wrestle him into the shower.

The man ordered an espresso, lit a cigarette, opened a notebook. Anna pretended to watch some children by the cathedral who were lobbing giant cigar-shaped balloons. He was studying her. Her skin tingled and she tried to convey *no* even as she knew that with a second margarita the answer would be *maybe.* Chastity, like abstinence, was a virtue best begun tomorrow.

"The children are beautiful," the man said in English.

Anna took in the particulars: his sideways smile, his shirt rumpled from wind, the dark circles under his eyes. Blue paint had dried in his arm hairs. On one thumb, he wore a silver ring, and on a chain around his neck, a small sphere.

"I like children at a distance."

"You are not ready for motherhood. I was once asked to be a father, but I declined. One must know his limits." He snuffed his cigarette. "You are American?" His presumption annoyed her. She'd like to pass for Swedish on a good day. German, on a lesser one. "You're on vacation," the man said, unfurling his hand. He knew her story by heart. "To see the museums, Monte Albán, buy souvenirs from indigenous children?"

"Actually, I'm working."

"Working?" He glanced at her margarita.

"I'm writing a book on Mexican masks." This lie came out smoothly. Her father had said the same thing at every *rancho* they'd visited. Years later, it sounded only slightly less convincing in English.

The man twirled his coaster. "A book about carvers?"

"Carvers, masks, the history of folk art . . ."

"You are here for Carnival." The man curled his hands into claws. "To chase the Tiger?"

Anna tilted her head. "I am always chasing a tiger."

He introduced himself. Salvador Flores. A painter. His studio was three blocks off the *zócalo*. He invited her to stop by. Anna wondered whether he found her attractive or whether he pulled the same charming-artist routine for all the *extranjeras*, like the spindly Argentinean she'd met in San Miguel de Allende who'd invited her to see his yarn paintings. She'd gone to his apartment—how had she been so innocent, so trusting?—but there were no paintings, just yellowing newspaper clippings about an opening a decade before. They talked. He'd tried to kiss her, his breath reeking of sugar and smoke. She got up to leave, worried he might forcibly stop her, but he'd just watched her go, as if she didn't matter at all.

"You've come to the right place for masks." He leaned in. "Did you know a mask is not considered authentic unless it is danced? Such a romantic idea. If you really want to meet carvers, you should hire a guide. Someone who knows the villages, speaks the language. I give tours, if you are interested."

So that was what he was after. Of course. Anna slid her finger around her spoon.

"I can manage."

"You speak Spanish?"

"Me defiendo." I defend myself. I get by.

"You have a car?"

Anna shook her head.

"You have been to Oaxaca before?"

"Just as a girl."

"No car, no Spanish, no experience. Oh"—he nodded with fresh understanding—"so it's a guide for tourists."

Anna felt compelled to defend her nonexistent book. "No, I hate tourists."

This was a ridiculous claim, and Anna blamed the painter for driving her to it. She looked like the quintessential tourist, with her flowered dress and margarita, an authentic drink turned cliché, ruined yet delicious. Anna liked to see herself as a traveler, not a tourist, but this was like claiming you were spiritual, not religious.

"With beginner Spanish, how can you ask good questions—about the soul of their animals, how God enters the wood, what it feels like to dance the dances of their ancestors? Or will you just ask everyone out for a margarita?"

He had a point, though it was rude of him to make it. Her father had complained of this very thing. Carvers were shy. They mumbled. Some spoke only Nahuatl. They didn't trust Americans, didn't want their pictures taken.

Two waifs in dusty clothes approached, selling gum. The painter brushed the girls away. *"No, niñas.* Tell your mother you should be in school."

He pulled in his lips, as if something were hurting him. Anna softened.

"Maybe you're right," she conceded. "But before I hire a guide, I'd need to check his credentials."

He sat up. "Of course."

"How well do you know San Juan del Monte?"

"I was born there."

"Do you have a car, or just a motorcycle?"

"I have a car."

"Do you speak Spanish?"

"Me defiendo."

"What's the most beautiful place in Oaxaca?"

"If I told everyone, it would no longer be beautiful."

"Last question. Do you know Thomas Malone?"

The painter set down his cup. "Thomas Malone?"

"The art collector."

"Never heard of him."

The painter flagged the waiter, who produced his check on a tiny tray. The painter's mood had abruptly shifted, teasing replaced by irritation. He didn't look at Anna, not even through his shades. Anna was surprised she cared, but she did. She saw the ball around his neck was a globe. She wanted to unclasp it and slip it in her pocket.

"You're leaving?"

"I have work." The implication was clear: He had real work and she didn't. The painter plunked down a gold ten-peso coin.

"Wait," Anna said. "Do you have a card? I'm going to Mexico City, but I might need a guide after."

"I usually work with professional tour companies."

"You just said . . ."

"Try Dolores on the square. She's cheap."

"Maybe I don't want cheap." Anna understood his ploy: Now that he'd convinced her she needed his services, he would have the pleasure of denying them.

"Really? Where is your hotel?" He touched his temples, a soothsayer summoning mystics. "Let me guess. The Puesta del Sol?"

Anna folded her arms. "It's a lovely establishment."

"My aunt is the *dueña*."

Anna didn't know what to say. To confirm the hotel's shabbiness would be to denigrate his aunt. To defend its merits would prove her foolishness. The painter laughed at her predicament. "Don't worry. I know it's ugly. *Pobrecita.* That hotel is all she has."

Pushing back his chair, he spoke in the punctuated Spanish of Chapter One. *"Buena suerte con tus aventuras."*

Good luck with your adventures. Anna caught the double meaning. She threw down her last card. "Tepito should be an adventure."

He stopped. "Tepito? In Mexico City? Don't go there. It's not safe."

"That's why I'm going."

He met her eyes. She had scored a point in whatever game they were playing. But then his phone rang and she lost him.

"Dígame, cariño." Tell me, loved one.

Coddling the phone, Salvador waved a distracted good-bye and made his way out to the street. His motorcycle hacked a smoker's cough before disappearing around the bandstand; then, oddly, he circled back. A victory lap. Or maybe he'd forgotten something. And then, definitively, he was gone.

Anna considered the empty chair. Loneliness blew through her. She was furious with herself and with him. Of course, she knew a danced mask was more valuable than a tourist mask for the same reason an English armoire was more valuable than a coat rack from IKEA, for the same reason old love was more valuable—and rare—than new.

She knew the back side of a mask was as important as its face: serious collectors sought a rich patina, wear marks built up from dirt and dancers' sweat. She could have lamented the persnickety powder-post beetle (a critter that drilled pinholes into masks) and discussed methods for fumigation. She could have talked about the African mask's influence on Picasso. Or discussed the James Ensor painting *Masks Confronting Death* and recited the artist's observation: *"The mask means to me: freshness of color, sumptuous decoration, wild unexpected gestures, very shrill expressions, exquisite turbulence."* She could have explained that her life was an exquisite turbulence she never managed to still. She could have told him she had come to Mexico to bury her mother and resurrect her father. She knew the fucking verbs to say this in Spanish, if he'd stopped speaking English long enough to listen.

She lit her 199th cigarette, scoped the patio for eligible men, but the place was filled with tourists fiddling visors and fanny packs. Screw it. He thought she was an idiot, and she was, for letting him think so.

A text rang into her phone. David. We need to talk. Drink @ Charleys @ 6.

Anna dropped her phone into her bag headfirst. On the corner, a shopkeeper hung stuffed toys from his awning. Bug-eyed Bart Simpson dangled from a hook. Yes, that was how she would leave David, twisting in the wind.

She flagged the waiter. *"Señor, otra margarita, por favor."*

A second margarita was a mistake, of course. The kind of mistake Anna was used to making. Her signature mistake. The one that always called her name.

twelve | THE HOUSEKEEPER

"*Madre María, mother of us all,*
it's Soledad. I have news. Señor Thomas sent me down to the English
library this morning to check on the ad. I hate that place. The Americans all stare at you like you're going to steal their purse. The ad was
buried by other notices, so I put it back on top. It's been weeks and they
still haven't found a replacement. If the *señor* had treated Señorita Holly
better, she wouldn't have left. Jealousy, that's what it was. The *señora*
misses Holly terribly, though she's too proud to admit it. Another postcard arrived yesterday from California and it set her off again. All
afternoon, she stomped around the garden snipping rosebushes, prick-
ing herself, taking it out on me. It's a shame, because Holly was such a
loving person and she kept the *señora* company in the afternoons, wearing that funny crown she made from a blue scarf and dried flowers.
She hung it next to the *señora*'s coat and put it on before work. 'The

princess has arrived,' she would say, and laugh. Yesterday, I caught the *señora* standing in the hallway, touching the empty hook. She hung a black umbrella there, but we all know what's missing.

"But oh, *Virgencita*, there's more. Yesterday I found a heart-shaped locket in Hugo's pants pocket. There was no picture inside. If I ask him, he might lie or he might tell the truth, and I don't know which would be worse. My heart is an empty locket. The red light in the chapel glows nearly every night. I am carving a hole in the window with a nail, each night, a little wider, making sure the glass does not break. Long past midnight, the *señor* works. Doing what, I cannot imagine. I hear water sloshing and a strange hum. Once I saw him carrying a bag of garbage to his car, but he quickly drove it away. This from a man who won't pick up a fallen napkin. Nothing is normal here. Everything is a secret in a closed mouth. Beloved Virgin, I remain your watchful servant. Even in my sleep, I keep my eyes open."

thirteen | THE GARDENER

Hugo stared out the car window at the passing countryside, dreaming of his yellow girl. Pedro, the pool cleaner, was driving, slurping orange soda and biting his nails like a starving man. The car smelled like the coffee they'd downed for breakfast and the cigarettes they'd smoked for lunch and the licorice Pedro chewed after his cigarette, red sticks dangling from his mouth. Despite such annoyances, Hugo enjoyed these road trips. This was their first pick-up for Reyes, but they'd made many for Thomas Malone. It was good to be paid to drive, stay in a hotel, a perk of working for the rich, touching what they touched, being the one to deliver what they coveted. On overnights, he and Pedro drank hard, letting out the ghosts, staying clear of women and their confusions. They were runners, men for hire, men willing to drive to Tepito.

Pedro was picking his nose. *No hay remedio.* There is no hope for a guy like that. "Say something," Hugo said. "Your silence is killing me."

"I am focusing on the road."

Nothing was before them except a straight line of cracked pavement framed by six lifetimes of cactus and dust.

"You are not focusing on the road. You are picking your nose and thinking."

"You still seeing that girl?"

Again, Hugo regretted spilling his secret. "I still buy a lot of paper."

Pedro shook his head. "She's a child."

"Who isn't?"

"Your wife knows?"

"No, gracias a Dios."

"That's what you think. She knows. Without a doubt." Pedro cackled. "Women may not say anything, but they always know."

"Soledad thinks we're moving to the North. I promised her."

"Instead you're spending cash on the girl."

"The girl is a girl. She's not expensive."

"Pussy is always expensive."

"I need some real money before I decide which way to go."

Pedro checked his side mirror. "Listen, my Tiger: *Better a rich man's dog than a poor man's saint.*"

Hugo smiled to hear his old nickname. "That's an expression?"

"Commit it to memory."

"You are getting so cynical. You used to be sweet. Our little angel, Pedrito. When we were boys, you'd cry over a stray cat. If you got a bad grade, you'd drop your homework in the arroyo. What happened to you?"

Something hardened in Pedro's face. With his index finger, he wiped his nose, horizontally, a gentle saw.

"I changed," he said.

They parked in the outskirts, locked the wheel boot, wove through the *tianguis* that stretched for blocks, selling handbags, boom boxes, and bongs. Most of the stuff was stolen or pirated, even the electricity, which vendors tapped to fuel tiny televisions blaring soap operas and soccer. Hugo had never been to Tepito, but he'd heard news reports compare it to Mumbai, heard people there were so poor and crazy from drugs they worshipped Santa Muerte, the Angel of Death, though the news footage didn't paint the whole picture. It was the difference between 2-D and 3-D, between watching sex and having it. Thin women sold used clothing for ten pesos. Rats darted between stands of child pornography. The air smelled of weed and incense and garbage. A banner across the street read: BEING MEXICAN IS A PRIVILEGE, BUT BEING FROM TEPITO IS A GIFT OF GOD.

People here had nothing but pride.

The pick-up was scheduled for four. With an hour to kill, Pedro suggested, then *insisted*, they visit the famous Romero shrine to Santa Muerte. Hugo was reluctant but agreed. You didn't have to believe in God or the devil to be nervous about seeing the Angel of Death. It was a circus outside the Romero house. Hugo pushed forward until he was looking right at her. What he saw disgusted him: a human skeleton dressed like a tacky bride in a white nylon dress. A jangle of crosses dangled from her bony neck. Her skull reminded him of a greyhound. Deep eye sockets, too many teeth.

Around her, a parade of the miserable whispered love names: *White Lady, Black Lady, Lady of the Shadows, La Flaca (Skinny One), Sweet Death.* Scarred men blew cigar smoke, spat tequila, offering her delights *boca a boca.* Shirtless machos flexed Santa Muerte tattoos. One mess of a woman crawled on her knees, hauling a baby on her back, her mascara smudged like someone had erased her face. Bums slid folded bills into the collection box to curry favor. Pedro was transfixed, mumbling prayers like a fiend.

Hugo grabbed his arm. "Asshole, she's not listening. She's dead. Let's go."

The pool cleaner crossed himself, kissed his fingertips.

As they pushed through the hot city, Hugo's courage returned. Pedro was right: *Better a rich man's dog than a poor man's saint.* The streets around Tepito were named after professions: *Pintores, Plomeros, Mecánicos.* This struck Hugo as funny.

"Mamá, I moved into an apartment on Prostitutas."

Pedro pulled a paper scrap from his pocket. "We're looking for Fifteen Jardineros. Some restaurant."

"Gardeners. Like me. It's a sign."

"Sign of what?"

Hugo shrugged. "I'm trying to figure that out."

"Get serious." Pedro snapped his fingers just in front of Hugo's nose. "You want money for the girl, stop fucking around."

Hugo didn't appreciate Pedro's tone. Hugo had a few years on little Pedro from the village. Hugo had gotten him hired as a pool cleaner for Thomas Malone and now as a part-time runner for Reyes. They were friends, nearly brothers, stepbrothers or half brothers, whichever was less. They joked around, pissed in Malone's pool, but here was Pedro, slapping his back like some rich uncle, saying, "If we do this right, we each take home half a grand."

"Why so much?"

"El Pelotas didn't tell you?"

"You call Reyes that?"

"Not to his face." Pedro pulled out a black face mask, held it over his mug. "What do you think?"

Hugo laughed, nervous. "It's Subcomandante Marcos. Where's your pipe?"

Pedro lifted his shirt. A pistol was wedged against his gut.

Hugo swore. "It's just a pick-up. What's with you?"

Pedro dropped his head. Pity. Exasperation. "The guy we're meeting stole this mask from Reyes. We're taking it back. Reyes is pissed. The guy is as good as dead."

"How does Reyes know he's here?"

"Gonzáles."

"Gonzáles is coming?

"Gonzáles never comes."

"You know a lot about this. How—"

"Reyes told me. It's complicated."

Hugo pushed Pedro's shoulder. "Since when do you talk to Reyes?"

"Easy, *cabrón. No manches.*" Pedro made eye contact, but barely. "Here's what is happening. This part is simple. I'll go up. You stay on the street. Something doesn't sound right, you howl."

"Since when are you the boss?"

"I am nobody's boss." Pedro spat over his shoulder. "And nobody's donkey."

Pedro glared, like the world owed him an apology, which it

probably did. Still, Hugo was surprised little Pedro had noticed. Hugo had assumed his friend was content to pour chlorine in rich people's pools. He'd never viewed Pedro as a man of ambition, but the cartels offered power, protection, a family. A way up, but never out.

For ten blocks, they walked in silence. Hugo counted backward. What did Pedro mean, it was complicated?

A boy in plastic sandals biked past them, legs so skinny his kneecaps stuck out. Hugo wanted to chase after the kid, warn him, tell him to ride out of Tepito and never come back.

fourteen | ANNA

She wore no jewelry. She carried no map. This was Mexico City, the largest metropolis in the western hemisphere, a city so dangerous tourists who climbed into the wrong taxi might never reach their hotel. The sky was slathered with a mayonnaise-like haze. Anna found a *taxi de sitio*, gave the driver the address.

"Tepito?" the driver muttered. "Not safe."

"Yes," Anna agreed. "I know."

The cab roared north past blockish apartment buildings with stacked terraces, past billboards of big-chested blondes hawking hair spray and sugary fruit drinks. Ten lanes of traffic skimmed along Reforma. It was hard to believe this megalopolis was once an island in the middle of a lake. Mexico City was literally built over Tenochtitlán, the Aztecs' glorious city of canals. By 1500, the population of Tenochtitlán was four times that of London, and for all the Aztecs' notorious barbarousness, their culture was advanced, with a 365-day calendar, poetry performances, a vibrant market selling gold and gems, feathers and spices. Produce grew in sunken gardens. Aqueducts transported drinking water. After the Conquest, the Spanish drained the lake, demolished the temples, or simply erected cathedrals over them. Today, like Venice, Mexico City was sinking. Drainage, subway lines, building foundations had settled and cracked. The Basilica of Guadalupe tilted so much the walk to the altar was uphill.

There's a metaphor, Anna thought.

Right on Matamoros. Anna sat rigid, focused. Red cabs scurried like the cochineal bugs Indian women crushed to dye wool. The wind was filthy and soft. She didn't chat with the driver. Not here.

David never did shit like this. The most dangerous thing he'd ever done was order sushi in Pittsburgh.

Anna double-checked the e-mail. She'd scarcely looked at the photograph of the mask. She didn't care about the object, only what it would fetch. A small fortune. Her father's reputation. Her mother's museum wing. The humiliation of her ex. She practiced the words she would need to complete the transaction. *Máscara.* Mask. *Comprar.* To buy. A regular *ar* verb. What the hell was she doing here? She ought to have her head examined. No, drilled. The way the ancient Peruvian healers did, boring into the skulls of sick patients to release the misery trapped inside.

The taxi swung onto Jardineros, stopped mid-block in front of a sketchy-looking joint with a sign reading TRES PERROS FEROCES. The place was closed. For lunch? For good? Chairs were upturned on tables. The picture window was smeared. By comparison, the cab felt safe and familiar, with its lingering smell of sausage and smoke. Anna had eight grand in a pouch under her shirt. A two-grand emergency fund in her wallet. No Gonzáles.

She paid the driver, asked him to wait. "I'm going to return to the bus station right after."

The driver gave her an odd expression, like he trusted her less and respected her more. "How long?"

"Twenty minutes, maximum."

He turned off the motor, left his meter running. Anna got out. A copper-colored dog limped down the road, followed by a wandering vendor selling *migas*. Pop music mixed with the hip-hop of mufflerless cars. Anna half hoped the restaurant door was locked, but it opened easily.

"*Aló.*"

No answer.

A meat carver lay on the bar, along with food-encrusted plates and discarded beer bottles. Garish orange walls were painted with cartoon dogs wielding pistols. The air smelled faintly of vomit. Anna tiptoed.

"*Aló.*"

The kitchen door swung open to reveal a face. Anna was expecting a Mexican, but this guy was Anglo. Jeans hung off his hips and belled around work boots. He appeared hungry, exhausted. His eyes looked like gumballs he'd popped in that morning. This was not Gonzáles. This was his twigger.

"*Soy Anna, de la parte de Señor Ramsey. El coleccionista.*"

He answered in English. "You're Daniel Ramsey?"

Anna nodded. Close enough. He waved her into the kitchen, the last place she wanted to go. She checked the window. The cab was already gone.

The kitchen reeked worse than the dining room. A sour-milk stink of defeat rose from stainless-steel sinks and bare shelving. Three windows struggled to let in light. A table had been dragged to the center of the room. Two chairs. A spit cup. A shiny cell phone. The twigger sat. His office. His face kept changing expression, film frames spliced in odd places. Who knew what he was seeing? Anna had read about meth. The idiots blew up houses. Lost their teeth. They were scab pickers, TV set disassemblers. The initial euphoria degenerated into paranoia and hallucinations. An addict would sell his mother for a high so rapturous it ruined his life.

"Daniel Ramsey sent me," Anna said, relieved not to have to navigate the encounter in Spanish. "Is Lorenzo Gonzáles here yet? He's meeting us."

The man checked behind him. "Not here."

Anna tamped her impatience. She didn't see the mask, but it could be anywhere. The freezer. The oven. "I have the money."

The looter made for the sink, his strides overly long, like he'd forgotten what little effort simple things took. He put a pot to boil for no apparent reason, returned to the table, tapping two fingers like a tuning fork.

"I wasn't expecting a woman."

Anna spoke the same basic sentences she'd rehearsed in Spanish. "You contacted Daniel Ramsey. He's my father. I'm his daughter. We would like to buy your mask."

"You're late." The digger scratched his scabbed arms. Meth users had the sensation that bugs were scurrying under their skin. Termites. Beetles. Ants.

"Actually early," she corrected. "We have until tomorrow."

"I already sold the mask."

"*What?*"

His head jerked. "You're late."

Of all the terrible scenarios Anna had imagined, this one had not occurred to her.

"We had an exclusive." She repeated this, the second time using the Spanish word, *exclusivo*, which sounded more emphatic. She checked the door, willing Gonzáles to walk through it.

The looter squinted. "Guess I lost track of time."

"We sent a deposit." Given the setting, this sounded hopelessly naive.

"I've got no record of that on my books."

Anna scanned the kitchen. There were no books. There wasn't even a pen. "Who bought the mask?"

"It's still here." More head-jerking, some botched reflex. "In back."

Anna used her sweetest kindergarten voice. "Since we're here first, I'll buy the mask *now*, and you can have your money right away."

The twigger slammed his fist into the table. Anna jumped. He slapped his face. Clarification. Reboot. This seemed to help. He loped into a back room and returned with a box the size of a toaster. A bungee cord held down four flaps.

"I have another offer, so the price has gone up," he said.

"How much?"

"Twenty-five percent."

Anna said okay. The guy was so cranked he probably couldn't count. She'd give him the full ten grand, which meant forfeiting all that delicious travel money, but oh well. Where the hell was Gonzáles? The looter hoisted his jeans. She looked at him, not the box. He seemed to appreciate this.

"Do you want to see the mask?"

Anna said she did. The looter put his finger to his lips, as if a baby bunny might be sleeping inside. Gingerly, Anna lifted the flaps.

The Mixtec were master stoneworkers, and this was a masterwork. Hundreds of turquoise shards had been cut, sanded, polished, and glued into place. The mask's seven teeth were fashioned from iridescent conch shell, neat as typewriter keys. One eye was missing. Had the looter smashed it? The intact shell eye was lined with gold leaf; its pupil was an elliptical black stone. The mask was surprisingly heavy, as if it carried metaphysical weight, a man's soul, his history, his quest for immortality.

Until now, Anna had pursued the death mask solely for what it could give her, but now she was overwhelmed by its cultural import. She remembered the facts she'd read. During his eighteen-year reign, Montezuma II wore sandals festooned with jewels, a nostril ring, a magnificent headdress with four hundred shimmering quetzal feathers mounted in gold. (This stunning relic was owned by Austria, which after five hundred years had agreed, in principle, to "loan" it to Mexico.) After his death, Montezuma's loyal servants placed a funerary mask with his urn so he would be ready to greet the gods. This journey had been disrupted by a twenty-first-century drug addict who needed a fix. It was unsavory to think about, so Anna didn't. She thought about how much she loved her father, how proud the mask would make him, how thrilled he would be to show the world this icon of Mexican history, to have it join the Ramsey Collection.

Her father was right: This mask would save the rest. All his journeys and bargaining, his forays into huts and jungles, his struggles with Spanish, his reading, his study, his courage, and even the death of his wife, had led him to this climactic moment. The death mask would not make Daniel Ramsey immortal, of course, but it might ease the sting of departure.

Anna dug up her money. It was her turn to shake as the looter counted the bills.

"My father told me you're an amazing digger," she said. "That you work hard and are trustworthy."

The looter puffed his thin chest. "I know where to look."

Anna wondered if he'd lost count. Sure enough, he started again. You could almost pretend this was okay. Buying vegetables at a farm stand. She was getting used to his face. He reminded her of a boy from high school, a lifeguard driving to the pool on a quarter tank of gas. This twigger guy was not much older than she was. Drugs had muted his sheen, but not extinguished all light. Her fear melted to sympathy. To give him money was to feed his habit, but she had her father to think about. Her mother.

"We appreciate the call, the opportunity." She was babbling.

An explosion cut in. Car or gun. The precariousness of the situation flew back at her: Mexico City, the addict, no cab. The mask sent a warning. *Get the fuck out of here.*

"Okay, then," Anna said. "Thank—"

The kitchen door flew open. A man appeared before them, black face mask, a pistol. They all just stood there, together. Two men, a woman, a mask, and a gun.

The gunman spoke first. "*¿Dónde está la máscara?*" He was looking right at it. His gun swerved. A mermaid tattoo swam up his forearm. "Who's she?"

Anna's hand darted in front of her face. A superhero, ready to catch bullets. With sickening clarity, she understood that of the three people gathered in this shitty restaurant, only one would get what he wanted.

"Another interested buyer." The digger looked proud, like he was dating the girl everyone coveted. The gunman walked to the table, nudged the cash with his gun. The water on the stove was boiling over.

"This hers?"

"Hers," the looter said. "Mine."

The Mexican jammed the bills into his pants, took the mask, aimed the gun at Anna, daring her to object. She swallowed the wing nut lodged in her throat. The gunman grunted. "Mine now."

Outside, life was still happening. Somewhere, a German tourist was buying a ticket to the anthropology museum. Somewhere, a mother was breastfeeding her infant underneath a woven *rebozo*. A world away, her father was watching the History Channel in his plaid chair, and here, at Tres Perros Feroces, a masked hit man was flexing his gun. Everything happened at the same time, but only certain things happened to you.

"I would appreciate if you didn't do that," the looter began. Anna winced. The drug-addict idiot was challenging the masked man who carried a gun. "It took me two days to dig that out, and I deserve—"

The Mexican interrupted. "I've been told to kill you."

The verb "kill" was *matar*. He'd used the future tense. Or some tricky form of subjunctive. The beginning of the verb was clear, the end less certain. And Anna thought: *A cockroach can live weeks without a head.*

The gun clicked. Anna ducked under the table.

"*Hombre. No hagas eso,*" the looter mumbled. Don't do this. "My mother wants to see her son in the morning."

"*¿Tu mamá?* Where the hell is your mother?"

The gun danced loose in his hands. *Beep. Beep. Beep.* A car alarm, then a siren. The sun came through the side window and made no difference. The gunman turned to the noise. The looter reached in a drawer and produced a pistol. His face ignited, no longer contrite but ecstatic.

"Aha, asshole, now what?" The looter zoomed his gun, a boy with a toy airplane. "*Pistola contra pistola.*"

Anna tried to look worthless. *Beep. Beep. Beep.* She thought of her mother and prayed. Not a real prayer, just a sloppy plea for more life. She was thirty. She could live three times this long. The refrigerator kicked on, then ranchero music, its shifty accordion sliding. And Anna thought: *Fire moves faster uphill than down.*

The gunman moved back, money jammed in his groin, mask under one arm. Boots, black, pointed, stepped back, back again, then disappeared in a clatter.

The looter dumped the gun in the drawer, the boiling water in the sink. The car alarm had finally shut the fuck up. Anna stood. Her legs nearly gave way. She needed to leave, but wasn't sure how to make that happen.

"Who was that?"

"Some Mexican."

There were twenty million Mexicans in Mexico City alone. "Yes, but which one?"

"Another buyer."

"He didn't *buy* anything."

"I didn't expect that shit. Armed robbery. I should have shot him."

"Why didn't you?"

"My gun isn't loaded."

"You carry a gun without bullets?"

"It worked pretty well. We're both still here." He rubbed his arm, confirming this fact.

"You could have *bought* bullets. We're in fucking Tepito." Cursing made Anna feel powerful, like her mouth was a gun.

The looter relaxed his face, innocence surfacing. "I guess I've never wanted to shoot anyone."

Anna's anger now had a focal point, and she let it rip. "No one *wants* to shoot anyone. You buy bullets to *protect* yourself, protect *me*. He took the mask and my money." She talked about shooting people like she knew something about it. She'd never even broken a bone.

The looter raised his voice. "He took *my* mask and *my* money."

"You have any clue what that mask was?"

"Of course. I dug it up."

"It belonged to *Montezuma*."

"Montezuma who?"

Anna glared. She wanted to rip his head off.

The looter caught on, got defensive. "Fuck that. Montezuma. Who says so?"

"Gonzáles."

"Bullshit." Pause. "What's it worth?"

"Priceless. No price. No one can even guess the price. Enough money for a lifetime . . . if it wasn't wasted."

The looter shot Anna a look that made her heart freeze. She saw how stupid she was being: arguing with an addict, a twigger with termites under his skin, a looter with a bulletless gun. This man had smoked his soul and eaten his heart and forgotten what his dick could do. They had a common enemy, but he wasn't going to help her recoup her losses or find the gunman or recover the mask that would keep her father sober. A drug addict, like a collector, thought only of himself.

"Who do you *think* it was?" Her voice was gentle.

The looter didn't look at her. "He thinks he's tricky wearing a mask, but I know that tattoo. He did a pick-up a few months back." The looter's head jerked. Explanation. Apology. Twitch. "He works for a pervert named Thomas Malone."

———

Out the bus window, endless desert. Moonlike. Abandoned. Anna draped her sweatshirt over her cold legs. Her nerves were fried. Even innocuous gestures seemed laced with foreboding: her plump seatmate crocheting, a nun engrossed in a thriller, a teenager in black jeans watching a B movie about zombies invading Manhattan. Starving, she opened a pack of orange cookies, ate them, one, two, three, four. She didn't dare drink water, for fear she'd have to pee. There were many reasons to hate herself, but Anna boiled it down to one: Thomas Malone had stolen the death mask out from under her, exactly as her father had predicted.

The bus slowed to a stop. Flat tire or bandits, Anna couldn't rally the energy to care. A wizened *vaquero* in a cowboy hat teetered on, carrying a cage with a collapsed chicken inside. Where did these people come from, and where did they go? No bus stop, not even a country road, just a man and a cage, waiting on the highway's edge. The cowboy sat sideways, boots and cage in the aisle. The chicken just lay there, red head like a wound. Feathers impossibly white. A gamy funk asserted itself. The chicken wasn't sleeping. It was dead.

Anna was close to tears. Over what? A dead chicken? The rancher carrying a dead chicken? She was leaky, a hapless colander. She'd lost her resilience, and now every little thing was getting inside, seeping into the places that hurt.

Her phone bleeped a text.

Did you get it left me know yiy are okay lovedad

Anna held the phone like a prayer book. Her father's first text. It didn't occur to him to punctuate or abbreviate. She should have written back but she didn't. She wouldn't lie and she couldn't tell the truth.

_____

That night, Anna paced her room, holding court with Duty Free. She'd promised to call her father, but worried the bad news might send him searching for ice. Instead, she texted: Delivery delayed but all good. Give me couple days. More soon!

Every liar needed exclamation points.

She pulled *Dancing with the Tiger* from her suitcase, looking for comfort, but the thrill of seeing her name in print had long been eclipsed. All she saw were mistakes. Lies her father had been told and together they had published. She balled up a pillow, slept, dreamt the blue mask was calling her. *Don't just lie there. Come find me.*

She woke up sweaty and exhausted. The sun came in the window. The book lay open to the fake Grasshopper masks. A thumb of tequila rested in her glass. She had a simple choice to make: Go home or chase the death mask. Two thousand miles away, her father was waking up in Connecticut, hobbling to the kitchen for coffee. His bird feeder must be empty by now. His masks were boxed in the basement. Old men and devils and hermits. The Ramsey Collection. One mask away from redemption. What did she have to go back for? No David. No job. No apartment.

There was no decision to make. Not really. Thomas Malone had stolen the mask from the Ramseys. Now Anna must steal it back.

fifteen | THE GARDENER

They left Tepito, driving south
through the outer wasteland of Mexico City, through a landscape so
bleak someone should set it on fire. Hugo held the turquoise mask in
his lap, thought about how each stone was like a day in your life, each
nugget forming a part of the person you grew to be.

He held up the mask, peered through the missing eye. "Boo."

Pedro looked annoyed, or skittish. "*No chingues.* You'll break it." He
slid his orange soda back in the drink holder.

"You're scared?" Hugo laughed. "I saw you praying to that skeleton.
Your lips were moving faster than a nun's."

"I pray to everybody. If you had any sense, you would, too. You
want to walk through Tepito without any protection? It's like a whore
not carrying a condom. I prayed to Santa Muerte for safe passage.
What do you believe in?"

"Money, women, chili, *cerveza*. Things you can hold and enjoy."

"My Tiger can't hold on to women."

"Actually, I hold on to two." Hugo lifted the mask's mouth to his ear. "The death mask is saying, *I don't want to live with the narcos.*"

"Smart mask."

"Malone would shit over this. Who's going to win? Reyes or Malone?"

Pedro chortled. The answer was obvious. "*Narco* only *thinks* he's winning, but he never wins. Gringo consumes more. Gringo blames more. Gringo pays in dollars. *Narcos* kill other *narcos*, but gringo kills *narco* in the end. I'm not talking masks. I'm talking big picture."

"Who kills gringos?"

"Cancer."

They were roaring down the *cuota*, the toll highway most chumps couldn't afford. Hugo said, "You didn't tell me what happened inside."

"Loser gave back the mask. Pathetic. Almost felt sorry for him. Reyes told me to pop him, but I don't need that on my conscience. Guy was too busy killing himself. He'll be dead in a month with a needle in his hand. If Reyes asks, say I shot him."

Hugo couldn't decide which was worse: promising to murder a man, or promising to murder a man and then not doing it.

"I don't like it."

"Listen"—Pedro jutted his chin—"if I am going to off someone, I'm going after someone important." He let that vow stand for a minute. "You hungry? I know a place in Puebla."

"We can't leave the mask in the car." Hugo didn't want to fuck things up.

"Stick it in the bag. We'll take it with us."

"This mask is worth a fortune."

"My stomach is worth a fortune." Pedro ran his finger under his nose. "I'll carry it. Trust me."

They ate cactus tacos in an open-air market. Hunched over his red stool, Hugo eyed the cook, who had nice breasts. Pedro had the mask in a bag slung over one shoulder. It was good to eat hot food, and Hugo relaxed in a way he hadn't all day. He'd be home soon, with money in his pocket, and he'd give the yellow girl the necklace he'd bought her, the kind with a locket you put a tiny photograph in. He'd find a picture where he didn't look too old.

Three tacos later, Pedro stood. "I need to take a piss."

"Leave the bag here."

"I'm not letting it out of my sight. I gave Reyes my word."

Hugo pointed to his right eye and warned: *"Ojos."*

Pedro gave a thumbs-up.

Hugo waited ten minutes. Paid the bill. Waited another ten, then got a bad feeling. Pedro didn't answer his phone. Hugo checked the toilets, circled back to the taco stand, asked the woman if she'd seen the guy he'd come in with. She hadn't. He looped around the market—all those vegetables nobody wanted—then fanned out to the side streets. His mind spun, furious and pleading. *Pedro, hombre, what happened to you? Did you screw me over, or did someone hurt you? Don't make me face Reyes without that pinche mask.*

He went back to the stand. Nothing. He went back to the john. Nothing. The curse of Tepito. Godforsaken place. People blowing smoke over somebody's mother. Desperate people will pray to anything. Desperate people will pray to a rock.

He found the car still parked on Providencia, door unlocked, wheel boot unlocked, keys under the mat. A friend's parting courtesy. Pedro's phone, the phone Reyes paid for, sat on the seat. Dead center.

Hugo waited an hour more, just in case. He had to admire little Pedro's *cojones*, even as he wanted to slice his throat. The thought of telling Reyes the news made his bowels run. He picked up a rock— gray, nothing special, but maybe that was the point. The gardener had not prayed since he was a boy, thin and sickly, when he'd prayed for a bicycle (he never got one), prayed his grandfather would not die (he did), prayed that dirty Lupe next door would show her privates (she didn't). In the intervening decades, God had been easy to leave behind.

Blessed God rock, Pedro fucked me over and now I have a drug lord up my ass. Help me, please. I don't know what to do. He wanted to say, *I deserve better than this,* but he wasn't sure that was true. Instead, he signed off with *Next time, I will do better.*

In Bible stories, after a prayer, the Lord sends a sign. Shooting star or parting waters. But all Hugo saw was graffiti and PRI signs and the dumb rock in his hand.

Reyes was going to kill him. Or maybe just cut off his hand.

He climbed into the car, gripped the steering wheel, and howled.

sixteen | ANNA

The clerk was wearing Carnival beads and a cut petunia behind his right ear. His eyebrows looked thicker than Anna remembered, and his fingers were clotted with rings. *He's working his way to Frida Kahlo,* Anna thought. *Pretty soon, he'll buy a monkey.*

She told him she needed to find an American couple living in Oaxaca and asked his advice. The clerk, whose name was Rafi, suggested she ask at the English library, six blocks west. "All the Americans go there," he said. "They have free coffee."

The English library had none of the grandeur of the expat library in San Miguel de Allende that Anna remembered from childhood, but it was still lively. Behind the green gate, a half-dozen visitors clustered around plastic tables and chairs. An *intercambio* was going on. A frumpy man who looked to be in his fifties recited Spanish verbs to a young Mexican woman, whose patience was as large as her chest. The librarian was British, officious, with a lavender scarf and purple reading glasses attached to a cord. Anna explained that she was trying to contact an American art collector, Thomas Malone.

"We're not allowed to give out the private information of our members."

"Is there some kind of expatriate directory?" Anna asked.

The woman pressed the spine of her novel. "Just word of mouth. You might come to our next board meeting in two weeks. I could introduce you round."

"It's for my father. He's not well. He and Thomas Malone are old friends. . . ."

The woman softened. She pointed across the room to a bulletin board. "They had a job advert posted for some time. I think it had their address, or maybe just a number. You might have a look."

The board was crammed with notices. Yoga. Tutoring. Deep-tissue massage. Apartments to rent. Mountain-biking excursions. Lost dogs. Pilates. Herbal cancer treatments. Tarot cards. Housecleaning—not one of its rip-off tags remained. Then, next to a notice for a bilingual barbershop quartet, was a handwritten file card.

> *Writer sought for art gallery guide. Excellent writing and editing skills a must for this collaboration. Six-week commitment. $15 an hour.*
>
> *Thomas Malone, 14 Amapolas, 513 6767*

Anna smiled to herself, an idea forming. She walked back to the circulation desk. "Do you think the job has been taken if it's still posted?"

The librarian looked warily over her readers. "No one ever bothers to remove things. You're looking for a position?"

Anna Ramsey didn't need a job, but Anna . . . Anna *Bookman* was broke. Yes, laid off from her editorial job. Divorced. Starting over in Mexico.

"Yes," Anna said. "Something part-time."

"Call. You might get lucky. They've put that same ad up before."

"What do you mean?"

The woman's mouth tightened into a beak. "Oaxaca has a commitment problem. No one wants to bloody grow up. Not even the retirees. Try keeping a library staffed. *So sorry, I'm going on a pilgrimage to Chichén Itzá to watch the solstice. So sorry, I'm going scuba diving in Belize.* Rubbish." She straightened the tape dispenser on her desk. "The girl who first had that post owes the library five hundred pesos. She'd had enough of Mexico and went home. Got a better offer, I suppose, or was tired of working for . . . tired of working. Everyone thinks, *Oh, Mexico. I'll just butter myself up in the sunshine. Loll about.* But you have to *live* somewhere. Pay rent. Have a proper flat. Not just flit about."

"How long ago was that? That girl who left?"

"I don't know. Before the Christmas holiday. But you should still ring, because even if they've hired someone, he's probably quit by now to pick coffee in Chiapas. Or start yoga school. That's the dream of all young people. Teach yoga." She pecked her gathered fingers toward the corkboard. "Live in your tights."

"Salutation to the sun," Anna said, egging her on.

The librarian lowered her eyes into her novel. "Down dog. Please."

———

"You'll have to find a housekeeper," Constance Malone said, as she squeezed lime juice into a blue-rimmed pitcher. "Someone you can trust, like Soledad."

Gazing at the sloping Sierra Madre, Anna tried to keep her envy in check. Perched in the foothills, the Malones' pink villa had a towering view of the city below. Behind the ten-foot security wall, no calendar, no tick of a clock, interrupted the pampered routine. The interior was tastefully appointed with exposed beams, hand-painted tiles, and folk art, although, oddly, no masks. No Thomas, either. He was late.

"Soledad seems wonderful," Anna agreed. The housekeeper, a dour soul in an apron, had greeted her at the door. "Maybe someday I'll be able to afford help, but I'm still in a hotel for now, until I find work."

"They clean, do laundry, *iron your T-shirts*."

The frozen vodka poured sluggish and clear. Anna hadn't expected her job interview to begin with cocktails, not that she was complaining.

"I have this liberal friend Lettie who refuses to hire help on principle," Constance rattled on. "She wants to clean up her own shit."

She tapped the screen door with her sandal. Anna felt a fresh pang of envy. The house was large, but the grounds were immense. The stone patio was surrounded by gardens, a lush mix of regal palms and fragrant bushes whose blossoms hung like swollen sexual organs. Beyond that, a long yard that ended with a swimming pool, a perfect turquoise rectangle. Outbuildings were visible in both directions. A pair of peacocks stood erect in a cage. Her father had spent many long afternoons on this patio, buying masks, trading stories, drinking. Anna's biggest fear was that she would run into the thug from Tepito, but she saw no one.

"This screen door is my private victory," Constance said. "Thomas likes everything cold and insists on roaring the air-conditioning every night. A bomb could go off on the front lawn and we wouldn't know. When he leaves in the morning, I open everything up. Let in the heat, the fresh air, the flies."

Constance sat in a pigskin chair, motioning to a hammocklike contraption. Anna dropped into it, sloshed her drink. Licking her hand, she appraised her hostess with a critical eye. Constance was in her late forties. Her graying hair was tied back in a ponytail. Her chin was set and her nose firm, an actress determined to age with grace. She draped her trim figure in a shapeless embroidered dress that reached her ankles, the kind that Indian women sold to tourists to hide the bumps of middle age. *When you start to wear muumuus, it's time to go home.*

Anna's phone beeped. David. Show got amazing reviews. Come home + celebrate.

Anna scowled. She was sweating. She hated him. Now more than ever.

"The way I see it, we have money," Constance rambled. "Mexicans need money. It's cruel not to give some away. So we have Hugo." She pointed to a gardener crossing the yard. Anna squinted, bracing herself, but it was not the thug from Tepito. This guy was leaner, with nice arms.

"We have Pedro, the pool cleaner. Soledad, who you met. A Spanish tutor. A masseuse. Thomas and I are single-handedly keeping this city afloat. Yesterday, I paid Hugo a hundred pesos extra to clean the dog mess off the driveway. Every mutt in town sneaks through our woods to make a donation. Maybe Lettie would like to clean up that shit, too. Poor Hugo is so eager for money. Either he's got debts or a girlfriend, but at least we treat the Mexicans like human beings. The previous *señora* made Soledad bring her own toilet paper."

Anna reminded herself she was no longer Anna Ramsey, the fact-checker, but Anna Bookman, the unemployed expatriate desperate for work. Anna Bookman would listen to any sort of drivel if it landed her a job.

A dog whimpered. Anna scanned the patio. "You have pets?"

"Morocco and Honduras." Constance pointed to the bench against the house. Anna bent to look. Two Yorkshire terriers were panting in the shade. "I refuse to go either place, so we named the dogs after them. I told Thomas, *Snuggle up, that's as close as we're getting.*" Constance took a long sip, frowned. Her cocktail was boring her. "Do you know anyone in the city?"

"No one, though I met an artist on the *zócalo*. Salvador something."

"Flores," Constance mused. "A painter. Unkempt. Unsuccessful. Pretty girl on the arm."

Anna grinned, committing this description to memory. "What a coincidence—"

"Hardly. Oaxaca is a city, but it operates like a small town. All the artists paint the same hideous things. Surrealist blobs. Squids, aliens, fetuses. That or skeletons, paying homage to Posada. Death. Death everywhere. Who wants to think about it?"

Constance shooed a fly, recrossed her long legs. Anna checked her watch. Thomas Malone was now fifteen minutes late. She pointed to a distant cottage shaded by trees. "What's that?"

"We rent that little place to Hugo and Soledad. They came with the house. Soledad knows everything, thinks the place is hers, but she's wonderfully useful when things go wrong."

"They're married? She seems older—"

"Yes, married."

"What's that other building?"

"That's the chapel where Thomas stores his masks."

"In a chapel?" Anna sat up. "I'd like to see that."

"Good luck. He doesn't let anyone in, and believe me, it's just as well. The place is a wreck. Falling plaster. Mice."

"I don't mind. I'd—"

"It's locked and even I don't have a key. Thomas calls it his *sanctuary*." Constance imbued the word with both sarcasm and status. "My husband is reasserting his faith. The Grand Restoration. For all I know, he's out there every night baptizing squirrels."

"What religion is he?"

"He *was* Presbyterian. Now he's tinkering."

"How did he get into collecting masks? Is he an anthropologist?"

"A drug rep." Her laugh was short and sharp. "Peddling Xanax in Philadelphia when we met at a society junket. I like to tell people I fell in love with my pusher. Would you like another?" Constance shook her empty glass.

"Another would put me over."

"Oh, go over." Constance reached for the pitcher.

Anna held out her glass. "Do you collect masks, too?" This seemed a stretch.

"I used to go with Thomas on buying trips, until last year. We went to Pátzcuaro for Day of the Dead, and it was horrifying. Dragged on all night. Everyone drunk and wearing hideous masks. No one spoke

English. Anything could have happened and the police wouldn't have lifted a finger. I told Thomas, *That's it. No more traveling. I'd rather stay home.* We have the pool, if we get hot. If we get hungry, Soledad will fix something. If we want art, we can look in books."

As if on cue, Soledad appeared with guacamole and chips. The housekeeper could have been thirty-five or fifty. Worry etched her forehead with three wavy lines.

"Soledad, this is Anna. She has come about the job." Though Constance spoke Spanish, her accent drained all beauty from the language, like chopping a rose into cubes.

Anna stood to shake Soledad's hand, but Constance signaled not to bother. Soledad gave a half smile, flashing the gold in her teeth.

"*¿Señora, qué se le antoja para cenar?*"

"Decisions." Constance sounded annoyed. "They won't slice bread without your permission." She turned to Soledad. *"Hablamos más tarde. Después."*

Anna tried to catch Soledad's eye, to convey, *Later, you and I will laugh about the señora,* but Soledad shrieked, *"La leche,"* and ran into the kitchen.

"It's boiled over again." Constance checked her watch. "Every day she scalds her hot chocolate. It's bad luck to let milk boil over. If that's true, we're all damned." She fanned herself with a newspaper. "Thomas has no idea what goes on. I manage the budget, the staff, the plumber, the dogs. Wait. There's Thomas. He's back."

In all the times Anna had imagined Thomas Malone, she'd pictured a younger variation of her father—pasty, paunchy, professorial—but the man who crossed the clipped grass was lean and groomed, a good fifteen years younger than Daniel Ramsey. He wore charcoal-gray trousers and a pressed long-sleeve white shirt, and he carried a wooden cross in his hand like a polo club. His crisp expression, compounded by his height, gave him an air of confidence and remote disdain. While Constance moved slowly, her husband's angular body glided over the lawn, leaving no trace.

"Thomas, come meet Anna Bookman. She's here about the job."

He shook Anna's hand, inspecting her, as if deciding whether to rent or buy. Though he could not have known she was Daniel Ramsey's daughter, the intensity of his gaze unnerved her.

The three of them sat. "Constance wants me to hire an assistant, but I'm not convinced I need one," Thomas began. "So what brings you to Oaxaca?"

Anna told the story she'd prepared. "I worked for magazines for five years. Fact-checking, primarily. But I got laid off, so I decided to come to Oaxaca to practice my Spanish. Make a fresh start. Find a job." She tried to sound as carefree as this biography implied.

Thomas scraped mud off his shoe with a penknife.

"Darling"—Constance pointed—"where did you get that cross?"

"On the road to Etla. There's a sharp curve where drunk Mexicans kill themselves. This little cross caught my eye."

He stuck it in the ground like a croquet peg.

Anna winced. "You pulled the cross from a shrine?" She turned to Constance for backup, but her hostess was measuring an inch of air to show Hugo how short to cut the grass. "Isn't that grave robbing?"

Thomas turned cool. "I am sure you're familiar with funereal arts."

Ever so sweetly, Anna said that she was. "How long have you been collecting?"

"I used to collect what other people found valuable. Now I create value by what I collect." His gaze scalded her skin. The implication was that he could do her a similar favor. Anna smiled and thought, *Fuck you.*

"How long are you staying?" he asked.

"It depends if I find work."

"Mid-March, I'm having the first public showing of my collection. More than a hundred works. Carved masks and antiquities. The gallery guide will be quite simple, a synopsis of each mask. History. Materials. Dimensions. Origin. Associated dances. An introduction to the exhibit. But we're behind schedule. The printing deadline is coming up quickly."

"How many masks do you own?" Anna knew this was like asking an alcoholic how many drinks he'd consumed. A collector would always equivocate, underestimate, lie.

"There are three kinds of masks. Masks made for tourists, masks made to be danced, and very old masks that circulate the antiquities market. I started collecting the second kind, but have moved on to the third. Basically, I appreciate, acquire, then let what I acquire appreciate. The castoffs I ship to my gallery in El Paso. Love and money should work together, don't you think?"

Anna met his gaze, daring him to act on what he was implying. A squirrel hopped across the lawn, tail swishing like a happy paintbrush. Constance chucked a dog toy at it, missed.

"Don't be modest," she said. "You drag things to the border every month. I worry about the bandits on the highways, but Thomas carries a gun. So do I." She pointed to a wood armoire. "In case some undesirable washes up from the city. My father is Texan. Guns are his pets. Darling, tell her about Reyes," Constance purred. Her pale skin had blotched in unattractive patches.

"Screw Reyes."

"Who's Reyes?"

"Óscar Reyes Carrillo, a fraud," Thomas snapped. "A drug lord who dabbles in art and antiquities. The press, the prestigious art world of Oaxaca, likes to call him my rival. It's true we often go head-to-head for a piece. He likes to send me taunting postcards of his latest purchases. Doesn't sign them, but I know damn well who they're from. Where's the latest?"

Constance got up, went inside, came back, handed Anna a crude postcard of a strange red clay figure, part snowman, part demon.

"Chupícuaro," Thomas said. "Fertility figure. Five hundred B.C. Found in an archaeological site now under water from the Solis Dam. Last year, they lowered the water enough to salvage a pair of church towers, long enough for a resourceful entrepreneur to snap up a few treasures. Sotheby's sold a comparable piece recently for $185,000. Private collection. 'Provenance unknown.' In the art world, no one knows where anything comes from." Thomas flicked his hand, poof. "Things magically surface."

The figure didn't do much for Anna, but you couldn't argue with passion. "It must be hard to compete with a mobster," she said, filling her voice with sympathy. "This Reyes has underground connections and you're stuck playing fair." Anna handed back the postcard, stole a glimpse at the chapel. Maybe Soledad cleaned in there occasionally. Maybe she left the door unlocked.

"For years I've kept a low profile, but Constance talked me into curating this show, and what does the great and powerful Reyes do? Schedules an opening *the same day*. Rents a gallery across town and says he's showing *his* mask collection. Let Oaxaca decide who's the more discriminating collector. The showdown is March fifteenth."

"Beware the Ides of March."

Thomas forced a grin. "If someone stabs Reyes, I rule Rome."

"How do you actually win?"

"The critics will decide, and the public." Thomas sniffed. "But there will be no contest."

Constance patted Thomas's thigh.

Anna asked, "Does Reyes know what you have?"

"*No one knows what I have.* Or what I'm getting. Publicity has never interested me. It interests my wife."

"It's time you were properly celebrated."

"Constance wants to impress her father." Thomas sipped his cocktail with a contemptuous expression. "Dicky Senior wants his son-in-law to *come* to something."

"No worries, dear, you're already something."

Anna smiled, smiled, smiled. Thomas Malone was earning in-law goodie points with a mask he'd stolen from her father. "But how can I write about the collection without seeing it?"

"You'll work here, and I'll bring you the masks. One by one—"

"I keep telling Thomas the guide could be expanded into a book," Constance said to Anna. "The definitive book on Mexican masks."

"There's nothing like that already?" Anna asked, innocent, breezy.

"There *was*." Constance dropped her chin. "But it's become a laughing—"

Thomas interrupted. "The author was a nice enough bloke, but drank too much. Bought any schlock that carvers offered him. I tried to warn him. Now Constance wants me to prove to her Texas relatives that I can write a better book *and* vanquish the *narco*."

His eyes circled Anna's shirt. It was hard to pretend nothing was happening. Constance gazed over the wall at the neighbors' knot of electric lines. Either she was oblivious of her husband's wandering eye or she had accepted what she could not change.

Thomas concluded his lament. "Call me Superman."

This was more than even Constance could take. "*Oh, please.* All I am saying is, Daniel Ramsey's downfall is your opportunity." With a frown, Constance rose. Her matchmaking was done. She grabbed the pitcher. "We're out of beverages."

The screen door banged. Thomas's expression grew lighthearted, mocking, as if they had both endured a comic ordeal. *Poor Constance,* Anna thought. *He's cruel.*

"So what do you think?" he asked. His expression was inscrutable.

"Is that an offer?"

Thomas stabbed an olive. "It's an offer. Come be my personal assistant."

"When would I start?"

"When you're ready."

"I came here ready."

"I could tell."

She wondered if she was going to have to sleep with Thomas Malone to get into his chapel. Anna Bookman ran her hand down her thigh. Fact: *Waitresses who wear red lipstick earn bigger tips.*

"Are you offering benefits?" she asked.

"You need insurance?"

"I had insurance once, but it made me sick." Anna spun her melting ice. "Have you had other assistants, or am I the first?"

"None that worked out. Collaboration is a tricky business."

"Not with the right partner. I'm a model employee."

"Should I check your letters of reference?"

"Just give me a minute to write some." She challenged him with her eyes. If Thomas insisted on references, the game was up, though she'd bet the only opinion he valued was his own.

"Did you come here alone," he asked, "or is some boyfriend straggling behind you?"

"I don't have a boyfriend, here."

"It's good to have a boyfriend who's not here. I don't imagine you suffer from a shortage of male company."

"I have been known to do some collecting."

Constance blew open the screen door. Her wrist sagged under the weight of a full pitcher. Anna pulled her shirt away from her chest to let in some air. Patio sex. A first.

"Thomas," Constance huffed, setting the pitcher down. "I'm blotto. It's the damn heat."

"Take a nap, puppet."

"I should really be going now." Anna put down her glass. "Thank you for everything."

Thomas stood. "So we'll see you Monday—"

Just then, a dog jumped over the wall and made a beeline toward the bench.

"There's that goddamn mutt—" Constance turned, muumuu billowing. She reached into the armoire and grabbed a rifle. "I've had it." The dog pushed its snout under the bench and growled. Thomas and Anna jumped up. Constance pointed the gun at Anna as if in a trance, her willowy body swaying. Thomas yelled his wife's name and lunged at her, but this only made her grip the rifle more fiercely. She fixed her aim on the dog.

Soledad stood behind the screen door, her face as blank as stucco.

The rifle went off. Anna jammed her fingers in her ears. The bullet missed the dog, but pierced the watering can, embedding itself in the woodpile. The dog scurried back over the wall. The watering can bled from its wound. Constance righted her muumuu, chambered another round.

"I have to do everything around here." Her voice rose. "Even the plumbing. Hugo's been banging all day—"

"Well, well. That was exciting." Thomas cleaned his hands in the air. "Anna, it's been a pleasure. Leave your number with—"

The rifle fired a second time. A squirrel collapsed in a bloody sack in the middle of the lawn. Its flesh resembled a human kidney or heart, some organ you couldn't live without. Anna's ears were ringing. Nobody spoke. The wounded air pieced itself back together.

"Thomas," Constance commanded, each word taking aim, "toss the squirrel over the Mendezes' wall."

Thomas tightened his mouth. "Hugo will handle it."

"He's gone. I am asking you."

"It's not their squirrel."

"It *is* their squirrel, their dog, their country."

All at once, Anna understood. Constance was an heiress. Texas oil money. Something. Thomas was a kept man. A kept man who kept other women. *Everyone picks someone smaller to dominate, like a set of Russian dolls. I am the last doll. The hard one that can't be opened.*

Constance held out a dustpan. Thomas retrieved it. Each step cost him. He'd made this walk before. Constance demanded the occasional concession. She knew her husband was unfaithful, and this was her way of reminding him who held the gun and who bought the bullets. It was hard not to feel pity for a man so compromised. Thomas knelt before the squirrel, his pressed pants wrinkling. Blood smeared the white dustpan. The air smelled like iron and compost. With outstretched hands, he scooped up the mess and chucked it over the wall.

Under the spigot, he washed the dustpan. Blood mixed with water. Soledad's face pulled back from the screen door.

"My pants . . ." Thomas turned toward the house. "Excuse me."

Constance collapsed in a chair. Anna crouched next to her, offering to fetch her water. Somewhere, a firecracker exploded. Constance grasped Anna's hand, interlocking fingers. This intimacy made Anna uneasy. Having decided the woman was nuts, she didn't want to muddy the waters with sympathy. Still, they had a few things in common: unfaithful men, Mexico, ambition—its disappointments. Anna could imagine Constance as a young woman, twenty-five, in white sneakers, tennis racquet in hand. Thomas had wooed her. Constance had been glad to share her money and long limbs with such an elegant man.

Constance blinked. "Do you know why they shoot firecrackers?"

Anna said she didn't.

"Each explosion is a call out to God. They are trying to crack open the sky and wake Him up. They want God to *do* something, but of course, He never does. Poor people. The wind just comes and blows the smoke away."

Walking up the drive, Anna weaved between piles of fresh dog shit. For the second time that week, she'd nearly been shot, but she was more exhilarated than scared. The death mask was in the chapel. She'd talk her way in there soon enough. After turning on the main road, Anna passed a *miscelánea* that sold soda and chips, passed an empty lot of debris and rusted cars, passed a ragged donkey, unmoving, passed an *abuelita* wrapped in a black shawl. When she reached the newsstand, she heard a third shot.

seventeen | THE GARDENER

Reyes was dressed like a '70s porn star. Fake tan. Baby-blue leisure pants stretched tight over his muscular thighs. Nylon shirt, four buttons open. Blond wig, flopping like a palm tree. His grubby eyes darted among the objects on his desk: laptop, cell phone, assault weapon, video monitor, Coke can, cigarettes, sausage sandwich stinking of chili, porn magazine, dead rose. Hugo told the story long because as long as he was talking, he was still alive. Besides, the story *felt* long, like he'd driven to Tepito one man and come back another. He turned the debacle into a parable of Good and Evil: faithful Hugo had trusted unfaithful Pedro, his childhood friend, who had double-crossed Reyes out of greed. Hugo ended with an apology.

Reyes held up a hand. *"Le cagaste, pero el problema no es insuperable."* You fucked up, but the problem is not insurmountable.

The gardener quickly agreed.

"Pedro will be back." Reyes's voice was hoarse, as if he'd been screaming for days. "When our Pedrito returns, you ask him nicely to return the mask. Then you kill him."

This was better and worse than Hugo had expected. The gardener shifted his weight, right foot to left. "*Con todo respeto, patrón,* I am a runner, not an assassin."

"Your job just changed."

"I don't even know where he is. He could be in Yucatán or Juárez." Hugo spread his arms, illustrating the distance.

Reyes massaged his chin. Pancake makeup came off on his thumb. "Remember, this is not an intelligent man. He's an animal who walks on two legs. It's February. He lives for his *fiestas.* He does what his father does, what the *pueblo* does. When do village boys return to the mother's teat?"

Hugo kicked the fake Oriental rug. The *patrón* was vicious but not stupid. He handed Hugo a wooden tiger mask. "Wear it to the dances. The carver said it was powerful. Are you superstitious? All the same, take a machete."

"But—"

"A tiger must earn his stripes."

"Someone with more experience—"

Reyes puckered his lips, a wedge of rotten fruit. "I need to write a letter today. Maybe I'll stop in that paper store by the viaduct. Shop-girls make such a tight fuck."

"*Patrón*—"

Reyes's face went apoplectic, fake hair bouncing. "You and that shitty pool cleaner are working together."

"I would not be here if that were true. I came to make things right. Out of loyalty to you."

Reyes pounded his desk. His gun shook. His sausage quivered.

"If that mask is not back to me by the end of Carnival, I will cut out your heart and hang it from a tree and watch the turkey vultures feast, and I will screw your little girlfriend and rape your ugly wife and kill your dog and cook your cat and burn down your house and blow up your car and throw your carcass in the Pacific, where the sharks will rip you apart and shit you out in pellets on the ocean floor. Have I left anything out? Do you have a mother? Or did she die from shame at having raised an incompetent? Gonzáles called. That was Montezuma's death mask. Do you know who the fuck he was? That American junkie stole that mask from *me*, and now that chlorine-head stole it from you *and* me. No one steals from Reyes. Not if they like to breathe."

Hugo kept his eyes on his boots. All a man ever really had were his heart and his shoes. How did Reyes know about the girl? How did Reyes know everything, show up everywhere? Hugo's hands tightened into fists. "I will bring you the mask by Ash Wednesday. I will kill Pedro, but please don't harm the girl. She is innocent."

He dared to look up.

Reyes was eating his sandwich. The guy was always eating. How much energy did it take to work a cell phone, arrange the next decapitation? Reyes gave his gun a friendly wave. "As the Americans say, *Halve a nize day.*"

That night, Hugo dreamt a fisherman approached him holding a dead crane. The bird's crest resembled a mirror, and when Hugo peered into it, he saw a dark field where night warriors rode on white-tailed deer, galloping, galloping, their hooves like heartbeats. The horsemen wore warrior masks, black holes where mouths belonged, black holes instead of eyes. Terrified, Hugo threw the crane into his bag and raced home, but when he opened it to show Soledad, the bird was gone.

When Hugo jerked awake in the wee hours, his dream did not fade as normal dreams did. He left Soledad sleeping and went to the kitchen. Self-pity overcame him. He had lost the mask and his best friend. He would soon lose the girl. Everything he'd done, he'd done for love, and now El Pelotas had his balls in a sling. Hugo pressed his lit cigarette into his forearm, seeing how much pain he could endure. A pink circle formed. The universe's tiniest planet. The burn stung. He fetched butter, which melted over the wound.

If one sin led to another, how could anybody turn back to grace? Maybe the world would be better without him. He listened to the darkness, a cacophony of creaks and chirps and twittering branches. At night, whatever you reaped came back to you. If you were at peace, the night felt peaceful. If you were wretched, so was the night. Nature didn't think much of man, didn't hold him in high regard. Why should it?

Where was Pedro with the pinche mask?

Hugo crawled back to bed, wrapped his cold arms around Soledad's waist. He longed to confess, but the list was growing unwieldy. *I am making money in ways that I shouldn't. I love a young girl in a yellow dress. I must kill my childhood friend. I don't know whether to leave you.* How much easier it was to watch his wife breathe, her nightgown soft as summer air, her skin smelling of lavender. How much easier it was to plant bulbs and wait for yellow flowers to grow.

Out the window, in the gray dawn, he made out the silhouette of the neighbor's donkey, motionless, tethered. *What freedom there is at the end of a rope.*

eighteen | THE LOOTER

The looter sat in a playground in Chapultepec Park, watching children swing in the sunshine. He'd found a bench under a shady tree with a view of Benito Juárez or Pancho Villa or Óscar Reyes Carrillo. It was hard to say which. He'd been bingeing for days, a final blowout before he returned to Colorado. His heart trembled but his mind was clear, brilliant, in fact. He'd figured out how the entire jungle gym was assembled, drawn a blueprint in his head. When he got back to Divide, he'd build one for his nephew. Scotty was the kid's name. Or maybe it was Luke.

Only the death mask held him back. Montezuma? *Christ.* He hadn't thought big enough. That was always his problem, not daring to imagine how good things could be. He missed the mask. The damn thing was mouthy, but they had gotten along. Objects could be good company, if you let them get close.

He popped his last pills.

He'd seen a movie about Montezuma once, done a half-assed report in high school, decided that if granted an afterlife, he'd come back as King of the Aztecs. Guy had his own zoo. Tigers, lions, songbirds, parrots, snakes rattling in jars. His cooks made him three hundred dishes each meal—frogs in pimiento sauce, oysters, and winged ants, topped off with hot chocolate served in gold cups. And a pipe. Always a fucking pipe.

The looter wiped his face with his shirttail. The sun was relentless. A bully with one decent idea. Businessmen strolled past, popping phones. Facebook. E-mail. Good night, my tweet. He kept an eye out for Reyes. Both eyes. Bastard could be anywhere. The trees were talking, but he ignored them, muttering: "I'm busy here. Shuffling my cards."

His father had taught him to play gin. Arnold Maddox, district manager of Pikes Peak Savings and Loan, had disinherited him, though he had nothing to hand down but a split-level and some waders. Arnold left his wife and kids. Started a rock band called the Wheelies. People built things, then didn't like what they'd built. Well, suck it up. *You were responsible for everything you made.*

The trees whispered, "He's an unhappy man. You're okay now. You're Montezuma, King of the Aztecs."

Or maybe he was just King of Divide. His homeland. *Center of the Known Universe.* Who thought that motto up? He laughed through his nose. Hell. Forget Divide. The new Montezuma should start a zoo right here in Chapultepec Park. Nab that tiger in the bushes. Design gardens. Bathe in the fountain. Where was the girl to help him undress? The parrots were making a racket. The dwarves were on strike. Cortés was whining about his cross. He wanted it higher.

"Forget Cortés," the trees whispered. "That death mask is *yours.* Go get it. It was made for your face."

On the next bench sat a plump woman with a kitty-cat T-shirt. Dark-skinned with a lighter boy playing nearby. A nanny, no doubt. Her bra cut into her sides. Her plastic watch matched her headband. Women without money made sure to match. The boy was throwing sand and she called, *"No, no, Manito."*

The looter got up, joined the nanny on her bench. She nudged away, gripping her phone like it was the battery pack for her brain. She tapped her watch. *"Ya es la hora."*

Nanny slid gum into her mouth. The smell of fake watermelon met the air. Her breasts shifted. His erection was as big as Mexico City. He needed her to take him in her watermelon mouth. People brought Montezuma gifts. Chocolate. Lizards for luck.

His hand reached to pet her thigh. His shadow arrived first.

Something dark caught his attention: three men, B-movie bad guys in leather jackets, ran toward him. Feo, Alfonso, and another goon. The looter took off, knocking a toddler into the sand. The harder he ran, the more nowhere he got. *Motherfuckers.* His pants were falling down he'd lost so much weight. He'd lost so much weight he could fly. He'd flown often in his dreams, soaring over villages and church steeples, peeping in the curtained windows where charcoal children slept. He had that kind of magic inside him. Buried. Waiting.

He flapped his arms. His sneakers lifted. He rose, up, up into the haze, until he was gazing down at the traffic on Reforma, the heaving buses, the spinning *glorietas*, the stoplights hanging like whistles. The boy from Colorado was flying high, two miles, three miles, a trillion, zillion miles into the stratosphere, the cosmos, where there was no need to breathe. Then, like outer space after the last star burned out, everything went dark.

nineteen | ANNA

Deception took more concentration than Anna realized. More tequila, too. Like Spanish, lies floated more freely off a lubricated tongue. Luckily, at Chez Malone, it was never too early for a drink. Her first afternoon, Thomas made Anna a frosty cocktail, then another, and Anna left 14 Amapolas pleasantly sloshed. Thomas had a sense of humor. He liked to slip on masks and do imitations. When Constance joined them, he did the same impersonations for her, defusing the possibility of marital jealousy lest it appear he was reserving his charms for his younger guest. Thomas was an extraordinarily busy man for someone without a job. The printer pumped out orders and his phone rang as he managed shipments with DHL. Throughout the editorial work, the flirtations, the elaborate charade, Anna kept her eyes fixed on the chapel.

It drove her crazy that the mask was so close yet unattainable. Anna had assumed Thomas would show off his prize or leave the chapel door ajar, but he entered and exited in the same methodical manner: locking the door, giving the lock a pull, slipping a ring of keys into his pants pocket. *Damn his meticulousness. His paranoia.* Her only hope was to steal his keys or persuade him to invite her in. Both scenarios made Anna extraordinarily thirsty.

The work itself was not hard. Anna took a Polaroid of each mask, then typed notes: character, origin, artist, materials, dimensions, date danced, and any information available about the dance itself. Some dances dated back to the Conquest, when Indians reenacted fertility rituals and mocked the Spaniards—these masks were painted bright pink, representing the Europeans' terrible sunburns. Thomas sometimes asked Anna's opinion, but then disagreed with whatever she said. The resulting debates were charged and flirtatious. Were the wavy carvings wind or water? Was the double-faced mask meant to be twins or to show the duplicity of man?

"No doubt the latter," Thomas said. "The Aztecs believed in man's essential duality. There were not good people and bad people. Every soul was good *and* evil. Sinners, saints, that whole fiction was a European invention." He stopped for a dramatic pause. "The Spanish brought the devil to Mexico."

"I think the mask is you," Anna said, laughing. "The dual faces of the art collector. You pretend something is shoddy to pay less."

"It's the same tactic you use with men."

"I don't know why you hired me." She challenged him with her mouth. "Cataloguing is tedious but not hard."

"I hate writing. I have dyslexia."

"Dog is God?"

"Which is why I order other parts of my life."

"Guess what 'Anna' is backwards?"

"Trouble."

Thomas's advances had a gradual progression. Monday, he touched her hand. Tuesday, her knee. Each morning, she dressed with him in mind, debating which blouse, which earrings. *What the hell are you doing?* she'd ask her reflection. *Working,* the mirror replied. She had to woo Thomas to finagle a key to steal a mask to give to her father, who would oversee the creation of the new Rose White Ramsey Gallery in the Metropolitan Museum of Art.

It was a lot to ask of one blouse.

How far she'd come from her twenties, when she'd hidden her figure in linen tent dresses. Men pursued her not because they knew or liked her, but because she looked like the girl they thought they deserved. As Anna took no credit for her appearance—just as a homely girl could not be blamed for looking plain—she felt unworthy of their regard, and was convinced they would be disappointed when they knew her well. She slept with men because they wanted her, because sex was pleasure you could count on. In a sense, she had waited her whole life to play Anna Bookman, to use her looks to get what *she* wanted, and Thomas Malone would fall for her because he was a shallow man in love with beautiful things.

The next afternoon, Constance drifted out to the patio at day's end. Sensing she was lonely, Anna stayed to talk. A minute later, Constance called Anna by the wrong name.

"Holly?" Anna said, confused. "Who's she?"

Constance coughed, stifling embarrassment, then said curtly, "She used to work here."

"With Soledad?"

"For Thomas." Constance slid her legs under her chair. "She was his assistant. Before you."

Anna tried to remember what the librarian had said. Something about Chiapas. "She found another job?"

"My husband can be difficult to work for. . . ."

"She left Mexico?"

"She went back to California." Constance gave her nose an irritated wipe. One of the dogs—Morocco? Or was it Honduras? Anna couldn't tell them apart, had never really bothered to try—came over, panting. Constance batted him away with her foot.

Something was wrong, but Anna couldn't tell what. "Were you close?"

"Not now." Constance's smile wobbled. "She's sent a postcard or two, like Reyes. *Thinking of you* sort of drivel." Her voice hardened, making clear that this moment of vulnerability had ended. She picked up a watering can. "Excuse me. I've got a few chores to do before tonight."

"I could help you."

Constance fastened a strand of flyaway hair behind her ear.

"No," she said. "Actually, you can't."

On Thursday, Thomas suggested that after work the next day, they go out for a drink to celebrate their first week. When Anna agreed, he excused himself to make a long-distance call. It was late afternoon and the neighbor's chain saw was roaring. Constance had taken the car to Soriana for groceries. Anna waited a minute, then, trying to look casual, headed across the lawn to the chapel.

She passed the pool, which desperately needed a cleaning, and, seeing no one, strolled to the chapel door. The padlock was old, took a skeleton key. No brand name. She yanked it. Definitely locked. She stepped back, circled the building. The pair of opaque windows on each side didn't appear to open. In back, the round window was set high, presumably over the altar. Behind the chapel, a flimsy wire fence marked the property line, where the land fell off dramatically. Down the bluff, a gaggle of children scampered about the neighbors' messy yard. Anna surveyed the landscape, then realized something surprising. The Malones' security wall extended to the edge of their property line, turned the corner inward, ran ten yards, and then stopped. Just stopped. While from the street, the wall gave the appearance of impenetrability, it was actually porous, if you were willing to trespass the Mendez property and hack through the woods. Had they run out of money? Was the embankment too unstable? Or had workers been lured to another job, then promised to return, but never done so? Perhaps, over time, the job had been forgotten, hidden by the woods that provided a natural buffer and deterrent, unless someone *really* wanted to sneak onto the Malones' property. Like the dogs. Like Anna.

The chain saw ground louder. Anna gazed into the woods. What kind of man kept secrets from his wife? Every man, she supposed. But this wasn't a private drawer or sexual fantasy, but an entire building Constance was forbidden to enter. It was creepy, sad too, as if Thomas Malone had locked up his soul or heart, his libido or intelligence, his greed or magnificence—some essential part of himself that he dared not expose.

A hand landed on her shoulder. Anna jumped.

"You wandered off," Thomas said loudly, straining to be heard.

"I didn't hear you with the chain saw." Anna tapped her ears. "You scared me."

The saw cut out with a snarl.

"What are you doing?" he asked her.

Anna did her best to look innocent. "Exploring. I wondered how far back the property line went. Who lives there?" She pointed down the ravine, hoping to distract him.

"Mexicans. Chickens."

"What do they do for a living?"

"The chickens?"

She punched his arm, light, playful. He guided her back to the house. They passed the pool, the peacocks. Behind the chain link, the male opened its plumage. Glorious blue feathers formed a monstrous fan. Its tail had a million black eyes.

"Your expression . . . You look odd," Thomas said. "Like a guilty child."

Anna laughed. "Guilty? No, just thinking."

"Thinking of what?"

"About what you'll bring me tomorrow and whether I'll like it."

They met in an underground café. The collector appeared the same but different, less husband, more businessman, an executive with squash trophies and gold cards, a man who drank Heineken and didn't recycle, a man who paid someone to walk his dog, who flew business class, read *Barron's*, did mini triathlons, bought art. His body looked thin, pressed, lonely in his clothes.

They sat under a hanging spider plant, next to a lugubrious painting of a disassembled woman. Luis Miguel crooned through invisible speakers. Thomas flagged the waiter, ordered two mescals, two beers, and guacamole, glancing at Anna to confirm. She pulled out a notebook. Thomas put his hand over hers, flattening her pen into silence.

"We're always talking about masks. Tell me more about you. What do you like to do? I mean, what are you really good at?"

Fucked-up relationships, Anna thought. *I am really good at those.*

"I like to travel."

"We could do that," Thomas said. "I need to go to Guanajuato before the show. Afterward, you could help me with new acquisitions."

"Acquiring what?"

"Objects of value."

"Just objects?"

Drinks appeared. Thomas took his shot in a single swallow. Anna matched him. Sade was cooing in the background. Fucking Sade. Always. Everywhere. Still.

Buzzed already, Anna adopted a more practical tone. "Wouldn't Constance want to do that with you? Traveling, I mean."

Thomas appeared unfazed by the mention of his wife. "Constance hates traveling and is a lousy bookkeeper. She would appreciate you keeping the proverbial eye on her peripatetic partner. It's a tongue twister."

A spider plant baby snagged Anna's hair. Thomas reached for the menu, revealing a tattoo above his wrist. It disappeared before Anna could make out the image. He pulled out his reading glasses. Tight rectangular frames. There was something endearing about the gesture, a small weakness. Anna was always looking for vulnerability. A place to insert herself.

His voice changed, turning almost sentimental.

"You're the perfect girl for me. I love masks. You love masks. I drink mescal. You drink mescal. I have money. You need money. I collect, and you need to be . . . collected."

Anna made her mouth go saucy. "All that older-man stuff. I like that."

The afternoon cocktail had met up with the evening cocktail and danced around her empty stomach. Anna thought back to the shower of the Puesta del Sol. That woman, limp and discarded, seemed miles away.

"Tell me more about Holly. Constance mentioned her."

"There's nothing much to tell. She worked for us and then moved back home to California. Oaxaca is like that." The collector tapped his menu. "Find something you like."

Anna tilted her head. "I already have."

His fingers had passed over his mouth, like he'd swallowed something.

"Are you all right?" she asked.

"Fine. Small headache. It will pass." He admired her. "You have beautiful cheekbones. The human skeleton is an amazing sculpture. What's that at the end of your necklace?"

"San Antonio."

"You're Catholic?"

"It was my mother's. He's the patron saint of the traveler." Anna held out the amulet. "I rub it when there's turbulence, or trouble. I don't know if it works, but I'm too scared to take it off. I'd like to believe in a higher power, but . . ."

"You can't. Organized religion is so damn conventional, so limiting. It makes me—"

Just then, four beaming mariachis in black suits with gold buttons appeared at their table, blasting "Guantanamera." Thomas put down a bill. More shots appeared. Thomas gave Anna a leading look that said, *I wanted to please you. Soon it will be your turn to please me.* The music was too loud to speak over. Anna let the mescal's roar meet the trumpets, ceding control to whoever took over when her inhibitions faded. She was a better date drunk than sober. More witty. More bright. One man had actually told her this.

Yo soy un hombre sincero
De donde crecen las palmas

Anna imagined sex with Thomas. Would he feel bony or kind, or kind of bony, a friendly skeleton? Would he maintain his avuncular scorn? Imagining sex made it difficult to speak. It was like trying to talk while watching a movie. Her mouth tasted like ashes. The guacamole lay untouched.

The mariachis drifted to the next table. Anna didn't know what to say anymore. She and Thomas had reached a new level. Beyond small talk and banter. Anna had done things like this, but not this. Thomas spoke in a whisper that felt like a spell: "Come with me, *mi flaca*. There's something I want to show you."

He led her up a staircase, following a sign saying TERRAZA. Anna watched her step, remembering the Hitchcock movie where Jimmy Stewart pushed a woman off a tower, or did she jump? All she remembered was, Kim Novak wound up dead. They reached a roof deck. He led her to the edge. The stars were scattered. Two fuzzy blue crosses shone above the distant cathedral. The air was soft as skin. Beneath them, cars jostled over cobblestones. Anna waited. The illicitness of the encounter aroused her, as bad things often did. There were many reasons to let this happen.

Her mother was dead. Her fiancé was unfaithful. The cute painter on the *zócalo* thought she and her father were American fools.

She was living in a city of masks.

No one was watching.

She wasn't Anna Ramsey. She was Anna Bookman.

There was no one to save her and no one to save herself for.

She needed the keys to his chapel. She needed the death mask.

His move was sudden. His arm pulled her waist and he kissed her and his hand crept up her shirt. Her nipples hardened.

"Can I trust you?" he asked her.

"I was going to ask you the same thing."

He scratched her back with his nails. Her hands felt his hip pockets for keys. Nothing. Dropping one hand to her clavicle, she touched San Antonio, patron saint of the traveler. Patron saint of lost people and things. And she thought: *I will write this man's book. I will break into his chapel.*

When they came down from the roof, Thomas disappeared behind the swinging door marked CABALLEROS. Anna couldn't find their table, circled the restaurant one and half times before recognizing his coat. She sat, drank water, made the room settle down. She tipped a glass. The final drop of mescal fell on her tongue without taste. She reached into Thomas's coat pocket and found his keys. Taking a wild guess, she circled loose a tarnished skeleton key. It fit in her palm and she studied it, wondering what door it opened.

twenty | THE GARDENER

On the papershop girl's final afternoon, Hugo undressed her, cut a lock of her hair, and slid it into his wallet. He stared at her nakedness, searching for something more to take. He had disappointed her. He had not left his wife. He had not punished her father. He had not found Pedro or the mask. Each strand of his story ended in failure.

She asked him: *"¿A dónde vas a comprar tu papel ahora?"* Where will you buy your paper now?

"I no longer need to write."

"Someday you will come into the store and there will be a girl in a yellow dress who looks like me."

"No one looks like you. I will come to Veracruz to find you."

"I am leaving today."

"I will buy you back."

"With what?"

"I will buy my paper in Veracruz. I will be there in thirty days."

"I will hate you every day until you come," she said, her eyes hard as obsidian. "If you do not come, you will be a stranger to me and I will forget your face. I will let my father watch me through the crack in the door and one day I will let him in."

Hugo grabbed her hip, hoping to leave a fingerprint any man would recognize. "You have gotten so serious, my little schoolgirl. Look how books ruin a beautiful woman. You do not have the father you claim to have, but I am flattered you take the trouble to lie. *No te preocupes.* In thirty days I will arrive in Veracruz and gold coins will fall from my pockets. God will smile down on us. I will make a great sacrifice for you."

"What do you know about God?"

"Nothing, but I am learning." Hugo did not know what he meant by this, but he liked the way it sounded.

The next morning, Hugo stood at the bus stop outside the girl's home. The sky was clear and traffic rushed by, commuters amped with coffee and adrenaline. The family's freshly washed car was parked on the street, an imported SUV with black windows, the kind preferred by corrupt politicians. It was peculiar that a rich man would allow his daughter to work in a paper shop. Hugo kicked the curb. He had never seen the father, and worried they would be the same age.

The front door opened. The mother, squat as a truffle, hobbled into the car. Father and daughter appeared next. The girl wore a yellow dress and lace gloves. She had dressed for him. Though the father knew nothing of their affair, Hugo sensed the departure was a performance. *This is my family. We are dressed in our good clothes.* When the pair reached the back of the car, out of the mother's line of vision, the father pushed back the girl's forehead and kissed her, lifting her body off the ground. Her feet dangled, untethered, twisting. When the man's grasp loosened, the girl fell back to earth. With wild eyes, the father glared at the passing cars, daring anyone to intercede. It was not the kiss a man gives his daughter.

The father was his age. They could have been brothers.

The father climbed into the car. The girl bent down, tied her shoe-laces, her face red with tears. Hugo ran toward her. She held up her gloved hand. *Stop.* When Hugo ran harder, she rushed into the car, slammed her door. The SUV accelerated, leaving Hugo flat-footed, panting. The birds sang. The oranges in the trees were ripe. The church bells would ring at noon.

Hugo fell to his knees, his gut rife with sickness and self-loathing. The girl had not been lying. He stared down the street, the center yellow stripe. Timeline. Tightrope. Arrow. He studied it until he made up his mind.

He would find the papershop girl and marry her. She would not go to university. She would fix his dinner and bear his children, as many as God sent, and have a closet full of yellow dresses. Each day she would wear a different one for him, like the rising of the morning sun.

Hugo stood. Cars zipped past, a blur of colors and chrome. The light changed. Traffic stopped. He stepped forward, froze. In the second car, behind a cracked windshield, the face of a man he'd known as a boy. Pedro. Different car, same asshole, waving, *fucking waving*, doing a little show-off dance, pumping his forearms like a *naco*. Hugo sprinted. The rusted red shit-bucket gunned forward. Hugo lunged at the door, grazed the bumper, fell heart-first on the pavement. His nose warmed with blood.

Reyes had it right again. Pedro was back.

That night, the stars were unusually bright. Tiger mask in hand, Hugo stood alone in the yard. For years, people had called *him* "the Tiger" because of the scars across his belly where his father had beaten him. For much of his life, Hugo had hated his father, but the old man was dead now and those feelings seemed childish and unimportant.

Vicente had been a small, tough man who worked in the *campo*. One day Hugo asked him why men wore tiger masks at Carnival, and his father had explained that every Aztec god had a *tono*, an animal counterpart. "Like a twin. Your other, worse half." The *tono* of the great god Tezcatlipoca was the jaguar, *el tigre*. Tezcatlipoca, who had created the world with the beneficent Quetzalcoatl, the winged serpent, had many names and personas: *Night Wind*, *The Smoking Mirror*, *The Enemy of Both Sides*, and *He by Whom We Live*. So immense was his power, so fickle his temperament, Tezcatlipoca could make a man rich or strike him dead.

"Like your mother," his father had joked. He wiped his hands on his jeans, slick with dirt and sweat. "Sometimes an angel. Sometimes . . . not."

To keep in Night Wind's good graces, the Aztecs built temples in his honor, and every year a handsome man without scar or blemish was selected to impersonate Tezcatlipoca on earth. For a year, the man was lavished with gold and servants until the grand festival, when priests led him to the sacrificial stone. Five priests secured his head, while the minister of death cut open his chest with volcanic flint and held his still-beating heart to the sun. The flesh was eaten and the head hung to dry. Immediately, another Tezcatlipoca was chosen.

The story scared the boy. He would never eat someone, not even to save the sun.

"For ice cream?" His father shook his knee.

The boy understood the joke. "If it was chocolate." He grinned. He seldom spoke to his father like this and so squeezed in another question. "But in San Juan del Monte, do they kill the Tiger?"

Vicente smiled at the boy's worry. "Now Carnival is just a party. It may look like they kill the Tiger, but the guy just rolls over and drinks another beer." He laughed, tousled his son's hair. "If it makes you feel better, sometimes in dances, the Tiger gets away. That happens in life, too. You do something bad, but only He knows." He pointed up, his face crafty, conspiratorial. "For good to prosper, evil must be allowed to escape."

Hugo closed this memory, put a name to what he'd committed to: He would kill a man to save his own skin. He would kill a man to rescue the papershop girl. He slipped the tiger mask over his face. It fit him, as he knew it would.

twenty-one | ANNA

Amapolas Street was empty and sepia-toned at two a.m. when Anna made her way to the Malones' home on the hillside. Turning on her headlamp, she entered the woods behind the Mendez property, bushwhacking, hands protecting her face. Her biggest worry was waking the dogs. Native American trackers could tell where an enemy had trod by reading broken twigs. Any idiot could have found her; she was leaving a virtual highway of footprints and trampled branches. At the incline, the chapel appeared on the bluff, a two-dimensional cutout, looming. Anna humped up the hill, touched the fence marking the property line.

A dog barked.

A second dog answered the first. A canine a cappella. Anna debated turning around, but instead pushed down the wire fence and threw over a leg. Her jeans snagged. She was stuck mid-crotch, a regular

Three Stooges moment, not that she was laughing. If Constance found her, she'd cock her rifle. If Thomas found her, he'd call the police. If the dogs found her, she'd be supper. Her pants ripped. Her forearm was bleeding, possibly her leg. She kept going.

In the distance, the pink house showed neither movement nor light. Even if the barking had woken them, the Malones surely would stay in bed. Surely, they did not suspect that the ghostwriter of Thomas's guide was breaking into his chapel with a stolen skeleton key.

Anna was thinking in *surely*s, because nothing was sure.

At the chapel door, she studied the dark, the trees, the sickle moon. The pool's quiet wake reflected the security lights. The dogs had slowed to an occasional yelp. She slid in the key. It wouldn't turn. She was bad with locks, could barely open her apartment door. Left, right, out again, back in, right slowly, left hard. She cursed. She'd picked the wrong key. *Surely*. Her hand hurt. She tried again. No. This was the key to the kitchen door or Hugo's cottage or a love shack in Puerto Vallarta.

She could jimmy a window. She tried this now, slamming each window with her palm, but they were all locked. Impenetrable. She swore, looked for someone to help her. A ridiculous idea. *Excuse me, but could you help me break into this chapel?*

She prayed to her mother and tried the key again. *Nada.*

Having failed completely, she'd leave through the front door. When thwarted, Anna got this way, daring another thing to go wrong. The way beige panties led to an e-mail attachment led to a video led to Clarissa led to Sandra and Fiona. Like that.

She passed the pool, patio, kitchen screen door, where, for once, Soledad was not watching. At the front gate, Anna lifted the latch.

Fucking Thomas and his fucking chapel. It was *her* mask. Not his. The death mask belonged to the Ramseys. Thomas Malone had all this. He didn't need more. Her anger needed someplace to go. She picked up a rock, chucked it at the front door. She had no arm. The rock fell short, stopping on the welcome mat like an uninvited guest. The rock had the same chance of entering the house as Anna had of breaking into the chapel. A second-story window lit up. A gray silhouette drifted past. It looked like a skeleton, floating.

Anna slept fitfully until ten, then dragged herself to the *zócalo* and ordered her three favorite drinks. If the waiter judged her for drinking a margarita before lunch, he was too polite to show it or too eager for a tip. The *zócalo* was almost empty. A street cleaner swept away yesterday's garbage with a stick broom. A man pushed a bicycle without handlebars. A circling truck broadcast the virtues of a tonic that cured arthritis and depression, constipation and grief.

Uno, dos, tres, her drinks arrived. She was driving a stick-shift car. *The coffee is the accelerator. The water is the brake. The tequila is the clutch.* Her first attempt at larceny had been futile, which meant Anna Bookman needed to snuggle up to Thomas Malone again, trade the wrong key for the right one. She'd call him after finishing her drinks.

"How is the girl with the masks today?"

Salvador, the painter, the pirate, in shredded jeans and blue bandanna. Anna felt a flutter of attraction, quickly followed by self-rebuke. *He didn't come looking for you.* The painter motioned *May I?* and joined her. Anna breathed in the pleasant aroma of new smoke. She could not help comparing him with Thomas. Their differences were striking. The collector. The artist. The aristocrat. The bohemian. The married man who wanted her. The single man who did not.

"Terrific," Anna said, pleased to report how well she'd gotten along without him. "I got a job writing a gallery guide for a collector."

"Let me guess," he said, playing soothsayer again. "You found Thomas Malone."

"I thought you didn't know him."

"The biggest *cabrón* in Oaxaca."

"Well, don't hide your feelings."

"Thomas Malone is a spoiled art collector who throws his money around. The real story is with the carvers. Have you seen the Old Gringo's collection?"

"A few pieces—"

"Of course not. You will have to sleep with him first."

Anna looked away.

"What? You gave in that easy."

Anna made a face. "Of course not."

An espresso was placed between them. Salvador sat back. His cotton shirt blew turpentine past Anna's nose.

"Wait a month," he said. "His collection goes up in March. The great battle of the Mexican masks. Lucha Libre. *Narco* against *cabrón*. Drug dealer versus art dealer. I place my bet on Reyes. You know, there are a couple books on masks you could read, though the biggest has some errors."

"*Dancing with the Tiger*. I know it," Anna said flatly. "The mistakes were not the writer's fault. Carvers misled him and sold him fake masks."

Salvador looked skeptical. "Why would they do that?"

"Money."

"Maybe the author did not speak Spanish. What was his name?"

"I forget," Anna said. "But believe me, I know that book. He trusted the carvers, and the carvers abused that trust."

"Which carvers?"

"Emilio Luna. Ricardo Rodríguez. Whole pages don't add up. Dances that don't exist. New masks made to look old. Fake rusting. It was all a big game, fooling Americans. They must have laughed and laughed—"

"That would be kind of funny," he said. "But I don't believe it."

Anna shrugged. "It's true. Go look. There are Grasshopper masks that supposedly date back to the early nineteenth century, but they are less than ten years old. Supposedly, they are danced at the Harvest Dance in Santa Catarina, only there's no such town. Or rather, there are plenty of Santa Catarinas, but none have a Harvest Dance."

Salvador stubbed his cigarette. "Do you still need a guide?"

"I never needed a guide."

The painter looked contrite. "The other day, I thought you were another tourist writing silly stories. Tuesday, there is a Carnival parade in San Juan del Monte. Have you been?"

"To Carnival, but not there."

"I invite you, then. While we are up there, we can investigate this book. I make you a bet the carvers are honest and the writer is guilty."

Anna paused, unable to believe what was happening. She was being asked to bet on her father's integrity.

"What are we betting?"

"If I lose, I give you a painting, and if I am right, you will give me . . ."

"A mask."

"I was thinking a copy of your book."

Anna looked into her lap. She'd forgotten her book. "That may take a while."

"That's okay. If you pay for gas, I will introduce the carvers and translate, and chase the dogs, and prove these artists are honest men. Sounds good?"

It did sound good. Who could explain chemistry? She liked his face, his messy rolled-up sleeves, his half-tied shoes. He smelled like paint cleaner. A little toxic, a little edgy.

"Thank you," Anna said. She meant it. They had broken through wherever they'd started. "Are you sure you don't mind?"

"If you write about a place, you should know it." He waited a beat, giving her a chance to mock him. When she didn't, he teased again. "Now, as your guide, I need to know: Are you easy to be with?"

"In what way?"

Salvador snaked his hand through the air. "Whatever way we might have to go."

Her phone bleeped a text. Her father. were are you#

She had missed an earlier text from David. Same question. Where R U?

She had nothing to say to David. There was nothing she *could* say to her father. She dropped the phone in her bag, looked hard at the painter, and told him the truth.

"Some men think I'm easy, but they're wrong."

twenty-two | THE LOOTER

The looter woke up handcuffed in the back of an SUV, a gun barrel pressed into his waist. Three Mexicans rode with him. Feo, Alfonso, the other punk from the safe house. The looter tried to figure how much trouble he was in. He remembered buying at Pico's stand, but after that things grew hazy. Cross-eyed, he could see his nose was swollen and pulpy. Blood caked his shirt. He wanted many things, but only asked for one.

"¿Un tabaco?"

"Por supuesto, mi cariño." Alfonso sat beside him, holding the gun. "Let me light it for you."

"Where are we going?"

"To see Gonzáles."

Gonzáles was better than Reyes. The looter had never met Gonzáles, saw no reason to meet him now.

"Where's Gonzáles?"

"Oaxaca."

"Why the handcuffs?"

"We don't want you to escape."

Alfonso put the cigarette in the looter's lips. The smoke felt close to bliss. An hour later, they reached Oaxaca, wove into the city. The SUV parked in a decent neighborhood: a good sign. Alfonso pushed him out of the car. The four men marched to the front door, banging buckets and sacks.

Alfonso rang the bell. Feo was his usual ugly self, so many muscles he could hardly lower his arms. His T-shirt read HECHO EN MÉXICO. A housekeeper opened the door, saw the handcuffs, looked alarmed. She was a wide woman with earrings running up one lobe, like someone had gone nuts with a stapler.

"Señor Gonzáles is not here," she said, closing the door. "He's away in Cuernavaca."

Feo drew a gun, pushed her aside. "Where's the bathroom? The master bath?"

The housekeeper pointed up the stairs. Feo grabbed her chin, making sure she was listening. "We're hungry. Make us some food."

The looter tried to catch the housekeeper's attention, to convey that she should call the police, but he missed her face by a mile. Her wide pants swayed as she drifted into the kitchen. A burner ignited with a whoosh.

The bathroom was marble, sunken tub, white tile. Feo threw the looter on the toilet. The punk filled the buckets with water, dumped in a bag of powder, stirred the sludge with a stick. Feo kept his aim fixed on the looter's head. The looter trembled. He understood. They would bury him in cement and leave him for dead.

An ice cream truck passed, playing a childish ditty. The smell of corn oil pushed up the stairs. This wasn't happening to anyone but him.

The mixer barked, "Help me, assholes."

Feo shot the kid a look, warning him to watch it.

They worked together, mixing and dumping. The cement, pasty and foul, was the color of elephants, not that the looter had seen elephants, but he'd drawn them as a boy, used up gray markers to fill their enormous hides. Fragments of his life appeared to him. Colorado. The mountains, the ranch houses, his mother. She had wanted him to be an accountant because he was good with numbers. Math. Algebra. Where had x gotten him? He'd dropped out of community college and drifted to Utah, started digging, dealing; his two passions went well together. After crossing the border, he did a few drug runs in Juárez, but always returned to digging. Underground, he was lucky. He was the guy who found stuff, the guy who wouldn't stop till he did. He had stamina. Charisma. All those words ending in a. America. Where was his country to save him?

"*Cariño,*" Feo said, unlocking the cuffs. "Your bath is ready. Take off your clothes."

"I'm leaving for Colorado today. I have a flight to catch."

"That plane has been delayed."

Trembling, the looter loosened his belt buckle. Now that his hands were free, he couldn't make them work. "Please . . ."

Feo lowered his gun to the looter's genitals. "Hurry up."

The looter dropped his clothing in a heap. His body was his only possession. Naked, he stepped into the tub. The cool cement covered his ankles. Who would think to kill a man this way? The human imagination had too much time on its hands. Feo produced duct tape, sealed the looter's mouth.

"Sit down, *señor arqueólogo,*" Feo said. "Relax."

Feo jammed his gun into the looter's ribs. It jerked but did not go off. The other two kept mixing. Arrowheads of sweat stained their shirts.

Feo swiveled on the toilet seat, grinding his jaw, reminiscing. "You fucking idiot. That mask was worth a fortune. You think Reyes is going to put up with that shit? No one steals from Reyes."

Cement covered the looter's skinny calves, the white legs his mother had once scrubbed clean, the legs that wound around women as he kissed their necks. The itching was unbearable. The sweat on his scalp itched and the hair on his splayed legs itched and his nose was running. He mumbled into the tape, used his eyes to plead for mercy. He had beautiful eyes. Every woman he'd slept with had told him so. But Feo turned away, exposing a scar on his neck, a dog on a choke chain. These men were not in their bodies.

It was time to pray, but all the looter could think was *Shoot me now,* the punch line from a joke he no longer remembered. The cement reached his armpits. These men were dogs. He'd heard of decapitation, of profanity scrawled on corpses, but not this. This was not intelligent.

An even more degrading idea struck him: He was being buried alive in a bathtub not because he'd stolen the death mask, but to send a message to Gonzáles. He was not Christopher Maddox; he was a dry-erase board, a human Post-it. Not even his death was his own. His bowels emptied. His ears rang. Sweat dropped from his chin. He was a young man, with gifts. *No one else finds the shit I do.*

He could run but they would kill him. He could scream but no one would hear. He could wait and someone might find him. He was a treasure buried underground, a looter who needed a looter. The Maddox Principle of Opposing Equilibrium had failed him in every way.

Shovel after shovel.

Closing his eyes, he was a boy again on the beach in North Carolina. His sister was burying him in wet sand. She'd dug a pit and arranged him inside it, then set about to cover him. The ocean surf crashed in regular intervals. His skin smelled like coconut. Sandpipers pranced in the waves. A day like this could last forever. On her beach chair, his mother checked her tan lines, pleased she was no longer white.

Cement circled his neck.

"Wait here," Feo said. "We'll be back after lunch."

twenty-three | ANNA

Thomas Malone drove fast, which didn't surprise Anna. What surprised her was how good it felt to be in his car, watching him shift the phallic clutch, feeling the breeze through the open window, going somewhere, anywhere, fast. Combat boots, swishy dress, lipstick red as Valentine roses, she'd dressed to get what she wanted. At a light, they stopped alongside a house painted a luscious shade of terra-cotta. A birdcage hung from the wall. Inside, a pair of canaries fought, a hideous, screeching explosion of feathers. Mexico was always doing that: beauty and cruelty shadowboxing.

"I'm glad you called," Thomas said. "Turn around. I packed cocktails."

On the backseat was a cooler with a thermos and two cups.

"Margaritas?"

"Para todo mal, mezcal, y para todo bien también."

For everything bad, mescal, and for everything good as well.

She filled two cups, handed him one, felt a chill as she slid hers between her thighs for safekeeping.

They nudged through traffic, past El Llano Park, where families pushed strollers, waited in line for flavored ice. Normal people doing normal things on a Sunday afternoon. Safe bet she was the only woman in Oaxaca seducing a nefarious art collector to steal an Aztec death mask.

"Have you made any friends yet?" Thomas asked. "Besides us."

Banking on jealousy to work in her favor, Anna said, "I met a local painter. Constance knows him. Salvador Flores. He's going to take me to Carnival in San Juan del Monte."

Thomas gave her a withering look. "I thought you were smarter than that."

"What's that mean?"

"Did he offer to be your guide and show you secret places that only he knows? Take you for a donkey ride? Sell you a rug from his grandmother for a very special price?" Thomas chortled. "I didn't know you wanted to go native."

"Okay." Anna folded her arms. "Enough. I'm going to miss work Tuesday. That okay?"

Ignoring the question, Thomas made a childish sad face. "Poor Salvador. He sits on the *zócalo* and pounces on the loneliest girl he sees. Was that you? Well, not anymore. I've rescued you." The collector patted her thigh. "Funny. He usually goes for college girls, present-tense girls on exchange programs. *Vroom, vroom* on the motorbike."

"Where are we going?" Anna said coldly.

"Cheer up. He's bamboozled the best of them."

"Where are we going?"

"There's a place near here I like. I thought we could talk."

"What kind of place?"

"You'll see. It's not fancy, but I didn't think you were into fancy."

"I'm not."

"Good girl."

This last comment annoyed her, like it was his job, *his right*, to recognize value and bestow it, to control her by praising the behavior he desired. She was a good girl when she affirmed what he'd already decided to do. She wanted to say: *You don't get to decide what's good or bad.* She wanted to say: *Just because you're older doesn't mean you're right.* But Anna Bookman kept her mouth shut. She was after his keys.

In the ugly outskirts of the city, Thomas pulled into the parking lot of a minty bunker called the VIP Hotel. A garish flamingo tap-danced across its façade. The long-legged bird wore a rakish top hat over a leering mascaraed eye. Thomas drove around back, nosed his bumper up to room 7. Without a word he got out, popped the trunk, grabbed a briefcase and a cardboard box.

"I brought you a present." He shook the box, teasing her into the room, before disappearing inside.

Anna sat, debating what to do next. The VIP Hotel was the sort of low-rent motel frequented by truckers and prostitutes, mid-level politicians and their mistresses. Anna didn't know whether to be flattered or appalled. She felt silly following him if they weren't going to have sex, but she also felt dumb sitting in the car, exposed, unclaimed, the last suitcase circling the baggage carousel.

Anna poured the last of the margaritas into her cup.

By the time she got inside, alcohol had loosened her misgivings. She liked how drinking made simple actions more difficult, and difficult actions unthinkable, thereby lowering her expectations of herself to a manageable level. Walking. Talking. Petty theft. She could manage these things with a buzz. She just needed two minutes alone with his keys, to return the bad one, snatch another. *Send him for ice. Dig through coat pockets. Have him take a shower. Dig through pants. Wait till he's sleeping. Dig through his fucking briefs.*

With a vague sweep, Anna took in the worn-out furnishings. They could be anywhere. Phoenix or Taipei. The dispassion of the place aroused her. They'd entered a box of anonymity and indifference. What happened here didn't count. Thomas reclined on the bed, feet up.

Anna said, "This is a funny place to talk."

She caught her face in the mirror. The circles under her eyes formed tiny suitcases of worry. Thomas had already opened a liter of mescal, poured two shots.

Thomas slid scissors across the nylon bedspread. "Open your gift."

Anna considered the box. To open it was to commit to the object inside. Hereafter, she would own something he'd given her. "You didn't have to do that." Anna always said this when given a present.

"I wanted to. Open it. Then decide."

Decide what? she nearly asked.

Anna ran the scissors through the tape. The flaps opened. Looking up at her was a mask of a sensual woman with wild orange hair and almond-shaped eyes. A golden fly decorated each sculpted cheek. Her fleshy lips whispered a secret.

"She's beautiful."

"I think so."

"Who is she?"

"La Malinche. Mistress of Cortés."

"The traitor? Thanks a lot."

"Seductress of the conquistador."

"The most hated woman in Mexico. The interpreter who sold out the entire indigenous race."

"The woman who helped Catholicism triumph over the pagan practice of human sacrifice and ensured that the Virgin Mary became the most beloved saint."

"*La chingada.* The whore." Anna finished her shot. Her tongue felt grainy and soiled. "If I'm Malinche, that makes you Cortés. Didn't he have syphilis?"

Thomas gave her a cool appraisal. "I thought a woman with your imagination would enjoy being Malinche, that you'd find a way to astonish a quiet boy from Ohio. I bet as a girl you liked the circus."

Anna's face tightened. Were her desires that obvious?

"Let's face it: You're done with artists from the *zócalo.*" Thomas touched her shoulder. "Put on the mask. Surprise me with a dance. I brought music."

Anna retreated into the bathroom, head spinning. She'd had sex for worse reasons. Self-doubt. Boredom. Pity. This might be the most heroic sex she'd ever had. The most satisfying. She'd screw Thomas Malone, then screw him over. A year from now, she'd slip on her little black dress and invite him to the grand opening of the Rose White Ramsey Gallery at the Met. She was a victim only if she lost. Of course, she knew what to do with the mask of La Malinche. Every woman did. The mask was heavy, but not impossible. She checked her face in the mirror. She looked like the kind of prostitute who worked the VIP Hotel.

And she thought: *It takes the average snowflake two hours to fall.*

She opened the bathroom door. Brazilian music bubbled caramelized pop. Candlelight made the room wobbly and golden. Full-dressed, Thomas leaned against the far wall. He tugged his cuff down over his wrist. Their every encounter, every glance and word, offer and counter-offer, had been designed to lead her here. He wanted her to dance a mask for him. All along, he had known she was willing.

Anna danced. Smoky, dangerous, smart. She was seducing him. She was seducing herself. Slipping an arched foot from her combat boots, she let her sweater puddle on the floor. When her dress dropped, she caressed her camisole. She touched herself. Men wanted to see themselves, then see how you were different. She wasn't naked. She was wearing a costume. Exposed but hidden, she was Anna. She was Malinche. Whore. Heroine. Captive. Insurgent. Forget the chapel. *She* was a goddamn new religion. Her breasts, celestial clouds. Her pussy, a burning bush.

Anna found her glass. Thomas refilled it.

"How am I doing?" She was hammered and didn't care. She was going to win this game. Take home the grand prize.

"Wonderful," he said.

"You know how the dance ends."

Thomas shushed her. "Strippers don't talk."

"Oh, I see." With mock seriousness, she recited an expression her Spanish teacher had always used. *"Con la boca caillita, te ves más bonita."*

With your mouth shut, you look more beautiful. She remembered the most ridiculous things.

Thomas pressed a finger over her lips. "Exactly."

Anna spun away, let the music stir her insides. A mask had no value unless it was danced. Maybe the same held true for women. She danced. She disrobed. She got down to a bra and panties. Thomas was still fully dressed.

"If this is strip poker, I seem to be losing."

"Shhhhhh."

She led him to bed, pushed him down, straddled him, reached around his hips. No keys. The mask was heavy and she took it off.

Thomas tensed. Her mouth grazed his, but got no response. He did not touch her. His face was remote. He was stiff, but not where it mattered.

"What's wrong?" She was pretty sure she was doing most things right.

"We should wait for the chapel."

"Is that what you do in there?"

"It all depends."

"I thought you didn't let anyone in."

"Someday. When we have a relationship."

"What do you call this?"

"An encounter."

Anna got up, found her dress. It took effort not to feel bad. She had been rejected by a man she didn't want. An oxymoron. Something. Her back to the bed, Anna jangled his jacket. No keys. That left the brief-case, open on the table. Through the blinds, a red neon sign blinked: MARISCOS AL CHEFF. She felt like a blonde in a Hopper painting, sexy to look at, broken inside.

"You brought me to this fine hotel just to dance?" She was trying to understand what was happening.

"We're building trust."

Anna turned sharply. "I trust a man who wants me. That I understand. I don't know what this is."

"We'll wait for the chapel. Anticipation heightens pleasure. Like virgins on their wedding night."

"Virgins?" Anna gestured around the room.

"Metaphorically speaking."

"This virgin needs another drink. Ice, this time. I saw a machine outside."

Thomas roused himself, smoothed his hair, then disappeared so quickly Anna wondered if he'd ditched her, but then she heard the clatter of falling ice. She found his keys in the pocket of his briefcase. She worked quickly, sliding the bad key back on. But which key should she take next? In the briefcase, a postcard caught her eye, a black-and-white photograph of a glamorous woman, whose face had been smudged with white paste. Another taunt from Reyes? Anna turned it over. *Juliet in Mud Mask* from the Getty. She jumped to the bottom. *Love always, Holly.* The card began, *Hello, you two, this card made me think of—*

"What are you doing?"

Thomas Malone stood in the doorway.

"Looking for a cigarette." Anna shuffled the papers, burying the card. "Did you bring any?"

"You were looking through my things."

"For cigarettes." Anna looked him directly in the eye, unblinking. "Why? You have secrets in here?"

"Of course." He handed Anna the ice bucket. She reached for the bottle. No key. No sex. Failure was killing her buzz.

"Put the mask back on," he said. "It becomes you."

"No, I become it. *Her.*"

He sat down, patted the bed. "Lie with me. I want to imagine us together."

"We are together. We *were* more together."

He tied on her mask. She let him do this. Thomas lay down, eyes closed, fondled her breasts through her dress. She lay with him, watched his face. His mouth quivered with pleasure. She was aroused, despite herself.

"What's happening?" she asked.

"We're making love in the chapel."

"Am I wearing a mask?"

"Of course."

"Then how do you know it's me?"

A police car streamed past, siren blazing.

When he didn't answer, Anna Bookman nibbled his ear. "I want you to show me the chapel."

"I'll take you soon," he murmured.

"I can't wait."

"*No veo la hora.* That's what Argentineans say. 'I can't see the hour.'"

"I can't even see a minute."

Time passed. Time passed as they lay in the bed of the VIP Hotel, two Americans in Mexico, while outside, a blue sign advertised the building's vacancy, while outside, a boy rode a bike with no hands, while outside, workers from the graveyard shift streamed out of the Coca-Cola plant, while outside, two nuns hunched in a doorway, selling dry sugar cookies, thirty pesos a bag. They lay in the dark and said nothing, a smiling man and a woman in a mask.

twenty-four | THE GARDENER

Hugo lowered his tiger mask and
felt the knife that lay over his heart. The sun beat down on him, filling
his groin with longing, one yellow recalling another. It was Carnival in
San Juan del Monte, and high on the dais, local dignitaries sat stuffed
like taxidermy. The brass band coddled their silent instruments beneath
tissue-paper bunting that hung limp, everyone, everything, hoping for
a breeze. Hugo kicked the dirt, wishing he had already done what he
came to do and could look back with the pleasant distance of memory,
but the mayor had gotten hold of the microphone, and his oratory blossomed like a miraculous poppy.

He thanked everyone for coming to San Juan del Monte, in the
great state of Oaxaca, in the grand Republic of Mexico. He reminded
everyone that these dances dated back to the Conquest, when the Spanish imposed Catholicism on the Indians, and the Indians mocked the

conquistadors with these same dances performed here today. "Yes, my friends, we gather to celebrate the beauty of Mexico, which lives in harmony as one *pueblo,* one *gente.*" The mayor's voice caressed the cobblestones and swept through the village and rose over the mountains into the clouds where, months later, it would rain down on the village. "Everyone should try the tacos. Everyone should taste the roasted iguana. But hurry. The dances are about to begin."

Hugo threw down his cigarette in disgust. *Once he climbs on the donkey, he doesn't want to get off.*

On his back, Hugo wore a two-liter soda bottle filled with *tepache.* He swung it around and drank, ocher spirits burning his nostrils. Sweet corn and brown sugar. He felt light-headed but clear, ethereal yet committed. He did not see the town drunk, sprawled in the dust like a dog; the chunks of beef cooking on the open fire, enough to feed the village; the teenage girl holding a baby, her eyes brown and empty as stained teacups; the children, cherry soda staining their mouths, faces glazed from sugar and boredom; the tourists, white as soap, who'd come to Mexico to snap their cameras, missing the very thing they tried so hard to see; or the prepubescent Queen of Carnival in her turquoise taffeta dress and paper crown, who slumped in her Corona chair, intent on her lollipop.

Hugo had eyes for only one man.

He waited as his country waited for prosperity, as children waited for Christmas, as women waited for husbands to return from the North, as husbands waited for mistresses to return to bed, as Mexicans waited for a president who did not steal, as they waited for a police chief who did not steal, as they waited for a priest who did not steal. They waited with the patience of a donkey tied at the side of the road.

At last, the mayor sat down. The band lit up. A streak of mirror-eyed cats streamed through the swirling, perspiring crowd. Hugo dropped his mask over his face. Every tiger danced the same dance. Every tiger wore the same face. They bent to the ground, rattled their maracas. The music quivered, shivery as the devil's violin.

Pedro wasn't hard to find.

The Tiger recognized his friend's posture, would have known his bare feet if they had been lined up with a dozen others. The Tiger inched closer until he was staring at the nape of Pedro's neck, its soft channel. Symmetry has a beauty you can't quite explain.

"¿Dónde está la máscara?"

Pedro jerked around.

"Yes, it's me, old friend," the Tiger snarled. "Those were delicious tacos. Where is the mask?"

Pedro laid his hand on his friend's shoulder. "Reyes?"

The Tiger showed off his machete.

"You going to hurt me?"

"Not if you give me the mask."

Pedro spun. The Tiger grabbed his arm, freed his knife. Another tiger, two hundred pounds of liquor and pride, careened into Pedro, slamming him gut-first into the waiting machete. The blade pressed into the pool cleaner's chest and hung there, perpendicular, a cartoon man with a knife in his chest. The body fell to the stones. Violins screeched. Dancers pushed downstream. Who could stop for a drunk? Let someone else clear the carrion.

The Tiger imagined Reyes's hideous face screaming *What the fuck? You were supposed to get the mask and* then *kill him.* Sweat rained down his arms and legs. The gardener gazed into the sky, waiting for divine retribution, but the Lord turned his back, refusing to intercede: another death, another day, a tiger who kills a tiger. *Qué le vamos a hacer.* What can we do about it.

Out of nowhere, a missile shaped like an ear of corn—a comet or UFO or weapon—shot across the sky. It made no sense, but there it was, burning northward, showering sparks like the tendrils of a firecracker. The Tiger cried out, legs buckling. He pointed. Nearby dancers gazed up but, seeing nothing, turned away in disgust. Moments later, the mysterious comet faded over the mountains and the sky returned to its faceless blue.

The Tiger pushed through the crowd, panting, falling, pants falling, afraid the police would arrest him, afraid Reyes would kill him, but he reached the edge of the crowd without incident. Fire roared in his chest and loins. He was crying.

He had killed a man.

He had made his first sacrifice for love.

twenty-five | THE POOL CLEANER

Pedro lay in the street, his moans lost in the cacophony of Carnival. Dancers often collapsed; the very drunkest had to be lifted—a three-man job—and swung to the curb like a dead deer. A ghoul leapt over his bleeding belly. A shimmery transvestite kicked him with her pump. Finally, a jaguar crouched, touched his bleeding chest, and yelled for help.

A fist of tigers descended to get a better view. *Something horrible has happened. Let me see.* In the chaos, dancers barked orders through the mouths of Christians and Moors, their wooden eyes unblinking. María, the baker, tenderly removed his mask and announced that it was Pedro, the *chavo* who cleans pools, son of Leonora Rodríguez, the old woman who stands at the fence.

Sí, soy yo. I am here. Don't leave me alone to die.

"He is breathing."

"Loosen his clothes."

María formed a tourniquet with her shawl. The butcher felt Pedro's wrist for a pulse. They did not love him, but they did not want him to die. He was a fixture in town, a champion of backgammon, a lover of orange soda, part of the landscape of home. He had no right to disappear so suddenly. It was like waking one morning to discover the cathedral was gone.

Pedro felt himself lifted. The sky reappeared, reflecting an ocean he would die without seeing. A woman said, "His face looks like foul milk." A man said, "He's losing too much blood." Children, giddy with questions, pulled their mothers, who shouted, *"¡Apúrate!"—Hurry up!*—dragging them away, as if death were contagious.

He was carried through the streets. Gossip buzzed like angry bees. *Who did this?* One man claimed a *moro* in sneakers had done it. Another blamed a tiger, but which one? Enrique Montoya García, an ancient man with a donkey, swore, *"El diablo lo hizo."* The devil had stabbed the boy with a knife and flown over the mountains on the back of an eagle.

Pedro could not see them, but he heard and tasted and smelled them, his senses heightened in an ecstatic farewell.

They laid him in a rusty truck bed. Pain flowered before him. He was cold. His friends presented their faces like gifts. They wept. *They do not weep for me. They weep for themselves. They know someday they too will die and they cannot imagine the world without themselves in it, a world that will keep dancing at Carnival.* If the death of Jesus could not ensure the salvation of man, what did the life of any one man matter?

Mi hijo. Who did this to you?

Mamá, be careful. They will come looking for you, too.

But he could no longer remember the men who wished him ill. And he thought: *I am Pedro Rodríguez Modica, son of Leonora, a man who purifies water.* And he thought: *There is no child to carry my name.* And he thought: *I was a good boy but not a good man.*

When he opened his eyes, he did not see his mother, or the Virgin, or the Angel of Death, just friends, who crossed themselves and mumbled to God. With sudden clarity, he could see who was shallow and who was wise, who would comfort his grieving sister by slipping a consoling hand under her shirt.

The truck's engine started with a kick, rolled forward, picked up speed, flying over *topes*, out of town, past the checkpoint of bored *federales*. Pedro took a last look at the sky. He was dying. The doctor had a degree from Tijuana. The man could not cure a sinus infection, let alone raise the dead.

twenty-six | ANNA

Anna ran behind Salvador. She didn't care who she bumped. She cared only about the person holding her hand. They hadn't seen the murder, hadn't realized anything was wrong until people started screaming and the police cars swooped in with sirens and red pulsing lights.

At a crossroads, Salvador stopped, pulled Anna close, cursing the whole *desmadre*, promising to get them the hell out of there, *hasta la quinta chingada*, to the fifth son of a bitch, which Anna decided must be quite far away. Her cheek rested against his chest. His shirt smelled bitter and sweet. Anna admired the trees. Their sturdy trunks supported branches, which grew leaves, which offered shade to two people, who held each other trying to feel safe as the trees.

Salvador said, "I know a place we can go."

On the last street in town, he pushed open a white metal gate. A gray-haired man sat on a concrete terrace, chiseling a chunk of wood he steadied with his bare feet. His entire body was covered with sawdust. It was clear he had no idea what had transpired in the village.

The man wiped his hands on his apron before giving Salvador a slap on the shoulder. His smile was tired but kind. *He works hard,* Anna thought. *He is both poor and rich.*

Salvador introduced her. *"Permíteme presentarte a Emilio Luna,* the most respected carver in San Juan del Monte."

Electricity sizzled down Anna's spine. Emilio Luna. The man who had sold her father thousands of dollars of phony Grasshopper masks. She'd expected a villain, not a kindly goblin, a sprite, a *duende.* The carver's hand was light in hers, cool and dry. He tapped a plastic chair, showing Anna where to sit.

Spanish leapt forward. Anna caught a few flying nouns: *tigre, machete, sangre, cabrón.* She watched the carver's face, trying to see inside. Had this old man swindled her father? If he had, did she still care? Maybe conning her father had been the only way for the old man to feed his family. Laundry hung from a clothesline. Jeans. A giant bra. Husks of unpainted tiger masks lay scattered, but no grasshoppers.

Salvador turned to her. "I know we've had a scare, but Emilio Luna will answer your questions. He is willing to be in your book. Speak loudly, he is a little deaf in the right ear."

Stupid book. Stupid lie. Anna fished out a notebook and pen.

"Do you want me to translate?" he asked.

Anna shook her head. She had her pride—and her dictionary.

Salvador gave her a leading stare. "Ask him about the Grasshopper masks."

Anna understood now why the painter had defended the carver's reputation. They were friends. This wasn't going to end well. Daniel Ramsey was either a fool or a liar.

"Please, sir, how long have you been carving?"

"My father was a carver. *His* father was a carver. People copy our designs, but we were the first in the village. Every fiesta, people came to my father for masks. 'I want an old man.' 'I want a tiger.' As a boy, I watched and practiced." The man spoke slowly to her. She understood him.

"What kind of wood is that?" she asked.

"Copal."

"Where do you get it?"

The man pointed to the hills, then picked up a tiger's head and held it between his thighs. With a metal tool and a mallet, he tapped the wood. There was a charming self-consciousness to the gesture; he would now perform for his American guest. A minute later, the tiger's eyeball emerged. Anna envied people who worked with their hands.

"Señor, how do you decide what to make next?"

He rubbed the grain with his thumb. "You listen to the wood. You dream." He touched his temple. *"El Señor te da la inspiración."*

God gives you inspiration. It bugged Anna how God talked to everybody but her. "Do you ever take commissions?"

"I sell tigers to the coasts."

"Just tigers?"

"Tigers, Moors, donkeys . . . and people from the town." He held up a dusty photograph of a girl. "I will make a mask of her for her birthday."

"What about grasshoppers?" She watched his face closely.

"Grasshoppers? No grasshoppers. My original work is in the showroom." The carver turned to Salvador. "Take her."

They stood, left the old man outside. Salvador pushed back a curtain into an unlit room with twin beds. Two dozen masks were laid out, each more gruesome than the last. A hag spitting out a baby, an old man with blond fur growing from his eyes. A red-faced man with swollen lips, who looked like he'd caught his wife in bed with his brother. A zoo of misfits. A menagerie of the damned, but not a single grasshopper. *Duende.* A *duende* was an elf, but it was also a term for art so intense, so passionate and dark, the artist's soul had touched death. A bullfighter could have *duende.* A singer went nowhere without it.

Salvador focused on Anna in a way he hadn't before. He was testing her. "I always thought it was strange a gentle man could make masks like these. As a boy, they scared me. Do they scare you?"

Anna had spent most of her childhood being scared: scared her parents would divorce, scared her father would drive into a tree or take off to Mexico and never come home, but she didn't see her father in these masks, she saw herself, the inner crud of her being. She would never tell Salvador how bad it had gotten before David. How she slept with men she didn't care for. How she'd left the men who loved her most. How she drank to forget. This had been her pattern, the way she danced Carnival.

Anna smoothed the hag's hair.

"No," she lied. "I don't scare that easily."

Outside, the men fell back into a conversation Anna couldn't follow. Emilio Luna had not created the Grasshopper masks. Anna was sure of it. When they paused, she asked if Ricardo Rodríguez lived nearby.

"He's dead," Emilio Luna told her. "But his widow lives down the street."

"She sells masks?"

"It's possible."

"Señora Rodríguez is special, but don't worry," said the carver. In Spanish, *especial* meant "strange." "She stands by the fence all day praying."

Salvador frowned. "You shouldn't go alone."

The three of them held still to listen. A turkey crowed. The breeze touched the trees. Anna said she would be just a few minutes.

"Do not lose yourself," Salvador said. "Or your guide will have to rescue you."

She smiled. "I've been waiting to be found."

On the street, walking away, alone, she checked her phone. Two texts.

The first, David: U in Mexico. WTF?

The second, her father: Success?

He'd mastered the question mark.

Just wrapping things up, she typed back to her father. How long could she sustain this bluff? Anna took two steps, imagined David and Clarissa, the guest bed. She grabbed her phone, typed furiously: Sex is the biggest nothing of all time—Andy Warhol. She pressed send, watched the phone deliver the text to Daniel Ramsey.

With her tattered dress and stick limbs, the old woman looked like a witch from a fairy tale. A black lace shawl encircled her gaunt face, and her lips puckered like the tie end of a balloon. She clung to the chicken-wire fence, muttering. At the sight of Anna, she beckoned with a shriveled hand.

"Ven. Ven. Se venden máscaras."

The yard was a mess of rusty cans and slops. A gray cat stood on a chair, tail curled like a question mark. The air smelled of burning plastic. Anna summoned her nerve.

"Buenas tardes." Anna opened the gate with forced cheer. Maybe the old woman had dementia. Had news of the stabbing reached her? Had anything reached her at all?

The crone motioned with an impatient *"Sí, sí, ven"* and led Anna to a hut across the yard. Anna ducked under a crossbeam, breathed in the stink of peat or feces. As her eyes adjusted, she saw they were in an outhouse shrouded with blankets. Plants dripped from the ceiling. The plastic toilet seat rested on a wooden box. A crusty-eyed bulldog appeared and perched at the woman's side, drooling.

The old woman had five masks: three tigers, a Moor, and a wolf. No Centurions.

"Qué bonito," Anna murmured, though they weren't *bonito* at all. She picked up a tiger, brushed off its dirty face. The paint job was sloppy. *How sad. This is all she has to sell.* Anna would make a lousy collector; the worse someone's merchandise, the more compelled she felt to buy it. She infuriated David by coming home with bruised apples and wilted bouquets.

Anna asked the name of the artist.

"Mi primo. I have one other mask. Very special. Wait here."

The woman evaporated into the gloom. Anna sighed. She should never have come. Just when she'd decided to buy the Moor out of charity, then make a graceful exit, the crone returned and thrust a heavy mask into her hands, saying: "Very old and valuable. Stone."

It was the death mask.

It couldn't be, but it was. Montezuma's death mask—or an excellent copy. She turned it over, incredulous. Snakes. Warts. Red back. Splintering resin.

Anna searched the old woman's face. Her yellow, bloodshot eyes. She might have hepatitis. She might be insane. The click of bugs grew louder. The dog panted. It was too much. The murder and now this. Anna couldn't figure all the angles, conjugate verbs, decide what to do.

"It's beautiful," she said again, buying time.

This mask must be a reproduction. A knock-off. The Tepito gunman had taken a photo of Malone's mask, made a copy, which had somehow wound up with this lunatic crone in an outhouse in San Juan del Monte. The crone must come from a family of frauds. No doubt Daniel Ramsey had stood in this very hovel and handed over great sums for worthless art.

"*Turquesa. Muy vieja. ¿Cuánto me da?*"

"I am sorry." Anna said. "*No puedo comprarla.*"

Her rejection set off a torment of wailing. The smell of basil and cigar lodged against the back of Anna's throat. She fought back a gag.

"*Mi princesa.* I make you good price. Fifteen hundred pesos."

Anna laid the mask on the floor. "*Señora*, this mask is not authentic." Her voice gentle, but firm. "It's a reproduction."

As soon as Anna had said the reasonable thing, it lost all power to convince. A glorious vision blossomed in its place. The looter had been wrong: The Tepito gunman didn't work for Thomas Malone. He worked for himself. He'd brought the mask to the mountains, to this woman, who was selling it because she didn't know its real value. Or she was scared of Reyes. Or she was desperate for money. All of which meant Anna had been seducing the wrong man, barking up the wrong chapel.

Montezuma's mask was here.

Ambition surged inside her. A desire not unlike cocaine, the toxic dribble that teases the back of the throat. She knelt, picked up the mask. Its good eye bored into her. *Take me before someone else does.*

Anna pulled out a thousand pesos. Her hands were clumsy. "*Bueno, señora.* This is all the money I have, but if it is sufficient, I will—"

The woman snatched the money and stuffed it in her empty bra. "*Que Dios te bendiga.*" She lifted a large wooden cross off the wall. Anna assumed this, too, was for sale, but the old woman swung the cross at Anna's face. She ducked but the edge of the wood caught her cheek. With a cry, Anna turned and ran out of the hut, across the yard, around a lumbering pig. *I am going to die here. Óscar Reyes Carrillo is going to jump out of that hut with a gun.*

Yard. Door. Street. Dirt road. Potholes. Only then did she dare turn around. The hag had returned to the fence, tobacco fingers twinkling as she crossed herself, mustard eyes rolling as she recited the incantatory prayer whose sorrow always filled Anna with unease. *Santa María, Madre de Dios, ruega por nosotros pecadores, ahora y en la hora de nuestra muerte. Amen.*

A short woman with a worried expression passed Anna on the road. In one hand, she carried white day lilies. In the other, a man's wallet.

Walking back to Emilio Luna's house, Anna composed herself, slowed her breathing. Best not to tell Salvador about the mask. Fact: *People lie most often to the people they are closest to.* Another fact: *Every fourth conversation contains a falsehood.* Besides, this wasn't a blatant lie, but a lie of omission. A slinky black dress of a lie. A push-up bra. A cigarette snuck in an alley. An affair in the guest room. Two people in a single bed.

What happened to your cheek?

I snagged it on a rosebush.

Did you get one?

One what?

A rose?

No.

Next time, then. Salvador would smile. *Next time you'll get even.*

A terrifying wail emanated from the old woman's house. Anna kept going, chanting her own sort of Rosary, a prayer that shot into the sky, a firecracker calling out to God, who answered only in smoke. *I have the mask now. Now I have the mask.*

When Salvador dropped her off back at the hotel, he invited her to visit his studio the next day. He was shy, almost awkward, until he kissed her. The kiss was gentle, but sure, and it spread through her body, warm, liquid, and she thought, *The simple things are the most amazing.* When he pulled back, he laid his hand over her cut cheek, as if he could heal her wound.

twenty-seven | THE COLLECTOR

Daniel Ramsey read Anna's text
five times, parsing each word, all four of them—*Just wrapping things up*—convincing himself this was good news. You couldn't *wrap up* unless you had accomplished what you'd set out to do. The word "just" was particularly reassuring. *Just* checking out of the hotel, perhaps. Buying souvenirs. But Anna had never come out and said, *I have the mask.* She was being evasive, making him wait to hear the long version in person.

He walked to the window. Frozen ground. Empty trees. The hush of the cold. Anna would be home soon.

And then what?

The Ramsey Collection would have a magnificent centerpiece. Word would travel quickly. Newspapers. The Web. DEATH MASK OF MONTEZUMA UNEARTHED. The shameless Addison Rockwell would call, tripping over himself, apologizing for the previous misunderstanding, proposing lunch at the Carlyle. Iced teas and club sandwiches all around. Rockwell's aristocratic countenance would express the museum's desire to renew discussion of the Rose White Ramsey Gallery. This time Daniel would set the terms. The book reprinted with corrections. An opening with international publicity. Symposium. Lecture tour. Yes, he wanted it all. Hot damn. There was reason to celebrate.

And Anna said, *I mean it. No ice.*

She was right. Many a slip between the cup and the lip. Maybe the looter wanted more money, or Malone or Reyes had gotten there first. How would Malone know about the mask? He wouldn't. How would Reyes know? He just would. Mexico City was a tough place and Anna was so damn pretty, like her mother. He should never have sent her— no, he hadn't *sent* her, she'd taken off, but still—his only child meeting a drug addict to purchase art on the black market while he sat snug in his living room, cowardly daydreaming of press conferences and punch bowls. What kind of father was he? What kind of monster?

And Anna said, *I mean it. No ice.*

He hadn't been entirely truthful with Anna. He *had* smuggled masks through customs. He had his regular tricks. You were allowed two bottles at duty-free liquor, but he'd buy four. When challenged, he'd argue. By the time they'd confiscated his Kahlúa, the line was backed up a mile and they would wave him through. Rose was a master of diversion, feigning fainting spells, the flu. The one time authorities searched his bags, he'd claimed he was opening a Mexican restaurant and needed wall decorations. He'd waved the phony blueprints he kept in his bag. He also carried fake provenance papers, as a last resort. Bottom line: Customs wanted drugs, not art. Still, it was so stressful his nose bled. He'd stop at the bar to calm his nerves.

And then they did get ugly, though not in the way he'd ever imagined. It was June, rainy season, the landscape lush and green. He was in the hotel bar, La Campana, nursing a queasy stomach and reading the wilted pages of a magazine, when Manuel López burst through the door, his face flushed yet pale, insisting the *señor* was needed on the phone. There had been an accident. Just then, the wind chimes rang, a metallic cascade of sound.

And the horror after that. The terrible logistics. The remains, yes, the body remained in a white-tiled funeral home festooned with crosses and Virgins, as if those things helped, and the *abuela* who placed her wrinkled hand on his, how good it felt to be touched, taken care of in this small way, the flight home, no memory, the urn he had pushed into the closet, how he'd sent Anna away to school so she would stop wandering room-to-room, touching her mother's clothes, smelling her soap, and the nights, the long nights after, finding dinner, eating dinner, cleaning up after dinner, listening for a cheery voice that never came.

How did everyone carry on, knowing all they were going to lose?

Just wrapping things up. And that strange second text, something about sex. *What in the world?* Maybe that was what people called spam.

February sank into his bones.

The birds attacked the empty feeder.

The ruined book sat on the coffee table.

The beauty one finds in fine art is one of the pitifully few real and lasting products of all human endeavor. John Paul Getty. His book was called *The Joys of Collecting*, but he was a lonely man. Estranged from his five children, he had refused to pay his grandson's ransom until the Italian captors mailed him the boy's ear. Getty would have wanted nothing to do with a death mask. He disliked funerary objects, because he was afraid to die.

Ramsey went to the bedroom. In moments of grief, he sat with Rose's urn and it comforted him. He slid open the door and reached, scurried his hand. The shelf was empty. Her journal was gone, too.

Anna.

He collapsed on the bed with an anguished sigh. He wasn't ready to give her up. The urn was not Rose, of course, just a symbol of Rose, but without a tangible object, all he had were memories, voices harder and harder to hear.

He wanted a drink. He gave himself permission. One drink to settle his nerves, one toast to the woman he loved. But he had nothing to drink. He'd have to go out. The Subaru sat in the driveway. All he had to do was scrape off the frost.

PART TWO

I go everywhere with my eyes closed and two
eyeballs painted on my face. There is a woman
across the court with no face at all.

—*Denis Johnson, "The Incognito Lounge"*

one | THE LOOTER

Heaven wasn't at all like he'd pictured it. No grassy fields or cool mountain lakes. No sex, no beer, no fishing. No, heaven felt like being skinned alive and looked a lot like Mexico. Cinder-block room, donkey blanket for a curtain. His angel was a stocky Mexican with a kindly expression, butch haircut, five or six earrings running up her right ear, breasts the size of mangoes. She sat on a stool like a milkmaid. A dog barked in the distance. The air smelled like dirt.

The looter closed his eyes, opened them, expecting this vision to disappear, but nothing budged. His whole body hurt. Neck, back, but mostly his skin, what was left of it. His legs and arms flowed with a pink river of pus dotted with half-cooked scabs. He remembered the cement. The tub.

"Where am I?"

The woman smiled, said nothing. He found his Spanish, asked again.

This time she answered. "In my house."

"Is this heaven?"

The woman laughed. "Hardly. The *narcos* buried you in the bathtub. I cooked them lunch and they went on their way. The cement had almost set, but you were still breathing. I called my brother. He brought acid, and we dug you out. I have been treating your wounds. You have been feverish with infection. I am doing my best."

The looter lay back, closed his eyes. It was a lot, not to be dead. More than enough for one day. His body trembled. He could still smell the cement, feel the cool ooze, see the daggers of sweat on the men's shirts. Tears wet his eyelids, followed by a violent rush of yellow lava that raced up his throat. Bile poured down his chin onto his stomach. He could do nothing to stop it. The woman wiped his lips, the wet on his chest. She offered him a joint and he smoked it.

two | ANNA

It was dark by the time Anna got back to the Puesta del Sol with the death mask. A white moth beat against her window. On the patio, a Norwegian family played cards with their towheaded children. Anna lowered the blinds, propped the mask on the bureau as if it needed fresh air. When she undressed to shower, it watched her. Montezuma's death mask. The prospect was both thrilling and vile.

She called her father, eager to share the good news. He didn't pick up. This was typical. He left his phone in the car half the time. Let the battery run out. Just as well. Better to wait for Gonzáles to confirm the mask. Authentication before celebration. No more Grasshopper debacles.

Anna lay in bed, placed the mask over her face and pretended she was dead. It felt peaceful. The weight on her forehead. Her limbs giving way. Anna was ten when her mother died and she'd been surprised how life had gone on. Holidays came. Lilacs bloomed. People ate lunch, got married, outgrew their shoes. At school, teachers whispered into her scalp, *Let me know if you need anything.* What was she supposed to need? In class, words drifted across the page without meaning. Numbers read like Chinese. In the restroom, Anna scrutinized her reflection. She looked the same.

And Salvador? She would visit his studio tomorrow. What did he think of her—if he thought of her at all? It had felt so good when he'd held her in San Juan del Monte. Not an exorcism. A blessing.

That evening, she called Lorenzo Gonzáles. His housekeeper answered.

"*El señor no está aquí.*"

Anna asked when he'd be back.

"Tomorrow, but he has no free appointments."

"Tomorrow at one is perfect."

"No, I am sorry. He is busy all day."

"Thank you, I will come tomorrow at one, then. Please tell him it concerns a mask."

Anna hung up before the woman could object. There were advantages to speaking bad Spanish.

Anna showed up early for work at the Malones' as if nothing had changed, except, of course, everything had. Hidden in her top dresser drawer was the most valuable pre-Columbian relic to surface in the past century. Or not. Until she knew which, it made no sense to sever ties with the collector.

Thomas did not acknowledge their motel tryst. No fond glance or touch, no prurient wink. He greeted her with a brusque "Welcome, Ms. Bookman. We have a lot to do." If anything, he acted unusually impatient, reminding her of their deadline. The gallery opening was three weeks away. The printer needed four days. They had catalogued only a third of the show. Thomas was disappointed she had to leave by noon. Their progress was often interrupted by phone calls he took in private.

Mid-morning, after one such disappearance, Thomas returned with several files jammed with papers and colored index cards. "Since we're behind schedule, I thought these might help. This is the work my previous assistant assembled. You can enter it into your database."

"Holly didn't use a computer?" Anna had dragged hers along.

"She preferred to write by hand."

"Because she didn't like computers or didn't have one?"

"Both."

The notes included the usual information: character, origin, artist, dances, and so on. Holly's handwriting was round and open. In the margins were sketches of birds.

"I feel like I'm plagiarizing," Anna said. "Are we going to give her credit?"

"I paid for the work. It's my property."

"But you'll cite her in the guide."

"She asked not to be mentioned. Really, the less said about her, the better. It upsets Constance. It's difficult when you become attached to people who aren't emotionally stable. As you've no doubt noticed, Oaxaca is a magnet for lost souls. Druggies. Divorcees. Mystics. Crazies."

"Which was Holly?"

This stopped him. A wry smile quickly replaced confusion. "Either a kleptomaniac or a thinly disguised opportunist. But that's how it is. Flighty people often fly away."

"Like a bird." Anna pointed to the drawings.

His mouth twitched. "Anyway, I hope you weren't expecting a byline. For all official purposes, the guide will be written by Lorenzo Gonzáles, a leading authority on Mexican masks and pre-Columbian art."

Anna narrowed her eyes. "So what are we—"

"Gonzáles will sign it, but he can't be bothered to write it. He's a busy man, as you can imagine."

Anna could imagine, did imagine, the whole picture. Thomas's upcoming show was not about pleasing Texas relatives. The easiest way to cleanse stolen art was to have it appear in a public showing with a catalogue endorsed by a respected dealer like Lorenzo Gonzáles. After this coming-out party, the stolen object had a legitimate paper trail, its sordid past forgotten amid the swirl of canapés and *prosecco*. Anna's own reputation had benefited from just such a cleansing. On David's arm, surrounded by the glitterati of the New York art world, she became respectable. Her dodgy romantic past, her checkered provenance, were all but forgotten, leaving only the pleasure of aesthetics.

Thomas excused himself again. Anna returned to work with a sigh. She wished she could leave right away, and wondered what the afternoon would bring. Gonzáles's assessment. Salvador's studio. Things could go terribly right or wrong. She opened a manila envelope from the files. A photograph of a young woman tumbled out. Even in the faded Polaroid, she was stunning. She wore a sleeveless blouse, feather earrings, the dangerous smile of a hitchhiker. An unlit cigarette dangled from her mouth. A tiara of flowers and a blue scarf encircled her head. Her expression was coy, daring, a little gonzo, a little come-hither. Definitely a girl without underwear. She sat at the same table where Anna now sat, bright note-cards scattered. The photograph had been glued to a sheet of paper, a profile created from the familiar mask headings.

CHARACTER: Holly Price, personal assistant

ORIGIN: Berkeley, California

MATERIALS: Flesh and bones

DIMENSIONS: Perfect

DATE DANCED: Last night

INFORMATION ABOUT THE DANCE: I think you remember

A Post-it had been stuck on top. "For your collection." Apparently, Anna wasn't the only personal assistant who had gotten personal with Thomas Malone.

Anna scanned the yard. Something was wrong with this place. A gloom or sadness shrouded the house, the distant cottage, the wall over which Thomas had dropped the dead squirrel, the pool no one bothered to clean, the chairs where her father had once sat, drinking, the kitchen where Soledad was frying bananas in corn oil, the grass Hugo cut down to two inches, the dog shit he scooped, and the chapel, locked. Had Holly been let in? Had they met there? Anna shivered. She didn't want to sleep with Thomas Malone, but for some crazy reason—and this made her question her sanity—she didn't want to be the only personal assistant who hadn't.

A construction van was parked outside Lorenzo Gonzáles's home. The dealer answered the door, apologized for the disarray. He showed

Anna to his office, saying he was glad things had gone smoothly in Mexico City.

"Actually, not." Anna was still angry. "I was held up at gunpoint. Where were you?"

He looked genuinely surprised, as he lowered his large frame into his chair. "How terrible. I had a family emergency in Puebla. I am sorry I couldn't be there, but you got the mask. What happened?"

"It all worked out in the end."

Gonzáles pulled out a magnifying glass. "Let me see."

She passed him the mask. The dealer scoured its surface. "This is either a legitimate antiquity or an excellent reproduction."

Anna rolled her eyes. This much she knew.

"Every object has a story. I will need more time to tell this mask's full story, but as our looter friend was trespassing in an archaeological site, this is rightly the property of the Mexican government. A foreigner caught carrying looted relics will be deported in forty-eight hours. By law, I should call the police."

He plucked the receiver and paused.

Anna recognized this bluff for what it was. She would bet her last peso Lorenzo Gonzáles had never given the Mexican government so much as an ashtray.

She kept it simple. "I don't think that would serve either of us."

Gonzáles leaned back. "Leave the mask with me. I can deliver the report in a week."

"I need information today."

"I prefer not to speculate."

"I can't leave the mask."

"With my new alarm system, no one gets in or out."

"Can you at least give me a date?"

Gonzáles frowned. "I can work with photographs, if I must. But you'll have to come back tomorrow before I could sign authenticity papers. I trust you could wait twenty-four hours?"

This service was another racket, like paid expert witnesses at a trial. While most art historians labored to document an object's history—its original use, the context of its burial or storage, its provenance since it was recovered (life, death, rebirth)—less scrupulous experts found creative writing a lucrative profession. It was amazing how many recently surfaced antiquities had previously belonged to unnamed Swiss collections. Anna did not know where Lorenzo Gonzáles fit on this ethical spectrum, but she had her suspicions.

Gonzáles held up a pencil. "You realize, even if I write, 'The death mask of Montezuma the Second has finally been discovered,' scholars will rebut my claim. Jealous collectors will deny it. But my review is the first step. The process starts here. With me." Gonzáles pointed his pencil to his desk. "While I work, I can give you a history lesson. Or are you too busy for that?"

Anna slid back in her chair.

"This sort of mosaic mask dates back to the postclassical period. Most masks were worn in religious services by priests, but the aristocracy was buried with masks to ensure safe passage to the underworld. The Maya had a saying: *A king dies, but a god is born.* Everybody wanted to live forever. You want to live forever?"

Anna nodded. She needed the papers.

Gonzáles produced a digital camera, lecturing on as he worked.

"Priests and royalty were buried with masks, gold, even dogs. Hairless dogs, Xoloitzcuintli, were slaughtered to guide the dead over the river. Today, masks are still used for celebrations. Carnival. Semana Santa. Día de los Muertos. Your typical *campesino* has no idea why he wears a mask. A *fiesta* is an excuse to get drunk. They wear masks because their fathers wore masks and *their* fathers wore masks, back, back." He leaned in. "Look at my face. What do you see?"

Nose hair. Veins. Exhaustion. She saw all this but said, "An educated man who knows a lot about archaeology and is proud of his country."

Gonzáles pulled back, smug. "Exactly. You see only what I want to show you. The human race has outgrown its face. The face no longer serves a purpose."

"And the body?"

"The body is not so good at keeping secrets."

The house was suddenly quiet. No housekeeper, no workmen. Just the tick of the hall clock. Anna wished he'd left the shades open. She thought of the dead tiger. An ordinary man, but to himself a whole world. Gonzáles held out the mask. His breath smelled of garlic. She could map his pores. She reached over and took back the mask. It was all she could do not to snatch it. Her shoulders shook, a warm chill.

"You are wearing a mask right now," he said. "Why is that?"

Anna set her jaw. She had no answer, but was sure Gonzáles did.

"Because, my dear, like the Aztecs, you are afraid."

three | THE GARDENER

With burning hands, Hugo pushed past the curtain into Pedro's house. He tore through the dead man's belongings—kitchen, closet, bed, dustballs, flip-flops, condoms—berating himself with a tickertape of expletives. His stomach churned a sluice of acid and nerves. He tried to think like a man with something to hide.

Outside, he searched the yard, studied the trees, the crisscross of branches, language he could not decipher. Finding nothing, he roared through the shitty house again, then collapsed outside in a plastic chair, pulled out a smoke. He could barely manage the cigarette. The logistics of fire and ash.

The *cabrón* would have needed to sell the mask quietly, without alerting Reyes. He might have sought help from his uncle Berto, a museum janitor who stole trinkets nobody missed, but such plans were delicate, took time. Hugo watched the clouds, pontoons of white nothing. A church bell tolled. The road was quiet, the entire town in mourning. Then he figured out the riddle, just like that: *The idiot had hidden the mask in his car.*

Pedro's house had no lock, but his car did. Locking the mask in the trunk would make sense to a simple man. *But where was the car?* Not here, where it belonged. Pedro must have snuck back to San Juan del Monte that morning. Parade roadblocks would have blocked his entry. The pool cleaner had not known he would die at Carnival with his car parked awkwardly across town, this basic chore left undone. (Hugo preferred to think that Pedro had died, not that he'd been killed, not that *he* had killed him.) The death mask was still inside the car, baking in the sun, waiting to be found.

Hugo had already discovered a spare car key in a pitcher. He snatched it and slunk into town, cap low, lest he be recognized. He worked systematically, block by block, moving out from the *zócalo*, carving ever wider squares.

If he didn't find the mask, Reyes would kill him.

If the police found him, he'd rot in jail.

Yellow girl made of yellow sun. What I do, I do for you.

Of the millions of sedans, he wanted only one. Blue Ford. Beat-up seats. They should invent a car that called your name. *Hugo. I'm over here, asshole, frying by the dumpster.* Or better yet, a woman's sexy voice. *Papito, I'm hot. Open my doors.*

Eight blocks from the *zócalo*, he found Pedro's car dozing under a tree. The way his luck was going, he half expected it to drive off when he got close. He slipped in the key. The door flew open. He checked the burning seats, dove under them, opened the trunk, weeded through the dead man's crap, cooler, spare tire, jumper cables, a bong. Nothing. He calmed himself, checked everything again. More nothing. He slammed his fist on the hood. Left a dent. Thunder shook his insides. He searched the sky for the reason God never saw fit to care for him. The sun would not stop shining. The trees didn't give a damn. Maybe he should pray to Santa Muerte. Whose side was that bitch on?

Back at Pedro's house, Hugo dumped drawers, smashed trinkets. His thoughts swarmed, dreams mixing with anxiety, worries sifting with memories, memories with omens of tigers and guns. He saw the girl's father lift her yellow dress. He saw Santa Muerte taunting him to *blow a little smoke on your mother.* He saw Soledad, lit in the doorway. *You are just pretending to plant dahlias.* He saw the burning comet disintegrate into sparks. He saw Pedro shoveling tacos, giving a thumbs-up.

Where was the *pinche* mask?

Everything was somewhere even when it was lost.

A fly landed on the lid of an orange soda can.

Hugo kicked a spare chair. Pedro's house depressed him. The *burro* had never learned to care for himself. His whole life he'd still needed his mother. By his bed hung a framed photograph of Señora Leonora Modica de Rodríguez, a twig of a woman, a living skeleton. The old woman grinned like she had secrets she'd take to the grave. Hugo smiled at his stupidity. *Motherfucker.* He'd never been a man of profanity, but he was no longer the same man. Of course—a Mexican with something to hide would give it to his mother.

Hugo picked up the fallen chair, set it straight.

At the corner cantina, he ordered a mescal, laid two coins on the bar. His knife was clean. His heart was clean. He was new water rushing over ancient rocks. He crossed himself, hitched his jeans, took a bus into the mountains.

four | THE COLLECTOR

He'd sit at the bar and have a Coke. He could do that. He'd lost his wife. For years, he had drunk to ease that sorrow, but she wasn't coming back. He had come to terms with this. *Just wrapping things up.* Three o'clock. Blinds carving horizontal strips of light. *What can I get you?* Bottles glimmered with mystery and warmth. Daniel Ramsey said something. Either he said a dry vodka martini or he said a Coke, no ice. He thought both and said one. His hands shook. He grabbed a toothpick, bit down, pulled the splinters from his mouth, crammed peanuts into his dry trap. Over at a booth, a woman in a narrow gray suit sipped seltzer. She kept adding the same column of numbers and frowning. He remembered La Campana, how he had been nursing his queasy stomach with Campari when Manuel López burst through the door saying the *señor* was needed on the phone. The wind chimes shook. *There has been an accident involving Señora Ramsey.* Daniel had not moved. He finished his drink. Manuel was nearly in tears, pulling his arm. *Señor, please. Come now.* He'd pushed the Mexican away. *I hear you. Don't rush me.* He was sick. The drink was helping. He tipped the glass to capture the last drop. The ice fell against his face. He ordered another. Just like now, he'd ordered another. Coke or vodka. One word could change your life. You jump. You bet. You marry. You quit. You drink. You ask. You buy. You touch. You remember. You say yes. You say no. You say *I'll have what you're having.* You say *one more, please.* You say *I'm buying.* You say *I have not been this happy since my wife died.* You say *another round.* You say *it's good to have friends.*

You say my daughter is in Mexico *just wrapping things up.*

You say, I must go and find her.

five | THE LOOTER

The looter spent all day in bed. It was the most peaceful day he could remember, but also the saddest. He understood, because he was not stupid and no longer high, that all that shiny good feeling, the rightness of his every move, the beauty of every moment, was the product of crank, and the only way to make that particular sun rise again was to smoke more, though he also knew, because he was not stupid and no longer high, that chasing that bliss would kill him. The unfairness of this conundrum blasted his insides. Once you had tasted the limits of human ecstasy, how could you settle for less?

He was lucky to be alive and tried not to feel sorry for himself or devise new ways to score drugs. The woman fed him chicken broth and dressed his wounds. He did not ask why she was helping him, for fear she would stop. No husband appeared. No children or neighbors. Her name was Mari, short for Marisol. Every few hours, she fixed him herbal tea from what looked like pine needles. He'd given up asking what it was called. Some Indian remedy with a fucked-up name.

Finally, his curiosity got the best of him, and he asked her why she was helping him. *"¿Por qué me estás ayudando?"*

She was sitting on her stool. Her heaviness inspired confidence.

"This is my penance. For Lent."

"What did you do?"

Mari shook her head. "I don't remember."

"I'll pay you back."

"I don't want drug money."

"You want sex?'

"With you?" This amused her. "They paid me to keep quiet, but I put the money in your wallet. You will need it to get restarted."

"Then what can I give you?"

Mari looked around. "Something for my shrine, perhaps. You should thank the Virgin Mary for saving your life."

The looter closed his eyes, wishing she'd asked for a new TV instead. "For your shrine . . . what? Like incense?"

"Burro. Incense costs ten pesos. Is that what your life is worth?" It was the first time he'd seen her angry.

"I'd like more marijuana." He hoped the formal name sounded medicinal.

"You take too many drugs."

"Pot is nothing."

"I can see everything you do in your face."

"More pot, *Mamá.*"

"I am not your *mamá*." The woman reached for a joint. "I am your lesbian aunt. Drink your tea."

The next morning, Mari roused him, saying he needed fresh air. Until then, the looter had left his room only to piss. Though it was still early, heat radiated off the patio in waves. He squinted, took her arm, tried to look brave. She picked up a basket of apricots and led him to a gate.

What he saw was a garden so magical it didn't seem real. Wild orchids, tongue-tied vines, ferns the size of giraffes, bird feeders, coral blossoms—a bit of the Amazon rain forest set in a parched middle-class neighborhood in Mexico. It reminded him of the drawings children make when they're told not to leave any white space.

"I must go to work," Mari said. "Sit down awhile."

The looter didn't want to stay alone. "What am I doing here?"

Mari pointed to a bench. "Recuperating."

She left him. He sat, sneezed. Manure. Lilies. A lot of goddamn pollen. Perfect place for a snake. He wasn't used to nature and couldn't decide if he liked it, though after a moment, he relaxed, stopped trying to be bigger than what was before him. He considered each plant in turn. Orange trees. Cactus like fireworks. A dozen kinds of pleasing flowers he couldn't name. At the far end, Mari's shrine, a three-foot stone statue of the Virgin, arms open, blessed the sheep, no, the flock, the garden, whatever. Votive candles dripped white wax.

Something gray darted past his face. A hummingbird, for God's sake. The bird landed on a tube feeder filled with red sugar syrup. His father had taught him about hummingbirds. Tiny things. Fragile.

Some weighed no more than a penny. Flying like maniacs to stay in one place. Chasing the sweetness of flowers. He knew the feeling. Sadness reached his eyes, watching the damn bird sputtering. Stupid little bird he could kill with his fist.

He missed being high. He missed it more than he missed his father, mother, and old girlfriend combined. He'd been born good, but something had happened. Burdens, failures, and now what could he do? Dig his way out? Put the goodness back? Plant himself like a garden? Every day, a new seed.

He ripped open an apricot, held out its juicy flesh in his palm, tried to look like a tree. Rooted. Strong. But the bird was fixated on the red sauce, dipping its needle beak and guzzling. *Here I am, little bird, with real fruit.* Maybe he should sing. His arm was getting tired. He divided the fruit, held out both hands, balanced. He was thirty seconds from feeling stupid, thirty seconds from jumping the fence to find Pico. Juice gummed between his fingers. The bird wouldn't come. Maybe hummingbirds didn't like apricots. Maybe he should buy the bird a fucking Coke. *No, idiot. Just stand there. Wait. Get used to waiting for good things to happen.*

In that quiet, waiting for the bird that never came, he figured out what to give Mari for her shrine—the most sacred object he had ever possessed—but he would need every ounce of cunning and courage, maybe even prayer, to secure it. Mari was right: *His life was worth more than a stick of incense.*

The college dropout from Divide, Colorado, was an international treasure.

six | ANNA

Visiting Salvador's studio had
seemed like a good idea, but now as she stood at his door, her visit
struck her as silly and presumptuous. What if his invitation had been a
mere pleasantry? Maybe the murder had created a false intimacy that
would now leave nothing but awkwardness. What if she hated his
paintings? Her friend Alice once joked that the trickiest point in a new
relationship was when your lover offered to read his poetry. Well, she'd
ask questions, hope he'd mistake curiosity for praise. She'd find her
favorite picture and make much of it.

The door opened. Salvador looked tousled. The stubble of his jaw
rubbed against her cheek when he planted a single air kiss. She smelled
vanilla, a whiff of turpentine.

"I am glad you came, but I feel nervous. Whenever I show someone
my art, I worry it is no good."

"Maybe it isn't," she said. "Just kidding. I'm sure it's—"

She ducked his mock punch. He led her across a terrace of broken bricks. He'd been expecting her. That was something.

"How are you feeling?" she asked.

"Tired. I couldn't sleep. All yesterday, I wonder what that dead tiger planned to do today. I want to do those things for him, but I don't know what they are."

"Are you friends with all these people?" Anna pointed to apartments along the garden. She pictured late parties with philosophers and sexy ceramicists.

"Not really. A few. Close your eyes."

Salvador guided her the remaining steps, then pulled back his hand. No dead babies. Salvador Flores painted still lifes. Plates and bowls and pitchers. The green of fresh peas. Butter yellow. The paintings were feminine; no, Anna corrected herself, domestic. The curve of a spoon. A mug by a white curtain. Simplified. Elemental. *Morning*, Anna decided. *His paintings feel like morning, even in the afternoon.*

She sat on the floor before a half-finished painting of a red bowl and a sky-blue pitcher. *They are a couple. A family in the making. The bowl is pregnant. The pitcher is proud of the bowl. It makes him feel strong to be at her side. They are not touching but they're together. The bowl is thinking. Expectant. Ready to be of use.*

"I would like to crawl inside your paintings."

Salvador sat next to her. "Crawl?" He didn't know this verb.

"Climb into your paintings and live there." Anna pantomimed with two fingers.

"Échame más flores."

This time, she was confused.

He cupped her knee with his palm. "*Throw me more flowers.* You are saying nice things, and I am asking for more. How is your cheek?"

"Better." Anna gestured to the paintings with her chin. "Is this what your life was like growing up?" She tried to contain her resentment. A happy childhood would make even friendship impossible.

"No, more like that." He pointed to his palette, a mess of colors, false starts, possibilities.

"You have a big family?"

"It only feels big. You would like my brother. He's smarter than I am, and better-looking. Even my mother likes him best. When we were young I was so jealous of Enrique, I once took *una honda*"—he mimed a slingshot—"and hit him in the eye with a rock."

Anna couldn't help smiling. "Was he okay?"

"No, not really. He can't judge distances well. He is a handsome man with a fucked-up eye." Salvador smiled, tentatively. "The women all baby him, and he likes that."

Anna covered his eye with her hand. "He looks like a pirate?" She laughed. "The other day, you looked like one."

"Me?" He considered this. "Enrique lives in Guatemala, but he says when he is forty, he will come back to Mexico, find a wife, become a *papi*, and make our mother happy. You want a family? Oh, I forgot. You don't like children."

"I like children from *afar*." Anna tapped her boots together. "Do you have a bedroom piece?"

"A what?"

"Bedroom piece. Artists hide their best work in the bedroom because it's not for sale."

"If I hung my paintings in my bedroom, I would never sleep. In the middle of the night, I would start painting, changing things."

"You're a perfectionist?"

"No. I just hate most of my work."

"That's crazy."

"Maybe," he agreed. "You like what you write?"

"I don't really write." She caught herself. She was supposed to be writing a book. "I'm just *starting* to write for myself. Before, I mostly corrected other people's mistakes. I was a fact-checker. I checked their facts."

"Facts." He shook his head, skeptical. "Never believe facts."

Anna felt affronted for no good reason. "So what do you believe in? Science? Religion? The lottery?"

"Children."

"But you don't have any."

"It's easiest to believe in something you don't have."

He took her hand in his lap. They sat there, leaning against the wall. The paintings didn't move. Nothing moved except the birds outside. They could not see the birds, but they could hear them. The sun from the window fell across Anna's face. They sat like this for a long while and didn't say a thing.

Salvador said there were two places he wanted to take her, if she had time. Anna said she did. They climbed into his gray sedan. Images of the Virgin Mary and Che Guevara hung from his rearview mirror. The virgin and the outlaw. He touched them both before turning the ignition. They drove into the hills.

"We grew up poor. Chicken poor. *Campo* poor, which is more hopeless than American poor."

"But now—"

"Slowly, my dad climbs up. I was the first in the family to go to university. My parents think being an artist is a waste of my education. They don't believe I can make a living. They think I deal drugs."

"Do you?"

"Only on weekends." He smiled. "I try to live economically, but it's hard. I was always greedy as a boy. I still fight this. Wanting things."

"Wanting what?"

"Art. Clothing. Food. I don't know. It's not the things. It's the safety of things."

"But your family was happy . . ."

"Not TV-happy, but yes. We were loved. We felt part of something—this big family. Cousins. Aunts. Not lonely or alone. Not hungry."

When Anna said nothing, he asked, "Why? You were lonely?"

"A bit," Anna said. "But we had a lot of things."

Ten minutes later, Salvador pulled in front of a stucco church. It was hot outside, but cool as they entered. They sat in a middle pew. He pointed to a fresco, a blurred image of a man's face, round as a basketball and no more expressive. A wool scarf wrapped around his head, like a cartoon character with a toothache. His mouth was smudged.

"Do you like it?"

Anna shrugged. "It's pretty rough. Folk art? It doesn't match the formality of the church." A pair of giggling teenagers snapped photos in front of the artwork. A boy scratched his armpits.

Salvador whispered, "This painting of Jesus was made back in the thirties. An art professor gave it to the church." Salvador pulled a postcard from his pocket. A classic rendering of Christ. Gentle expression. Crown of thorns. The stucco had chipped in places, leaving ragged patches of white. "This is how it used to look." Anna compared the postcard and the painting. No resemblance.

"What happened?"

"An old woman restored it."

"She's an artist?"

"A believer."

Anna muffled a laugh. "Wow. That's the worst restoration job I've ever seen. Even I could do better."

"That's what people call it. *The worst restoration job ever. Un fracaso.* The old woman says the priest gave her permission. He denies it. They are bringing in experts to see if it can be saved. The piece is an Ecce Homo. Behold the man. But people now call it Ecce Mono. Behold the monkey."

Anna laughed out loud.

"Art disappears from churches all the time," Salvador said. "Thieves cut paintings from the frame. They steal statues. They even rob the collection box. Drug lords have figured out there is money in antiquities. The government doesn't pay enough for guards or security. You have to care for art . . ." He paused, searching for a word. "What is the boy who watches the sheep?"

"Shepherd?"

"We need more shepherds."

Anna blushed. He couldn't know about the death mask and she was bursting to tell him. To confess. Here, in church, before the Jesus monkey.

"Every once in a while, there is good news," he went on. "A few years ago, the widow of an American dentist gave back eight thousand objects to the Mexican government. For years, her husband bought pre-Columbian art on the black market. Some pieces had been removed with a power saw. He repaired them with dentist glue."

Salvador laughed unhappily.

"We destroy so many things with our touching." He lifted his hand, changed his mind, put it back in his lap. "Starting with the things we love most."

They drove to another village and parked, walked past olive trees, trash bins, a giant Coke sign urging TOMA LO BUENO. Salvador led her to a circular clearing surrounded by a hip-high stone wall. An amphitheater. No, an old bullring. The city below them looked like a Christmas card, nestled and calm. No firecrackers. No dogs. No smoke. Salvador produced a blanket, a bottle of red wine, and cheese.

"This is the most beautiful place I know in Oaxaca. Remember you asked me? When I was a boy, *novilleros* practiced here. I tried to build my own museum. I collected arrowheads and feathers and arranged them. One time, I tried to make Enrique pay to see them, but he hit me and stole whatever he liked. I worried if I didn't collect things, they would be lost. I didn't want to step on the ground and kill an ant or a flower. Then my family took a trip to Monterrey, three days in the car. When I saw how big the desert was, I cried. What difference could I make in a place so big?" He shrugged, offered Anna some cheese. "Now boys bring their girlfriends here to . . ." He twirled his hand.

"That's why we're here." Anna twirled her hand.

He gave a happy shrug. *"Depende."*

The sun was going down. Ragged orange patches of light scarred the sky. The wine warmed Anna's insides. Feeling playful, she pulled Salvador to his feet, turned her fingers into horns, pawed the ground with her hooves. The torero pinched his arrogant nose, shook his red cape. The brave bull charged and the torero spun the animal, carving veronicas in the dust. His shirt buttons twinkled like the sequins of a *traje de luces*. Together they danced before the falling sun, as the crowd thundered, as the women tossed roses, as the band oompahed, as the queen smiled behind her black fan, beneath her lace mantilla. The matador could not harm the brave animal. He lowered her to the ground, wiped the dust from her brow, and laid his head on the animal's heaving chest. A man in love with a woman calls her *mi cielo*. My heaven. My sky. In that moment, the sky looked like heaven, and heaven seemed close.

seven | THE GARDENER

The old woman was not hard to find. Black dress, black head scarf, she rattled the chain link with clutched hands. The yard was a dump. Garbage. A pig passed out in cornhusks. Hugo tied on his mask. When he opened the metal gate, the woman rushed toward him. *"Que Dios te bendiga y te guarde."* May God bless you and keep you.

"Where is the mask?"

He watched a lie form on her lips. "What mask?"

He shook her shoulders. Her frailness disgusted him. She was half dead already.

"No games, old woman. Your little Pedro stole a mask from me. From Reyes."

The woman swore, fire in her eyes. "He was a good boy."

"The mask, woman."

"You're too late," she spat. "It was cursed. I wash my hands of it. You killed my boy. *Santa María, Madre de Dios, ruega por nosotros pecadores . . .*"

The Tiger stormed through her shack, the chicken coop, the outhouse. He slashed shrubs with his machete. He was tired of looking in vain.

Finding nothing, he shook the old witch. "I ask you for the last time. Where is the mask?"

"I sold it to an American."

"What American?"

"The one who stays with young Flores." Her dog wandered over and she pulled its long ears. "He was an innocent boy who made a mistake. A boy who needed his mother. I got rid of it right away. He didn't have to tell me. I knew."

The Tiger couldn't listen anymore. He pushed her hard, away from him, and the old woman tumbled backward. Her head slammed against the chicken coop and she collapsed without a word, limbs splayed like a broken kite. The Tiger knelt. With a surge of tenderness, he pressed his palm to her forehead. *Come back, old woman. I am not as bad as I seem.* And he thought, *I should get a doctor,* but he did not move.

He watched her die. She died as he watched her.

He put a finger under her nose, waiting, to be sure. The stink of pig and lye was overwhelmed by his own stench. The dog whimpered, dug its snout under his mistress's hip. A crow crossed the sky.

He got up, built a fire.

The Aztecs cremated the dead to speed their journey to the afterlife. He owed the old woman this much. A week before, he would have recoiled from this task, but now he felt neither fear nor revulsion. When the fire caught, he dragged her body into the flames. She weighed nothing. Her black dress parachuted in the updraft. He watched the crone's spirit rise. Her wailing voice wrapped around him like a shroud. *My beloved sons, we are all going to die.*

That night, Hugo dreamt he was an Aztec executioner working in the Temple of Fire. Blood tasted rich in his mouth, and his arms ached from lifting his flint. A storm blew in. Wind bent the trees. In a cataclysmic flash, a silent lightning bolt struck the temple. The great building shook and leapt into flames. In the fire, of the fire, he cried out for God.

Hugo jolted awake, his shirt damp with sweat. Soledad had not woken. Wired, he went to the kitchen, opened his Aztec history book. *The fall of the Aztec Empire and the death of Montezuma were foretold by eight omens.*

An Aztec fisherman harvesting a crane with a mirror on its forehead.

His heart quickened. In his dream the night after Reyes gave him the tiger mask, he had seen a fisherman holding a crane.

A comet shaped like an ear of corn scattering sparks over the city.

A wailing woman.

A noiseless lightning bolt destroying a temple.

Fear nipped his chest. He'd seen a corn-shaped comet at Carnival. The crone had wailed into the wind. In his dream tonight, a silent thunderhead had destroyed the Temple of Fire. The next four were unfamiliar.

A boiling lake.

A comet in the night sky.

A two-headed creature.

A burning temple.

Hugo glared at the kettle, the oven. Every object seemed capable of treason. *I am having visions. I am losing my mind.*

He walked outside, threw himself on the damp grass, stared at the stars, a thousand nicks of light stinging the sky. For months, he'd thought of nothing but the papershop girl, but now he was confronting a new kind of danger. Four omens. Four more before the empire fell. But what empire? Was the price of his sins that he would go mad? Were the spirits demanding the death mask's return? He wanted to ask Soledad, but he was alone with these visions, his sickness, forced to follow the mask wherever it led him. Staring into the night sky, Hugo made two fists and waited for the next missive from the dead.

eight | THE HOUSEKEEPER

"*Santísima Virgen, es tarde otra vez,* but I cannot sleep. Hugo says we will leave soon for the North. I don't want to go. The place I dream of living is Real de Catorce. Real is a holy city, a ghost town. The Huichol say ancient spirits live in the hills, and they eat peyote and walk into the desert with their offerings. Catholics go on pilgrimage to the parish church to worship San Francisco de Asís, the miraculous El Charrito, who cures the sick and maimed. The mountain air is so pure it cleans your insides in a single day. Though I was only eight the summer we went, I remember the beauty of the land. We climbed up from the town into the ruins, and I could imagine how men once mined for silver, how the elegant city once bustled with shopkeepers and craftsmen. All that is left now are crumbling walls, and spirits who refuse to leave. We children sat inside the remains of a stone house, just walls, no roof. Concha said it was three hundred years old. I lay back in the grass and the sky was stained-glass blue and the tuna flowers hung like pink earrings on the prickly pears and a tree shaped like a woman shook in the wind.

"Those mountains felt like heaven, and every fallen candy wrapper was a jewel from a queen's crown. All summer I collected trash to make collages. Princesses and dragons. At the end of the summer, my mother threw my art away, saying we couldn't take it with us, and I cried and rescued my artwork and brought it to you. *Mamá* got mad—*hija*, you can't bring trash to the Virgin—but I knew you would like it. Do you remember? Saints must have memories that go on forever.

"One more thing. (Are you still listening?) In Real de Catorce, we saw crosses everywhere. The cactus grew into crosses and the trees looked like crosses and the electric wires were crossed and we children spun in the mountains, arms wide, until everything got blurry and we fell down in the sun. Beautiful, spinning children in the shape of crosses. Can you see us, beloved Virgin? I am still that girl.

"Now I want a child of my own. (I am trying to be patient.) If I have a girl, I will name her Azura to remind me how it felt to stand on the mountaintop of Real de Catorce and hear the goat bells ringing like Sunday morning, and how I scoured the ground for beautiful trash, a bottle cap or a yellow candy wrapper caught in the thorns, waiting for someone to save it."

nine | THE PAPERSHOP GIRL

She liked her new bedroom in Veracruz with her Romeo Santos poster and chartreuse beanbag chair. At night, a towering eucalyptus tree stood guard out her window. In the morning, the sun lit her Betty Boop bedspread. The girl had no friends at school. She had arrived midyear and cliques had already formed. Girls who were friends traded charms from their bracelets, shared spearmint gum, slept at one another's houses on weekends, gossiping about sex.

During class, boys stared at her chest, but she refused to slouch. Let them imagine all they were missing. She wore lace gloves and tight jeans, and on special days, a yellow dress. At lunch, she ate alone, and her math teacher, Señora Barreto, nodded at her encouragingly, but the girl pretended not to see or understand this kindness.

Each day after school, she straightened her room, stacked her sweaters by color, aligned brush and comb. Before the move, her mother had begged her to throw out her stuffed animals, but she refused, so ducks, platypuses, and puppies sat next to her algebra book and tampons and the Bible she never opened. She missed Hugo. She did not love him, but she missed his attention. His desire pleased her. If he wanted her enough, he would do her bidding. He had promised to come in thirty days. She would marry him if he bought her a ring.

At dinner one night, her parents argued over money. There was something foul in the air, the stink of resentment. Her mother served chicken soup. Her father ate in his undershirt. His left hand never left his beer. Her mother said: *Why must you spend so much money at the dry cleaner's? Wear your shirts twice. Hang them up and they won't wrinkle. I wear mine three times and wash them by hand, and you throw money away.* Her father said, *A man must look professional or he will not appear trustworthy.* Her mother said, *It is vanity.* Her father said, *You should have the same pride in your appearance.*

The papershop girl carried her plate to the kitchen and left it in the sink underwater. She went to her room, lay down, stared at the ceiling panels covering pipes. When the knock came, she scurried to the edge of the bed, placed her bare feet on the tiles, careful not to touch the cracks. Her father closed the door, sat next to her, pant leg brushing her thigh. His cologne smelled like oranges dipped in chocolate. Her comforter wrinkled under his weight. He placed his hand on her leg. Her skin paled under his grasp. She trembled. His face looked like that of a man who was sleepwalking, awake but not seeing, and he whispered: "My little girl. How beautiful you are."

ten | ANNA

Inside the cloistered home of Lorenzo Gonzáles, Anna felt miles away from the bustling streets of Oaxaca, the ATMs and tour buses, the commerce of jicama and mangoes. She had hoped the dealer would pronounce his verdict right away, but instead he delivered a windy lecture about the repatriation of antiquities, how "source countries," like Italy, Greece, and Turkey, were increasingly willing to challenge the predatory practices of "collecting countries," those with the money and desire to expand museum collections. With all the lawsuits, the major museums were exporting more art than they acquired. Gonzáles made his disdain clear, characterizing the efforts of source countries to recoup lost art as thinly disguised nationalism.

"Maybe Greek museums should only show Greek art?" He gave a large shrug. "Maybe the Metropolitan Museum should give away its whole collection and limit itself to Native American art? Does the international art market encourage looting? Maybe, but there has been looting ever since man invented the shovel. Mexico has eleven thousand archaeological sites. Guard them all? Good luck."

The telecom tycoon Carlos Slim was his hero. "Richest man in the world. Worth seventy-four billion. Builds his own museum, the Soumaya, named after his wife. Sure, he's got Orozco, Tamayo, but he buys van Gogh, Matisse, the biggest collection of Rodin sculptures outside France. Why European art? Because most Mexicans cannot afford to go to Europe. *So he brings the art to them.*" Gonzáles shook his head, impressed. "And what does he get for his efforts? The press rides him like a donkey. Call his collection second-rate. They hate the building. Too shiny. *Naco.* They are so envious they can only spit."

Anna kept her eye on the death mask. She didn't like seeing it on his desk.

Gonzáles picked up a newspaper, batted it with his middle finger. "Another museum was robbed. San Luis Potosí. No alarms. Three Diego Riveras removed. One oil. Two watercolors. The night guard disappeared as well."

"That's terrible—

"And now this mask shows up, out of the blue. That's the expression, right?" Anna nodded. "It has long been rumored a funerary mask was made for Montezuma the Second the day he took power." His voice dropped. "If authentic, this mask would represent a stunning archaeological discovery. . . . You could sell it to Carlos Slim for the entranceway of the Soumaya. He could put it next to *The Thinker.*"

Adrenaline washed through Anna's insides, dangerous, sickening. It was time for something to go right.

Gonzáles beamed. "But unfortunately, I'm afraid, your mask is not that treasure."

His words slapped Anna's face.

"It is not a bad little reproduction." He chuckled. "Actually quite clever." His pencil pointed. "See the flatness of the nose, the earplugs. This line of red stones represents bloodletting—all signs of royalty. These bumps are cabochons. Nice touch. But with a legitimate pre-Columbian relic, the stones and glue would be older, the cedar wood more decayed. Look at the holes. Too small and even. This mask could fool amateurs, maybe a few collectors. I'll buy it to show my archaeology students. See if they lose their heads when confronted with the possibility of glory."

"Are you sure?"

He fished a five-hundred-peso note from this wallet, held it out. "Go buy yourself a nice dinner on the *zócalo* tonight."

Anna didn't even look at the money. "We paid, *we lost*, fourteen thousand dollars on this mask. What happened to our deposit?"

"I sent—"

"He never got it."

The dealer looked away.

"I flew here because you told my father it was legitimate." She wanted him to acknowledge his complicity.

Gonzáles frowned. "I told your father I couldn't promise the mask's veracity without seeing it in person. I told you that, too. Ventures like this are always a risk."

"You still collect a commission."

"Two thousand dollars?" The dealer sniffed. "Since we are being honest, I will tell you exactly what happened. This digger e-mailed me a photograph of the mask. He was very agitated and wanted to sell it right away. I think: *If legitimate, this is the mask of the century.* Frankly, your father needs a discovery this size to restore his name. I write him. *He* is the one who gets excited, claims it *has* to be Montezuma's death mask. I express reservations, but agree to broker the deal, for less than my usual fee because I like and respect your father."

Anna's indignation collapsed. It was a new version of the same lousy story. Mexicans had taken her father for a ride. Or he had taken himself—and then taken her.

"Did Montezuma even *have* a death mask?" she asked.

Gonzáles interlaced his hands behind his head, as if they'd reached his favorite part of the story. "I am a dreamer. I continue to believe in the mask." He paused, staring into the half distance. "And when it is discovered, I plan to collect the commission."

"So this mask is worth nothing?"

"Not necessarily." His smile was friendly, corrupt. "A reproduction can bring its owner as much pleasure as the genuine."

"I bet for the right price, you'd declare it authentic." Her insinuation was insulting, but she didn't care.

Gonzáles did his best to look indignant. "Despite what Americans think, not all Mexicans are for sale, Miss Ramsey." More gently, he added: "Your father's enthusiasm is an enviable quality. Most collectors have given up on the legend. I am glad your father has not."

It still didn't add up. "But why would the gunman in Tepito go to the trouble of stealing a worthless mask? It makes no sense."

"He probably works for Reyes." Gonzáles shrugged. "We cannot guess what story of revenge was being played out. Even small disagreements are settled with guns. *You owe me money, I shoot you. You look at me funny, I shoot you again.* I did not call Reyes, but no one *has* to call Reyes. Reyes just shows up."

"But he didn't shoot the looter—or me—he took the mask."

The dealer hung his head. "I am sorry to involve you in this ugliness. I should not have called your father, and he should never have sent you. Take this bit of money as an apology. I will hang the mask in my office as a reminder not to abuse my influence."

He held out the money. Anna didn't budge.

He sighed with sympathy. "If I may offer you some advice: Go home. You are not safe here. To carry around a mask that looks valuable is as dangerous as carrying the real thing. In Mexico, politicians are shot dead in the morning sun, *panzas* full of tamales and mescal. Their bodyguards step aside to be sure the bullet reaches its target. The streets are crowded, but there are no witnesses. The art world is just as brutal."

Anna stuffed the mask in her pack. She was pissed. She was thirsty.

Gonzáles walked her to the door. "Be careful," he warned. "Every day, priceless art is broken by careless hands. I would hate for you to be one of those things."

Anna pushed through the city, disgusted. The worthless mask bounced against her back, a chiming reminder of her own stupidity. She hadn't thought herself capable of fetishism, but when a masterpiece had been dangled, she'd jumped, rushing headlong into danger. Chasing the mask had made her feel important. Without it, she was just another tourist, like the hideous group in front of her now, slogging along in their Bermuda shorts behind a guide hoisting a closed umbrella.

"The oil in the peppers can burn your eyes, so you'll want to wear gloves." A foodie tour. Have mouth, will travel. "Of course, the larger ones you can stuff. . . . What? Yes, you can put anything inside a *poblano*. They are docile, grandma-friendly. As I said earlier, *ancho*, *pasilla*, and *guajillo* form the holy trinity of *mole*."

The holy trinity of mole. Why were tourists so incredibly annoying? Some twisted form of self-hatred. A mirror? Your own inanity reflected?

Anna squeezed past them, steering to the *zócalo*, practicing the phrases she would need to order her three favorite drinks. At her usual café, she saw something alarming and froze. Salvador was sitting across from a gorgeous woman. She wore skinny jeans, high-heel sandals, a silk scarf. Her dark hair shone like polished rock. A regular beauty pageant contestant. Miss Venezuela. The two of them were holding hands. Both hands. Four hands on the table, a confessional scene from a *telenovela*. The woman was weeping. Salvador was gesturing *No, no,* reassuring her, patting her arm. Only someone delusional would read the scene as anything other than what it was: a man pleading with his lover for forgiveness.

Anna pivoted hard. Sweat rose off her back. She hadn't realized how hard she'd been hoping.

In and out of shops she drifted, touching things she didn't want, indignation collapsing into despair. How naive she had been. *I thought you were smarter than that.* No, in fact. She wasn't. Or had there been a misunderstanding? Maybe the woman was a friend or some clingy ex. Maybe Salvador was leaving the goddess for Anna. *He likes you. He'll explain. Just give him a chance.*

Later that afternoon, she marched to Salvador's apartment. The fact-checker. The woman scorned. She rang the bell, waited. It would take him a minute to leave his apartment, cross the central patio, reach the entrance that fronted the street. Finally, the giant door inched open. Salvador's expression moved so quickly from pleased to peeved that

Anna wasn't sure the pleasure had been there at all. A woman's navy cardigan rested over his shoulder.

"I was in the neighborhood, so I stopped by."

He winced. "I am glad."

He was lying. He was not glad.

"Would you like to get a coffee?" Anna asked, already retreating from her original plan. She would not ask about the woman.

He didn't meet her eyes. "I am sorry. I can't right now."

"You have company?" Anna nodded at the cardigan.

"Something has come up. I'll be busy for a while."

Anna was sweating. She hated him.

"I will call you," he promised.

He would never call her.

"Okay, well," she said, stepping back. *"Buena suerte con tus aventuras."*

His shoulders dropped. "It's not like that."

"No," Anna agreed. "It's probably not."

At the Buen Viaje travel agency, Anna booked a flight home. Monday. Four days. That gave her the weekend to deal with her mother's ashes. She'd come to terms with the idea of scattering her remains. Life was scattered. Life was a crazy mess of particles.

She should call her father, but she didn't have the heart to kill his dream. She'd bluff a text or two until she got home, then break the bad news in person. She pulled out her phone. One voicemail. One text. She took the voicemail first, neck hairs prickling. From thousands of miles away, she heard and smelled and tasted and touched and saw the air where her father was standing. Salt. Lime. Beer. Ice. His voice was sloshy.

"Hello, Anna. It's your father. Listen, I hope this isn't too late. Don't come home yet. I'm coming down there. Damn the knees. I realize we never talked about *customs*. If you're stopped, you need to know what to say. I will handle everything. Jesus, it's loud in here. Can you still hear me? Your mother usually carried the masks through customs and she'd tell the officers . . ." He was laughing now. "She was an amazing woman, the only person who really understood me."

Anna dropped the phone. She missed the next few phrases, but what did it matter.

"I'll find you at the Sunrise. Okay. Signing off. This is your father. Thank you. You're a wonderful daughter. Be careful. Okay. Bye-bye."

As she walked home, Anna dug up a cigarette, inhaled a pale green rush. She'd lost count of what number this was. Back at the Puesta, she poured a mescal, lay down, watching the ceiling fan spin. Her father was drinking again. How silly she'd been to think he could change. That she could. He would never make it to Mexico.

She remembered the text. David. The florist wants a security deposit. Please advise.

Anna recognized the dangerous feeling growing inside her. This was how she had felt before David. She'd hurt herself to prove no one else could, self-destruction being its own sort of revenge. Tonight, she would go out. *The fact-checker does the big city.* Read my rough draft. Count my words. Highlight my best passages. Fix my bad grammar. Reposition my transitions. Sharpen each point. Punctuate. Tighten. Control. Command. Shift. Return. Delete.

———————

At Macho Tacos, it was *hora feliz.* Expats with brash voices and empty cargo shorts swiveled on barstools. Anna downed two strawberry margaritas for the price of one and met Kathy from Minneapolis, who introduced her to Steve, whom people called Bigfoot. Anna asked Bigfoot if he was big and he said, "So I've been told." Kathy backed off to hang with her flip-flop girls, and Steve bought Anna a happy-hour shot, and they played some *Gilligan's Island* drinking game that Anna kept losing. Pretty soon, he was calling her Ginger.

At sundown, they staggered outside, past the ladies closing the market. The air smelled like raw meat. Anna told a banana joke, but couldn't remember the punch line. She kept falling off her sandals.

They climbed to his apartment. Bigfoot was a slob. Deodorant on the coffee table, pistachio shells scattered on a plate. He tried to undress her, but couldn't figure out the buttons and, more confounding, her bra that opened in the front. Bigfoot was used to women being one way, and Anna was another. "What about some music?" she said. "Right-o," Bigfoot said, and put on Jimmy Buffett. Anna did a tiki dance, her blouse askew. She wished she had another drink, then magically, she did. She felt almost beautiful. Beauty being its own sort of mask.

Bigfoot popped a beer. "I like how you dance."

"I moved here to join a convent."

"Sister Ginger. I'll pray for you."

Bigfoot put his palms together, pushed down her panties, making the final swish with his foot. He was not a natural athlete or lover. His erection was the boldest part of his body, one pure idea—*I know how this thing works.*

Jimmy was singing about changes in latitude.

Bigfoot guided Anna to the bedroom. He dug up a condom, wore it like a third sock. He smelled like gel. They fell on the bed. The closer Bigfoot got, the farther away he seemed. When he got real close, Anna gripped his shoulders, ready to dream up some tawdry Mexico erotica, all firecrackers and smoke, but before she had patched another man's face on his body, he was done. Hiccup sex. A wet dream without the dream.

They lay on their backs. Bigfoot told her she was sexy, promised to do better next time.

"Thank you for being with me," he said.

Anna whispered, *"De nada."* It was nothing.

Anna was good at nothing. It occurred to her what she'd had with David had been nothing. Just a rhythm, parallel play. *I'll go to the gym and you make dinner and you stop at the store and I'll have a drink with my friends and we'll meet and floss our teeth and have sex and sleep.* They didn't talk about difficult things. Or rather, they talked about other people's difficulties, not their own. They never fought; they left, calling a friend, running. She knew who David was. Vain, selfish, careless with people, but he also had many gifts. Intelligence. Humor. Ambition. Generous—but he gave only gifts that required no sacrifice; he would spend money, but not be inconvenienced. Perhaps somewhere deep down inside her, wherever the subconscious, that blind mole, lay hiding, she'd known he would fail the Clarissa test. Maybe she had wanted it to happen, because she needed their demise to be his fault.

What the hell was wrong with her?

She often wept after sex. Sometimes she was happy and sometimes she was sad and sometimes, like now, she had no idea why she was crying. Maybe because sex was a metaphor for something you could never really have. That, and knowing her single kiss with Salvador had meant more than this. She should have outgrown these cheap stunts: using men to prove her worth. Because she knew better. Because they never worked.

Bigfoot looked sort of dear, drinking his glass of water, messing with his phone. He wasn't a monster, just another Steve who liked pretty girls. She pointed a finger gun at his back. No, that wasn't right. Turning the gun, she pressed her finger muzzle hard against her sternum, pulled the trigger, and thought: *This is the way I hate myself.*

eleven | THE LOOTER

The looter grew impatient waiting for his skin to heal. He liked the garden—the mottled sunlight, the Virgin Mary—but fuck it. It was time to go. On the fourth morning, while Mari slept, he made his escape. His life had new purpose. He had someone to thank and someone to screw over. Both goals formed part of a singular campaign. Forget Jesus. Resurrection didn't make you a saint. He had returned from the dead the same man: A looter. A man lucky with treasure. A man with the patience to dig. And yet he had new energy, because he was ready to prove that the Maddox Principle held water. Cultivate the good inside him. Turn himself inside out.

He took a bus to Mexico City, beelined to the juice stand. When Pico saw him, his face fell away, confusion, then fear.

"*Hombre,* you are supposed to be dead."

"I was dead, but I didn't like it."

Pico shook his head, full of objections. "They said you were buried in a bathtub. Now you're here. It's not right. If Reyes sees you, he's going to kill you."

"Again?"

Pico laughed, like the looter was a disobedient dog he couldn't bring himself to punish. "I am not seeing you."

"I'm not here."

"Okay, then. What do you want?"

"Weed."

Pico looked doubtful. "That's it?"

"New Year's resolution."

"It's almost March."

"Late start. Hey, what's that on your shirt?" The design looked like a jigsaw puzzle.

Pico shrugged. "Some Aztec god. Hummingbird something. God of sun and war, a real *cabrón*. You had to kill a lot of people to keep him happy."

"Like Reyes."

"Nah. Reyes doesn't kill for sport. Reyes is family. You just can't leave him or fuck up."

"I did both."

Pico started up the juice. His hands shook, like he was about to cut himself and make blood orange juice.

The looter thought of Mari and made a fresh connection. This was a pilgrimage. He was a pilgrim. Sunday-school stories flooded back to him. The worst sinners crawled on their knees. The looter dropped to the pavement, testing his joints. His skin was gossamer thin. Dirt and pigeon mess splotched the sidewalk, but pilgrims weren't supposed to mind. The looter crawled a few paces, to get the hang of it.

Mid-squeeze, Pico peered down, shook his head. "Get up, man. The juice isn't that good."

Pico had half an orange in his hand. The sections formed a circle, equal parts of a whole. The looter admired its perfection.

"I can see everything now," he said. "More than everything."

Pico folded his arms. "What are you on?"

"You just need someone to hate."

"That won't work."

"An asshole gives your life purpose. An angel or an asshole, and I've got both."

"Not Reyes . . ." Pico wagged his knife. "He's an octopus. You are no match for him, my friend, dead or alive."

"What about dead *and* alive?"

The looter pushed off one knee and rose. He did a little jig to prove he wasn't wrecked yet. His pants slid under his hipbones. He hoisted them, jammed his shirt inside, making his clothes behave.

"I'm going to Colorado after this," he announced. "That's the endgame. Settle my debts. Hey, throw me an orange. This time I'm going to eat it."

The fruit fell *thump* into his waiting palm. The looter peeled back the skin to where the sweetness was waiting.

He bought a ticket on a second-class bus. The death mask was somewhere in Oaxaca, but that was all he knew. He had no luggage, just his satchel, his lucky toothbrush, and now, mercifully, most of his skin.

He smoked a joint before the bus took off.

Reyes thought he was dead. It had been worth the trip to confirm this. So long as he remained a ghost, he was free, provided he stayed clear of the safe house, and Pico kept mum, and he didn't run into Reyes. The drug lord had a house in Oaxaca. A summer home. An assassin's retreat.

When no one sat next to him on the bus, the looter stretched over two seats, pillowed his sweatshirt, read the passing graffiti claiming various political candidates were prostitutes, assholes, and frauds.

The girl across the aisle seemed to be pregnant. She had braces and reddish-brown hair. In her lap, she coddled a basket. Two round things. The belly. The basket. You couldn't call her face pretty. Too many freckles. She smiled at him, as if she had a few phrases in English she wanted to try out. *How do you do? My name is Gloria. I like the city more than the country.*

The looter couldn't think what to say. It was hard to be aroused by a girl someone else had knocked up, though he'd heard pregnant girls wanted it bad, hormones all jazzed for one last dance. She looked like a woman who worked hard. He wanted to ask her, *Are you good with a mop?* But he couldn't think of the Spanish word for "mop" or even "broom." He didn't know the word for "braces," either, the other obvious topic. He offered her a tab of gum, saying, *"¿Dónde vas?"* It was a lame question. The bus went only one place.

"Oaxaca." She smiled again. Once you got used to her freckles, they were sort of attractive, like God spent some serious time painting her face.

"You live in Oaxaca?"

The girl gave a tiny nod.

"Oaxaca is pretty?" He was buying time here, deciding what to do next.

"*Sí.* Very pretty." The girl looked ahead, like she didn't want the other passengers to see her talking with an American man with no luggage and bad skin.

"I need a room to rent. Do you know one?"

The girl stared at the back of the seat in front of her, blue fake-leather nothing. Maybe he'd gone too far. Clearly, she had run into trouble with men. She wasn't old. Maybe twenty-one tomorrow.

"My aunt has an extra room in the garden," she said, shyly.

"How much does she charge a night?"

"Thirty pesos."

Two bucks. He could afford it. He couldn't tell if she was happy about this room idea or reluctant. "Then I will go with you when we arrive in pretty Oaxaca and you can show me the room."

The girl nodded into her basket. The looter wondered if women still found him good-looking. They used to, before he spent so much time digging in caves. He didn't talk to the girl the rest of the bus ride, so she wouldn't think he was trying to get in her panties.

He turned his face to the window, hoping to tan through the glass. The desert was an empty place for being so full. He wondered if real pilgrims took the bus or whether this was cheating. Maybe he should pray. He hadn't prayed in years, give or take a decade, and wasn't sure how to begin, especially on a bus. Maybe he'd pray to Mari. Thank her, in his head. Women were always saving him. The Virgin. Mari. This knocked-up girl with the basket.

The world of men had only led him underground.

The girl pulled sewing out of her basket, squeezed yarn through a needle's eye. Needlepoint. His mother had been into that, covered a bench with flowers, then wouldn't let anyone sit on it. His mother probably missed him, even though he'd stolen her VCR. She'd probably cry if she saw his face. Jug wine. Saran wrap. Aerobic sneakers. His mother wasn't as bad in person as she was in his head. Banging out cube steaks, losing herself in romance novels and reality shows, like all that love and money was real. The snow in the Rockies never melted. Not completely. His mother was a mountain peak. Chilly. Inaccessible. But there was warmth under her surface. The earth's core was a ball of fire. Use your imagination. Dig with your fucking heart.

And now he was crying, face to the window, back to the girl. No one saw his baby tears but the agave, the prickly pear, the thistle flowers streaming past, and none of them were talking. Not anymore.

His mother thought he was dead.

twelve | ANNA

The death mask was fake. Her father was boozing. She'd slept with Bigfoot. Her trip had been a *fracaso total* and now she had to dispose of her mother's ashes. There wasn't time to purchase a grave site, and she wasn't sure her mother would have wanted one anyway. No, she would have to find a tree in the countryside, a mystical, magical, heavenly shade tree, like O'Keeffe's Lawrence tree, where she could scatter her mother's remains. She'd take a photograph to show her father, so they could visit the spot.

Anna knew only one person well enough to borrow a car.

Constance agreed to lend the old Fiat, but insisted she come to lunch. Anna accepted. A Last Supper, of sorts. She would not tell the Malones she was leaving the country. She didn't owe Señor VIP an explanation. Let him ring up Holly, have her finish the guide.

Soledad buzzed open the gate at the security wall, then waited for

Anna to walk down the driveway to the front door. Frowning like a sour nun, the housekeeper refused to make eye contact. Inside, Anna set down her pack. The death mask was still inside, her burden to carry. She walked through the vestibule, past the living room.

"Anna!" Constance called. "We're all in here."

In the kitchen, a man and woman in their fifties were dipping cocktail tomatoes into herbed sauce. Constance leaned against the tile counter, wearing a freshly ironed tunic and white pants, glass cocked, staring into the attentive eyes of a handsome man who Anna realized with a sickening jolt was Salvador.

Oaxaca was smaller than small. Oaxaca was a *telenovela*.

Constance planted an air kiss. "Meet our friends, Margaret and Harold Fuller. Marge leads tours and Harold is retired from insurance."

Marge Fuller was a doughy matron in a wraparound skirt and Birkenstocks. A chopstick secured her silver hair in a bun. Harold, a feeble-looking specimen with wide hips and narrow shoulders, reminded Anna of a blown lightbulb, the kind you shake and hear a distant ping. Anna recognized Harold from the English library, where she'd seen him taking Spanish classes from a ravishing Mexican. *Yo voy. Tú vas. Él, ella, usted va.* Having now met Marge, who managed to be both fat and flat, Anna understood the allure of Spanish lessons.

Constance guided her arm. "I believe you know Salvador Flores."

Salvador looked amused. *Now I get to see you in your natural milieu.* His attitude infuriated her. Having lumped her with all the other silly expatriates, he now expected her to apologize for a tribe she didn't claim.

Anna offered a cool smile. "We've met."

"It is a pleasure to see you again." He kissed her and touched her arm. Anna had always considered sending mixed messages her personal forte—never commit to anything you can't take back, never reject someone you might want later—but Salvador made her look like an amateur. She scouted the room. No sign of Miss Venezuela. Salvador winked. "I am learning where to buy organic peanut butter."

Constance handed Anna a cocktail and the keys to the Fiat. "Let me know if that drink is too sweet. Here's Thomas—"

Dressed in black and scowling, Thomas cast a shadow over the room. He spotted Anna, and kissed her cheek a little too firmly before peeling off to find Soledad and discuss the scarcity of ice cubes.

Anna sipped her cocktail, sprinting through the afternoon's intricate dynamics. She'd nearly slept with Thomas, but had a crush on Salvador. Constance was setting her up with Salvador—who already had a *cariño*—to stop her husband's philandering. Salvador and Thomas hated each other. No one knew Anna was Daniel Ramsey's daughter or that she was leaving Mexico in three days. Anna needed to borrow Constance's car to spread her mother's ashes. The trick was to survive the meal and secure the vehicle without alienating her tipsy hostess, who kept a rifle in the patio armoire. The plot had more twists than a French farce. *It's a Mexican farce. With guns.*

"My," Thomas said, rubbing his hands. "What a festive menagerie we've assembled."

Yes, Anna thought. *Welcome to the zoo.*

They ate at the long kitchen table. The house had a formal dining room, but Constance complained it was too dark and stodgy, too far away from the food should you need something, though Soledad was present at all times during the meal, scurrying to fetch and clean. Anna and Salvador faced each other at Thomas's end, while Marge and Harold clustered on either side of Constance. Each plate arrived with a slab of meatloaf, a bunker of mashed potatoes, an arsenal of peas. By each setting lay a mini American flag. The guests huddled, waiting for the hostess to lift her ceremonial fork.

"Take up your flags, troops," Constance commanded. The guests glanced at one another. "Don't you remember? Monday was Presidents' Day. Or today is National Tortilla Chip Day. Take your pick."

Anna shook her flag with mock enthusiasm. She needed the Fiat. Salvador tilted back in his chair, contemplating world peace or apocalypse. It was impossible to tell which.

Glass raised, Constance gave Harold a fond glance. "To old friends and new friends. To art and artists. To collectors, who have the eye and discretion to recognize beauty—"

Thomas finished her sentence. "In objects and women."

Harold chortled an appreciative "Hear, hear."

"And to Soledad, for her fine cooking."

As Soledad didn't understand English no matter how loudly it was delivered, Constance repeated herself in her plodding Spanish. Soledad flashed her golden teeth, went back to the sink.

"Did I miss anything?"

Anna jumped into the breach. "To our hostess for bringing us together."

With a rousing *"Salud,"* the guests drank, set down their flags, thankful the humiliation was over and no one had seen fit to take a photograph.

Thomas addressed Salvador: "I understand you took Anna to San

Juan del Monte. Did you see anything worth buying? My show is in three weeks. I'm still acquiring."

"Thomas is ruthless," Constance said, sucking her dry cubes. "Buys masks right off a dancer's face." It was impossible to tell if she was proud or disgusted.

"Where is your collection?" Salvador looked around.

"There's a chapel on the property where I store everything." Thomas gestured behind him.

"I'd like to see that."

Thomas gave Anna a coy look. "My collection is private. I find keeping things secret heightens their pleasure."

Anna considered her fork as if it were a new invention.

"Art should be shared," Salvador objected. "Not locked up."

"The artist shared his art with me."

"Just you?"

"All artists should be so lucky as to make art for an appreciative patron who pays well and stores their work in perpetuity."

Salvador gripped the stem of his glass. "So art is only for the aristocracy?"

"Look at the Medicis, the Salon. Poor men make art for rich men. The artists' angst, their struggle, is what makes their art powerful. Frankly, I prefer to pay someone to struggle for me. I don't collect a mask unless it's been danced. Let the tourists mop up the ornaments. All the great museums were built by powerful collectors—"

"Who robbed poor countries to decorate their . . ." Salvador couldn't find the word he wanted.

Thomas interrupted. "The desire to collect is a basic human instinct. Every man wants to surround himself with the things he likes. Some men just have better taste than others." Thomas turned to Anna with a triumphant expression. "It is no crime to love beauty."

"Changing the subject"—Constance tapped her glass with her fork—"have you been reading the papers? Oaxaca is the new Juárez. Two murders this month alone. Some dancer was stabbed at Carnival."

"Three couples have dropped our butterfly trip," said Marge. "The paper said the killer was wearing a tiger's mask." She gave Thomas a leading glance.

"Anna and I were there," Salvador said.

Thomas squinted, considering. "It might make a good footnote for our book."

"*Our book?*" Salvador raised an eyebrow. Anna pushed peas around her plate.

"Anna and I have plans to collaborate on a book. You've—"

"What was the second murder?" Anna cut in. She didn't want to talk about books, hers, theirs, real or imagined. To her surprise, Salvador answered.

"You met her. Leonora Rodríguez. The old widow near Luna's. Who would want to hurt her? It's crazy. Someone saw a man with a tiger's mask walking through the woods."

"Wait. The same tiger killed them both?" Marge asked.

Harold patted his mouth with his napkin. "A serial killer is roaming Oaxaca."

"San Juan del Monte," his wife corrected.

"A serial tiger," Malone corrected again.

"Fabulous meatloaf," Marge said.

"Reminds me of my mother," Harold said. "She made a bread pudding—"

"Someone is licking my toes," Marge said. "Thomas, is that you?"

"I'm afraid Honduras beat me to it."

"So what happened?" Anna pressed, trying to steer the conversation back around. "No one has found the killer?"

Constance gave her an *Oh, please* look. Her face was flushed, on its way to mottled. "Here's the worst part: The tiger not only kills an old, defenseless woman, *he sets her on fire.* The crazy newspaper ran pictures! The poor woman is dead, and do they run a nice photograph from her wedding day? No. They show her charred body lying in embers. Remind me never to be murdered in Mexico."

Harold turned to Marge. "Things like this don't happen in Shaker Heights."

"I have the paper somewhere." Constance got up, disappeared into the hall.

"Puppet, let's change the subject. We don't need to see—"

Constance returned, passed the newspaper to Harold, who passed it to Anna without looking. It was her, all right. Head scarf, wizened features frozen in rictus. Anna set down her fork. How could anyone eat? Her horror was coupled with a sinful tingle of excitement. There was only one reason to murder Leonora Rodríguez. Somebody had come looking for the mask. Why had she believed Lorenzo Gonzáles? Why did she believe anybody?

"Constance," Thomas chastised, shaking his flag like a pompom, "it's Tortilla Chip Day. Not Day of the Dead."

His wife's pale hair formed a frazzled nimbus. "Go ahead and kill me if you have to, but don't set me on fire."

"Puppet, can we move on to breezier topics? Taxes? Scorpions?"

Heat rose to Anna's forehead, her neck. *The good news is, the mask in my pack is worth a fortune. The bad news is, someone may kill me to get it.* Her flight home left Monday. The trick was to stay alive until then.

One of these two men could help her. The married, egomaniacal American collector. Or the moody, womanizing Mexican painter. Some girls had all the luck.

"Actually," Constance said, ignoring her husband. "There was a third murder. I almost forgot. An American fellow was cemented into a bathtub."

"Oh, come on." Marge rolled her eyes. "Now you're making things up."

Constance made a Boy Scout pledge. "I squeezed the story out of Soledad, who got it from the housekeeper. Some guy Gonzáles—Thomas knows him, a dealer with a mail-order Ph.D.—comes home and finds a strange man buried alive in his bathtub. Drugs, I suppose, or a shady art deal. I've always wanted to find a naked man in my bathtub, though I'd prefer he were alive." Constance smiled at Thomas, who considered his reflection in his knife. "I am sending the mashed potatoes around again. You know there's no word in Spanish for 'leftovers'? It simply doesn't exist."

Thomas leaned into Anna and whispered playfully, a boy with a frog in his pocket. "Buried alive in cement. Hell of a bath."

Salvador watched this exchange. Anna blushed. There were times when being an American was the world's most embarrassing affliction. A million U.S. citizens had relocated to Mexico—all of them looking for something. The most cynical came for the exchange rate. The romantic came for the scenery, the color. Retirees came for the weather. Surfers came for waves. Hippies for weed. Liberals wanted to escape the American capitalist machine. Poets sought a simpler life, a humble dirt road.

Settling in the prettiest cities and seaside resorts, they re-created the culture they'd left behind while complaining about all the ways Mexico disappointed them: the bad plumbing, the slow Internet, the wait for a phone, the aggressive drivers, the pollution, the toxic water, the firecrackers, the parade of saints' days, the strikes, the bureaucracy, the corruption, the *mañana* syndrome, the blind religiosity, the poverty. *Aprovechar*—an essential Spanish verb with no satisfying English equivalent. "Take advantage of" came close. That's what expatriates like the Malones did. They came to Mexico to take advantage. So had her father.

As if he'd read Anna's mind, Thomas called down the table, "Look at us, greedy Americans. All that fine food and we forgot to say grace. Constance, will you do the honors?"

His wife flung her cigarette hand. Her charm bracelet jangled: London Bridge, the Eiffel Tower, Chichén Itzá. "You should have thought of that earlier. It's too late for grace now."

The guests had laid down their forks. No one wanted to be the first to resume eating. They reached for their drinks instead.

Anna excused herself. In the bathroom, she splashed her face with water, wondered whether she was going to vomit. She hoisted the window to let in fresh air. Just how much danger was she in? Pressing her palm to her chest, she slowed her racing heart. Outside, everything was still. The only person in sight was Hugo, on break, smoking by the pool, which, presumably for lack of sufficient chemicals, had turned a faint shade of green.

Anna went back to the table. Her mind churned useless facts. *The average cremated body weighs five pounds. The human brain is often the most active when it's asleep. A woman's heart beats faster than a man's.* How was she going to make it until Monday?

Salvador looked left, then right, waiting for traffic to clear. "I am taking a trip to the Sierra this weekend. Marge, do you know a good hotel in Benito Juárez?"

Marge licked the underside of her spoon. "We always stay at the Refugio Galeano. Not fancy but functional. They have cabins with glass roofs so you can lie in bed and look up at the stars."

"You going alone?" Constance asked.

"Unless I could persuade Anna to come with me. Have you seen the Sierra? I could introduce you to some carvers . . ."

Anna had never met a man who blew so hot and cold.

Thomas mumbled to her, "I know a sweet old lady who sells Indian rugs." Then louder, "I wouldn't recommend the Sierra. No masks worth—"

Harold chimed in, "The mountain air is very good for clearing the sinuses—"

"So you won't need the car after all," Constance said, as though things had been decided.

"Thanks for the invitation," Anna said to Salvador. Aloof. Non-committal. "Let me think about it."

"Anna, why don't you come with me to the basement," Thomas said. "I need more mescal. I want to show you the wine cellar."

Four faces turned to Anna.

"The cellar?" she said.

"I know you appreciate a good mescal. I have quite a collection."

Anna looked at Salvador, hoping he'd object, but he was gazing out the screen door to the patio. "Sounds like a real opportunity," he said.

"Go on," Constance said bitterly, her face a trampled rose garden. "It will only take a minute."

Salvador muttered, "Maybe less."

A flurry of twigs and leaves fell past the window. The bottom half of a man was visible on a ladder. Hugo was cleaning the gutters.

"Maybe another time. I really should be going." Anna checked her watch, though she had nowhere to be.

A single drop of sweat rolled down Thomas's temple. "Puppet, I heard rumors about apple pie. Let's move outside and watch you shoot the neighbor's dog."

Debris tumbled past the window like dirty rain.

"Fetch my gun, darling." Constance's wineglass was full again. "I'll give you a lesson."

"Little did I know I'd married Annie Oakley," Thomas joked to his guests.

Constance snapped. "I am tired of cleaning up shit I didn't make."

"Ask Hugo."

"The Mexicans, yes. They solve all our problems."

Harold lifted his glass, before he realized it was empty. Marge fished a postcard from a ceramic bowl in the center of the table. "What's this mask, Thomas? This yours?"

Thomas grimaced. "The latest missive from Reyes, the neighborhood drug lord. Claims he's acquired Montezuma's death mask."

Marge looked put out. "*The* Montezuma?"

Salvador wadded up his napkin. "If someone found Montezuma's death mask, it went straight to the black market, like everything else."

Thomas spoke to Marge. "Every collector working Latin America has been looking for this mask for decades. Reyes, Ramsey. Everyone."

Anna took a sudden interest in her water glass. How had Reyes gotten a photo of the mask? Nothing made sense.

Thomas fingered the postcard's edge. "Imagine. The greatest pre-Columbian discovery of our lifetimes is in the hands of a monster."

Anna swallowed.

"I guess Reyes wins your little mask bet, your face-off," Marge said, sounding pleased at her pun. "Drug lords always win, I'm afraid."

Thomas smiled. "Reyes wins until somebody kills him."

Dirt fell from the gutters. The peacocks squawked. Soledad's milk bubbled on the stove. Anna handed the postcard to Salvador, who inspected the postmark. As they stood to say good-bye, he slipped the card into his pocket.

Salvador offered her a ride home on his motorcycle. He gave her his helmet, instructed her to keep one hand on the grip, the other on him. Slowly, he built up speed. Her thighs gripped his. Her helmet bumped his head. It felt as if they had become one person. She didn't want to stop riding, but in a few minutes he rolled up to the Puesta del Sol.

"You have my number, if you change your mind." He surveyed the lobby, sickly blue in the light. "I worry about you, staying here. My aunt was robbed once."

"The gay clerk has a baseball bat and knows how to use it."

"I don't know why you spend time with them."

"Rafi?"

"The Malones."

"Then why did you go?"

"To see you."

This stopped her. She looked down the street. Pink buildings. Iron balconies. Cobblestones. Bougainvillea. Some days, some nights, Anna was sure no country was as lovely as Mexico. Salvador was lovely, too. Complicated.

"Come with me tomorrow." He said this twice.

"I can't, but thank you."

Resigned, he hugged her and started his bike, then drove off with a wave. She watched him take the corner, confident she would never see him again.

She crossed the patio. Something was hanging on her door. *A hat. How odd. No, not a hat. A mask.* A carved wooden mask of a woman. Arched eyebrows. Full lips. Anna would have called her pretty if not for the bullet holes piercing each temple. Painted blood dripped from the wounds. A note had been jammed in her mouth. Anna translated.

*Put the mask in the box on the northwest corner
of El Llano Park and no harm will come to you.*

—The Tiger

Anna whipped around, took a hard look at everything. The dark trees ruffled and swayed.

thirteen | THE LOOTER

The guest room was actually an outbuilding that doubled as laundry room and bunkhouse. Washing sink. Clothesline. Bed shoved against the wall. The girl looked proud and apologetic as the looter tested the mattress, though he was taking the room no matter what.

Outside, the aunt, a boxy woman with a safety-pinned skirt, hunched on a stool, sifting through dry beans. Her hands were bear paws. He wondered what women like that thought about. Did they ever want sex? What if he snuck up to her in the middle of the night? Maybe she would bless him like a prodigal son.

"*Gracias,*" the looter said to the girl.

The girl smiled back, relieved that the room met his standards.

"*Éste es mi primer viaje a Oaxaca,*" he said. "Would you show me the city? Or do you have a map?"

The girl blushed. "We don't have a map, but I could show you the bus that goes to the center."

The looter pretended to need help getting up. She took his hand.

For the first time, it occurred to him that she might have a boyfriend or husband. He braced himself to see some macho swagger across the yard. She must have sensed his unease, because when she let his hand go she said, "Just me and my aunt live here. I will tell her that you will take the room. How long will you be staying?"

The looter produced three hundred pesos, enough for ten nights. The girl closed the bills in her hand, went out to the patio, whispered to her aunt. The two women giggled. The girl picked up her needlepoint. A white cat circled her, bending its tail.

The looter lit a joint, blew the sweet smoke out the far window. The pot was Pico's best stuff, and right away, he was parched. It was only the second joint he'd smoked since the accident—that was how he had come to think of it—that Mari hadn't lit for him. He missed Mari, but was glad to have the girl. He liked having a woman close by. Women brought him luck. You didn't have to fuck them all. That's where he'd been wrong. Your first instinct didn't have to be the one you followed.

What would the mask say about that? Being a death mask, he'd probably advise banging the girl now because life was short and once the baby came her crotch would be trashed, but when the looter pictured the blue mask, the shattered face surprised him: *Be kind, motherfucker,* it said. *For once in your life, be kind.*

He rode downtown with the girl, bumping about in the hulking bus, their hips touching. Sunny day. No surprise there. They traveled into the city's colonial heart with its candy-colored buildings and umbrel-laed cafés, shops selling black clay angels and Guatemalan worry dolls. *Gua-te-ma-la.* That dream felt as distant as childhood.

The looter was feeling good. Stoned, but not paranoid. Reyes didn't ride public transportation, so even if the drug lord had come to Oaxaca for some assassin downtime, there was zero chance of seeing his hideous face. The looter had his Spanish up and running—past, present, even future.

"When's the baby coming?" He had to talk loud over the bus's whining gears.

"One month."

"Is it a boy?"

"No lo sé." The girl shrugged, laughing now, the happiest he'd seen her, like maybe she was ready to talk about the baby instead of pretending it wasn't there. She had changed clothes for the trip downtown. Her dress was the color of watermelon, cheap and cheerful as a Popsicle. Her breasts were hidden but still there.

"You look pretty in your dress." He was practicing nice.

She thanked him with a shy smile. The other passengers sat sullen and slumped. Guys who had to work and weren't happy about it. She was the best thing on the bus by far. It was good to have her full attention. He wondered if she smelled sweet, but all he could smell was coconut from the sunblock he'd slathered over his new baby skin.

"Where do you want to go?" she asked.

"I need to find someone, actually something. That's why I came to Oaxaca."

The girl looked confused. "What do you want to find?"

"A present for a friend."

She brightened at this idea. "We can go shopping at the market. I could help you pick something out."

"This is a special thing. Someone has it and I have to pick it up."

"Who has it?"

"I'm not sure. Could be a couple different people."

"What is it?"

"I'd rather not say."

The girl looked at him, and then way beyond that. "I will help you," she said, committing to each word. "We will figure it out together."

He shook his head, amazed. She was more than he deserved, but he wasn't going to argue. "I can tell you're going to bring me luck," he said.

The bus stopped to let off passengers. The looter said, "Tell me your name."

fourteen | THE DRUG LORD

"Mi nombre es Óscar Reyes Carrillo,
and I am making this videotape because people may hear stories about
me when I am dead and I want them to know the truth. The doctor
says I have cancer and do not have long to live. There is also the possibility I will be shot. I sit here before you, stripped down to my *calzon-
cillos* to show you I have nothing to hide.

"I was born in Juárez, the oldest of six children. My father worked
construction and odd jobs. We often went to bed hungry, but Mother
took us to church every Sunday in clean clothes. People have heard the
story of the poor Mexican child so many times it has lost the power to
stir pity. I am nothing to you. I am nothing to anyone but myself.

"When I learned to drive, I took trucks loaded with marijuana over
the border. The drugs were hidden under crates of fresh fruit. The border guards let us through for a fee. The cartel paid fifty dollars a trip. I

gave my mother half the money. When she asked where it came from, I told her I had a job. This was the truth. The rest of the money I spent on expensive sneakers and on girls at nightclubs so they would let me touch their pussies. I was an adolescent drug dealer who thought he was a man.

"At eighteen, I enrolled in the police academy. The cartels have infiltrated the system to the maximum degree. Recruits are plied with money, drugs, and women, so when they graduate, they are too spoiled to work a normal job. At the academy, young men learned marksmanship, surveillance, security, and interrogation, torture. The best graduates work for the *narcos*. If they prove disloyal, arrogant, or incompetent, they are shot.

"For years, I was a paid assassin. At first, I was paid three thousand dollars a hit, but my fee grew to five times that. Sometimes we were instructed to hold or torture captives while we waited for ransom. There are many ways to hurt a man. We'd hook cables to a captive's big toe and turn on the electric current. We'd wrap people in sheets laced with gasoline and light them on fire. We pulled out fingernails. The suffering is immense. I prefer not to torture women, but sometimes those were the orders. It helps to be high. It's like watching a movie. There is no guilt.

"When we received the ransom money, we shot the prisoners and dumped the bodies or placed them in a specific location to send a message. Facedown. Faceup. Finger in the mouth or anus. Every gesture had meaning. It is better to cut people after they are dead so they bleed less. Gangs used to not kill women or children, but people no longer adhere to those niceties. I would go on drug binges and would not sleep for days. I was too high to regret what I was doing. This is not an excuse but an explanation. Maybe the drugs gave me cancer. Or maybe it was the pressure of the life I was leading. Or maybe God is punishing me. A hundred? Two hundred? I do not remember how many people I have killed. I do not take drugs anymore. They are a young man's game.

"Maybe I sound like an animal. I am not. I am a *patrón*. This is a term of respect. Every *patrón* works for the *patrón* above him. I collect art and direct the antiquities trade for southern Mexico. My *patrón* does not understand this sideline, but he does not stop me. People call me van Gogh, not because of my ear, but because I know about art. I dropped out of school in eighth grade, but I have taught myself art history. Mostly, I look at a painting, or whatever, and decide if I want it. I can't describe what I like about a piece. I just do or don't. Like a woman. I have stuff in storage that would make museums drool. I could be a decent painter. If I painted my life, no one would believe it. My childhood was beautiful in its own way because we had so little. Children and chickens, sticks and stones. We played *narcos* against *narcos* in the dust.

"There is an American asshole in Oaxaca who collects masks, and I enjoy making him miserable. When I get a mask he might like, I send him a photo. I steal his runners. Someday I may slit his throat or rape his wife, but I haven't yet because he amuses me. Soon we will each have an opening to show off our masks. The fool doesn't realize that no one beats the cartels. My *patrón* wants the American to drive for us, smuggle shipments over the border. He is corruptible. We will appeal to his ego and greed and taste for sex. This works ninety-nine percent of the time.

"With money, you can make the dog dance. Without money, you dance like a dog.

"The best mask I ever had was the death mask of Montezuma, but it was stolen from me. This kind of betrayal is unacceptable. I buried the American digger in Gonzáles's tub. The next time Gonzáles screws up, I'll fix him a bath. An American girl has the mask now, but I will take it back soon. You cannot be sloppy when you kill an American, or the FBI will fly down and make soup. I want to be buried with the mask. It will set me apart from the dogs. With that mask, I could look God in the face.

"People think being a drug lord is all cocaine and women, but actually it is hard work. I never sleep in the same bed two nights in a row. Sometimes I sleep in a tunnel. Sometimes I check into a five-star hotel under the name Jesús Máximo. I have disguises. My bathtub has a trapdoor. My cook keeps a gun in her breadbox.

"Some men take prostitutes to bed. I take art books and a pistol. I look up words in the dictionary. Maybe I should pay a naked woman to do this for me. Ha. When I know enough about art, I will off Gonzáles. No one likes a know-it-all. There's another reason I take art books to bed: If I am shot in my sleep, it comforts me to think I saw something beautiful before I fell into the arms of Santa Muerte."

fifteen | ANNA

When Salvador drove up to the
Puesta del Sol, Anna didn't care whether he was motivated by sex, money, revenge, boredom, mockery, pity, or kindness. She was simply grateful he was taking her into the mountains, where no tiger could find her. Salvador had sounded surprised when she'd called and confessed a change of heart. She'd slept only three hours, cell phone in hand, front desk number entered, chair propped under the doorknob.

"You seem stressed." Salvador shifted gears.

"Shy," Anna said.

"That is something new." He smiled, friendly, teasing, cute.

"You are nice to do this."

She couldn't think what to say next. She wanted to fall into his lap, confess everything, but he would want her to turn over the mask to

Mexican authorities. He would make no distinction between her father and Thomas Malone.

She checked the side mirror. No Tiger.

"Someone had to rescue you," he said. "Also, I wanted to show you the mountains."

For a change, Anna said what she was thinking. "You hurt my feelings when you threw me out of your apartment."

Salvador rapped the steering wheel. "I did not throw you out. My family needed me. I thought, *Why spend time with a woman who is sleeping with Thomas Malone?*"

"I am not sleeping with Thomas Malone."

"Are you sure?"

"I think I would know."

"So there's hope?"

His sincerity disarmed her. "I thought I was the only one interested." She rubbed his neck. "My mother used to do this for my dad when he drove."

He made a happy animal sound. "Lucky man."

"Not really. Not now. He's drinking again."

She told him about her father's addiction. He listened. It felt good to share a difficult part of her life, though she was careful not to mention her father's name.

"He says he's coming to Mexico, but it will never happen. When he's drinking, he can barely get out of his chair. He would have missed my wedding if—"

"You are married?"

"I was engaged, but not anymore."

Her face must have looked distraught, because he touched her knee. "Are you okay? Do you want to go back?"

"Go back?" Anna stuck her elbow out the window. "No. I want to go faster."

Benito Juárez was a Mexican version of small-town Vermont. Marching schoolchildren carried a flag around the village square while a bugler played a patriotic anthem. Log cabins lined the thick woods. The air was clean and brisk.

Their room had not been cleaned yet, so they decided to hike to a *mirador* that offered a spectacular view of the valley.

"You might want to leave that here," Salvador said, eyeing her pack. "What do you have in there?"

"My life."

"Dámelo."

She hesitated, then carefully handed him the pack, warning him fragile things were inside, and then, worried she sounded unappreciative, added, *"Gracias."*

And he said, *"El gusto es mío."*

Up a trail they zigzagged, past farmhouses, cornfields, and sheep. Anna decided her worst fears were unfounded. The Tiger had not followed her here.

Salvador was hiking in dress shoes and jeans. Anna felt a rush of affection. She could love a man who hiked in dress shoes long before she could love a man who hiked in ripstop and fleece. Screw Miss Venezuela. She wasn't here. Anna was.

Salvador stopped, panting. She took the pack back from him. "Sometimes I want to travel forever," she said.

"I have always wanted to follow the *camino* of Che Guevara," he said. "Ride south through Argentina. Smoke and drink and sleep with beautiful women."

Jealousy rose inside Anna, juice through a straw. She said she wanted to come.

Salvador swatted the air. "You don't want *one* man. You want whoever is next. I know what you think: 'Salvador, he is okay in Mexico.'"

Anna laughed. He had her number.

Salvador wiped sweat off his lip.

"After Mexico, you go home and marry an American man and have American babies and live a happy American life until you have an American divorce and come back to Oaxaca and sit on the *zócalo* with your sad margarita and hope to see your old friend Salvador who you abandoned years ago."

"I may never go back to America." Her plane left in two days. "Look at that."

She pointed to a shack with colorful laundry drying on a line: a man's pants, toddler shirts, baby socks. Anna sighed. "One day, I want to make a book of photographs of only clotheslines."

"You think it is beautiful, and all they want is a dryer."

The view at the top was lovely, a panorama of distant mountains, a patchwork of parceled land, everything dazzling in a silvery haze.

"Por fin." Salvador stabbed his walking stick. *"Llegamos.* Too much clean air. I need a cigarette."

Anna checked over her shoulder. No Tiger. She was being ridiculous.

Salvador tugged her arm. "Sit with me, woman."

Back against a boulder, he opened the backpack's outside flap and pulled out a warm beer.

"Where did that come from?"

"Magic," he said.

Anna sat between his legs, leaned against his chest. Her mother would have loved this landscape. *You are what you notice. What you see, you can keep. Whatever hurts is your beginning.*

"What's wrong?" Salvador nudged her.

"Being on the edge like this makes me want to jump."

"Put your bird mask on first."

"You think people in those little houses are happy?"

"If you ask me are those people happy because they live in a house that looks pretty to tourists who climb the hill with their boyfriends, then I think the answer is no."

Anna's stomach registered the word "boyfriend." "What about the pigs?"

"Very happy. Speaking of pigs, don't see Thomas Malone anymore. He is not a nice man."

"No es un hombre sincero," Anna half sang. "You've told me."

"He will not help you."

"I was trying to get your attention."

"You have it."

Salvador stroked her hair. She liked the way he made her feel: like a traveler, a conjugator of irregular verbs. He pulled up a blade of grass, nibbled the tender end. He looked less jostled, a glass of water come to rest. *Under different circumstances, this could be a love story.*

Anna pulled her mother's journal from her pack. "My mother kept a diary when she was in Mexico. She collected all these great quotes.

Here's one. '*I had expected to see the town of my mother's memories, of her nostalgia—nostalgia laced with sighs. She had lived her lifetime sighing about Comala, about going back. But she never had. Now I had come in her place. I was seeing things through her eyes, as she had seen them. She had given me her eyes to see.*'"

"*Pedro Páramo*," Salvador said. "'*You will hear the voice of memory that is stronger than the voice of death—if death has a voice.*' That is not quite right, but almost."

He kissed her. And she thought: *I don't ever want to move.* And she thought: *So long as we stay on this mountaintop, we are both seeing the same thing.*

Salvador lifted her head. "I need to tell you something."

She braced herself. Here it comes. Miss Venezuela. "Listen, it doesn't matter. I understand—"

"Thomas was right," he said. "There are no great carvers in Benito Juárez. None, in fact."

"Then why are we here?"

The answer was written all over his face.

sixteen | THE GARDENER

The Tiger checked his hands for blood, checked the rearview mirror, checked the time, checked his machete. His hands itched. A rash. It was late afternoon. He cracked his neck. His car was headed into the mountains. *Veinte kilómetros a Benito Juárez.*

Find the mask.

Save the girl.

Kill her father.

What sacrifice would you make for our love?

An old man on a bicycle pedaled on the side of the road. The Tiger snuck his car up behind him, gunned the accelerator. The man toppled into the weeds. The Tiger laughed. He was an invincible animal.

He hadn't slept since he'd killed the old woman. Whenever he closed his eyes, visions appeared: dreams and faces, the past and present overlapping, the comet, the crane, the crone, the yellow girl, Reyes, Soledad, the wounded Montezuma carried to safety, his handsome face bloodied, his golden robes torn. It was getting hard not to think of everything at once.

Was it possible to kill without guilt or remorse? If so, were you a man or an animal?

He had to find the American. He'd been certain that the mask would scare her, that she would follow his instructions—*Put the mask in the box*—but she'd run off with her little artist friend. His phone rang. A text. Reyes. Where the fuck is my mask? You are late.

The Tiger threw the phone across the car. He was shaking.

Lago Azul was blue as the sky. Families played along the sandy edges. Something strange was happening. Steam rose off the lake. The water started to boil, slowly at first, then faster, bubbling, hotter by the second. Families shrieked and rushed to shore. The lake was convulsing. A cloudbank wiped out the sun. Wind whipped across the Tiger's car, shaking the chassis. Dead bathers floated to the surface, cooked in their own skin. A tsunami-size wave appeared, two stories high, pressing toward the shore, inexorable as death. Over the road, black water swarmed around his wheels, rising, stalling out all motion. The Tiger jammed the brakes. He was in the wave and of the wave, trapped in its cold, black grasp. Water poured into his lap, filled his ears.

He let go of the steering wheel, tore the mask off his face.

When he opened his eyes, the lake was blue again, calm, dotted with vacationers, dead-man floating, face to the sun. A flirty husband splashed his wife, trying to get something started. Children spat watermelon seeds, tossed rinds onto the sand. He was driving on the wrong side of the road, heading straight into a moving van.

Hugo jerked the wheel just in time, crossed himself. *Oh, little yellow girl. What I do, I do for you.*

He had seen the fifth omen. The boiling lake.

The dead could fuck up the living. The dead had nothing but time.

seventeen | THE PAPERSHOP GIRL

I do not blame my mother. The birds were clear about it, flying in a nervous, broken X, going west on a Sunday, *qué mala onda*. Then Mamá's egg broke in boiling water and a dead bird appeared at the front door, etched feet and a wasted gray eye. Mamá shrieked and would not touch it.

So we're moving closer to Manny. Only an hour drive, instead of five. Nice, I guess, not that Manny will thank us, but maybe the omens will calm themselves, leave my mother alone before she goes completely *loca*.

Last time we went to the cemetery in Xalapa, someone had placed a giant stuffed bear on the gravestone next to Manny. The bear looked pathetic, slumped over, getting dusty, but still I felt bad that Manny had only plastic flowers. Maybe the other kid had a *narco* for a father. Those people could buy a pinball machine and leave it out in the rain.

Sometimes I go back and pick a different ending, see us sitting at dinner, laughing like people in a milk ad. I have never written down what happened, but I will now so I don't forget. Your memory will forget anything if you let it.

We were on vacation in Acapulco. It was morning, hot already. Mamá wanted new sandals because her strap broke, and the three of us were walking the strip. We were all tired, the way a vacation can feel like work. Mamá had bought Manny one of those shiny balloons, which he didn't deserve, and I said so. He had it tied around his wrist. He was dragging behind so we wouldn't see him scarfing red hots, and I was deciding whether to rat him out or whine for a new bikini. I didn't notice the men drive up, or the guns, until Mamá screamed and dragged me under an awning. By then, a guy had scooped up Manny, who was howling, his face a runny mess.

The thug held Manny in front of him like a shield. A six-year-old. It was crazy after that, screaming and gunfire. People crawled under cars. Someone stepped on my back. Mamá ran into the street. You can scream, but if the noise around you is loud enough, you make no sound at all. That coward thought they wouldn't shoot a child, but the *narcos* just used more bullets. Manny died in his arms. Mamá threw herself on top of Manny and let his blood seep into her dress. His stupid balloon didn't pop. Daffy Duck, floating like it was a fucking parade.

You don't expect something like that at the beach.

Manny was a good boy. Spoiled but good inside. He ate chilies from the jar. He had a pet turtle, Donatello, but he let him go free. I bet Manny would have been a doctor when he grew up. He put Band-Aids on my cuts. He liked superheroes because they could fix problems and punch out bad guys. He had Superman undies and would tie a towel around his neck and jump off the couch and smile because he didn't know what to do next. There really isn't much a little boy can fix.

Papi doesn't believe in signs, but after Manny died, Mamá started having visions. That's when Papi began coming into my bedroom. One bad thing leads to the next. The door closes. The window closes. Pretty soon, you're in the dark. Maybe Papi stopped believing in God. Sometimes I hear Manny whisper, *I will protect you.* He would if he could but he can't.

Manny would be eleven now, but instead he's six forever.

After he died, for a year or so, I wore a lot of clothes, layers on top of layers, all together. Two or three shirts and a sweater and socks and tights. It drove Papi nuts. Kids called me Mummy Girl. Luckily, that name died out. I still wear gloves no matter what. I don't touch people even when I'm naked. I don't tell anyone what I am thinking. My thoughts are my own. I am a piñata with candy inside.

The name Manuel means "God is with us."

This is a lie.

God is a drunk sleeping under a cactus.

eighteen | THE LOOTER

They wandered the city until dark.
The looter was letting things evolve, the SAT word for letting shit flow downstream. Outside the market, crones sold baskets of chili peppers, their scrawny legs crossed beneath their rumps like knitting needles. Some clown was hawking Calderón puppets. The girl wanted hair combs. They searched for one of those discount stores where everything costs ten pesos and breaks before you get it home.

"*Mira. Hay uno.*" The girl pointed.

"*Te espero afuera.*" I will wait for you outside.

The girl looked doubtful, like maybe he'd ditch her. He kissed her forehead, all those peppery freckles. He hadn't meant to kiss her. It just came up.

The girl waddled into the store. *Chelo.* He had a hard time remembering her name. He leaned against a kiosk, glanced down a side alley, where a haggard guy was smoking a hand-rolled cigarette, eyes like jumping beans. The looter didn't need to smell the piss to know what the guy was selling. Old cravings yanked his insides. *Walk away. Walk away now.*

He darted in the opposite direction, hungry for distraction. Underwear shop. Penny candy. One of those document joints where you can laminate an ID, wire money, have credentials forged. Once in D.F., on the Plaza de Santo Domingo, he'd bought a fake driver's license under the name Nacho Rico. Forget the U.S. of A. These shops were the land of opportunity. For a hundred bucks and a passport, you could walk out a dentist.

He circled back to the kiosk, read the posters, blinked in disbelief. *Mask exposition at La Fábrica. The collection of Thomas Malone. More than a hundred masks from all over Mexico.* A second poster had been stapled over most of the first. *Óscar Reyes Carrillo opens his mask collection to the public.* Seeing Reyes's name in print brought back the sickening smell of wet cement. A foot-odor smell, muggy and human. The looter spun around, nerves jumping. Daylight had its shadows. He touched the poster, making it real. *Thomas Malone is here, which means the mask is here.* The scabs on his arms pussed through his shirt, leaving pale pink moons.

The girl called out, "Cruise."

Cruise? She was looking right at him. She must have misheard his name or forgotten how to pronounce "Chris." He smiled. Cruise Maddox. He liked it. *Come cruising with the Cruise. Welcome to the Cruise Ship Lollypop.* He chuckled. Chelo looked hurt, wanting in on the joke. He took her hand. "I'm in the right place. The man I'm looking for is in Oaxaca. We just have to figure out where he lives."

The girl looked pleased. "God helped."

"But the man I am *not* looking for is here, too."

The girl scanned the street. "Then we'll stay away from him."

And the looter said: "Where can we buy a gun?"

He didn't know squat about guns, and Chelo wanted nothing to do with it. When the pawnshop clerk presented two pistols, he chose the bigger one without question. He remembered to ask for bullets. What else did you need? Aim wasn't for sale.

Chelo waited outside until he was done. "No good comes from that."

"But with a gun, no bad comes either."

"Son peligrosos."

"No, guns aren't dangerous," he argued. *"Lo contrario.* A gun makes you safe."

She sighed. "You think like my father."

"Where is he?"

"Dead."

They held hands as they walked. Her fingers were sticky but warm. The looter felt braver with the gun, though he wasn't sure where to put it. It seemed careless to store it in his satchel and worrisome to jam it into his pants. At a hardware store, he found a cheap fishing box, dumped its plastic trappings in a trash can, laid the pistol inside, then carried the box with his right hand, slung his satchel, leaving his left hand free for the girl. Voilà.

They kept walking, past Chinese slippers and rainbow tupperware. The gun made the looter feel oddly festive, a sheriff leading the world's smallest parade. He wondered if he was a good shot, wished he'd paid more attention the time his father drove him to the salt marsh for target practice. The sun had been setting, and the air smelled like skunk cabbage, and his father drank can after can of light beer, using the silver empties as targets. A bully trying to look tough. *Packing heat.* The looter gave a half laugh at the cliché of it all. With a gun, you could be whoever you wanted, and if someone objected, you could blow him away. A clay pigeon. A white bird that turns into dust.

nineteen | ANNA

Dinner was a comedy, sweet, really.
There was nothing on the menu—there wasn't even a menu—just a shy woman with a lazy eye offering them vegetable soup, hot chocolate, rice, beans *de la olla*, and *tlayudas* with chicken. The *tlayuda* was the local specialty, a crispy tortilla shaped like an elephant's ear, layered with beans, cheese, shredded lettuce, and *pico de gallo*. They ordered two of everything, asked if there wasn't a beer. There wasn't. They ate the hot food, which, like all food in the mountains, no matter how simple, tasted delicious.

After dinner, they cut through the woods. Salvador had requested a private cabin, but they ended up the only occupants of a dormitory designed for tour groups. Six rooms of bunk beds, a long corridor, a common room big enough for a county square dance. The kitchen smelled like soup and crackers.

"I feel like we're on a Christian retreat," Anna said, peering into the empty fridge. "Hello. Hello."

Salvador groaned. "The owner promised me a bungalow. It's typical. You make your reservation and then it's 'I am sorry, there are no cabins available.'"

Anna wondered what Salvador expected of this evening. Bunk beds made the logistics more complicated. Either they squeezed into a single bunk, which seemed premature, or slept stacked like campers. The thought of negotiating these possibilities made Anna extraordinarily thirsty. She slipped a bottle of wine into the fridge.

Salvador looked wistfully at the cabins nestled in a bluff below. "Look at the other people in their *casitas*."

"Let's make a fire."

"We need *bon-bones*."

"What are those?" Anna asked.

"Those white candies you put on the fire."

"Marshmallows?"

Salvador shrugged. He didn't know the word in English, and she didn't know it in Spanish. "Let's go to the store."

They wound through a wooded shortcut. Branches thatched the darkening sky like lace. Anna tried to see everything before it saw her.

At a small store catering to campers, an effeminate boy fetched marshmallows, chocolate bars, and no-name vanilla wafers from wooden shelves. Anna's friend Mercedes often complained that all the nice Mexican men were gay. While this seemed a stretch, Anna was quite sure it was true of all nice clerks. On the way back to the dormitory, they gathered kindling. Anna hummed, stuck close to Salvador's side. The night smelled like dirt and trees.

Salvador held up two handfuls of sticks. *"Basta, ¿no?"*

He went inside, but Anna lingered on the stoop, watching the stars, searching for meaning or pattern. The longer she looked, the more lights she saw. Patience rewarded. Distance overcome. *Slow down,* she told herself. *Be where you are.*

It felt good to be sitting on the lap of Salvador Flores in a chair before a fire in a dormitory in Benito Juárez. Anna impaled a marshmallow, lit the sugar on fire. They jousted with their burning sticks, shadows towering on the wall. Anna pressed her marshmallow into a cookie lined with chocolate. She bit in, made a face.

"Another lousy American invention. More fun to make than to eat." She yawned, chucked her s'more in the fire. "I'm ready for bed." She wanted to get that part over with: who was sleeping where. Sometimes you couldn't enjoy the middle until you knew the end.

"We have thirty beds, *mi amor.* Which do you prefer?"

Anna led him into the farthest bedroom, no longer unsure what she wanted. The moment might have been awkward, but wasn't. They climbed to a top bunk and held each other, staring through the glass roof at Orion's Belt and a hundred other stars Anna couldn't name. It was cold away from the fire, even though they were dressed.

Anna fingered the globe around his neck. "Does this have a story?"

"A present from Enrique. From Guatemala."

"You wear it all the time?"

"I like the idea of it."

"What idea?"

"I don't know. I can't think when I am in bed with you."

Anna wrapped her legs around him, hoping to make his concentration even worse. Their heat was building. She palmed the planet in her cold hand.

"Do you have a girlfriend?"

Salvador chuckled. "Why am I here if I have a girlfriend?"

"I saw you in the *zócalo* with this beautiful woman."

"A tall girl with crazy brown hair?"

"Long legs."

"Look at you," he teased. "All *celosa*."

"Jealous?"

Anna was about to deny this, when above them, on the glass ceiling, something moved. She tensed, unsure, and then terribly sure. A man was crawling across the glass, apelike, on all fours. He was wearing a tiger's mask. His mirror eyes caught the beam of the security light. So did his machete. Anna gave a muffled scream: "It's the Tiger. Get up." Salvador fell off the bed, sputtering, *"What?"* Anna fell after him. "The one who killed the old woman." Salvador couldn't find his car keys. Anna couldn't find her shoes. They fished around wildly, cursing. Her heart seemed to be beating outside her body while her mind throbbed *nonono*. Keys found, shoes in hand, they raced through the common room, past the dying orange embers, down the long corridor, through the soup-and-cracker kitchen. Salvador slid the dead bolt and sized up the shadows.

The salamanders watched them, scales frozen.

The moon had nothing to say.

They ran.

Salvador unlocked the car, wheeled into reverse, swearing, *"Hijo de su gran putísima madre."* When they reached the town square, Anna half expected ghost children to be practicing their marches, but everything was hushed and gray. A spotlight illuminated the Mexican flag, the Oaxacan flag, both limp. On a stone wall, the store clerk, wearing a wedding dress, twirled a lavender paper flower.

"What is happening?" Salvador was leaning so far forward his forehead almost touched the windshield. A road sign said fifty kilometers to Oaxaca.

"That's the tiger from San Juan del Monte. He's chasing me." Whatever Anna's heart was doing didn't feel natural. "It's dangerous to drive so fast."

Salvador let up the accelerator.

"Don't slow down."

Salvador said, "He knows you have the death mask."

Statement. Not question. Anna held her breath, thinking she misheard.

His voice turned grim. "That tiger knows you've been carrying the death mask around with you. Reyes wants it, so he will do anything— including killing us both—to stop you from smuggling it over the border."

Anna tapped the window with her knuckle. "How did you know?"

"Lorenzo Gonzáles is a friend of mine."

"He's not a nice person."

"Neither am I."

Out the rearview mirror, black.

"Your friend lied to me." She faced him, indignant. "Offered me five hundred pesos, like I'm a complete idiot."

Salvador shifted, taking the switchbacks hard. "Give me the mask. I will make sure it goes to the right people. What do you need it for? You have Malone and your book."

Anna resented this description, start to finish. "I am not writing a book. I came to Mexico to buy this mask for my father, and I've worked damn hard to get it."

"Your father?"

"Gonzáles didn't tell you that part?"

Salvador asked what part.

"The idiot who wrote the messed-up mask book. Daniel Ramsey. He's my father. I helped him write that book."

Salvador took his foot off the accelerator. *"Me lleva la chingada."*

Anna kept going. She was losing her voice. "We need this mask for the Ramsey Collection. The Metropolitan Museum was *planning* to open a gallery in my mother's name. With this mask, they might still do that. My father comes back, a hero. Do you get why I had to do this? My name was on that book, too. Imagine how I felt. I'm supposed to be a fact-checker."

They'd reached the valley floor. Salvador rolled to the curb.

"What are you doing?"

Salvador killed the ignition. "I don't feel like driving anymore. I am not safe with you. Not in my car. Not on the street. Not in bed. *Everything you have told me is a lie.*" He was yelling. "That tiger is crazy. You think you can beat Reyes?"

"I don't know Reyes—"

"You know what he does to people? He doesn't care. *Ni una madre.*"

Not even a mother. The essence of nothing. Anna checked the rearview mirror. Her voice chilled, cool to subzero. "Why are you with me?"

Salvador met her tone. "Mexican museums look professional with their locks and security cameras, but every day art disappears. Hands go and take. A little of this. A little of that. It all goes to the black market. Lorenzo and I saw this every day, but we could not stop it. Now we work together—underground—to keep the best art in Mexico. *For the public.* Away from people like Thomas Malone."

A glow appeared in the rearview mirror. Light finding strength. Anna pleaded with him. *"We need to go."*

Cursing, he started the car, careened onto the road. Anna didn't speak, for fear of distracting him. She didn't dare look behind.

"You've got it all wrong," she said finally. "Gonzáles *runs* the black market. He called us."

"That was a mistake. He didn't believe the death mask was real. You choose your battles. You let some pieces go, to save what's most important. We work closely with the few honest museums left. If the press writes about a piece, it cannot disappear so easily. But always we are fighting Reyes." He glared at her. "And people like him."

So this is what he thought of her. She was just another looter.

"You were trying to steal the mask back from me?"

"Steal it? No. Convince you to do the right thing. *Keep the mask in Mexico.* That's all I ask. In Mexico, where it can be seen in context."

"That's why you took me to the Ecce Mono. You didn't just happen to stop in my café. Gonzáles sent you. You never cared about me, you were keeping an eye on the mask. That's why you're here now. Not for me. For the mask."

Salvador's face looked grim in the dashboard light.

"Yes," he said. "That's why."

He turned to her, his eyes lifeless. "I've never given a tour in my life."

———

They did not speak again. Anna focused on the Virgin and Che, wondering which force was more powerful. Reverence or rebellion. They lost the Tiger somewhere on the city outskirts. To be sure, Salvador drove a crazy loop past an abandoned mine, around a baseball field. This was his city. He would not be outdriven. Home, on the safe side of the security wall, Salvador dropped his duffel.

"What do you want to say to me?"

It was late, past midnight. Anna's fear felt both vivid and distant. She was close to tears. "Thank you for getting us out of there."

Salvador appeared smaller outside his car. Not a great Mexican muralist, a Rivera or Orozco, just a man cobbling together enough beauty to survive the day. She might love him, though maybe only because she'd never see him again.

"Tell me you won't see Malone," he said. "We can work together to find a safe place for the mask."

"I won't see Thomas Malone, but I need the mask."

"Then forget it. Forget—"

A woman in her late fifties padded out in a flowered terry-cloth bathrobe. Her brown hair was streaked with copper highlights. Thick face cream gave her worried face an oily glow. She coddled her large breasts to keep warm.

"*Hijo. ¿Qué haces? Ya es tarde.*"

"*Mamá. No te preocupes. Estamos bien.*"

"*Mamá?*" Anna looked incredulous.

Salvador's shoulders fell. "*Mamá, te presento a mi amiga, Anna.* Anna, this is my mother."

The woman glanced unhappily at Anna.

"You didn't tell me you lived with your mother."

"I don't."

"You live *next door*. You never introduced me?"

Salvador rocked to one hip, defiant. "You prefer to be with Americans."

The mother pulled a pack of cigarettes from the pocket of her robe. She looked like a woman who drank coffee all day, like a woman who had dieted for thirty years and never lost a pound. *"Hijo, dime lo que está pasando."* The mother's brow tensed. She fingered the collar of her robe as she smoked. *"Me preocupaba—"*

"Todo está bien. This is the woman I took to see Tío Emilio. She is a writer, writing a book about masks."

"Tío Emilio?" Anna had the sensation of falling.

Salvador crossed his arms. "Emilio Luna is my uncle."

Anna assimilated this new fact. She was not the only liar. He had not *really* wanted to discover the truth about the carvers. He was protecting his family from scandal. No doubt Emilio Luna had a second workroom filled with Grasshopper masks, one that wasn't on the tour.

"I should go now," she said.

Salvador responded with furious calm. "I am a simple man. I live here and take care of my mother. My masks are for my wall, not my face. I don't even know who you are."

His mother arced a pink slipper over the stones.

"That's right," Anna said. "You don't."

She walked out to the street. A pregnant mutt limped past her. Anna followed the dog. Somewhere in Oaxaca, a murderous man in a tiger mask was stalking her, but Anna wasn't scared. Pity the tiger who crossed her path.

twenty | THE GARDENER

It was one in the morning when he parked outside the Puesta del Sol and slipped on the tiger mask. He was angry with himself for losing the girl. Silly people. Everyone knew how this was going to end. He jumped the wall, crossed the patio to her room. The curtains were drawn. He lifted the flimsy screen from its track, hoisted himself inside. The room was empty, bed made. He checked the bathroom, the armoire, a twist of dirty clothes. No death mask. In the closet, he found a ceramic urn, peeked inside, closed it. In the bathroom, he sprayed her perfume inside his mask, sat on the toilet, door ajar, machete across his lap. He was four days late delivering the mask to Reyes. Not good. Not at all. His insides stirred with hunger. He let his eyes close, imagined the gentle touch of the paper-shop girl.

Acércate. Come close and be with me.

An hour later he woke, looked out the window. A strange, missile-like shape arced across the night sky. East to west. Orange. Aggressive. A reminder that man was mortal, not in charge. He shivered with recognition. A streaming comet. The sixth omen. That left only two.

He fired off a text to Reyes: Patrón, Will have the mask in your hands soon. Excuse the delay. Your humble servant. The Tiger.

twenty-one | ANNA

One in the morning and the streets
of downtown Oaxaca were empty, except for a line of parked taxis,
whose dozing drivers slumped over their steering wheels like men who'd
been shot. Anna marched up the marble steps of the Excelsior, the city's
only four-star hotel, and handed the concierge her emergency credit
card. A room cost 3,800 pesos a night. At that inflated price, Anna
assumed, the staff didn't allow guests to be murdered.

The lobby was opulent. Burgundy wallpaper. Gleaming baby grand.
Mahogany chairs with eagle talons for feet. Gregorian chants rose up a
spiral staircase. In wall-size mirrors, Anna caught sight of her own
bedraggled face. Matted hair. Eye sockets like golf balls.

If the wiry man at the desk was surprised to see an American check
in after midnight without luggage, he hid his curiosity behind a veneer
of good manners and perfectly enunciated Spanish. He passed her the

guest book. She filled out her name, address, e-mail, then paused at "Emergency Contact," momentarily stumped. If there had been such a person, she wouldn't be here in the first place. Aware of the concierge's questioning gaze, she scribbled: *Constance Malone.* He handed her a giant key attached to a red velvet ribbon. Third floor. Room 303.

"Desayuno de cortesía comienza a las siete."

Anna asked if the bar was open. The concierge bowed his head with great regret. "Not at this hour, but we have room service."

"I would like a bottle of mescal."

The concierge blinked. "Shall I get the wine list? We have several varieties."

"I have confidence in your taste." She wasn't sure she'd said this right, and so added: "It doesn't matter." But *No importa* sounded rude, so she added: "What I wanted to say was, 'Yes, it matters, but I am sure whatever mescal you bring will please me.'" Having made a hash of the transaction, she turned, unspeakably tired.

The tiny elevator headed to the third floor. A mosaic of mirrors cut Anna's face into diamonds. Her lips had lost all color.

At the second floor, the elevator stopped. The doors opened to a short, acne-scarred man wearing black silk pajamas and a crimson dressing robe. His feet were jammed into yellow socks and black leather slippers. His head was wrapped in a turban, beneath which pinprick eyes glimmered with Hugh Hefner smugness. The man held an enormous martini, garnished with a pair of spiked olives.

Anna pointed up. *"Arriba."*

The man signaled down with his unlit cigar. *"Abajo."* He ogled her indecently, as though she were the one in pajamas. He lifted his glass, an invitation. One eyelid twitched. The elevator doors closed. And Anna thought, *Jesus Christ. It never ends.*

Her room was both understated and grandiose. Thick white mold-
ings, oil paintings of milkmaids, French doors opening onto a balcony.
A vase of pungent tiger lilies sat on a marble-topped dresser, along with
a saucer of chocolates, and amazingly, already, a bottle of mescal. It
was a room for honeymooners, opera singers, Japanese businessmen,
who would pair their wingtip shoes outside the door to be polished.
Anna set down her things, poured a shot. She wanted to reach a place
where she would not see the Tiger's machete, or Salvador's face saying,
I am not safe with you. She drank, dreaming up clever rebuttals. All the
other ways she was right. She said them in English, translated them
into Spanish. She checked on the mask. Its face looked like she felt:
shattered.

Her phone had a new text from David: Call me. U not only 1 hurting.

Anna typed: No quiero verte ni en pintura.

I don't want to see you even in a painting.

Fortified, she wove into the hallway. The banister circled down to a
round Oriental rug. She peered over the edge, imagining what she
would look like falling. The art of it. The spectacle. She'd wear a dress,
mint-green taffeta that would balloon and cocoon for a glorious instant.
Mescal rose in her throat as archangels supplicated in Latin. Fact: *The
two most common dreams were of being chased and of jumping from a
high place.* And she thought: *I am living the dream.*

She was drunk, eager to be drunker. Behind her, a display case
showed off luxury items available for purchase: silver tea set, porcelain
cherub, silk scarves. When her room key wouldn't turn the lock, she
fetched her phone and a Swiss Army knife. She unscrewed the case's
hinges and, feeling ingenious, wiggled out the scarf, then swiped a
brass candlestick with an embedded jade angel. She was collecting art.
She was an art collector.

She left the door hanging, climbed higher, chanting, *Tiger, tiger, burning bright.*

What kind of coward signed his name "The Tiger"?

On the fourth floor, she found a chapel. How strange. How magical. Four rows of pews fronted by a life-size crucifix. Jesus was a bloody mess, tangled beard, gloomy eyes. She thought about praying, but took pictures instead. *Flash, flash, flash.* A blizzard of green dots. The room was spinning. Clutching the angel candlestick, the scarf ringing her neck, she lay down and watched the fairies, no, Furies, dance across the ceiling, snakes in their hair. Adultery. Incest. Murder. They came to earth to drive the guilty insane.

She'd sleep here. Wait for an angel to find her.

When she opened her eyes, a kindly-looking woman was gazing down at her. She wore a black uniform and a pressed white collar. Another face appeared. The concierge. Also, the elevator man with the bad complexion. The woman said: "Shall I call the police?" The voices of the archangels rose in chorus, but Anna could not answer or move. She let sleep soothe her. Thick and warm.

She dreamt Thomas was undressing her. She dreamt she enjoyed it.

twenty-two | THE LOOTER

The bus groaned up the hill as the driver manhandled a yard-long stick shift that resembled a frozen snake. They held hands in the dark. Chelo's braces shone like jewelry. He hadn't done this since he was in high school: taken a girl out, picked up the tab, held hands. The innocence of the moment moved him. Life could be a love song. A safe place where good people stuck together.

Every lit room in the city had people inside.

Back at her house, he kissed Chelo *buenas noches*. Quick, on the lips. Turning away, he was proud of himself. For once in his life, he hadn't pushed things too far.

He fell hard into bed. The air smelled like straw and animal hide, a regular manger. The night was alive with sounds. Dogs. Fireworks. Ranchero music. Sergio Vega, again. They played his hit song every five minutes. Poor bastard. The king of *narcocorridos* made a killing singing ballads about drugs lords. One day, rumors started that Vega had been murdered. The singer did an interview to put the gossip to rest. Hours after the denial, he was gunned down in his red Cadillac. You couldn't make this stuff up.

A mosquito dive-bombed the looter's head. No fucking screens. Where was Chelo to keep him company? Forget the gallant routine. Who did he think he was? Frank Sinatra? Heart attack, aneurysm, bullet in the head—you never knew when the red Caddy was coming for you, so screw the girl. Screw the girl *now*.

He lit a joint, tried to name every dark shape. Reyes was out there, but as long as the looter stayed dead, he was safe. Car door. Motorcycle. Cowbell. The night would not shut the fuck up. The pot was good, but he could do better. That dude at the kiosk, a dealer, for sure. If he left now, he'd be back in a half hour. Chelo wouldn't miss him because *she was already sleeping*. Selfish of her, but people were like that. Putting their needs first.

His girl appeared in the doorway with a soft *"Hola."* The security light lit up her nightgown, exposing her swollen silhouette. Her belly looked like Neptune.

"Come here," he said. "Lie down with me."

He'd never been close to a pregnant woman and he wondered if she was going to feel like a fat girl, but she was hard all over, in the bony parts, in her belly, too. She smelled soft, though. Shampoo flowery, a turn-on. She was wearing panties but they weren't much. He nuzzled her neck. She moved into him like he was doing something right. Her stomach was so large it was awkward, so he rolled her over, spooning, resting his hands in the warm space between her stomach and her breasts. His scabs still hurt. A strange sadness washed over him, déjà vu or premonition or warning, quickly replaced by joy. He was not dead like Sergio Vega. Any day, you could start over. Any day you could say, *I am not doing that anymore. I am doing this instead.*

A man could populate the United States in a single ejaculation.

A man could meet his wife on a bus.

The looter practiced her name. It was hard to remember, because it didn't mean anything.

"*Chelo.* What type of name is that?"

The girl gave an amused peep, then squeezed his hand. She spoke patiently, like she wouldn't mind teaching him things for the rest of her life.

"'Chelo' is the nickname for 'Consuelo.'"

"*Consuelo?*"

Consolation. He wasn't even sure he knew the meaning in English. Except "consolation prize," not something a mother would name her kid. He kissed her spine through her nightgown. "And what does *consuelo* mean?"

Chelo buried her head in his chest and whispered, "This."

twenty-three | ANNA

Anna woke up naked and hung-
over, sprawled on a bed she did not recognize. Gregorian chants
had been replaced by the buzz of a black fly. The sun was up. Her
backpack lay on the floor. Her clothes were folded over a chair. On
a bedside table, toothbrush, toothpaste, aspirin. She used all of them.
Her head hurt. She tried to remember. The hotel. The spiral staircase. The Furies. Outside, the burr of a motor cut out. Workmen doing
something. She figured out where she was, but had no memory of
arriving. Anna had always told herself drinking was her father's problem, not hers, but she was starting to wonder about the size of that
particular inheritance. She guzzled water, fell back asleep.

———

The second time Anna woke, Thomas was kneeling at her bedside. His eyes looked brighter than usual, almost kindly, or maybe triumphant. The gray tufts at his temples shot up like flames from a disposable lighter. Pots crashed about the kitchen. Soledad.

"How did I get here?" Anna asked.

"I rescued you. Do you remember?"

Anna draped her arm over her forehead. The pressure helped a little. "Not much. I was so tired."

"You were so drunk. You stole trinkets from a display case at the nicest hotel in Oaxaca and then passed out in the upstairs chapel. The hotel was going to press charges, but I slipped them some cash. They were happy to avoid the embarrassment of arresting an American guest. I drove you home and you attacked me with gratefulness. Being a gentleman, I reciprocated, though I put my marriage in grave peril."

His hand brushed her stomach and breasts.

"Thomas!" Constance shouted. Thomas sighed, pulled back.

"Wait. Why did the hotel call you?" Despite her best efforts to extract herself, all roads circled back to Thomas Malone.

"Don't you remember?" He pressed his thumb on her chin. "You listed Constance as your emergency contact."

Anna dressed. A car pulled into the driveway. She peeked out the window. Police. Thomas greeted the two officers, nodding. She snuck out to the hallway window, which had a better view. What was all this about? Who cared? It was Sunday. In twenty-four hours, she would be flying home with the death mask. All she had to do was find a hotel room at the airport. Hunker down for the night where no tiger could find her.

The day was hot already. She slipped off her cardigan, unzipped her backpack, then panicked. *God, no, please.* She thrashed through her things, dread rising, rising, flapjacking around her insides. It wasn't what she saw that horrified her, but what she didn't see. The death mask was gone.

twenty-four | THE COLLECTOR

If he was going to Mexico, he needed a suitcase. Daniel Ramsey gripped the banister, planting each foot with care. Steady on his feet. Just fine. The basement had gotten cluttered over the years. Rusty patio furniture, outdated appliances, and the biggest squatter of all: forty-two boxes, numbered, stacked in rows on flats, the entire Ramsey Collection.

Well, there's your museum.

Miraculously, his suitcase was where he remembered it. He pulled it down, tested the wheels. Somewhere in this mess was his Mexican travel gear, money belt, walking stick. He pushed a box aside, feeling his patience for this particular quest drain. He would rather be upstairs with a fresh drink. Any second he was going to hurt his back. A bin of Christmas cards, another of clothes, then a box labeled OAXACA.

His travel notebooks were inside. His past, his life with Rose, his trips, his purchases. Ever since he'd received the Met's letter, he had debated reading his journals, but had been too angry, too afraid.

But now . . . He reached in his hip pocket for his flask, just touched it, assured by its presence.

He opened the box, pulled a chair under the light. The first notebook was dated 1995, three years after Rosie died. He'd been on a tear, racing through Mexico, as if movement could bring her back.

Spent the last week in Pinotepa National. López family. Bought two decent Moor masks. Overpaid but didn't have stomach to bargain. Left my card, and Jorge, the son, promised to keep an eye out. Malone and I are traveling together. He is introducing me around as El Coleccionista and having a good laugh about it, meanwhile his "chapel" must be packed to the gills. Promises to give me a tour someday. Not holding my breath. He's been flirting with every waitress under thirty, leaving bills on the edge of the table. I pretend not to notice. He's always been lousy to women. Amazing Constance puts up with him. Tomorrow, San Juan del Monte. Following Gonzáles tip on elusive Centurion masks . . . Ah, drinks have arrived. Malone is buying . . .

Daniel Ramsey squinted the past into focus. He kept reading.

Rodríguez had only one Centurion left, in his family for a century. Malone and I argued over it, but he backed down. I overpaid, perhaps, but it was a remarkable mask, wildly imaginative. Rodríguez sensed our enthusiasm and

asked five times what I've paid for any mask this trip.
Malone pouted, but I sense it was a play for sympathy.
Gonzáles had been feeding me tips, says he prefers to work
with me, which I understand, as Malone is difficult and
sometimes too cheap to pay for quality masks. The
craftsmanship on the Centurion is astounding. Later,
Malone conceded I'd gotten a steal.

He stood, opened the suitcase, dumped the notebooks inside, zipped it closed, staggered up the stairs, careful not to fall. In the living room, he poured himself a vodka, sank into his armchair to read.

After an hour, the pattern was clear. After two hours, no doubt remained. He had been duped, but not by Mexican carvers.

Outside, the sky was up to no good. Snow maybe, or freezing rain. Daniel Ramsey's hands trembled as he opened his desk drawer and reached for his passport.

twenty-five | ANNA

The death mask was gone again,
and Anna was nearly positive that Thomas Malone had stolen it. Not
that he was letting on. The collector was all sweetness and light, crack-
ing a joke about food poisoning as he escorted her to the front door.
Behind his eyes, a glimmer, taunting her, daring, or was she just imagining another mask?

Her only hope was the Excelsior. A concierge, a different one,
greeted Anna with a bow and fetched the manager. He was a jolly man
with a domed forehead and a mustache that twitched with concern as
he listened to Anna's story. (Apparently, he had been briefed when he
had arrived that morning.) She apologized, offered to pay for the scarf
and the candlestick—a bluff, she didn't have that kind of money—but
the manager said the *señor* had taken care of everything. Anna asked if
anyone had found a turquoise mask. The manager made a big show of

grilling the chambermaid, a terrified girl, who curtsied her denials. *No, señorita,* she had not seen a mask. *No, señorita,* nothing in the room. The manager checked the *oficina de objetos perdidos.*

"I am sorry," he said. "We have not seen the mask that you are describing."

And with that, Anna was done. So very done. The Ramseys' dream of redemption ended in yet another failure. Thomas Malone had the mask, and neither Anna Ramsey nor Anna Bookman could extract it. By now, Thomas had figured out that Anna was not an underemployed ingenue, but a rival collector. Hot, hungover, hopeless, Anna wandered the parched streets of Oaxaca. Forget imperial booty. She would give her life for an aspirin.

Only one pharmacy downtown was open on Sundays. The line barely moved. Anna was counting the customers when another horror struck. Skinny jeans, black heels, sunglasses tucked into cleavage, Salvador's *cariño* was the first customer in line. Anna ducked her face, feeling slovenly, hideous. Her breath could have ignited a good-size hibachi.

The pharmacist spoke in a hushed voice, then fetched a box of pills. When the *cariño* turned to pay, Anna nudged in close enough to read the pink label. Prenatal vitamins.

Water, coffee, a margarita.

The second round, Anna skipped the water.

A jet cut a white contrail across the sky. Her flight home left the next day. She tallied her scorecard. She'd lost the death mask. She'd lost the Rose White Ramsey Gallery. She'd lost David. She'd lost Salvador.

She'd lost $14,000. She'd lost her father. But there was still time to do one thing right: that afternoon, she would take a cab into the hills and scatter her mother's ashes at the old bullring, the most beautiful spot in Oaxaca. Salvador had been right about that.

She opened her bag and found a note folded inside. It read like an old-fashioned telegram:

> *Malinche. Stop. Feel the need for further collaboration.*
> *Stop. Meet me at the VIP Hotel at 9. Stop. I have*
> *another present.*

What the hell was Thomas up to now? She balled the note and left it in the ashtray, resisting the temptation to set it on fire.

The Puesta del Sol lay fat and full in its Sunday post-*comida* slumber. Anna hadn't been back since she found the bloody mask on her door. Surely the Tiger would not show his face in broad daylight. She just needed to pack her things. Anna told the weekend clerk she was checking out and asked him to help her with her bags in *cinco minutos*. She peered in her window. Nothing amiss. She turned the key, threw her clothes in her suitcase, not stopping to fold or inventory. When she knelt to check under the bed, a hand palmed her head: *"No te mueves."*

Anna screamed. The hand slammed her face to the floor. *"Si gritas, te mato."* If you scream, I will kill you. *"Dame la máscara."*

"No la tengo."

The hand released. Anna turned slowly around. Her attacker was a man in a tiger's mask, the man who'd stabbed the dancer, set the widow on fire, chased Anna in the mountains. He was pulling stuff out of her bag. Anna cowered, knees to chest. Her cheek was bleeding again. The pain felt good, familiar, hers. *See, you've hurt me, that's enough now. Go away.* The Tiger yanked a chair over and sat, twirled a machete on his thigh.

"Where is the mask?"

"I don't have it."

"It's here somewhere."

"Someone stole it from me." Her Spanish was disintegrating. Masculine. Feminine. Who the hell cared?

"Déjate las macanas." Cut the crap.

"I swear someone stole it. Don't hurt me. It is dangerous to hurt Americans." Anna couldn't remember whether *herir* was the right verb. She might have just told him it would be dangerous to boil Americans. "If you hurt me, there will be . . ." The only word she could find was "consequences."

"¿Señorita?" The clerk.

The Tiger hacked his machete down her shirt buttons, cutting an inch of fabric. "Answer him," he hissed.

"Todo está bien." She hoped the clerk could hear the subtext, the fear. "I have changed my mind and will stay another night."

"Bueno. Como usted lo desea." Footsteps drifted off. The idiot had left her. The Tiger went to the closet and lifted her mother's urn. "What's this?"

Anna whispered, *"Nada."*

He tipped it, threatening to pour the contents on the floor. "Do you think I'm stupid?"

"Stop. It's my mother," Anna cried out. "She's dead. She wanted to be in Mexico."

"Then I will take your dead mother with me. When you bring the mask, I return her."

"I am leaving tomorrow."

"Not anymore."

"Please."

The Tiger righted the urn, but did not put it back. "I give you until Friday. Meet me at Monte Albán at midnight. By the Danzantes. Come alone. If you do not come, I will pour this dirt down a toilet in a whore-house on the highway to Guerrero. You understand?"

Anna repeated her mission. "I am going to bring you the mask." This was the easiest way to form the future. *I am going* to find the mask. *I am going* to die in this crappy hotel room. *I am going* to lose my mother forever.

The Tiger wedged his machete into the chair. "If you trick me, I will kill you and your pretty boyfriend and his ugly mother."

Anna risked a joke. "The mother, too? You promise?"

"A present." He stood, stopped himself. "Are you a virgin?"

"Do I have a Virgin?" She fingered San Antonio.

"No. *Are* you a virgin?"

She had thought this nightmare was nearly over, but perhaps it had just begun. "No," she said, her voice barely audible.

He jiggled his knife between her legs. Anna gave a short cry. Skin. It was no protection at all. "Too bad," he said, turning away. "I have no interest in *la chingada*."

For a good while, Anna didn't move; then she got up and couldn't stop—pacing the patio, circling the maimed angel, smoking, swearing, messing with her hair. She had come to Mexico to bury her mother's ashes, but had lost them instead. Well, technically, she had not lost them. They were being held hostage by a drug lord's hit man. It was terrible. Crazy. Terrible crazy.

Two cigarettes later, she collapsed at a table, head buried in her arms. *Mom, mom, mom.* After twenty years, she had so few memories left. Tea parties. Her mother poured sweet apple tea in little cups she'd painted by hand. She'd put on a corny southern accent. "Bless my heart, Miss Anna. You are a sight for sore eyes." Her mother, who loved the beach, who taught Anna to sing periwinkles out of their shells. Her mother, who knit doll blankets, collected vintage tablecloths, ferried spiders outside. Her mother, who felt none of the same sympathies for criminals. "Throw away the key," she said, as she refolded the newspaper after reading about some murderer. "Just make him go away." (She would have abhorred the drug violence in Mexico. *How much money does anyone need? Are these drug lords happy? Sleeping with guns. Their own children aren't safe.*)

When Anna's father traveled, she and her mother stayed alone for long stretches. Her mother seldom lost her temper, though nothing made her angrier than when Anna complained she was bored. "Read. Draw. Write a letter. Ride your bike." The list had infinite variety, but always ended with *Go climb a tree,* her mother's way of saying, *Leave me in peace.* Her mother was earning a degree in museum studies, and spent hours poring over dull books, taking notes, pleading for Anna to give her an hour of quiet.

So Anna climbed trees. Until one day she climbed a pine tree so high she couldn't get down. Twenty feet up, she got stuck on a branch, sap smeared on her jeans, palms sore, so high she could see the shingles on the roof. Climbing up had been easy. *Don't look down.* And she hadn't, until her mother ran out and stood beneath her, small and worried, hands on her waist.

"Sweetie, you're up awfully high. You think you can climb down?" Her voice was serious but calm. She was wearing her favorite thrift-store shirt, red checks, rolled sleeves.

Anna sat sideways on a branch, like a swing. She didn't dare turn to dangle a leg to the next limb down. The branches were making her dizzy. The wind had picked up. Rain was coming. She tried not to cry.

"Can I jump to you?"

Her mother looked horrified. "Jesus Christ. Don't move." She tore off to the house, hair flying. A minute later, she was back.

"The firemen are coming. Just hold tight."

"What fire? I want to come down now."

What happened next surprised Anna even more. Her mother started to climb. Anna had never seen her mother climb a tree, but her arms were strong and she made short work of it. She was athletic, a tennis player in college. She could still do a split.

The branches thinned at the top. When her mother touched Anna's blue sneaker, she stopped, and together they waited for the bucket truck, breathing in the earthy scent of needles and bark. "Two Christmas ornaments hanging off a pine tree," her mother would say later. "All we needed was a star."

When they were down, her mother rocked Anna in her arms, whispering, "I'm so sorry. It's all my fault." Anna decided it was worth feeling that scared to feel this safe.

"What did you learn today?" her mother asked when she tucked Anna into bed that night. Her hands smelled like Nivea.

"Don't climb trees?"

Her mother shook her head, then kissed Anna's cheek. "Next time you climb a tree, take me with you."

The laundry girl rolled past with a cart full of dirty towels. Anna missed her mother so much her teeth hurt. If only it were possible to summon the dead, from dreams and stories, memories and photographs. A solid made from ether. Even for a day.

Next time you climb a tree . . . Take me *with* you. Take *me* with *you*.

And Anna thought: *That tiger can have the death mask, but not my mother.*

She would do what she had to. She would do what she must.

Anna walked to her room, opened the closet, removed the Malinche mask Thomas had given her. What had Doña Marina done when the murderous Spanish conquistador Hernán Cortés and his army of marauders attacked her beloved city?

La Malinche had slept with the enemy—and survived.

twenty-six | THE GARDENER

Hugo took a seat facing Jesus.
After leaving the American, he had stumbled into the first church he'd
come to, exhilarated and ashamed. True, his rock prayer had gone
nowhere, but maybe for a prayer to succeed, you had to get out of your
car. He bowed his head. He prayed he had not hurt the girl. He prayed
for the dead. There were so many. The dead outnumbered the living
tenfold: the Mexicans who died at the border; the young women of
Juárez who disappeared, *feminicidios*, sold, some believed, for body
parts; the police gunned down by drug dealers; the dealers gunned
down by police; Hugo's own father, dead and gone; his mother, too.
The dead haunted his sleep. Pedro's mother, wailing as she cleaned
Montezuma's floors. Pedro hammering. His revenge. In the afterlife,
he'd become a blacksmith, fashioning hooks and latches and skeleton

keys. He prayed for the girl's mother, ashes in an urn, hidden in the backseat of his car.

Billions of people had died the world over, and still all these souls believed their lives were precious. Men and women dreamt and loved and ate and saw the world through their eyes and watched their bodies age, wither, and return to the ground, all but a lucky few forgotten, trod upon by the living, who labored and fucked, burdened by the crushing weight of their endless desires. The living owed the dead their peace. What right had he to steal their finery?

Hugo turned to the Virgin. The Mother of God soothed him like a balm. When he looked into her face, he knew what he could not do: when the American brought him the death mask, he would not give it to Óscar Reyes Carrillo or Thomas Malone or Lorenzo Gonzáles. Not for love or money, guilt or gratitude. Not even to ensure the caresses of the papershop girl. Only two omens remained—the two-headed monster and the burning temple. The empire, Hugo now understood, was his own sanity, the delicate kingdom of his mind. The path to salvation was so simple it was childlike. He could hear his mother scolding him after he'd left his toys strewn: *Hijo, put things back where they belong.*

When he barged into his house, he found his wife collapsed on the floor. Sliced apples lay scattered around her.

He knelt before her. "*¿Qué te ha pasado?*"

"I felt dizzy, but I am okay now. Resting. I have good news."

He shook her arm. "Are you crazy? You are sick on the ground. What good news?"

"The Virgin sent us a child."

Hugo fell back on his heels.

"I am pregnant, but don't worry." His wife's voice gained strength. "We can still go to the other side. The baby will be born with an American passport. The Virgin answered our prayers."

Hugo assembled some kind of expression. Proud husband. Proud father. Where did a man go to procure such a face? He laid his hand on her stomach. "I don't feel anything. Are you sure?"

"He's only a few weeks old. A grain of rice."

Hugo helped her to bed. "Rest now. I'll check on you in a bit."

He escaped to the yard, picked up a fallen orange, and hurled it into the darkness. The stars blinked a message he could not decode.

The mature man:
a heart as firm as stone . . .

From his Aztec history book, he was memorizing the Huehuetlatolli, the ancient truths and teachings of the Nahuas, lessons designed to teach young men how to live a good life. They were recited in school. They were recited when a loved one departed.

Tears filled his eyes, for himself, his wife, his unborn child, for the American girl carrying her dead mother, for the papershop girl in her yellow dress, the sun around which his world revolved, beautiful, young, and bright.

He wished the baby were hers.

His phone rang a text. Reyes. I'm waiting. Your wife has beautiful hands.

With a moan, Hugo rolled into a ball, pressed his face into the dirt.

twenty-seven | THE HOUSEKEEPER

"*Santísima Virgen, take pity on me.* I told Hugo a lie. The words rose up before I could stop them. Forgive me. Allow me to prove myself worthy of your blessings. I have seen inside the chapel and understand now why the *señor* needed water. Every night the light in the chapel shines, I watch and pray. Gruesome things call my attention. Evil is as confusing as goodness is plain. The *señora* refuses to see. Sometimes the bravest thing you can do is open your eyes. I understand the test you have laid before me. This good work I do in your name. In return, I beg you, *Virgencita,* make me an honest woman. A lie is a lie only as long as it remains untrue. I could be a good mother."

twenty-eight | THE COLLECTOR

Frost covered the open fields of
Connecticut as Daniel Ramsey drove to the airport, where his elec-
tronic ticket was waiting. His dry eyes shifted from road to speed-
ometer to vodka bottle in the passenger seat. Damp wind smacked
his face. *Wake up, wake up, wake up.* He had not slept. Thomas Malone,
the name a curse in his mouth.

Route 1 was backed up. Accident or roadwork. He shifted into
park, plotting his revenge. He'd be cordial, shake hands, accept a patio
chair, before calmly levying his accusations. *I think you sold me some
worthless masks a while back. You and Gonzáles.* If Constance heard, so
be it. Let her know what kind of man she'd married, a liar, a cheat.
Thomas would feign confusion; deny everything in his creamy voice: *I
realize you've had a tough time, and I'm genuinely sorry for that, but surely
you don't blame me for your troubles?*

Traffic picked up, but barely. He was late. He should have taken the interstate. The last thumb of vodka sloshed about. Sometimes a man needed a drink to get off his ass. Shakespeare had known this. Churchill, too. His knees ached. The vodka was annoying him. *Finish the damn thing.* In a single swallow, he did.

The accident was impressive. A white sedan lay in the median like an enormous wounded gull. He passed the carnage, accelerated, making up time, going fast enough that at the intersection he sailed under a red light. Cars careened forward, greedy bastards, not waiting for traffic to clear. A maroon minivan shot into his path. Through the window, he made out a child's pale face in a pompom hat. He swerved, overcompensated, ran onto the curb, then crashed back to the road. He gave a girlish cry. His hands trembled as he patted his chest, checking himself, his heart. No accident. No injury. He merged into the slow lane, chastened but still moving, and that's when he heard sirens. And he thought: *Thomas Malone is the devil and no one can stop him.*

twenty-nine | THE LOOTER

He could tell it was a big deal for Chelo to be out at night with a man. She ordered limeade and a slice of chocolate cake. He had a beer with a side shot of whiskey. They had spent the day strolling the city, stopping for shaved ice, snapping silly pictures of each other. By six, they collapsed in a café. Tomorrow, he'd track down Malone, but he wasn't feeling ambitious today. He bought a rose from a woman with a basket on her head. Full price. No bargaining. Chelo pressed her nose into the flower's curled heart, set it down, as if she had many suitors, many roses, as if she had a collection.

The looter tried to relax, but paranoia chipped away at his good feeling. Who knew when Reyes's ugly face might materialize? If Chelo could show up on a bus and make everything good, then Reyes could show up in a café, guns loaded. Chelo had promised to help him, but she couldn't protect him from Reyes or take him to Malone. Maybe he should pray.

"*Tal vez debería rezar.*" The looter skimmed the pride from his voice. "For help finding this friend of mine, this thing."

The girl nodded like she'd been expecting this. "God could help if you asked."

"What should I say?"

The girl tapped her painted nails against her straw. "Speak in your own voice. Nobody else's."

"What voice?"

"Who you are."

"What if that's not good enough?"

The girl pursed her lips. "Be a better man. Earn his respect."

This comment pissed him right off. He'd been looking for reassurance and she'd made him feel small. She was knocked-up but playing it chaste.

"What do *you* know?" His voice came out mean and he didn't try to fix it. He would not be judged. Not by a girl who couldn't scrape two pesos together.

The girl's eyes turned cold. "I know God."

"Nobody knows God."

"I do."

The looter scoffed, fished for a cigarette. Chelo sat centered, hands on her Buddha belly, like everyone should rub her stomach for luck. All at once, the looter didn't care if he hurt her—or the baby. She was nobody to him. She was a tramp he'd met on a bus. She didn't know he'd dug up one of the greatest treasures in Mexican history. She didn't know that he'd sold it, stolen it back, sold it a second time, and now, even as she sat sipping limeade, was devising a plan to steal it a third time, not for profit but to honor the Virgin of Guadalupe, *her Virgin*. What had Chelo done in her life? Spread her legs, peeled potatoes, passed judgment. He didn't have the Spanish vocabulary to express all the ways she was inferior to him. He just said: "And what does God say about your baby?"

The girl's face hardened, a security wall eight inches thick. Her lips covered her braces. "God says my baby is His son."

"Your son is an *hijo de la chingada*."

It was one of the most insulting things you could say to a Mexican. *Your son is a son of the whore*, not any whore, La Malinche, the Indian who slept with Cortés. The girl bent her head like he'd smacked her.

He threw down his money and left her, too furious to steer. When the market appeared, he dove in, pushing past synthetic T-shirts, past chorizo dangling like vulgar necklaces. He hated this country. Mexicans had nothing. Nothing but land they soiled. Nothing but animals they killed, relics they pawned, drugs they pushed. Nothing but God, who did nothing. The looter shoved past sleepy children awake too late at night. *Go to bed. Go to school. Stop eating candy.* He thought of his mother. The calamity of his life was her fault. She had not made him into the man he wanted to be.

The meat stalls went on forever. A skinned pig's head stared at him, a regular Supreme Court judge. Its lips moved. The looter rubbed his eyes, hoping to shut down the weirdness, but the foul, fleshy, avuncular, chalk-colored, blue-eyed swine resting on the butcher's table was communicating over the chasm of species and language. *Listen to the girl*, it said. *Believe in something. I know. I'm a pig.*

The looter glared at the beheaded turkeys, the skinned rabbits, the whole dead menagerie, daring other animals to offer two more lousy cents.

The butcher turned away from the chicken parts on his scale.

"Can I help you?"

"Your pig is talking to me."

The butcher wiped his hands on his apron. A red splotch covered his heart. He looked down at his pig, amused, impressed.

"If my pig is talking to you, you'd better listen," he said. "He never tells me anything."

The looter put his ear to the pig's nostrils. Not a peep. What had it said? *Listen to the girl.* He pictured Chelo, the moon of her belly, her constellation of freckles. Why had he lost his temper? He no longer remembered. With a stab to the gut, he realized he wasn't sure where she lived and didn't have her number.

He ran out of the market now, knocking into people, not caring. What he wanted mattered more than what he upset. Chelo was the house he would live in. The children he would father. The love he would make. The proof he was a man, alive, no longer a twigger buried underground. Breathless, he reached the café, scanned the tables, *their table*, but the girl was gone.

The pain of her absence took his breath away.

He picked up a rock and hurled it. Something snapped in his shoulder. Something snapped in his heart. He was unloved and unlovable. Both things were his fault.

thirty | ANNA

Room 7 of the VIP Hotel hadn't
changed anything but its sheets. Same sad desk where no letters were
written. Same lamp, its shade tilted and frayed. Anna didn't want to
think about who had slept here in the interim, and the many ways what
they had done was different from and the same as what she was about
to do. She was going to seduce Thomas Malone and, while he slept,
steal his keys. All of them, not one. She was done being subtle. She'd go
to the chapel, swipe the mask, take off like Holly, meet the Tiger on
Friday, retrieve her mother's ashes, fly over the border and never return.

Thomas lay on the bed, peering into his phone. Anna drank mescal
from a recyclable cup. At the foot of the bed, another box, unopened.
Maybe Thomas was giving her back the death mask. She smiled at the
absurdity of the idea. The thing you wanted most was never inside
someone else's box.

"Open your present."

"I will." She didn't move.

"Open it now."

Anna studied him, debating whether at his core, beyond his vanities and greed, he was a good man or a bad man. She cut through the tape with scissors. Her desire for a happy ending was so strong she slowed down. As long as the box remained closed, her wish still might come true.

"You didn't have to do this."

She lifted the top of the box. It was a mask, all right—a mask of a skull, a grinning chalk-white *calavera* with sloppy red lipstick and gnarly clenched teeth. Beyond ugly.

And Anna thought: *I used to date nice boys.*

"Put it on."

Anna shook her head, slid the box across the cheap comforter. "It's too much. What's next? A donkey?"

"I want you to wear it. You must."

"I must?" The ridiculousness of his statement gave her an edge. "Why?"

He set his mouth. "I was looking for a woman to go places with me. I thought you were her."

"You really want me to wear this?"

"It's Calavera Catrina. Posada mocking the Indians who wanted to be European, putting on airs. You'll be the height of fashion. The elegant cadaver."

"In bed?"

"Sex, death, religion. They all go together. Why do you think the French call the orgasm the 'little death'?"

"Because they're French."

"Don't be so conventional. We're playing. You like the circus." From his cigarette case, Thomas produced a joint. This surprised her until she remembered he'd been a drug rep. Who knew what combination of substances kept him afloat?

He inhaled, passed the joint to her. "You like?"

Anna took a hit. Sweet smoke filled her lungs. She remembered a lacrosse player she'd dated one summer, a bully with a tapestry belt. She exhaled. "Like has nothing to do with it."

Two minutes later, she was stoned. Not high, but low, like a stone, a stoned stone, or maybe the creature that lives under the stoned stone, a slug with no eyes.

She volunteered to fetch ice, a pretext for fresh air. The parking lot reeked of diesel and fries. At the ice machine, her phone bleeped a text. David.

I heard yr dad's sale fell thru. Sorry. For everything. Come home. Be w/ me.

Ice cubes dropped into the plastic bucket. Anna searched for her feelings—love, regret, fear—but she was as full and empty as the parking lot of the VIP Hotel. Was David really sorry? Did he love her? Did she love him? There were no facts to check. No book, no census data, no website that confirmed sincerity, that diagrammed the tricky arteries of the heart. She pictured David, asleep in bed, when she'd lain awake nights, sifting through what she lacked the nerve to say. So many things. Or maybe just one: *I wish you loved me enough to make me tell you the truth.*

She walked back to room 7, hugging the ice bucket to her chest. It wasn't too late to start over. Anna was good at beginnings. She would start by being honest with Thomas Malone.

She closed the door behind her. The collector patted the bed, his expression enigmatic. The room grew smaller. She was frightened. Honesty had this effect on her. Any mask was safer than no mask at all.

"I need your help," she began, joining him on the bed. "I've gotten myself into a real mess."

He toyed with her hair. "I am an expert at cleaning up messes."

She swallowed, pushed the words from her mouth. "That night, at the Excelsior when I blacked out, I lost something—"

"Lost what?"

"A death mask I bought in San Juan del Monte from that old woman who was killed. I had it with me that night, but when I woke up at your house, it was gone."

His face registered no emotion. She continued. "A man in a tiger's mask came to my hotel. The same tiger who killed the old woman. He threatened to kill me if I don't give him the mask. He works for Reyes. Did you take the mask that night? I don't care now, I just need your help."

"The death mask in the postcard?"

Anna nodded.

"You had Montezuma's death mask and didn't tell me?" His voice was high and brittle. "Though you worked for me, though we'd shared intimacies, you said nothing. You wanted the mask, I suppose, for the Ramsey Collection."

A stone fell through Anna's body. She saw three versions of everything, none of them good. "How did you know?"

"How dumb do you think I am? Stealing my key. At that ridiculous dinner party, your face was so transparent. Scurrying off to the bathroom to compose yourself. I called Gonzáles. *Who is she, and what does she want?* In two minutes, I'd dragged it out of him. So Anna Ramsey came to Oaxaca to spy on me. She's sick of her father's incompetence.

She's ambitious, wants to join the real collectors. She gets her hands on a treasure, but there's one complication: Reyes has already hung a nail over his heart-shaped bed for this particular trophy, already sent a victory postcard to his rival." Thomas paused. "How am I doing so far?"

Anna reached for a cigarette. She might be sick.

"But poor Anna loses the mask. Maybe she was drunk. Maybe she trusted someone she shouldn't have. Now Reyes wants it back. He sends his tiger to do his dirty work, and now scared little Anna wants Thomas Malone, the man she has lied to, the man she has seduced and betrayed, to save her. Thomas Malone becomes attractive when there's something Anna needs or wants."

Anna looked up at the door. No cross. She prayed to the ice bucket.

"To answer your question, I don't have the death mask. But could I help you? Maybe. I could call the American embassy or smuggle you over the border in my truck. Hire a bodyguard. Contact Reyes and plead your case. Anything is possible, but why don't you first show me why I should care?"

He held up the skull mask.

"I'm sorry," Anna began. "I thought it was a silly knockoff. The tiger stole my mother's ashes."

"Anna. You're a writer. Show, don't tell."

"Will you help me?"

"Help yourself."

It had come to this. Perhaps she'd always known it would. She took the skull mask, stumbled to the bathroom, sat on the toilet, wiggling her bare toes. Half-moons of color. If Thomas didn't have the death mask, who did? If he did have the mask, the only way forward was to see the night through. Catrina was heavy. Anna's breath warmed the wood as she tied the mask over her face. *He's got some sexual fetish. He thinks this is fun. How does a skeleton dance? I'll walk out like a zombie and—*

A woman screamed. A gun fired. The television announcing its presence. Maybe Thomas had changed his mind and they'd snuggle up to a nice mafia movie. Anna opened the door. He'd turned off the lights. By the TV's light, she made out the bed, bureaus, blinds, but Thomas had disappeared. The room swept past in unstable rushes. Whatever she'd smoked had clouded her insides, leaving her limbs heavy and numb. She called into the dark. "Thomas . . . I don't feel well all of a sudden."

The blow to her neck came from behind. She blocked her fall on the bed with one arm. Then he was on her. His weight crushed her spine. His hand clamped the mask over her mouth. They struggled. He tore her clothes. *Thomas, you're hurting me!* but her voice had no power and Thomas was chanting gibberish, *Dueña y señora de la vida, Ángel que nuestro Padre creó.* He dropped his pants. Through the mask, she caught snatches of the ceiling, square panels, removable. The mirror reflected the headboard, his back. Everything happened quickly. Everything happened slow. He was going to rape her, this horrible man. She kicked and struggled. Did she scream? She clamped her thighs. His face glowed, frantic eyes not seeing. She braced herself but nothing happened. She wrestled high enough to see his groin, pale and limp, and he saw her see this, his failure.

With one furious motion, he hurled her to the floor. Her head smacked the desk. He kicked the mask on her face. Her cheek split open. She moaned. Car chase. Broken glass. Gunfire. Family entertainment. The room door slammed. Face pressed to the carpet, Anna felt the vibrations of traffic, the single car that merged, disappearing into the night.

Out the window, the MARISCOS sign pulsed. Above it, the moon, half in light, half in shadow. The moon, where the footprints of astronauts would remain forever because there was no wind to blow them away. Anna held herself in the only place he hadn't touched. A Mexican saying floated up from memory. *El que con lobos anda a aullar se enseña.*

He who walks with wolves learns to howl.

thirty-one | THE LOOTER

He was an empty man. How had he deluded himself for so long? All this time, he'd believed he carried an internal flame. He'd believed in his own honor, his place in the world, but that belief had crashed on the cobblestones of Oaxaca and he now understood who he was—a worthless junkie living in a country that did not love him. The Maddox Principle of Opposing Equilibrium was bunk. His outside had corroded his insides. Drugs had hardened his heart, consumed his decency. He could not be close to another person, except sexually, and barely that. He didn't know what to say to a woman or how to behave. *Nice . . .* another four-letter word for trying to get what you want.

He found the kiosk. The dealer with ping-pong eyes was conducting high finance in the alley. His T-shirt read MEXICAN HAIRLESS DOG. His client was a muscular guy in a leather coat and shiny white high-tops. A small man hoping to feel large. The looter caught the buyer's profile. The sight of his hideous face made his legs go weak.

Fucking Feo.

The dealer jerked around, paranoid someone was cutting in on his territory.

Feo looked ashen, like Jesus Christ had risen from a manhole. Recognition. Disbelief. Panic. A triptych of *What the fuck?* The man he had buried alive had returned from the dead.

Nobody moved.

thirty-two | THE DOGS

It was past midnight and the dogs of Oaxaca were howling again.

The first dog howled at the scent of danger.

The second howled because his stomach was empty.

The third howled to one-up the other two, playing the dozens, singing the blues: *You think you've got problems, listen to this.*

The fourth dog howled in empathy—*We are all dogs together.*

The fifth howled to let everyone know he was a big dog.

The sixth howled to not feel so alone.

The seventh howled hoping to attract a sexy bitch who enjoyed late-night perambulations.

The eighth howled to hear the beauty of her mezzo-soprano voice, a legacy of her mother, a Neapolitan mastiff.

The ninth howled to express his inner dog. *I am learning to be me.*

The tenth howled because the night was lovely and fleeting and, one day, no matter how grand his contemplations, no matter how majestically his howl echoed through the valley, no matter how many rabbits he killed or how furiously he copulated, there would come a night, much like this one, when he would no longer howl.

PART THREE

We must remove the mask.

—*Michel de Montaigne*

one | ANNA

Orange numbers ticked by on the digital clock. A minute lasted forever.

He was gone, but still present.

Thomas Malone was still on the sheets, still pressing her wrists, still closing the door behind him, leaving her stranded at the VIP Hotel, discarded like the white towel he had used to dry his hands.

Anna lay with her fear, scared of the dark, scared of the light. Did knowing the man make it better or worse? With a stranger, the violence was anonymous, pure, but this evening had started with a drink and a present. He *knew* her, but had done what he'd done regardless. Without regard. And the masks? Erotica, a ruse that no longer worked, and he was growing more desperate and violent, furious with himself, with women. How much did Constance know? Did they share these secrets, or were they locked in his chapel, his sanctuary, his private collection?

Murmurings drifted through the motel walls. Men and women, and who knew what else. Boxes with people inside. People coming together, pulling apart. Mouths open. Hungry. Breathing. All that desire, barely contained. Snuff motels. Ending things was a choice people made when oblivion became preferable to pain, but taking your own life was like tossing aside a half-read book, something Anna never did. Even the worst stories could improve.

She hobbled to the bathroom. Her cheek was bleeding again, her eyelids swollen, but otherwise she looked remarkably unscathed—her hair covered the bump on her head—proving once again that people who looked okay often weren't. The Aztecs understood this. Their healers placed water under a patient's chin. If the reflection was shadowed, a man had lost his soul.

Anna showered. She held herself. A wisp of water scalded her back.

She thought about the Tiger, but was no longer scared.

She thought of her father, but was no longer angry.

She wondered where her mother was, spirit and ash. She sifted through her memories. Christmas morning, the smell of bacon, her mother's thick robe. The tentative way she put on makeup. "Good?" she'd ask Anna. "Or too much?"

Es mi bandera, la enseña nacional . . .

Up from memory floated a song. A Mexican flag salute, of all things, the anthem her mother sang at dinner parties to prove her Mexican chops.

Son estas notas su cántico marcial . . .

Anna sang, careful of her pronunciation, her accent. Shower water dripped off her cut lips. The Spanish shook loose something inside her and she thought: *This is as far down as I am going.*

———

She walked the dark, narrow streets, nipping mescal from the bottle. Her right heel was bleeding. She gave up trying to find a cab. The worst had already come to pass. Despite the shower, she felt soiled. She should have thrown out her underwear. She should have sliced the skin off Thomas Malone's face with her Swiss Army knife and worn it like an Aztec mask.

The cathedral appeared, soft in the darkness. She walked up to its oak doors studded with iron. The padlock stopped her, a dead end to her only idea. The city slept, except for a trio of goth waifs crashing skateboards. Anna sat on the wide church steps. When she closed her eyes, the VIP Hotel rushed back at her in lurid strobe-light flashes. His grasp. His breath. His vacant eyes. What was the word for unconsummated rape?

A man joined her on the steps. Thirties, with a gaunt smoker's face. Beanie hat. A satchel hung from his shoulder. A fishing box sat at his feet. A man, any man, was the last thing she wanted to see.

Anna turned away, but he didn't take the hint.

"Is the church locked?" he asked.

She gave a half nod. Of course, he'd known she spoke English. She had an American face, the kind people swore they'd seen before.

"You want to get in?" he asked.

Anna shrugged.

"You cut your cheek."

"It just got worse."

The man dug into his shirt pocket for a cigarette. His meaty thumb rubbed his eye socket. He looked exhausted, like a man who had never learned to take care of himself, and no woman had volunteered for the job. Then it came to her, an electric realization. She knew him. He knew her. He held out a cigarette and a lighter. She took both. Still, no recognition. *How can you be so fucking unobservant? Look at me, idiot. Look at my face.*

Anna inhaled, mustering her strength. "So what are *you* doing here?"

"Mexico?" He gestured outward to nothing. "Looking for something I lost. Sold, really. I need it back. Then, tonight, I lost my girlfriend at a café."

"You should be more careful."

"I'll get it all back."

"What did you lose? The thing, not the girl."

The man hesitated, like he was debating between the long and short version. "A million-dollar mask." He gave a quick grin.

Maybe it was the way his hoodie hung off his shallow chest, or the fact he didn't recognize her from five feet away, or how the only thing he had to brag about was something he'd lost, but Anna felt a wave of sympathy. Things weren't going to end well for this guy. He had burned his mind for kindling. He wore his sadness like clothes. Still, she couldn't resist playing him.

"Let me guess. You lost the death mask of Montezuma."

He recoiled, amazed. "What the . . . How did you know that?"

"Simple," Anna said. "So did I."

When each story had been told, retold, parsed and compared, when the last of the mescal had been drunk and cigarettes shared, when they'd lain on the steps and gazed into the night sky, gotten philosophical about the passage of time and astrology, how little we humans knew, when they had talked about death and the trickiness of being fully alive, like they were right now, staying up all night, stargazing, when exhaustion set in and they got giddy and made fun of themselves, two American fuckups who'd met at church, two American fuckups who'd lost everything, the same priceless art treasure, the loves of their lives (Anna exaggerated this fact to keep him company), when they'd reviewed the impending threats, Thomas, the Tiger, Reyes, when the looter told her Reyes was missing half his right ear, when they'd laughed about this, speculating where the missing piece had gone, when Anna described the assault and the looter vowed to avenge her, when he lifted his fishing box and told her his gun now had bullets, when the sun ushered in the new day and the birds would not shut up about it, when they agreed to go for coffee, but couldn't move, Anna turned to the looter and said exactly what she was thinking: "We both want the same thing, but only one of us can have it."

"I've been thinking about that," he said.

"This whole story is like *lotería,* that Mexican bingo game." The looter nodded vaguely. "Only we've got The Tiger, The Dealer, The Expatriate, The Drunk—"

"Who's that?" He looked hurt.

"My father."

The looter shook his head. "We'll flip a coin."

"I know a trick how to win."

"No tricks. No lottery. Just fate."

"We need the mask before March fifteenth. After Thomas's opening, everyone will know it's his. Game over. We've got what . . . a little more than two weeks."

The smell of breakfast grease beckoned, but Anna had no desire to

331

leave. She felt oddly close to this man, as if they'd taken a long car trip together, shared junk food and confessions, or seen something big, like the Grand Canyon, and decided not to take any photos, just remember whatever stuck and let the rest fall away. You could tell strangers things you could never tell a lover.

The looter lay on his back, ankles crossed. "Malone has the mask. We just need a plan." He'd said this many times.

A priest scurried past them, purring good day. He unlocked the church, propped the doors. Anna said, "If I don't find the mask by Friday, the Tiger is going to kill me." How many times in her life had she tossed out this expression? *So-and-so is going to kill me.* Only now, it was true. "*And* chuck my mother's ashes in a dumpster."

The looter pointed to the church doors. "I'm going in. Get some advice."

"From him?"

"No, her."

Anna hadn't expected this. A pious junkie. He'd told his whole life story without mentioning addiction, but you didn't get a face like his from sunbathing.

"You really think the Virgin is going to help you?" She resented his confidence. Other people had God and she didn't. It was like having family money, health insurance, a back hundred acres. Maybe her father needed religion to stop drinking. God was one of the Twelve Steps, she seemed to recall. Maybe the first step. Maybe the whole staircase. "She's saved your life once. Now you're back asking for more. Maybe she's got other customers."

The looter shrugged. "Why wouldn't she help?"

Anna could think of a half-dozen reasons. Or none. "That's Chelo talking." He looked peeved. "No, that's good, I mean. You're doing it." She had no idea what "it" was. "I'll wait here. Let me know what she says."

He walked up the steps, toe dragging. As soon as he left, Anna missed him. The rest of the city would work today, ferry children to school, come home tired, sleep in their beds, as the donkeys brayed, as the dogs howled, as the moon rose, as water refilled the cisterns, as corrupt coyotes led Mexicans over the border, as gangs trafficked narcotics, as *putas* disrobed, as mariachis blasted their trumpets, as moths banged against flimsy screens, desperate to reach the light. None of it would stop for her, just as none of it had stopped for her mother.

Anna remembered something she'd read in the guidebook. This cathedral was famous for its *retablos*, small oil paintings done on slabs of tin or wood, thanking saints for blessings and miracles. Her father owned a few. She dragged herself vertical, went inside, found a chapel jammed with paintings, each the size of a hardback book, each relating a story of calamity and salvation.

I give thanks to the Virgin for saving my life. I was working in the circus when an elephant went crazy—

I give thanks that I found work as a prostitute here in La Merced. Take good care of me so I can send a few pennies to my parents.

San Judas Tadeo, I bring you thanks because my magueys are giving me lots of delicious pulque.

Thank you, sweet Virgin of Juquila, for Viagra.

Thank you, blessed Virgin, for sending me in time to rescue my son who was hanging himself.

Blessed art thou, San Sebastián, because my father accepted my homosexuality.

Thank you for getting the gang off that glue-sniffing shit.

There was an earthquake,

A lightning bolt,

A brutal storm at sea.

My friend's hair accidentally caught on fire.

Thank you, San Isidro the Plowman, for sending the rain.

Pablo lost his hand to a pig.

Esteban fell in a lake.

I had blasted rheumatism.

The iron fell.

Our nopales are better than last year's.

Thank you, sweet Virgin, for curing my sheep.

Anna walked outside. Her heart felt filled up, overflowing with the ten million ways life could go wrong—and then, miraculously, be saved. She sat, holding herself, rocking just a bit, imagining the *retablo* she would paint should her own string of calamities be resolved. *Thank you, blessed Virgin, for helping me rescue the death mask of Montezuma, for saving me from the Tiger, for getting my father off booze, for bringing my mother's ashes to rest in Mexico, the country she loved, for making the fickle painter from the zócalo fall in love with me, for sending Miss Venezuela on a Mormon mission to Bora-Bora, for burning Thomas Malone at the stake.*

There would be no room for a painting.

The final gratitude was the hardest to admit: *Thank you, blessed Virgin, for saving me from a marriage that would have failed.*

She wished she were eating a steaming plate of huevos rancheros. She wished she were wearing more clothes so that none of her skin was exposed. *Endure,* she thought. This moment will lead to the next. She must have looked pathetic, because when the looter reappeared, he patted her back tentatively, as if he wasn't sure he was doing it right. The small kindness broke her down.

"Don't worry," he said. "We'll get the mask back."

"It feels like everything . . ."

She stopped herself, rubbed her forehead, thankful for this person, whoever he was. He couldn't solve all her problems, but perhaps he could help her with one.

"What did the Virgin say?" she asked.

The looter said, "She told me to dig."

two | THE LOOTER

The dirt moved easily. The looter had to laugh. If his Divide buddies could see him now, humping for Jesus, digging for Guadalupe. To keep his mind off his aching back, his knees, his thin skin, he remembered the books he'd read about brave warriors who'd faced danger or challenge. *Half a league, half a league, Half a league onward.*

The plan was simple. A tunnel. The chapel's hillside location was perfect, miraculous, really. He could dig forward without first having to dig down. The woods hid his mess. The church's foundation was already crumbling.

He thought of Anna. Nice girl but a wreck. She seemed fearless or maybe numb. Malone had attacked her. Reyes's tiger was chasing her. He had tried to reassure her—*Reyes would never hurt an American—*

but the truth was, heads were rolling down the streets of Acapulco, seventy-two immigrants blindfolded and shot in Tamaulipas, six tortured and dumped in a cave outside Cancún, hearts carved from bodies like cantaloupe balls. This was the new Aztec nation, only these killings had nothing to do with the sun. Had Feo told Reyes that he was still alive?

Theirs not to make reply, Theirs not to reason why, Theirs but to do and die . . .

It was easy to be a hero in a poem.

By noon, his stomach hurt. The looter located a cigarette, sat back, smoked. He pictured Chelo. Lovely Chelo. Like a cello. He wondered if she looked like a cello, but couldn't remember what a cello looked like. He should have taken orchestra in high school. Another regret. He could stack them like poker chips.

He picked up his shovel, his mind caressing her body. He wanted her, all of her, even the baby. The straightness of her hair broke his heart, the openness of her forehead. They made a good pair. She had faith. He had experience. He'd traveled. She did laundry. She'd ironed his shirt that first morning. It was still warm when he slipped it over his chest.

Fucking tree root.

He crawled out for a saw. He'd like to take his girl to the beach, make love in the waves. He'd seen that in a movie once. As he dug, he tinkered with this fantasy. Sometimes her bathing suit evaporated in the water. Sometimes Chelo wasn't pregnant anymore. The baby was napping in a hammock. He'd been a proud fool. Let the girl have her religion.

A dog barked. The looter grabbed his gun, scampered out. On the bluff, a scrappy white dog pressed its snout through the wire fence. The looter aimed, thought better of it, chucked a rock instead. The dog went nuts.

"*¡Faustino!*" Angry Spanish. Maybe the housekeeper.

The looter retreated to the tunnel. He could kill the dog, but not the maid.

"*¿Qué haces ahí?*"

Branches crackled. More barking.

"Someone's digging. Who's down there?"

The looter closed his eyes, pictured the Virgin. At Mari's house, he'd memorized the folds in the Virgin's green cloak, her face, which conveyed serenity and motherly love. Now he asked her to make the housekeeper leave, for her *señora* to call, her kettle to boil, her period to start. Praying gave wishes someplace to go.

"*Basta,*" the woman snapped. "Let the workers alone. You're covered in burrs."

The dog whimpered. Footsteps retreated. Birds. The knife sharpener's beckoning song. The looter dropped his shovel. Forget the tunnel. He wanted the girl.

He couldn't find her house. The streets all looked the same. He stopped a few people and asked if they knew a girl named Chelo. "About so high. Freckles. *Lunares.*" The women shook their heads, scarcely masking their distrust. When a plump woman pushing a stroller asked, "Is Chelo in trouble?" he knew he had her.

"No, no. I am a friend, a visitor, and I lost her address. Maybe I should yell, *Chelo, Chelo.*" He pantomimed calling her, hand to his mouth, wondering if he looked insane. She told him her house was two blocks ahead. Number 48 did not look familiar until he saw the white cat tiptoeing along its wall.

He needed a present. There was a *papelería* on the corner, but that wouldn't do. *Sorry I was a jerk. Here are some crayons.* Next, a shoe store. One summer he'd worked in a shoe store, and he knew the difference between leather and man-made uppers. He'd like to buy Chelo decent shoes, but didn't know her size. After that, a flower shop, thank God. He bought pink tulips and a toy puppy with a red felt tongue. Mexican girls like stuffed animals. He'd noticed this. He was proud of himself, spending money on the girl, thinking about what might please her.

He rang her bell. He was sweating, but who wasn't?

The door opened. Chelo looked like a stick figure a child would draw. Moon belly. Thin arms and legs. Straight hair. A splatter of freckles. A dopey smile took his mouth by surprise. He might love her. Or maybe this was the part before that, before love had a name.

"I found you." He held out his gift. *"Lo siento."*

He'd learned *Lo siento* back in grade school. *Hello. Good-bye. I would like. I'm sorry.* A man could travel the world with four simple expressions. Let his dick and wallet handle the rest. It was easier to apologize in Spanish. The words slid off the tongue. *Lo siento. Lo siento* could be the sound track of his life.

The girl accepted the gifts without expression or thanks. He couldn't read her face. Dirt smudged her cheekbone. She'd been gardening. His grandmother had gardened, had let him drop seeds into holes he poked in the dirt. When sprouts emerged, he'd felt like a father. His pride curled inside him. He might lose his temper or melt at her feet. He gazed past her, hoping the aunt wouldn't show up, hoping the aunt had a debilitating case of elephantiasis.

He tried again. "I prayed to the Virgin and then a pig told me . . . You were right. I came back because I was wrong and I missed you."

Chelo consulted her womb, like the baby had equal say.

He would not grovel. *"¿Puedo pasar?"*

Her hand dropped from the door. He cupped her hip with his palm. A cello. He could picture it now. He didn't deserve this girl, but he could become a man who did. The Maddox Principle of Opposing Equilibrium maintained there was always time to turn the boat around. Work hard. Care. Live by his word.

He kissed her cheek, his lips brushing the dirt. When he pulled back, she was smiling. He could draw her with six easy strokes. Two circles, four lines. But she was simple only on the outside.

She touched his face. "Can you help me in the garden? I can't bend over anymore." She giggled. "I can't even see my feet."

"From now on, your feet are my business."

He said this. He meant it.

three | THE COLLECTOR

Daniel Ramsey couldn't sleep. Nausea. Regret. The stale metallic taste in his mouth. He gazed through the prison bars, into the hallway, which, through an unseen window, was shifting from darkness to light.

A man appeared outside his cell. Six-foot, lanky, with the soapy good looks of a baseball player, a catcher maybe, a man who could call tricky pitches, throw out a runner on first. His cap shadowed everything but the strong line of his jaw. He gripped the bars, hesitant, making up his mind.

"You related to Rose Ramsey, the art teacher?"

Daniel hadn't expected this. "She was my wife."

"Mrs. Ramsey taught me art in middle school. Nice woman. Patient with kids with no talent, like me. She that way with you?"

"Who are you? The warden?"

"Night guard."

"I was on my way to bury her when the cops pulled me over. Damn fools." This was mostly true.

"How long has it been since Mrs. Ramsey passed?"

"Twenty years."

"Took your time."

"She wanted to be buried in Mexico. I was flying there."

"Been saving up?"

"In a way."

"But now you're in jail with a DUI." The guard tapped the door with his foot. "You're supposed to drink *after* you get to Mexico."

"I wasn't drunk."

"You blew a .15."

"I can handle that."

"Report says you nearly smashed a van full of kiddies and ran up over the curb."

"That makes it sound worse than it was. I'll pay the fine."

"You'll pay with your license. Three-month suspension."

"Can I leave the country?"

"You'll have to speak with the judge."

"I'll be back in a week."

"It depends on his mood. Connecticut state law demands two days in jail. Two days to six months. I'd count on a week. Friday, if you're lucky. I wouldn't tell the judge about burying Mrs. Ramsey. It doesn't ring true."

"You got a better story?"

The guard thought for a minute. "Tell him you just retired and this trip was a present from your kids. You're a nervous flier and went a little overboard self-medicating. Tell him how sorry you are, but you can't get a refund on your tour. Promise you won't drive in Mexico."

Daniel nodded, patted his vest, felt his antacids, his compass that glowed in the dark.

The man tilted back, holding the bars. "What do you do for a living? You teach, too?"

"I'm retired and my children just gave me this trip to Mexico—"

"That's good, but I mean really."

"I'm an art collector."

"Paintings?"

"Masks. Pre-Columbian objects. Some folk art."

"Masks?" The man held his palm over his face like a starfish.

Daniel nodded.

"What does an art collector *do*, exactly?"

"You study art, travel, meet dealers, visit artists, locate works of value, or works that will accrue value, either monetarily or culturally, pieces that are exceptional in some way. Rare or old. Unusual. Striking."

"How do you make money?"

"You can sell the collection or sell individual pieces for a profit."

"So you deal art?"

"No, more collect."

"While Mrs. Ramsey was teaching?"

"While Rose was teaching." He wasn't going to explain the economics of their marriage. This was another thing he and Thomas Malone had in common. They had both married money.

"But do you ever finish collecting? What's the end point?"

Daniel sighed. He was tired of explaining. His head hurt. "With masks, you're done when every village or style is well represented. Or you could lose your passion, start collecting something new, or run out of money or make one particularly large purchase, a capstone."

The fact that he was a prisoner struck him with new force. He didn't belong here. His tone grew irritable. "A collection is complete when the whole becomes more than any one part. When it fuses into something meaningful and lasting."

The man chewed this over. "Like family."

Daniel frowned. "Some families. Not all." He was in no mood for sentimental comparisons. "Actually, no collection is ever complete. *I have every stamp. I have the perfect collection of Tiffany glass.* There are always subtleties, offshoots, curiosities. A collection ends when you die. Even then, it isn't done. You are."

"Always more to want."

"More to *learn. Appreciate.* It's like love. Where does that end?"

"You buying more masks when you're down there burying Mrs. Ramsey?" The light was getting stronger now. Dust mites swirled in the air.

"Am I going to buy more masks?" He repeated the question, realizing how the truth would sound. "No, burying my wife. That's it."

The man released the bars. "I had your wife's class twice, I mean for two years. She decorated her classroom with all these posters and quotes. I only remember one. Monet or Matisse, maybe. You might know since you study art."

Daniel couldn't remember Rosie's classroom. Had he ever been to see it? These little resurrections were gifts—as when a friend uncovered a forgotten letter, a photograph or story—and he could add this new memory to the mix of old ones, another collection, forever dwindling, as he and his memory aged.

"What was the quote?" he asked, nervous somehow. Afraid this artifact would prove disappointing, unworthy of her.

"What have you done for color today?"

"What?"

"It was a question: *What have you done for color today?"*

Daniel looked around the cell. "Not much. How about you?"

The man shrugged. "So far? Nothing. But I'm getting off work. Start by cooking my wife breakfast. It's her birthday."

"That's color?"

"Red watermelon. Green rind. I don't know. I'm not an artist."

Daniel Ramsey pictured Rose sitting in her chair, surrounded by art books. Rose had brought color to his life. Love, yes. But spirit and vigor. And Anna, of course. But more than that, Rosie noticed things. Like how the fuchsia blossoms of bougainvillea were not in fact blossoms, but leaves. The actual flowers were tiny and yellow, buried, nearly lost in all that showiness.

He looked up, ready to share this detail, but the man was gone.

Daniel Ramsey listened to the sounds of morning. Crackling scanner. Coffee brewing. The horrors of the previous night belonged to yesterday. Color. What had he done? What would he do? He leaned against the bars, straining to see the window where the light was coming from.

four | ANNA

Emilio Luna looked confused. He had done commissions, but never in stone. The carver kept gazing past Anna as if Salvador might appear. He studied the photograph.

"Lo necesito rápido," Anna said, spinning her hands. The ugly American. It had come to this.

Emilio Luna lowered his chin, his voice soft as dust. "It's not my specialty. You need to go to the coast, where they work stone."

"I don't have time."

"I have other work." The carver gestured to a pile of heart-shaped boxes. "My brother Javier would have to help. It will be too expensive."

"¿Cuánto?"

Emilio Luna looked through the trees. "Four thousand pesos."

Anna winced. "Three thousand?"

His dog sauntered over, settled its rear in the dirt. The carver looked in its blue eyes, letting the animal decide. "Three thousand, five hundred."

"Three thousand."

"The stone is very expensive. *Sería mucho trabajo.*"

"Three thousand five hundred. Three days." She held out her hand. He grasped it with a feathery touch.

"Do you want a deposit?" A bluff. She had only five hundred pesos. Emilio Luna shook his head. No deposit.

One more thing, Anna said. "If you please, *señor*, this is a secret. Don't tell anyone. Not even Salvador."

At the bus stop, Anna's phone rang. Constance Malone.

"You didn't come to work today. We were worried and finally I said, 'I have to call.'"

"Montezuma's revenge," Anna said. "I could barely form sentences. Please tell Thomas for me. I hate to miss work."

Constance invited her to dinner Saturday night. "You'll be human by then."

Saturday night. That would put Anna on the Malones' patio a day after her meeting with the Tiger, assuming she survived that encounter. The timing was perfect. The party would keep Thomas clear of the chapel. The noise would mask the looter's racket.

"I'd love to come," Anna said. "Tell me what to bring."

"Just you," Constance said. "And Salvador."

"I'm not sure I can. We've fallen out of touch."

"Then bring another handsome painter."

Anna promised to try.

She climbed on the local bus, feeling tall and blonde and thin, a flamingo in a duck pond, the wrong color and all out of proportion. As the bus rumbled out of San Juan del Monte, she took pictures through the window, not stopping to focus or compose. Super Medino. A *bici-taxi. Papel picado* hanging like lace. Blue wall. Green wall. Canary-yellow wall. And she thought: *There is more color on one Mexican street than in all of New England.* And she thought: *I belong in this place where I do not belong.*

five | THE LOOTER

*Touring the tunnel was more dog-*like and humbling than he'd imagined, the two of them crawling on their knees. The looter rapped the chapel's foundation with his flashlight to show where he would bust through the floor. Anna looked strung-out in the half-light, like she hadn't slept, or maybe didn't cotton to being alone with a man underground.

"I tried to dig during the day, but the damn dog would bark. Still, at night, sometimes he showed up."

"The dog?"

"Malone."

"Where?"

The looter pointed up, then spun his finger around his temple, the universal sign of crazy. "He talks to himself and moans."

Anna made a face. "He makes me sick. Constance invited me to dinner Saturday night."

"That asshole invited you—"

"No, she did. But it's perfect. He'll be out of the chapel, and we'll make lots of noise."

"You should make a toast. To . . . what's her name?"

"Constance."

"To Constance and her husband, the rapist."

"The impotent rapist." Anna laughed, stopped herself. "I'm worried about the Tiger. What if the copy doesn't fool him?"

"Reyes doesn't remember the mask. He just remembers he wants it."

Anna ran her hand along the chicken wire lining the ceiling. Powder showered her hair. "This is a great tunnel. You could go into business."

"After the mask, I'm out of here."

Anna asked where. He stroked his jaw, considering. This Anna was easy to talk to. Or maybe it was the tunnel. "Back to Colorado. Open a business."

"Marry Chelo?" she teased.

He couldn't stop smiling—Chelo on the brain. He closed his mouth so she wouldn't see his fucked-up teeth.

"You went and saw her, didn't you?" Anna poked him. "I can see it in your face. You two made up."

Not to jinx anything, but he was making plans. He'd fly back to Denver and introduce Chelo to his mother. She would cry she'd be so happy. She'd hang their coats in the closet, show them the powder room. That's what she liked to call it. *The powder room.* Chelo would blush, say something polite in English that she'd rehearsed. *It is a pleasure to meet you. You have a beautiful home.* On the patio, they'd circle chairs, and for once, his mother wouldn't pepper him with questions. Beers in hand, they'd admire the Rockies, stone pyramids sugared up with snow. The looter would point out Pikes Peak and brag to Chelo how he'd once hiked twenty-six miles up and back, stood on the tippy top, and his mother would let that lie stand because he'd gotten close to the summit, close enough. His mother wouldn't ask directly about the baby—*Is that my grandchild?*—but she'd be hoping a girlfriend and baby would bring her prodigal son home. He'd leave the money he owed her by the coffeepot. Not explain a thing. Just let the magic stand for itself.

"Hey"—Anna tossed a stone in his lap—"where are you?"

He grinned. "Underground."

"I need you to be alert. Saturday, seven o'clock. Be here. I'll be there." She pointed up, behind her, to the house. "So long as the Tiger hasn't . . ." Anna dragged her thumb across her neck.

The girl looked unhinged; it made him nervous. He wasn't used to relying on girls for anything but sex and sandwiches. Getting over rape took time, the looter understood that much. His sister had been jumped once and she never liked men again, but maybe she never had. She'd always liked books more than people.

"You got your phone?"

"I got it, but I keep it turned off." He pulled it out of his pocket, regarding it suspiciously.

"Well, turn it on. What if I need to reach you Saturday?" The looter hesitated, then moved the power switch. Anna fingered the ground, as if she'd lost something. "Maybe we should bless the tunnel."

Before he could object, crazy Anna had crawled outside. A minute later, she was back with two sticks and a vine. "The tall stick is you and the shorter one is me. Our paths have crossed."

She looked wild-eyed, but the looter went with it. "Give them to me."

While Chelo was religious, this chick was making shit up on the fly. He wrapped the vine around the sticks like a Boy Scout. He was earning his Rudimentary Christianity in the Wild Merit Badge, his Humoring the Date-Raped Girl Merit Badge. He could add these to his earlier badges in Archaeology, Advanced Tunnel Building, and Scoring Drugs in a Foreign City. He was on his way to Eagle Scout.

The cross looked pretty damn official, he had to admit, resting against the tunnel. He didn't have the heart to tell Anna that the Virgin hadn't actually spoken to him in the cathedral. Digging had been his idea.

Anna eyed the cross. "Do you think it will protect us?"

In the distance, a donkey belched, as though he was tired of being a jackass, thank you, it was someone else's turn. The looter palmed Anna's boot.

"Protect us against Reyes?" He remembered a line from some country song, or maybe this was his own voice, a baby step closer to wise.

"I'm sorry, little darling," he said. "We're too far gone for that."

six | THE DRUG LORD

"¿Vivo?"

Reyes scratched his fake mustache. He was bald today, in a politician's suit, looking like Carlos Salinas, the exiled former president, the Harvard fucker who rigged ballot boxes, whose friends and relations often wound up dead. Reyes checked his reflection in the gilded mirror. Okay, maybe not Carlos Salinas. Maybe his chunky brother Raúl, the *cabrón* whose wife was caught withdrawing $84 million from a Swiss bank account.

"Alive?" Reyes repeated. "I wanted him dead."

The drug lord poked his sandwich. Sausage with chili. Heartburn seared his chest. He burped up a tamale from three days before. Who needed to keep a diary with a gut like his?

"Are you an assassin or a nun? Do I need to show you?"

Reyes pointed a pistol out the open window, shot at nothing. Birds jumped out of the trees, discombobulated, flapping.

"Feo. That's me. Shooting you. Can you hear it? When I want to kill something, I kill it."

He bit into his sandwich, opened his desk drawer, wiped his greasy fingers on a five-hundred-peso bill.

"How the hell would I know where he is? Look where drug addicts go. Just find him before I find you."

Reyes propped his feet on the desk, leaned back. It was good when things went right, but also good when things went wrong. If everything always went right, he'd be out of a job.

"Feo? You know what? *Con todo respeto,* you're ugly. That's the only reason I keep you alive. You make me look good. You're my point of comparison."

Reyes stood, shook out his pants.

"Maybe you saw wrong? Now you're backpedaling. If you saw his ghost, kill the ghost, too."

Silence. The birds scurried back into the tree. He fired. They took off like crazy. Too much shit inside those birds. No manners at all.

"Feo, you're killing me, and I'm already dying."

He clicked his laptop. His screen saver was his favorite prostitute, Suerte. Breasts like mountaintops. Made killer *pozole.* What they had was special. They would sit outside under a *palapa* at his villa in Acapulco and watch the sun drop into the sea, hire a gypsy guitarist to sing his heart out, sand everywhere, rum, hot tub, pinball, pork rinds, caviar, cocaine, trumpets, bodyguards, Viagra, helicopter humming. Yes, it was romantic. He was not ready to give up this life. Cancer could take a number. He was busy.

"*Cabrón*, that's a joke. I am not dying until I kill you. Then I can rest in peace."

He caressed his chest. The birds were back in the trees. Let them shit in peace. He could be generous, but not with the digger. That emaciated, drug-addicted American asshole was going to learn a lesson he'd be too dead to use. Like the last Salinas brother, Enrique, found murdered in his car outside Mexico City, plastic bag over his head.

"Bring me the head of John the Baptist. . . . I saw it in a movie once. And a painting. Caravaggio. Ever heard of him? Stupid question."

He rubbed his bad ear.

"Okay, if you can't bring me his head, then bring me your dick and I'll eat that for lunch. Good thing I'm not too hungry. Ha ha."

A *patrón* had to be ugly. People expected it. It gave them courage to follow through. You could never talk to a person the way you talked to a video camera.

"I want him dead. More dead than last time. No more bedtime baths. Bullets."

He hung up, called Suerte.

"I need you, baby. I don't want to die with you left undone."

seven | ANNA

Emilio Luna sat shirtless in the
shade, sanding heart boxes. Seeing Anna, he hopped into his house,
returned wearing a shirt and carrying a turquoise mask. He handed it
to Anna.

"*La máscara es bonita.*" She bit her lip, fishing for the right words.
"But it doesn't look the same as the other."

The carver considered her critique before disagreeing. "Javier works
stone in Mitla. They have worked stone for hundreds of years."

"Yes, but the face looks different. Where's the photograph?"

The carver fetched it. Anna held photo and mask side by side.

"It is better this way," the carver said. "You don't want an angry
mask."

Anna resisted the urge to smash the mask over his head. She was
meeting the Tiger in two days. A dry breeze blew between them. She
had no more money, so she tried flattery instead.

"Your brother is famous, a real artist. I know he can handle even the most delicate jobs. The two masks need to be . . ." The heat had melted her brain. *"Idénticas."*

The carver muttered something, prayer or curse, wiped his face with his shirttail. "Javier is away."

"When will he return?"

"Depende."

Anna wanted to climb into a heart box, close its perfect wooden door. She looked into his eyes. "If you do the work by Friday afternoon, I will be very content and will tell all my American friends about your remarkable masks."

She hated herself as she said this. Emilio Luna waved away this stupidity, sat back on his stump and resumed sanding. Anna reeled with dizziness. She hadn't brought any water. She was hungry and had to pee. *I would be so grateful.* That was what she wanted to say. But the conditional of *agradecer* was beyond her, given the heat, her anxiety. Instead, she said the one thing that might persuade a Mexican carver to help a demanding gringa.

"Por favor, señor. It's a present for my mother."

The man looked up, saw something in her face he recognized. That she was lying but had no choice.

"Viernes por la tarde."

Anna thanked him, turned, stopped cold. Salvador was leaning against the fence, wearing a gas station shirt embroidered BOB.

He sized her up, gave her a half smile, as if he found her both charming and despicable. "You are a good liar."

"So are you."

"Me?" He reached for her hand. Anna spun away. Salvador followed her to the street.

"I came to apologize," he said. "I have a bad temper. I can help you sell the mask to a good place for a reasonable price. We can work together, if you let me help."

Anna wasn't ready to relinquish her anger.

"You're too late. The mask is locked in Thomas Malone's chapel, but we've got a plan to get it out."

"*We?*"

"The looter and I."

"What looter?"

"Christopher Maddox. He's a twigger, a rather *famous* twigger in some circles." Seeing his confusion, she added, "A meth addict who digs relics." Salvador looked horrified. "But he's straight now and he's digging a tunnel under the chapel. It's almost done."

"You think that is safe?"

"The tunnel?"

"The twigger."

Anna shrugged. "I trust him. *He* hasn't lied to me yet. You could have told me about your girlfriend, or is that how things roll with cool Mexican painters? Everything easy. *Todo azul.*"

She'd picked up this expression somewhere. Everything's cool. All blue.

"What girlfriend?"

"The *fresa.*" Anna fluffed her hair. "Strawberry" was a disparaging term for a spoiled Mexican woman.

"My sister?"

Anna scrunched her face. "C'mon. Your sister?" She imitated his accent. "*I was once asked to be a father, but I declined. One must know his limits.*"

358

"Híjole." He looked down the road after a chicken. "You drove here?"

"I took the bus." This, too, seemed to be his fault. The heat was his fault. The Tiger was his fault. He had not helped her in any way.

"I need to show you something," he said. "After that, if you still want to go, you can."

"How did you know I was here?"

"Uncle Emilio is a good man, but he can't keep a secret."

Anna kept her eyes on the fence, debating. She wanted to believe in him, in someone, and she really didn't want to take the bus.

They walked to his car. The seats were scalding. He fished up a CD. "Since we are fighting, we will listen to music."

Mercedes Sosa sang "María, María" as they drove out of town. Anna's father had this CD. As a girl, Anna decided it was the world's saddest song. María deserved to live and love like other people but couldn't. She didn't have the force, the dreams, the desire, the grace . . . Anna ticked through her own shortcomings, one for each telephone pole. *I am impatient. I drink too much. I want to be the most beautiful woman in the room. I pretend to be happier than I am. I want to believe in God, but don't know where to start. I love to travel, but have no sense of direction. I can't imagine being a mother. I am careless with everything but words. I hate to spend money, and worry I will run out. I don't listen when people tell me their names. I sleep with men I don't like because I don't want to hurt their feelings. I'd rather be unhappy than cause someone else unhappiness, but then I resent people who make me unhappy. Sometimes I look at people I love and feel nothing at all.*

To be Anna. To be loved. To be loved as Anna.

It would require a fucking saint.

———

He took her to a bank in the city. Miss Venezuela was helping a customer. She wore a navy blue suit and her hair was piled into a crown, fallen strands artfully framing her face.

When her customer left, she came around her desk to greet them, kissing Salvador's cheek. In that instant, Anna hated them both, for being Mexican, for having more in common with each other than with her, for leaving her out of the cheek-kissing world of colonial Mexico with its church bells and picturesque decay.

"Victoria, this is Anna, the friend I mentioned. Anna, this is Victoria."

He said this in English. The implication was clear: Victoria's English was better than Anna's Spanish. Victoria had it all working. Victoria was Mexican and beautiful and spoke English and was pregnant with Salvador's child. Victoria probably stuffed her own tamales. She offered Anna her hand, soft as a bird. Her femininity made Anna want to howl.

"Anna observed you were pregnant." Salvador's voice had an edge.

Anna glared at him. Heat fanned down her body.

"She wants to know if your baby is mine."

Victoria tilted her head, confused. Salvador clarified. "She saw us in the *zócalo* last week. You were crying and I was holding your hands. She thinks you are my girlfriend."

Victoria gave a sympathetic tsk-tsk, as if to remind Anna that any Mexican woman has more in common with any American woman than with any Mexican—or American—man.

"Oh no, Anna." Victoria shook her index finger. "This is a mistake.

Salvador is not my boyfriend. The father of my baby is an even bigger *cabrón* than my brother."

For dinner, they ate rice and beans, and avocados sprinkled with cilantro and lime. Anna could not stop touching him, his hands, his shoulder, his lips. They discovered a scorpion the size of Anna's pinkie climbing the wall. With a piece of cardboard, Salvador tipped it into a jam jar filled with rubbing alcohol. The creature floated to the surface. A snow globe. Deadly. Clear.

Victoria had considered an abortion. The day Anna had seen them, she'd asked Salvador to drive her to Mexico City, but he had urged her to wait a few days, and in that time, she had changed her mind. Telling her mother had been difficult, but a grandchild was coming, and the excitement of this fact overshadowed their mother's contempt for the baby's father, whom she called "the rhinoceros from Monterrey."

Anna and Salvador agreed to start over. She told him about her father's collection, the looter, the Tiger. He told her stories about art disappearing in Mexico, none more egregious than the theft of Lord Pakal's death mask, which disappeared from the National Museum of Anthropology, along with one hundred other artifacts, on Christmas Eve in 1985. No alarm. No fingerprints. Almost four years later, the jade mask was discovered in an abandoned house in Acapulco. The thieves were two vet school dropouts who had climbed through an air-conditioning duct.

"Your looter friend is part of the problem. He steals from the dead."

"He was an addict. He's getting better."

"A drug addict does not change day to night. You put too much trust in him. One day, he will pull a gun."

"You have a better idea?"

Salvador looked away.

They couldn't agree on a course of action. Practically. Morally. In the United States, the mask would be safe, but Salvador was adamant that Mexican art should stay in Mexico. "Once objects are taken from their context, history is lost."

"You're saying we shouldn't have museums?"

"We need museums for the same reason we need zoos, but animals still need to live in the wild. Ancient people were buried with treasures. Should you dig up every grave when there is no money and no place to care for these things? We don't have to *see* everything. We can imagine them. We can wonder. We can leave them for someone else."

"But the mask was already dug up."

He stood, started to pace. "Right. That is the problem. Now it has to *belong* to someone. It used to belong just to itself."

Anna was getting irritated, too. There was no right answer. "Okay. Let's leave it with Thomas Malone. He'll watch over it."

Salvador laughed sharply. "I can ask around, see if any of my museum contacts would accept it."

"Why wouldn't they?"

"Would you want to be on duty when Reyes arrives to take back his treasure?"

Anna frowned. "Until we have the mask, it's all moot."

"Moot?" Salvador scowled. He was in no mood to learn new words. He stood up, sat down again, took her hands. "Forget the mask," he said. "Tell me more about you. Tell me how your mother died in Mexico—"

"I've forgotten so much."

He said tell me what you remember.

Her father was ill with a stomach bug. Rose had taken Anna to La Esperanza to pick up some masks. It had rained all day, but her mother was
cheerful. Every time Rose popped back in the car, her flushed face
looked younger. Anna sat with a bag of chips, licking chili off her fingers, eyeing a cardboard box holding several scary masks they'd bought
earlier that day. Anna had asked her mother why the carvers never
made princess masks. Her mother had promised to find her a mask she
liked, and now this promise had escalated into a challenge. Rose looked
all afternoon without success, and her expression tightened with each
disappointment.

"Let's go home," Anna had whined. "To the hotel with Daddy."

"You mean the bar?" Her mother's eyes snapped. She touched
Anna's knee. "Sorry. I'm going to find you a nice mask."

Eventually, she gave up, headed back. The road narrowed to barely
two lanes. It was raining. Anna drew hearts in the misty windows.

"Be careful," Anna said. She was pretty sure she'd said that.

Her mother flexed her fingers over the wheel. "I am. Very careful."
Or maybe she'd said, "Don't worry. I've got it."

Anna's eyes closed. She was cold and wanted to be back at the hotel,
eating a quesadilla, watching dubbed cartoons.

"How much longer?"

"Halfway. Take a catnap."

There was no quicker way to kill the desire for a nap than to be told to take one. Her mother pressed the brakes, cursed softly. "Someone's slid off the road."

A van had skidded perpendicular, blocking their lane and half the opposite one. Its hazard lights blinked red.

"Don't stop. You can get by."

"We'll fall into the ravine." Her mother shifted into park. "Wait here. I'll see if they can move. If not, we'll have to turn around."

"I don't want to go back." Anna pouted.

Her mother looked into Anna's eyes. "Me, neither."

Those were her mother's last words to her: *Me, neither.* Anna had been complaining about a situation her mother could not change, and her mother had reminded her that she didn't like it, either, that neither of them wanted to go back to the village, a place where you couldn't find a beautiful mask no matter how hard you tried. Years later, Anna read more into those words. Maybe her mother didn't care much about masks. Maybe she was exuberant that day because she liked having a quest of her own, instead of traipsing behind her husband.

Her mother opened the car door and ran. The van's driver lowered his window. Her mother gestured to their car. Her pants were getting wet. Rain was such a crazy idea, if you thought about it—clean water falling from the sky. The van started up. Why had it stopped if it wasn't broken down? Why hadn't the driver righted his vehicle and driven on? Her mother was still talking, practicing all those verbs she'd memorized. *They're like a song. You have to sing them.* How many verbs did a mother use in a day? Eat, sleep, work, want, dream, listen, teach, thank, hold, hope, comfort, be.

They could have left earlier. They could have driven around.

Five minutes earlier or later and her mother would not have been standing in the road when a drunk man in a dented truck swerved around the Ramseys' car and lost control. Five minutes earlier or later and her mother's soul would not have flown over the mountain on the back of an eagle.

Salvador massaged her temples, and the sound muffled his voice saying he was sorry.

Anna said, "I saw then how a family could disappear in an instant. The more you have, the more you can lose."

"Children at a distance."

"Everything at a distance. That's my problem." Her head was hot and achy. "I don't even like masks. I helped write that book and I don't like them. I like one or two, the plain ones, but the Ramsey Collection can go to hell."

"Now you are blaming the masks."

"Okay, should I blame Mexico? This country made my family and destroyed it. I said I was never coming back here, and here I am."

"Where was the accident?"

"The highway to La Esperanza. My father put a cross in the ground there, the kind Thomas Malone likes to collect."

That night, she borrowed a green T-shirt to sleep in. Its boyishness pleased her. How cool it would be to wake up and find a note inside its pocket. Someday, she would do that for him. Put a note in the pocket over his heart. He tucked her in with great care, like she was another artifact he wanted to save.

———————

Anna woke first, made coffee, crawled back into bed. Salvador pulled her close. His body felt tense. A church bell tolled, one, then another. "The plan is no good," he whispered into her scalp. "Why is he inviting you to his house? He's going to kill us all and dump us in the chapel."

"You just don't want to wave the American flag again."

"Go U-S-A. Go Disneylandia. Go bomb—"

"If you hate the U.S., then screwing over the American should cheer you up."

"I don't like your country, but I like some of its people." He kissed the part in her hair. "But he will be suspicious. Why go see a man who attacked you?"

"He's so crazy he probably thinks I liked it."

Her phone bleeped. She reached for it. David. So the wedding is off?

She hesitated, her stomach tightened with dread. She hated to cut strings. *Never commit to anything you can't take back, never reject someone you might want later.*

Salvador pulled her arm. "What?"

Anna passed him the phone.

"May I write him back?"

"If you let me see it first."

"He asked you a question. A stupid question, but a question. 'The wedding is off?' So you write back. 'Yes.' What's his name? David. 'Yes, David, the wedding is off.' Because he is a *burro* and may not understand, you add this." He passed her the phone. "This is what you say to a liar."

Te he visto la cara.

I have seen your face.

"He doesn't speak Spanish."

Salvador nodded. "Good."

They drove back to San Juan del Monte to see Emilio Luna. The second mask was not *idéntica*, but was convincing enough, they hoped, to fool a tiger. And just in case it wasn't, Salvador borrowed his cousin's gun.

eight | THE GARDENER

Monte Albán looked majestic in the
moonlight, the stone platforms, the ball court, the palace, each rock a
gravestone of a fallen culture. He dug and gazed down at the two val-
leys of Oaxaca—Tlacolula, Zimatlán. He dug and the night spoke to
him, murmuring in Spanish, in Nahuatl, rattling prognostications of
doom. When he slept, he dreamt he was awake. Awake, he dreamt of
the Aztecs. He did not feel safe—at home, in bed, on the street. Trees
pointed their branches. Squirrels smelled his stink. He'd killed Pedro,
the old woman. (Accidents, or were they?) The girl, he feared, was next.
Mexico, Mother Mexico. Take me in your arms. His breath against his
mask warmed his face.

The grass rustled. He spun around with a cry. A strange creature with
four legs and two heads was sauntering toward him. Llama or mythical
beast. A two-headed creature. He gave a stifled cry of fear. *The seventh*

omen. The demons had followed him here. As the beast approached, it pulled apart, morphing into a man and a woman. The American and a Mexican, though he had told the girl to come alone. The Tiger touched his machete. They stopped ten meters from him, uncertain.

The Mexican called out, *"Trajimos la máscara.* We trade it for the ashes."

"Have the girl bring it to me."

The man stepped forward. "We don't want problems."

"Her, not you."

She walked forward, set down a bundle before him. He caught her arm, threw her down, pressed his machete against her bare neck.

"Don't touch her," the Mexican yelled.

The Tiger swung the knife, marking time. "I am keeping her until I see it."

The Mexican produced a gun.

The Aztec voices grew louder, interrupting, overlapping. The Tiger cut a lock of the girl's hair, let it float to the ground. The Mexican widened his stance, gun nippy in his hand. The Tiger squeezed the girl's wrist. She was sobbing. *"Déjame.* Let me go. I am close to Reyes. We have relations."

This was either a lie that sounded true or a truth that sounded like a lie. It was true Reyes had no taste. He bedded the daughters of the Mexican elite. He bedded transsexuals from Tepito. If stranded in the desert, he'd put his dick down a snake hole.

"Estás mintiendo." You are lying.

"Look at me." The girl pushed forward her ruined face. "If you hurt me, he will kill you."

"¿Es verdad?" the Tiger called back to the Mexican, who held still for a moment, then lowered his gun.

The girl bit the air, doglike, feral. "Part of his right ear is missing."

The eyeholes of his tiger mask let in two fallen moons of light. It was hard to breathe with the heat and the voices. Only one omen remained—the burning temple. He was a sick animal. He had not understood this before. Did the papershop girl love him, or was he simply the evil she preferred? He lifted the machete over his chest. To die in sacrifice to the gods was the highest honor, the Aztecs believed— a guarantee you would be reborn and live in the house of the Sun. The sins of this life mattered little. What mattered was how you died.

"Don't do that."

The girl rose, yanked his arm. The machete fell. She grabbed the urn, ran to her boyfriend. The Tiger slashed the plastic. Turquoise. Shell eye. Warts. Looter to Reyes to Pedro to crone to girl to Tiger.

"Vete derechito a la chingada." The Mexican's voice cracked. He was propping up the girl. "Stay away from us."

The pair retreated with the gun and the urn, morphing back into a shuffling, two-headed, primordial creature. Hugo wished he could ride that animal all the way to Veracruz. He dropped to his knees, offered Montezuma's mask to the moon. His father looked down with his scythe and empty belly. A fox blinked. A lynx peeked around a rock. He laid the mask in the hole.

He was betraying Reyes as Pedro had betrayed Reyes. The drug lord would put a contract on his head. So be it. Only by resistance would the bloody reign of the *narcos* end. It would not be the United States or the Mexican army and certainly not the Mexican puppet president who set things right in the country he loved. It would be a million hearts refusing to obey orders. The gardener bowed his head. *God will save a man who has done one brave thing.*

nine | ANNA

The man who had pressed a machete to her throat now looked downright pious as he hoisted the death mask to the moon. How small, yet how large. Small as man, large as man's loneliness on a night when he speaks to God and wonders if anyone hears him. For a moment, Anna forgot that the mask was a forgery.

The Tiger picked up his shovel. Dirt flew in graceful arcs. "Who *is* that?" Anna hissed. She hugged the urn against her chest. They were hiding behind a bluff, peering out. "Why's he digging? Is that for the mask? He's supposed to give it to Reyes."

"Not our problem."

"Why bury the thing you've been trying to find? It makes no sense. Maybe he's Indian."

Salvador looked at her like she was nuts. "So what if he's Indian? We're all Indian. He's a murderer."

Anna shut up. What she'd meant was, maybe he's spiritual, or he had a purpose beyond money or drugs, a purpose higher than her own. The Tiger laid down his shovel, laid the mask in the hole. Anna pointed. Salvador made a face she couldn't read. She didn't know him that well, really. They were just beginning. Setting out in the evening. Travelers. Traveling together.

The Tiger stomped the ground, made the sign of the cross, and walked off toward the ball court. Anna and Salvador waited to be sure he was gone. Anna surveyed the grounds. The South Platform. The North Platform. The tombs. If the dead were alive, they were here tonight. And she thought: *Clouds fly higher during the day than at night.*

"We need to dig up that mask."

"No, we don't. *No vale.*"

"*Sí, vale.* I need two masks. One for me, one for the looter."

"You can't give the fake. He will know you cheated him. He is the one who dug it up."

"He was crackers on meth when he dug up that mask. He didn't even recognize me. He's not a mask guy. He's a drug guy."

"*He's a very famous twigger.*" He was mocking her, quoting her to herself. "I thought you were friends. *We talked all night long.* You would feel bad tricking him." Part statement, part question.

"It's a victimless crime." Bogus expression. Something guilty politicians said. "He wants the mask for a shrine. For decoration. In church, people pray to figures of Jesus. You don't need Christ's *real* body. They use *representations.*" That sounded better. "Besides, what he doesn't know won't hurt him."

The double negative lost Salvador. It reminded Anna of the cryptic

Mexican expression *No hay mal que por bien no venga,* a grab bag of negatives that roughly translated to *Nothing bad happens without creating some good.*

Salvador rested his hands on his hips, as if he needed support to stay vertical. She liked looking at him. Every single time.

"Will you help me?" she said.

"No tenemos una pala."

Anna wiggled her fingers.

"Hijo de puta, qué mujer."

"Give me a boost."

Anna secured the urn against a tree trunk, then hoisted herself up the bluff. She saw no one, and the quiet filled her with relief and dread. The patch of broken dirt was easy to find. She knelt and dug with her hands. Salvador used his foot. The irony of the moment did not escape her: She'd come to Mexico to bury her mother and instead was robbing a grave. Her father had several burial artifacts, but it was different to dig up something yourself, like killing a chicken instead of buying it at the store. Here was the really crazy part: Even though the mask was a copy, she felt a rush of excitement. A treasure hunt. Dog after bone. She wanted to be the one to find it. So this was the high, the tantalizing elixir that had mesmerized her father all those years, that kept him plunging into the countryside to find a certain Señor Martínez Gómez Hernández Rodríguez who made Grasshopper masks. Anna crawled over the dirt to kiss Salvador. His lips were cool. His mouth, warm.

"I dig you."

He looked confused. There would always be this gap. Nuances of language and culture. *But you get more, dummy. You get everything he can teach you.* She kissed him again. She was good at beginnings, so-so at middles, terrible at the end. *We won't end, then. Every day, we'll walk to the train station with our suitcases and travel someplace new. Every day, we'll leave. Start over. It is a pleasure to meet you. My name is Anna. I am good at beginnings.*

Their toil warmed them. Anna imagined the looter digging alone in a dark cave. That required real courage, real drugs. She struck something hard. A lost bit of shell saw the moon and smiled.

They drove down from Monte Albán in silence, the urn snug at her feet. She held the mask in her lap, wondering whether Salvador now thought less of her or more. As they took the third bend, Anna gasped and sank. "It's him." The Tiger's sedan was parked on the road's edge. A man bent over the open hood with a flashlight. Salvador kept driving, face rigid.

"We need to follow him," Anna said.

"You have the mask."

"But I want to know who he is."

"No importa."

"Sí, importa. I want to see him."

"Forget him."

"Right. I want to see him so I can forget him."

They pulled off the road. Three minutes later, the car streamed past. The place the Tiger led them could not have surprised them more. Not a slum on the edge of the city or the gilded palace of Óscar Reyes Carrillo. No, the Tiger's car stopped someplace utterly familiar. Salvador shook his head, incredulous. "You Americans all come to Mexico to lose your minds."

They parked as close as they dared, lowered their windows. The

Tiger was preoccupied with the lockbox, punching in the numeric code. The wrought-iron gates swung open. He climbed back in his car, pulled in a yard or two, changed his mind, turned off the ignition, his car poised just inside the gate. Anna heard the front door open, the familiar cursing as Thomas shuffled the dogs out of the way. Footsteps. Spanish.

"Where have you been?" It was Thomas. Their voices were faint but audible.

"Visiting my uncle."

"I got a postcard from Reyes today. He says you work for him now."

"No, señor."

"All this time I hired and housed you and Soledad, you were running for Reyes. You brought him the death mask. You knew my show was coming up and you brought the mask to that—"

Eyes wide, Anna mouthed to Salvador, *Hugo.*

"Señor, it wasn't that way. I never gave a mask to Reyes."

"My own gardener is working for a drug lord. Do you take me for an idiot? Were you going to kill us? Murder us in our sleep? Rob us and run away?"

"He said he would kill me. Take pity. *No me—*"

A gunshot rang out. Anna buried her head in Salvador's chest. Every bad thing kept getting worse.

"Thomas!" Constance yelled from the second floor. "Was that fireworks?"

Which man had been shot? Anna didn't know what to hope for.

"No worries, puppet," Thomas called up. "I shot a squirrel that was brazenly, shamelessly, eating your basil. I'll be right back. Let me dump it next door and we'll have a drink."

Hugo's car backed up, drove down the road, then disappeared into the abandoned lot at the end of the block. A minute later, Thomas emerged, strolled past their car, not hearing the two slumped people breathing inside.

"Puppet, come sit with me," Thomas called up, closing the gate behind him. "I've got a lead on a mask from this Canadian tribe. The Wild Woman of the Woods. Can you hear me?"

"What? I can't hear you."

"I feel like a Shakespearean actor calling my lover through an open window."

"Talk louder. I'm doing my face. I've got this cream on. Ungodly mess."

"My new mask, it's is called the Wild Woman of the Woods. She's got a beard, and a mouth like a bullet hole, and goes *wuu, wuu* like an owl. They say she kidnaps children and eats them."

"Eats the children?"

"But she's got a good side. Every so often, Dzonoqua, that's her name, picks a few lucky souls and makes them rich as Croesus. *And* she can bring back the dead." Thomas cackled. "I'd better hope that trick doesn't work."

The screen door slammed. The sounds of the night rose around them—the fizz of the mosquito zapper, the discordant stew of ranchero music, the barking of hungry dogs.

Salvador drove three blocks to a neighborhood church. Anna could not remember feeling so awake or so tired. Thomas had killed Hugo. It was hard to feel too bad, and yet in the battle between the American collector and the proud Indian—rightly, wrongly, that's how she thought of him now—she sided with the Indian.

"We need to check on Hugo," she said.

"Someone will find him in the morning."

"We should call the police."

"They are the last people to call."

"We can't leave him there like roadkill."

"What's that?"

"A dead squirrel."

"He could shoot us."

"You said he's dead."

Salvador tensed. "We need to go."

"What if he's alive? We could call the hospital."

"We are going to save the man who tried to kill us?"

"Yes," Anna said. "We are."

They crossed Amapolas and crept into the empty field, stepping around bombed-out appliances, knots of barbed wire, an upended bathtub. The Tiger's car formed a vague shape in the distance. *All over Mexico, there are fields like this where bodies have been dumped.* Anna couldn't fathom that the Tiger was dead, and she braced for him to leap out of the darkness, machete in hand. Salvador reached the car first. He peered through the back window, holding up a hand to stop her. She waited. She hated waiting, but she waited. He checked the driver's seat, hand still raised.

"You won't believe it," he said.

"He's dead?" A sudden sadness struck her. A tingle of emotion.

"I don't know if he's dead," Salvador replied. He looked uneasy. "There's blood everywhere, but the car is empty."

ten | THE GARDENER

Hugo awoke to his wife's face.
Maybe he was dreaming, but this wasn't like his Aztec nightmares. This dream felt three-dimensional, alive. Through tree branches, stars winked and the night air cooled his nostrils. Soledad opened his shirt, laid her hands over his shoulders. She shook him gently.

"Wake up. What has that bastard done? Speak to me."

He could not speak, but he could smell: iron and apples, perfume and flies. His gut was torn and his arm was bleeding. He was lying in a wheelbarrow in a thicket near his house. His pain was as big as the sky, and blacker.

Soledad untied the tiger mask roped to his belt, spat in its wooden hull, threw it in the bushes. She kissed his forehead. Hugo knew he was the only man his wife had ever loved, yet he had treated her like a dog. She had repaid his cruelty by saving his life.

She helped him sit up. The tendons in her neck strained with the effort. Her hair was matted to her face with his blood. She wrapped her apron around his side to slow the bleeding, muttering something about a doctor.

"I brought you this far," she whispered. "Can you walk a little? Lean on me, my love. I will carry you home."

eleven | THE COLLECTOR

Daniel Ramsey walked out of jail
into a new day. Tree limbs silhouetted the pale sky. The morning sun
shyly asserted itself. This cab was going to cost a mint, but what did it
matter? Nothing mattered except what did. February was behind him.
The snow had nearly melted. The air smelled like mud, something
green growing. When the taxi swerved into the lot, he opened the door
and collapsed inside, his body wracked with stiffness, his knees a confusion of grousing cartilage. He was thirsty for comfort he knew only
one way to find. The driver asked where he was going. Daniel told him,
then urged him to hurry. "Is it Friday?" he asked the driver. "March
second?" The driver confirmed it was. They pulled onto Route 1,
passed big-box stores, fast food, then out to the country. He admired
the landscape, the colors, distinguishing gray from beige from ecru.

twelve | THE LOOTER

The looter sat by a fountain,
waiting for Chelo to get her hair cut. Ever since his trip in Chapultepec
Park, he'd been mesmerized by fountains. The way water rose and fell
and rose again. The swirl of rainbows and bubbles. The spare change
tossed in the basin. The currency of wishes. The sound of running
water reminded him of Mari's garden, a place that had changed him, a
place he might have to revisit, now and then, for that change to stick.

His phone rang. Force of habit, he answered it, before the long
name on caller ID—Fernando Regalado Manuel—registered and he
realized his mistake. He listened. Just breathing. The looter's heart
ached as he wondered if the three-letter word on the other end could
deduce his location from the ambient noise.

"Feo?"

"*Señor arqueólogo. ¿Dónde estás?*"

"Here. I am here."

"And where is that?"

The looter looked around, getting his bearings. "I don't know, but I'm starting over. Clearing house. *Cleaning* house." Language poured out of him. Explanation. The miracle of it all. He wanted Feo to understand, be happy for him. "I found a nice girl. She's religious. I'm going to find a real job."

Feo laughed. "Altar boy?"

"Tell Reyes to find a new digger. Tell Gonzáles, too."

"Gonzáles may take a bath."

"Okay, well . . ."

"I have to kill you."

"No, you don't. I'm nobody. No body. No face. Forget me."

"*Ya es demasiado tarde para olvidar.*"

"No," the looter argued. "It's not too late to forget. There's lots of fucking time left." Was he pleading? The bushes. The branches. The spaces between them.

"You make a life and then you don't want to live it anymore. Doesn't work that way."

The looter was pacing, making circles. "This is a clean break."

"*No, arqueólogo.* We see you soon. I'm tracking your cell. Is that water I hear?"

The looter dropped the phone, stomped on it, hurled the cracked plastic into the fountain. He jumped up, feet together, a human pogo stick. *Alive. Alive. Alive.* The smartphone was his last tie to Reyes and it was underwater now, a black box surrounded by pesos.

He stared at it and made a wish. Or maybe a prayer.

One of those ugly hairless Mexican dogs jogged toward him. Its torso was solid flank muscle, dirt-brown and gleaming. The dog made eye contact, if you could call it that, fixed its gaze on him. Its cigar tail wagged impatiently, like it had an appointment, like it was already late.

thirteen | THE PAPERSHOP GIRL

Her mother dragged her to a
Frida Kahlo show. Lola scowled the entire way there, huddled in the
backseat as Esmeralda drove. Since moving to Veracruz, her mother
had become good friends with the plastic surgeon's wife, who sparkled
just like her name, all starry nails and Styrofoam hair. They liked
museums. Clutching each other, the two women teetered along, utter-
ing stupidities, like which painting would look good over the couch
and which they could have done better themselves.

Lola had no interest in Frida Kahlo. Her hideous mustache and
unibrow were silkscreened on every tourist tote, as if she was the only
Mexican woman who mattered, as if all the rest were peasants or under-
paid undersecretaries to undersecretaries to Señor Nada. The most
famous women in Mexican history were:

The Virgin Mary

La Malinche

Frida Kahlo

Selena

Salma Hayek

A virgin, a traitor, a freak, a murdered singer, and Salma Hayek, who was smart and sexy, but, of course, had to play Frida Kahlo in the movie. She would play the Virgin Mary someday, too. Work her way down the list.

Lola called out: "Regina says Frida Kahlo was a drug addict."

Her mother said, "Nobody's perfect."

Esmeralda regripped the leather steering wheel. "Who's Regina?"

Her mother murmured something under her breath.

Lola tried again. "Regina says Frida Kahlo hated the United States."

"Who could blame her?"

"Diego Rivera slept with Frida Kahlo's younger sister."

Her mother sighed. "Men have no self-control."

"Frida Kahlo had an abortion."

Her mother crossed herself.

"Frida Kahlo had surgery just to get Diego Rivera's attention."

"If you dress better, you won't have to do that."

The show was crowded. Paintings, of course, but also photographs and drawings. Quotes in calligraphy swooped across the walls. *"Surrealism is the magical surprise of finding a lion in the closet when you were sure of finding shirts."*

And Lola thought: *Surrealism is the magical surprise of finding your father in your bedroom when you were planning to masturbate.*

Her anger felt fresh and vivid. So did her sadness. She wanted to tell her mother about her father's visits. She wanted to tell her mother she had a lover. An older man, like the *cabrona* Frida Kahlo. But she kept her mouth shut, knowing her mother would blame her. One way or another, she'd lose even more.

Frida Kahlo's biography was printed on the wall. Polio as a child. When she was eighteen, the bus she was riding was hit by a tram. Her spine and pelvis were crushed. She wore a cast, endured endless rounds of surgery. She had planned to be a doctor, but became an artist instead. Diego Rivera was twice her age. They married. He slept around. They divorced. They remarried. *"There have been two grave accidents in my life. One was the trolley, and the other was Diego. Diego was by far the worst."*

Frida Kahlo spent her life painting Frida Kahlo. Frida with monkeys. Frida with Diego like a bullet in her brain. Frida Kahlo could not have children. She slept with women. She slammed tequila. She arrived at her first solo exhibit in an ambulance, sirens blaring. She had a leg amputated. She died at forty-seven. She may have killed herself. She had to share her husband with every woman who turned up in Coyoacán. Her husband's prick was part of the Grand Tour. Who wanted to have sex with a three-hundred-pound, frog-faced *cabrón*? The last words in her journal were: *"I hope the exit is joyful—and I hope never to return."*

Rebellion rose in Lola's throat. Frida Kahlo was not scared to show the places that hurt. This is my aborted child. This is my pregnancy of death. This is the man I love, who does not want me. This is my divorce. This is my friend's suicide. Her final directive: Cremation. *"I don't want to be buried. I have spent too much time lying down."*

"Let's go."

Lola jumped. She had forgotten her mother. "We just got here."

Irritation cut a wedge between her mother's eyes. "Who wants to see such ugliness? We're leaving. Esmeralda is in the gift shop buying chocolate."

"But Frida Kahlo is the most important female artist in the world."

"I've changed my mind. Frida Kahlo was a communist, a slut, and a lesbian. We should not have come."

"I've changed my mind, too." The girl set her chin. "I like her."

Her mother pointed her index finger like a dart. "Watch out or you'll end up like her."

"Famous?"

"Miserable."

"I already am."

A lion in the closet. There was always a fucking lion in the closet. A lion, or a tiger.

fourteen | ANNA

At six p.m. sharp, Anna dressed for dinner at the Malones'. She slipped on a little black dress, zipped up the back, dabbed perfume, brushed her wrists, making heat. She plucked her eyebrows, scrubbed grit from under her nails. She painted her toes, blew her hair dry. *I will go to the party. Christopher Maddox will break through the chapel floor and steal the death mask of Monte-zuma. We will meet back at the hotel. No one will be shot or killed. Like that. It will all happen just like that.*

She sat down at the typewriter, punching keys. *Dear Dad, I am writing this letter in case anything happens to me . . .*

This was the other extreme, should the night go terribly wrong. She would type the complete story and give the letter to Rafi, with her father's name on the envelope, should he call, or even arrive at some later date, should he ever emerge from the coddled cocoon of vodka.

Just in case, she would leave a record. At the front desk, she explained to Rafi what she wanted, but most of it was lost in translation. "If" clauses were a bear in Spanish. Hypothetical circumstances demanded high-tech verb constructions. *Hubiera.* The introduction to regrets.

"Para su padre," Rafi confirmed. *"Cuando venga."*

"No, my *padre* doesn't *venga.*" Anna shook her head. "But if I don't come back, read him the letter over the phone." She mimicked this, holding her hand to her ear.

"The letter is in Spanish?"

"English."

Rafi shrugged helplessly.

Anna sighed. "Just keep the envelope for a few weeks and then throw it away."

Rafi slid the letter into his soap opera magazine. "I understand," he said, though this was impossible. Mexicans told you what you wanted to hear. Americans heard what they wanted to hear. A perfect marriage.

fifteen | THE LOOTER

That evening, the looter lay on his bunk and tried not to think about Feo. The scene felt pleasantly animal with the chicken coop out back and the white cat curled at his feet and the faraway dogs barking their heads off about nothing. He regretted killing his phone. He was supposed to text Anna, but the plan was set: He'd leave in an hour, take a cab across town, break through the chapel floor, steal the mask before eight. He liked having a purpose, like back in the cave, only now that he wasn't cranked, things moved slowly, sort of boring but not really, because he was jacked about screwing over this joker Malone.

Mari was right: His life was worth more than a stick of incense. He was going to honor the Virgin. He was going to honor himself. *Hey, Reyes. My life is as valuable as that blue mask.* Shit, every life was. Life was a treasure, every stone of it. He liked the way that sounded. Profound, churchy. He could have been a preacher. The Sermon of Montezuma's Death Mask. He pictured himself in the pulpit, explaining life in the cave, how you had to go for it—whatever "it" was. They might have heard that before, but *it bore repeating*, twice, a million times, because people forgot, they watched too much TV—

Chelo appeared in the doorway with a soft *"Hola."*

She was bigger than yesterday. Belly big as Saturn now. Her amazing solar system. The best churches let you have pussy and God.

"Ven aquí, nena. Quédate conmigo."

The girl dropped the blinds. He liked watching her move. She cozied up, pulled needlepoint from her basket. He leaned in. The Virgin of Guadalupe. Of course. This girl was seriously religious. He was a little put off by this particular threesome. She'd finished Mary and was working on her halo. Two shades of yellow. Or maybe gold.

"How do you do that?"

"It's easy," she said. "You should try."

He meant, How do you have the patience to do that, but he let this misunderstanding pass. "It's what? A pillow?"

The girl laughed. "No, you frame it. Hang it on the wall."

Virgin art. No home could have too much. Each time the needle went into the hole, the strand got shorter. Each stitch, more color, less yarn. He could turn that into a sermon, too. He laughed. The girl laughed to keep him company.

"Tómalo." She pushed the canvas at him. "A man should know how to sew. If you become a pirate, you'll have to mend your socks."

The only needle he'd navigated was the other kind, but he wasn't going to bring up that bliss. "Where do I go?"

"That little square. Go up."

He stabbed the Virgin in the eye, pushed the canvas back to Chelo. "Forget it. I'll mess it up."

"We'll do it together." She guided his needle into the correct hole. "Now pick up the needle on the other side. Slowly. Don't pull too hard. Now go down over there."

This direction was easier. From the top, you could see where you were headed. He reached underneath to tug the golden yarn.

"There." She beamed. "Your first stitch."

The second was easier. The third, easier still. His aim improved, her hand on his, her belly warming his side. Needlepoint. Well, all right. Anything could be interesting, if you let it. They sewed until his hard-on got the best of him. He pulled her horizontal.

"You feel good."

She curled into him.

"You know, this baby is going to need a daddy," the looter murmured in her ear. "What if it's a boy?"

Their heads lay on the same pillow and he felt sleep coming on. Here in the fat aunt's backyard, surrounded by dumb chickens, lying on a lumpy cot with a pregnant girl in braces, the looter was content. *So this is happiness. So little. So much.* He touched her full breasts. She pressed his hands to her stomach. It was tight. Something freaky was happening. Little eruptions bubbled under her taut skin. Then he knew. He and this baby had something in common. They'd both been buried alive.

sixteen | ANNA

To Anna's relief, Marge and Harold were ensconced on the patio when she and Salvador arrived at the Malones' at seven. Harold sat stiff in a rocker. Marge, surrounded by clusters of honeysuckle, resembled a grotesque version of a Botero painting. *Mother-in-Law on Swing.* If the collector had a massacre planned, surely he wouldn't invite spectators from Shaker Heights. Even now, Anna was wowed by the flowerbeds, the looming palms, the hysterical cactus. The only discordant note was the swimming pool, thick with pond scum.

The foursome traded air kisses before sitting down. The Malones had gotten a phone call, Marge explained, they would be down in a minute. Anna took a seat facing the chapel. At any moment, the looter would tap through the chapel floor. Salvador, the adorable fraud, set about making loud small talk: the sculpture exhibit downtown, the police chief murdered in Acapulco, the dryness of the croissants at La Parisienne. He compensated for nervousness by appearing extravagantly casual, leaning back in his chair, laughing too loud. Harold complained about his Internet service, then moved on to another annoyance: The teachers were striking again. Protesters had set fire to a bus on the *periférico*, blocking traffic for blocks.

"We got in before the worst of it," he said. "But really, sometimes you might as well walk."

Anna fired off a text to the looter. Leave early. Traffic.

"Sorry we're late." Constance breezed across the terrace in flowing cotton pants and an embroidered tunic. Scarf at the throat. She smoothed cream into her chapped knuckles. Thomas followed her out. Freshly shaven, he wore black pants, a purple shirt, each sleeve fixed with a silver button. He resembled a stick of black licorice.

"Hello, wonderful guests."

Anna hadn't seen Thomas since the VIP Hotel, and had expected a tacit apology, a flicker of embarrassment or shame, but he circled the group, doling out pleasantries, as if nothing had happened. Anna touched her sore cheek. The funk of mescal rose in her throat. She reminded herself why she'd come. *The chapel. The chapel.*

"Thomas bought a new mask," Constance gushed. "He's floating around the house like Tinker Bell."

No, that's not why. He's happy to have the death mask. He's happy to have gotten away with murder.

Thomas rubbed his hands together. "Now who would like an Expatriate? It's my newest cocktail."

Marge frowned. "What's in it?"

"House secret. My most lethal concoction. Guaranteed to ensure an early and peaceful retirement."

"Sign me up," Marge said. Salvador and Harold nodded.

"Anna?" Thomas considered her for the first time. His lips tensed. He had to wonder if she'd keep their secret. He had to be nervous, if he was human at all. Anna considered his hateful chin, his deep-set eyes. She wanted a drink. A kamikaze. A B-52. Mescal from the basement.

"I probably shouldn't," she said. "A nasty virus attacked me Sunday night."

"Something is going around," Thomas agreed. "It knocks you flat, but most people recover."

"Stronger than before," Anna agreed, touching her cheek.

He turned, went inside. Anna felt her strength drained. She wanted to go home. She wanted her mother. Conversation simmered around her. Salvador found her eyes, offered a supportive nod. Thomas re-appeared. The Expatriate was the color of poppies. Anna savored its sweet release. She checked her watch. 7:23.

"Thomas," said Marge, her mouth flattening into a hyphen. "The show opens in two weeks. Enough suspense. It's time to share a few masks."

Thomas shook his head playfully. "You'll just have to wait."

Marge yanked her skirt, searching for a little give. She turned to Constance. "He's getting obsessive, if you ask me."

"Thomas has been obsessed for years, but you can't do anything of quality without being obsessed. Otherwise, you are a dabbler."

Harold perked up, hands fluttering. "My Spanish dabbling has been so rewarding."

Anna looked at Salvador with an *I can't believe this* eyebrow. Salvador patted the air, *Paciencia, mi amor, con tiempo todo se arregla.* In time, everything will work out.

Soledad announced dinner was served, and they walked inside to find a Hoosier picnic. Potato salad. Steak. Salad. Watermelon. Rolls. Anna had no appetite. She finished her drink. Soledad stood at the sink, washing her hands. Did she know Thomas had shot Hugo? If so, why was she still here? Where *was* Hugo?

"Wait!" Constance cried as Harold reached for his fork. "A toast to Thomas." The collector peered over his shoulder, pretending her praise had been directed to a better man standing behind him. "Who, after more than a decade of collecting, will soon display the finest collection of Mexican masks in the world."

Thomas tapped his fork against his glass and stood. Anna cringed. He was going to make a speech. She steadied herself, tipsy already. She pressed out the creases in her black dress, trying to clear her head. They had a job to do. The mask. The chapel.

"Friends, I'm honored. When I began collecting ten years ago, I had no idea how fascinating the enterprise would be. Masks convey a part of the human spirit that cannot easily be put into words. The mask peels back our daily façade and reveals the tragedy of the human condition."

Anna slipped the phone out of her purse. 7:55. No text. She ticked through all the ways things could have gone wrong. *The tunnel had collapsed. The mask wasn't in the chapel. The looter had stolen the mask and bolted for Colorado. The looter was shooting heroin and didn't remember his own name.* Salvador was leaning back on two chair legs. Soledad was making a racket with the pots.

"A man in a mask is above the law. He makes his own rules, his own moral code. He is free to transgress, anonymous, unknown. Be someone else. Be yourself. Be God. This, my friends, is freedom. Jesus died for our sins. Masks live for our fears. *Man is least himself when he talks in his own person. Give him a mask, and he will tell you the truth.* Oscar

Wilde died for his beliefs, savaged by Victorian society that could not stomach a man who—"

Salvador dropped his chair with a smack. Thomas surveyed his guests' bewildered faces, cleared his throat. "You don't want to hear all this. We have this fine potato salad—"

"Show us something," Marge hollered, sounding a bit drunk.

"Well"—Thomas shook his head, relenting—"I will show you one mask, my newest. The Wild Woman. She's out in the chapel. Eat, everyone. It'll just take a minute."

Anna jumped up. "Let me go with you."

"Stay put. No need for help."

Salvador tried. "I would like to see your place out there."

Thomas held up a hand. "I've got it."

8:05. No text. The screen door slammed.

"*Finally*, we're going to see something," Marge said. "I was beginning to wonder if his collection was pure fantasy."

"Thomas never makes anything up," Constance said. "It's one of his best qualities."

Anna sent a frantic text. Hes coming.

Salvador raked his hair, started humming. Soledad put milk on the stove.

Marge's face puckered. "But what's all this business about Jesus? If you ask me, he's gone over the deep end."

Constance did a yogi impression, turning her wrists skyward. "It's his new spiritual practice."

"Spiritual practice," Marge said mockingly, "like yoga practice. You don't need to practice what you believe, you only need to practice what you *don't* believe until you *do* believe it, and then you don't have to *practice* anymore."

Constance shook her head. "I've had too many Expatriates to follow that. Here's my problem with religion: If God exists, why doesn't He take responsibility? Give us a miracle now and then. A little good PR. Something to hang on to. If you're God, be God."

"Sounds like a bumper sticker," Harold said dryly.

Anna clutched her phone in both hands. She listened past the voices to the wind, trying to feel the ground move, the reverberation of broken tile.

"What I'm saying is," Constance said, "God needs to man up."

Thomas strolled into the kitchen. He did not look like a man who had just shot a meth addict in his chapel. He handed Marge a mask, a bearded woman.

Marge howled. "She's hiiiiiideous. Is that pigskin? I would never keep such a thing in my house. It probably has fleas."

"It's not in our house," Constance corrected. "It's in our chapel."

Marge whooped. "What kind of religion are you practicing out there? Voodoo?"

"Excuse me," Anna said. "I need to use the ladies' room." She circled the table. Salvador grabbed her hand. She mouthed, *Stay here*, then went down the hallway into the vestibule, snatched her backpack, slipped out a side door, and sprinted across the lawn. The grass was wet. The moon was full. The trees buzzed in the dark. Her friend was lost underground. She'd check the tunnel opening and—she stopped short. Fortune had smiled down on her.

The chapel door was ajar.

It was so unlike Thomas. A rare misstep. Now that she'd had a bit of luck, Anna didn't trust it. She moved cautiously toward the chapel. Hand on the door, she hesitated, fear overwhelming her. Murmurs from the party filtered down the long lawn. She breathed in hard, mustering her courage. Of course she would go inside. She was a girl who climbed trees.

The door flattened the weeds enough to let her slip in. Her eyes adjusted to the darkness, and she saw that Thomas had lied again.

His chapel was not a storage room for art, but a congregation of ghouls.

Masks, dozens of masks, lined the wooden pews. Masks of jackals, wolves, and tigers hung from the walls, mouths frothing. Every inch of space was covered. Startled Moors squeezed next to ashen Christians. Toothless geezers leered at beauty-marked whores. Creepy wooden figures the size of children, some missing forearms or feet or hair, crowded the aisles, their chipped eyes begging for rescue or deliverance. A headless woman supplicated. Amputees wept. On the ceiling, bones were glued in decorative patterns, medallions and flowers, light as lace. On the altar, a long table lined with twelve skulls, fists of stale bread and chalices, forming a Last Supper of the dead. Presiding over this macabre centerpiece was a life-size skeleton in a wedding dress and flowered garland. In one bony hand she held a scepter and, in her outstretched palm, the death mask of Montezuma.

Santa Muerte was Thomas Malone's new religion.

Take the mask and run.

Anna staggered forward past glass eyes, painted eyes, empty sockets. No sign of the looter; the floor was pristine. A video camera was perched on a tripod. A security camera? Or was Thomas Malone another inspired director? Anna stopped. Another surprise. Grasshopper masks. A dozen identical to the one she and her father had featured in their book lay in a pile. Nearby, long sheets of silver metal leaned against a wall with half-finished Centurion masks. It all made sense now. Constance was not Thomas Malone's sole source of income.

He was manufacturing bogus masks, fobbing them off on trusting collectors, like her father. *Daniel, I see a real opportunity here, a find.* The men's friendship had been a ruse, a con job. The crafty opportunist dances circles around the well-funded drunk.

Take the mask and run.

The Angel of Death was even more unnerving up close, not some cheap replica, but a model that med students would use, anatomically correct, each bone fastened with wire or nylon string. *The human skeleton has 206 bones.* A fact Anna had checked, remembered. *The only bone not attached to another bone is the hyoid, which facilitates speech.* Each truth reassured her. Science was a safe refuge in this cauldron of perverse religion, just as religion was a safe refuge when science— Anna froze. The bride's garland, she recognized it. Dried flowers spun around a blue silk scarf. Holly's tiara from the photograph. Thomas had pinched it for his sick memento mori. Anna touched the skeleton's arm. It was smooth, almost waxy. She tapped it with her knuckle, felt herself go weak. Real bones. The remains of some poor woman from Juárez, no doubt, the creation of a covert Santa Muerte factory. Even in death, Thomas Malone procured the rare and remarkable. Even in death, the collector put his own desires above another person's soul. Anna steadied herself against the table, silence loud in her ears. *This was somebody's child.* She focused on the turquoise mask, whose lopsided expression seemed more kindly than usual. *Take me and run.*

Anna lifted the mask, expecting alarms to ring, but the only sound was her own jagged breath. Fumbling, she wrapped the mask in her sweater, stuffed it in her pack, turned to leave. Her legs and lips had swelled. Objects swayed and dulled. She felt drugged. It didn't seem possible that a house filled with people she knew lay beyond the chapel door.

"C'mon, Morocco, Honduras. Keep me company."

Thomas.

Anna slid under a pew, making herself small and quiet. What would Thomas do if he caught her? Shoot her. Laugh it off. Claim the chapel was an art installation, and they could both pretend to believe his lie, pretend this wasn't fetishism, the occult. The chapel door opened. A dull light went on. Anna's heart was a crow, flapping, cawing, out of her chest. Fear played visual tricks. Everything shattered into multiple images. The pews, the cracks in the tiles, the dust. Already, she was willing to surrender. *Let the worst happen now.* His orange aftershave met her nose. Anna prayed to the only dead person who loved her. And she thought: *Fish never close their eyes.*

"Where shall we put you, my lovely? A woman as grand as you needs an escort. Sit next to the mendicant."

Anna held still, held on.

His footsteps approached. She stopped breathing. A hand touched her shoulder. "What are you doing here?"

Anna did not move or speak.

He repeated the question.

She whispered, "I wanted to see the collection."

"For God's sake, get up. You look ridiculous." Anna rose, steadying herself on the pew. Thomas was smiling, furious, bashful, proud. Maybe he'd secretly wanted to show off his creation. This could be another dark secret they shared.

"What do you think?" he asked. "I left the door open for you."

"It's amazing. Scary, of course." She was slurring. She didn't feel right. "All these faces. That's what you wanted, right? A haunted house, performance art."

Thomas's face went blank. "I'm not mad."

"You believe in Santa Muerte." Each word took effort.

"Of course not. A religion for paupers and thieves. The saint of last resort. You might want to give her a shout." Thomas grabbed her wrist, twisted it.

Anna fell back into the pew, too weak to stand.

"I am going to take back the death mask now." He reached into her pack. "I can see you're tired. You should sleep soon."

He had drugged her. Anna understood, but could do nothing to stop the chemicals easing into her bloodstream.

"I had high hopes for our collaboration, but your editorial skills were lacking. I am ready to enjoy you this time. I feel comfortable here in the chapel."

He sat beside her on the pew, marking her veins with a finger.

"You are mad," she said softly.

"I told you I am not mad."

"I am not having sex with you."

She was ill beyond speaking. Where was the looter? Where was Salvador? Thomas fetched a rope, tied her arms and legs. Anna watched this happen. She tried to scream but heard nothing. The chapel had bloomed into a cathedral, arches of light soared above her, and she floated, warm and remote.

"I will tell the others you fell ill and took a taxi home. Would you like to pick your mask tonight, or are you too tired? I am losing you, my dear. You are lost. Stay here with Holly while I dispose of our guests."

Anna whispered the name. *Holly.* Sickness rose up her throat. She understood now. Yes, at last.

"Marvelous woman. Laugh like a bird, pout like a pin-up. I'd have given her anything, left all this, but she denied me. The more I begged, the harder she laughed. *I'd rather run away with Constance.* So many games. *You can touch me here, but not there.* Her little mouth. Her dog-teeth. She wore my masks."

He had forgotten Anna entirely. His voice thinned to a pitiful whine.

"I don't ask for much. A little relief. A moment of pleasure. But each time, it gets harder. I paid her, but still she tortured me with her flirtations. *Think how much you'll miss me.* Nothing would change her mind. I brought her here. She wanted to see inside. They all do. But she wouldn't be quiet. She wouldn't obey. She was lovely. Blue scarf. Silly, vain crown. But she is lovely now, too. It took so much water to clean her, but I did it joyfully. She's a saint now. The center of attention, just like she always wanted."

"You killed her."

Intoxicating Holly with her tart smile and feather earrings was now a skeleton, festooned, hung up, revered in a perverse mix of religion and sex and obsession. The Grim Reaper. Lady Death. La Flaca.

"Don't be ridiculous," Thomas scolded, with a burst of charm. "I'm a collector. I live for my collection, and I live with it."

Thomas tugged each sleeve at the wrist, bowed before the altar, and left her. The chapel door clicked shut. Anna fought to hold on to consciousness. She pictured Salvador's face, marveling: *You Americans all come to Mexico to lose your minds.* Anna had not buried her mother's ashes. She had not told Salvador how happy he made her. Her father was drinking again, unattended. She was forever leaving things undone.

seventeen | THE HOUSEKEEPER

Soledad was rinsing plates in warm dishwater when Señor Thomas returned, letting the screen door slam, his eyebrows low and ugly over his eyes. The *señora* wanted to know where he had been, that much English Soledad understood, and she could tell by the *señora's* coiled body and tense voice that she was livid. "Where's Anna?" The *señor* stood at the end of the table, a corrupt senator, making a speech. Soledad caught only a few words. *Anna. Hotel. Taxi. Sick.*

The *señora* was drunk, her jaw hanging like a car door, while the guests sat straight as cactuses, napkins folded, ankles crossed. The turnip one reached for his wife's hand under the table and gave it a squeeze.

The *señor* poured himself a brandy. The guests started talking, all but the Mexican, who looked like someone had punched him in the *panza.* Soledad caught his eye, telling him, wordlessly, that Thomas Malone was a liar.

"Soledad, make us some tea, *por favor,*" the *señor* said.

She filled the kettle, lit a match, watched the orange flames jump to life. The simple force of fire. Elemental. Purifying. Farmers knew this. Fire could clean a field or an entire city. Sodom or Gomorrah. She thought about Hugo. How pathetic he looked, thinner with his chest wrapped, the first gray hairs peeking over his bandage, how he had been weeping, like a man who wasn't a man at all, just a small boy who'd lived for decades. She fixated on the window, the mullions, crosses, the long sill. Timeline. Tightrope. Arrow. The housekeeper studied the window until she made up her mind.

Her hands fumbled the key in the moonlight. She looked back at the glow of the big house. At any moment, the *señor* might appear. At any moment, the *señora* would summon her. The key had a tag saying CAPILLA, but she couldn't make it work. She had never dared use the key, never admitted to anyone she had it left over from the previous *señora*, the cheap one, who counted bananas. Soledad closed her eyes. *"Querida María, Madre de Dios y de todos nosotros . . ."*

The key turned. She lifted the gas canister.

Inside, the chapel was even more terrifying than the glimpse she'd seen through the peephole. She kept her flashlight trained to the floor, afraid to look around, look back. The girl was laid out on a pew, a maiden in a fairy tale. She was pretty, even here. Soledad had a pang of envy that the girl lived in the United States and had the freedom to travel, trade lovers, spend her dollars wherever she pleased. Americans cared little for family, which is why this Anna had wound up drugged in a chapel, reliant on a Mexican housekeeper for rescue. She could leave the girl here. There was no good reason to save her. And yet, of course, there was every reason. *Faith, without works, is nothing.*

Something creaked. Soledad turned sharply. Devils, dragons, whores, lecherous Spaniards leered. The bones on the ceiling hung like poisonous mushrooms. Heart hammering, she lifted the girl by the shoulders, dragged her down the aisle. She was heavy, dead weight. Breathing hard, she set the girl down, then chastised herself for wasting time. She lifted her again and pulled her through the door, collapsing on the threshold. It was dark. She was alone. *He will shoot you, too.* A second voice inside her, which was her, another version of her, the brave Soledad who was on speaking terms with the Virgin, whispered, *He who knows the right thing and fails to do it, for him it is sin.*

She counted to ten. This was her new habit. Many good things could happen between one and ten. Water boiled. The butcher took her order. She remembered how much she loved her husband, how lonely she would be without his touch. She could decide to forgive him for falling in love with a girl who sold paper.

A chill swept over her shoulder blades.

Someone was walking toward her. In the distance, somewhere in the hills of Oaxaca, a dog began to howl.

eighteen | THE GARDENER

Hugo sat at the kitchen table of the cottage and pulled out the stationery he'd purchased from the paper shop so many months before. He lit a single candle. He picked up his pen.

Mi niña de amarillo,

Though much has happened since you left for Veracruz, my love for you has never wavered.

He touched his bandage. The doctor at the public hospital had asked no questions. He knew how such things happened. Hugo knew he was lucky to be alive, and though Thomas Malone thought he was dead, Reyes did not, and the drug lord would not stop until this task was completed. Hugo had no right to put the girl in danger.

But I must let you fly away, little bird. I am too old
for you. Too poor and too old. You will sing for a
better man. Stay strong, my papershop girl. Remember
me in your dreams as I remember you. The Aztecs
chose the most beautiful young girls to be sacrificial
maidens. I read this in your book. The girls would
sing and care for the men chosen for sacrifice, making
sure their final hours were blissful. You are such a
maiden. I am that happy man.

Con gratitud,
Hugo

The gardener put down his pen. *If you were sacrificed, how long would your heart beat for me?* He would find out soon enough.

He thought of Soledad. His brave wife had gone to work that morning, weeping faked tears, confiding to the *señora*, who later told the *señor*, that Hugo had disappeared, run off with a younger woman. The *cabrón* had comforted her with soothing lies and rum in her tea while Hugo hid in the cottage, *callado como un muerto*. Silent as a corpse. They could not leave until he regained his strength. All day, hatred in her heart, Soledad had cooked and cleaned and fixed the Americans special coffee made with water from the toilet, brushing shoulders with a killer. But now it was past midnight, and where was she? The party had ended thirty minutes before.

The door burst open. Soledad stood before him, her expression ethereal, formidable. He quickly covered the letter.

"Where were you?"

"Doing God's work."

"It's late. God is working overtime." Hugo unfurled his hand, teasing out the story. "So tell me."

"It's a secret."

Hugo frowned. "It's dangerous out there."

"The Virgin watches over me."

"And what does the Virgin think about this work of yours?"

"She says, *'Buen trabajo, Soledad.'*"

"The Virgin sounds like a nun."

"No. The Virgin is a rockstar."

Hugo shook his head. "You know nothing about music."

"I sing."

"You are a beautiful woman blessed with a terrible voice."

"A broken heart makes beautiful music."

"Don't say that. It hurts me." He reached into his pocket and removed a silver chain. A locket hung from the end. "This is for you."

Soledad opened the locket, saw his picture inside. She smiled. His wife smiled upon him.

Hugo wrinkled his nose. "You smell gas?"

Soledad pushed her hands in her apron pockets, shook her head. No.

"Listen," Hugo straightened in his chair. His body hurt all over. "I have memorized a poem. It's from the Huehuetlatolli, the lessons Nahua elders gave young boys. I have been studying them.

"The mature man:
a heart as firm as stone,

a wise countenance,

the owner of a face and a heart

who is capable of understanding."

He meant the words as a prayer, a promise. His wife wiped her tired eyes. "I want that man." She held out a hand.

Hugo hobbled to take it.

nineteen | ANNA

Anna woke up inside a car. Her head hurt. The digital clock said one in the morning. Someone was holding her hand. She snatched it back, then heard Salvador's soothing voice. *"Gracias a Dios, estaba tan preocupado."* She fell into him and they held each other, tight as a planet, a circle of rock with its own weather and delicate clouds, light-years away from all they knew or who they had been.

"What happened?" It took effort to speak.

Salvador whispered the story, how he'd left the Malones', snuck back to the chapel, saw Soledad dragging her. Together, they carried her to the car.

And the looter?

Salvador shrugged.

And the mask?

"Still in the chapel, I guess." He was caressing her forehead. "You don't want to . . ."

"No, I don't want to . . ." She sat up, kneaded her face, trying to think. "But Thomas can't have the mask. Anyone but him."

"So we go *de ramate*?" That meant all the way.

Anna closed her eyes. She pictured the holes that scarred her father's living room walls, where the hooks had hung, the masks. She pictured her mother standing under an umbrella outside the van on the highway from La Esperanza, chatting in the window, pointing back to Anna. The car windows had filled with warm condensation, enough for Anna to draw hearts. She pictured a gallery with her mother's name, their collection, an homage to Mexico, to this amazing death mask, ferocious as God's spirit, resilient as man's spirit in a godless world. *Don't give up,* the mask told her. Or maybe that was her mother's voice. So far away now, difficult to hear. Anna breathed in, put a name to what she'd committed to. She was risking her life to save her father, to honor her mother, to protect the mask. She was risking her life to screw over Thomas Malone. Each reason was reason enough.

"*Vamos de ramate.*"

Salvador grinned. *"A todo dar."* We give it all up.

Anna narrowed her eyes. *"A toda pinche madre."*

The whole fucking way.

"You're getting quite Mexican."

"But how do we get inside? We're right back where we started."

"*Un regalo* from Soledad." Salvador dangled a key.

"Where did she get—"

"Housekeepers . . ."

Anna touched his arm, stopping him. "There's more." She told him about Holly. Salvador didn't believe her. Malone must have bought the skeleton somewhere.

"No, it's her. He cleaned her down to the bone and dressed her up like Santa Muerte. He's sick, crazy."

"There's no way—"

"He said, *'It took so much water to clean her.'* We need to bring her out. For evidence."

Salvador shook his head, disbelieving, believing. "So you are saying we need to steal a death mask *and* a skeleton?" The next string of swearing contained a *puta*, a *chingada*, and a *cabrón*.

Anna said, "I'll take that as a yes."

Two a.m. The moon shined bright as a coin. Tree frogs chanted. They pushed through the Mendezes' woods, frazzled and sweaty. The Malones' yard was silent. The pink house, the cottage, the chapel, the pool. Anna imagined the course of events after the dinner party dispersed. No doubt Thomas had returned to the chapel, been stunned to discover she was gone. Would he look for her? Unlikely. No, as the mask was safe, he'd keep up appearances. Slip on cotton pajamas. Steady his lips as he pecked Constance good night. Take a sleeping pill to soothe his brittle nerves. He had nothing to fear from Anna. Nothing that could not be explained away with a lie.

In the darkness, the pink house sulked like day-old cake. Anna and Salvador stood braced, checking the yard for signs of life, for Thomas, for Morocco, Honduras, but the only sound was the whirl of industrial air conditioners churning white noise and cold. Salvador gave a tense nod. They crept to the chapel. Anna jiggled the key in the door. It turned. She hesitated. She could still see Thomas's remote eyes, feel his weight on her wrists. The stink of mescal.

Sensing her distress, Salvador pushed past her. "Wait here. I will do it."

"No," Anna said. "You can't carry her alone."

As they entered, Salvador let out a hushed *Híjole*. Using his phone as a light, he scanned the masks, the ghouls, the bride, the banquet table set for dinner, then focused on a black stone mask hanging by a window. He moved closer, lifted the mask from its nail, flipped it over. "I don't believe it."

"Believe what?" Anna had reached the altar. The death mask glared at her. *Time to stop fucking around.*

"We bought this mask four years ago. It's from Teotihuacán, five hundred years after Christ. The face is a young boy, maybe a prince. It's supposed to be in Puebla, but here it is. Gonzáles *used* me. Salvador Flores, the great protector of Mexican art, was another idiot Gonzáles . . ." He couldn't find the right verb.

"Screwed over." Anna stuffed the death mask in her pack. "He screwed both of us."

"And where's your looter?" Salvador hissed. "Smoking his pipe?"

"Hurry." Anna ripped the skeleton's dress. It smelled like bleach. Her heart was going nuts. Her hands felt like oven mitts. At any moment, Thomas Malone might appear. "Help me with this. It'll be easier to carry without the stupid dress."

Salvador scowled, which meant yes, the same way *gracias* can mean no. No sooner had she removed the dress than she realized her mistake. Without it, the skeleton was floppy, hard to maneuver. Salvador crossed the arms over the chest. Anna grasped the ankles, trying not to feel squeamish. Salvador held one hand under the back, cupped the skull with the other. The bones were surprisingly light. They hustled down the aisle, like EMTs without the stretcher. The masks watched them, hundreds of eyes and open mouths, horns and fangs and nostrils, seeing, seething, smelling, breathing.

Through the chapel door they went. The lawn was quiet. Fog had rolled in from somewhere. There was no way they could navigate the back woods, which meant having to leave through the front gate, a football field away, past peacocks, past the pool, past the pink house, which might, at any moment, light up. Salvador mouthed, *Apúrate*, but it was hard to hurry without dropping the skeleton or making a racket. At first Anna felt disgust—she was carrying a dead body—but her revulsion faded to tenderness for this puzzle of moving parts, each bone separate but connected. *This is who we all become. No, this is who we are now, underneath.*

She kept her eyes glued to the house. If they were caught, she would tell Constance everything, every sordid detail. They'd nearly reached the pool, a tapestry of algae, when she looked behind her, gave a muffled cry.

A man had emerged from the woods.

Anna froze, ready to run, but it was not Thomas's angular frame. This man was smaller, slower, his face a blur that sharpened as he approached. Older, white, he looked a bit like her father. Then an entirely impossible thing happened. A fact beyond checking. Daniel Ramsey appeared through the fog, gave a short wave and a smile of recognition. He was limping, favoring his left side, the way he did when his knees hurt. His explorer's vest bulged with God only knew what. Eyedrops. Compass. An expired EpiPen. Anna did not move to embrace him, because she wasn't sure he was real.

"Dad?"

"I got to the Sunset late and—" Anna frantically shushed him. He began again, quieter. "Finally, a new clerk came on duty, a real pansy, and he gave me your note."

Anna set down the skeleton, hugged her father, smelled his breath. Clean. She couldn't name her feelings. She wanted to pound his chest and she wanted to cry. Salvador's eyes danced with impatience, but he pulled back, giving them privacy.

"Did you bury her already?" her father asked.

Anna looked at the skeleton, confused.

"Your mother. The ashes."

She wanted to say, *I've been a little busy.* Instead, she said, "I couldn't decide where . . ."

"I want to be there."

Anger curdled dangerously inside her. The fallen man had conveniently resurrected himself and now demanded a starring role. He wore a necktie. This detail touched her. He'd dressed for the flight. She looked at his knees, the ones that didn't like to fly.

"We need to go."

"You shouldn't have to do everything."

"But I already *have*." She reached into her pack and handed him the death mask. His mouth pinched as his fingers traced the warts, the grout. He turned the mask over, his thumb stroking the patina. After a quiet moment, he gestured to the skeleton. "What's that hideous thing?"

"It's too much to . . ."

Branches rustled. The woods. Anna swung around. It had taken her a moment to recognize her father, but she knew the looter at once: square shoulders, the drag of his right toe. The pregnant girl had to be Chelo. A child with a child inside. It was getting to be quite a party by the pool: Anna, her father, Salvador, the looter, Chelo, the skeleton. The dead, the unborn, the living, all gathered at the home of the murderous American. Someone ought to serve drinks.

"Is that him?" Salvador murmured to Anna. Not waiting for the answer, he whispered loudly, "Where have *you* been?"

The looter glared at Anna. "Where's the mask?"

"Where were *you*?"

"Tied up."

"I was tied up, too."

"Did you use the tunnel?"

"It had no opening."

"Where's the mask?"

Daniel Ramsey gave the death mask a teasing shake. The looter's shoulders shot back. His eyes set. Anna watched the house. They couldn't stay here. The night could explode in six million ways.

"We need to go now!"

The looter cursed. The patio light turned on. Anna's legs melted beneath her. The kitchen door opened. Fireflies danced in the dark. Anna saw just how foolish she had been, trusting air conditioners to keep them safe. Marching across the lawn in long, confident strides was Thomas Malone. He was holding a pistol.

They waited, transfixed by the gun and its deadly potential. Anna picked up Holly, as if to say, *She's mine now, not yours.* Five people had trespassed the Malones' enormous lawn, but when Thomas reached the group, he spoke only to Anna, his voice grim and mechanical.

"Put her down. Give me the mask."

Daniel hesitated, then obeyed, all exuberance drained from his face. Malone took the mask. This loss felt predestined. No matter how many times Anna found the mask, she would lose it again. Like love. Lost.

Found. Lost and Found. *La oficina de objetos perdidos.* She ought to rent a room there.

Her father held up a hand, an elder calling for peace. "Thomas, you have what you want now. Put the gun away. You and I have known each other—"

"Shut up, old man. You're in over your head." The collector pointed the pistol at Anna. "Put her down."

Anna didn't budge.

"Anna," Salvador pleaded.

She set down the feet, backpedaled a few yards. Thomas stooped, lifted the skeleton, stepped backward. He was taking his dead lover hostage. It was a lot to manage—a skeleton, a mask, and a gun—but he was getting away, getting away with everything. Anna watched, amazed by her own poor judgment. She had craved this man's admiration, wanted to prove she could keep pace, shot for shot, determined to succeed where her father had failed, and this vanity had put them all in peril.

A second-story window lit up. A miraculous sight.

Anna said, "Constance is awake."

Thomas wheeled around. He ran in an awkward series of hops, but the skeleton was sluggish in the grass, arms flopping to either side. Eyeing the pool, Thomas shuffled past a planter to the water's edge and gave the bones a mean push. In the commotion, the gun dropped into the pool. Gone, in an instant. With a final, frantic heave, Malone shoved the skeleton into the water. To Anna's amazement, perhaps because of the algae or simple physics, it didn't sink. Thomas threw a rock at it, but the rock bounced impotently off the ribs and sank, joining his pistol in the deep end.

Holly made a regal sight, lying on her green tapestry beyond everyone's reach. *Tibia, fibula, sternum, scapula.* It had been years since Anna had taken human anatomy, and the words drifted back to her, as foreign and lyrical as Spanish. The pelvis resembled a butterfly. The ribs, May Day ribbons. Holly's blue tiara drifted a few inches off her head. Free of Thomas and his atrocities, released from interpretations of the living, she floated, alone, at peace.

Across the lawn, Constance swooped toward them, her robe white and ghostlike. She carried her rifle.

Thomas called out before she arrived, his voice jaunty. "I'm sorry to wake you, my dear, but I'm afraid we've been robbed."

Constance looked older without her usual grooming. Her light hair was pulled back in a headband and her pale eyes hovered, no longer anchored by a firm eyebrow pencil and mascara. She glared at each guest in turn.

"Why are all these people here? What's that in the pool?"

Thomas held up his hands, palms open, an innocent man. "It's just inconceivable. These felons broke into the chapel, stole a priceless mask, and were dragging my skeleton across the lawn. She's the centerpiece of my show, my Calavera Catrina, and they've ruined her. Chlorine is terrible for—"

"Which mask?" Constance's voice turned steely.

"A death mask," Thomas said. "Montezuma's death mask."

Anna was about to object, but stopped herself when Constance pointed her rifle at the tiara and said, "What's that?"

With a pitiful cry, Constance clambered to the side of the pool. She crouched and paddled the water with cupped hands, drawing the tiara closer, nearly falling in. When the crown was a yard away, she hooked it with the barrel of her rifle. The drenched scarf dripped black water on the flagstones. She set down the gun and held the tiara, fingered the scarf, held it briefly to her nose. Her hands trembled. She turned to her husband, her face drained of color and expression, features flat and stony as a Mayan mask. Her eyes begged for reassurance, explanation. *What happened here? What has been happening?* She was ready to believe, to follow his story wherever it led. Any peg to hang her coat on. Any wisp of plausible fact.

Thomas's mouth twitched, formulating a fresh confabulation, but then he seemed to change his mind and gazed over the wall, down to the glittering lights of Oaxaca, like he was already down there, gone.

Anna turned to Salvador. He and the others watched Constance, wondering what she would do. The chapel, the masks, the petty affairs, the disappointments and deceit, all these she had borne. But this? Anna stepped forward, but for a second time stopped herself. *She doesn't want you.*

Time slowed. The skeleton floated, white as alabaster, water licking its rib cage, its skull, its delicate fingers. Still crouched, Constance seemed unable to rouse herself. Her cheeks trembled. Her chin quivered. She held out a hand, then dropped it. The night's silence was broken by a wretched sob. She crumpled, chest heaving, crushed by the weight of what she now understood. All masks had been lifted, and she saw her husband and she saw herself. A sadist and a sycophant. Two Americans lost in Mexico.

She twisted, her face runny and red. "What did you do to her? What have you done? You hurt her. You hurt me. Everyone." Using the gun as a crutch, she staggered to her feet. "All those girls I pretended not to see. For what?" Tall again, she hoisted the rifle to her shoulder, braced her legs, took aim squarely at her husband.

For the first time, Thomas looked worried. He patted down the air. "Now, puppet, don't fly off the handle. Holly gave me the crown before she left. It was a present. I didn't tell you because I knew how upset you'd be—"

Constance cut him off. "You are a liar. You lie over and over again. I can't stand the noise that comes out of your mouth. Give Anna the mask."

Thomas did not budge.

Constance shook her rifle. "Squirrel, I am not asking you."

The look Thomas gave Anna could have killed a snake. He shoved the mask into her chest. Its one decent eye rolled: *You again.* Thomas turned. A gunshot exploded. Anna screamed. Thomas buckled. Blood seeped through his pants. Daniel ran to his side. "*Jesus Christ,* she shot him." Chelo backed up, hand protecting her belly. The looter stepped in front of her, a shield, arms spread, but Constance kept the rifle firmly aimed at Thomas. "That's enough," Daniel shouted. "You've hurt him." With his belt, he fashioned a tourniquet around the sodden leg, murmuring about mistakes and violence and ridiculous and what the hell kind of circus was going on here anyway. Thomas was shaking, an animal in shock. Salvador spun behind a tree, frantically whispering into his phone, *Amapolas . . . emergencia . . . accidente.*

Finding herself unscathed, Anna rushed to check on her father, the looter, the girl. This moment of calm was shattered by the sound of crashing glass. An eerie *whoosh* swept across the yard, followed by a loud crack as the chapel burst into flames. A second later, the right side of the roof blew off. Masks flew across the lawn, and a series of low blasts shook Anna's insides.

Salvador shouted at Anna to go to the house, then ran across the yard for a hose. Ignoring his directive, Anna went to stand by her father. Together, they watched.

The chapel burned quickly, as if by divine ordination. The wooden beams and pews kept the fire stoked. The soaring flames animated the masks' ghastly faces, their charred mouths gaping. Skulls rolled in the embers. Daniel darted about, trying to save a few treasures. The two dogs barked themselves hoarse, and the peacocks screeched from their cage, and the neighbor's donkey brayed in terror. Soledad appeared, breathless, still in her apron, hair frazzled. At the edge of the patio, she fell to her knees, crossed herself, lips moving, all sound lost in the chaos. Salvador yanked the hose across the grass and shot a stream of water into the blaze, without any noticeable effect. He was screaming, *"La casa, la casa,"* and the Mendez family appeared and formed a bucket brigade. Anna joined in, horrified to see that the fire had reached the woods. Thin branches sizzled like tinder. It had not rained in weeks.

A fire truck roared up the street, followed by police and an ambulance. Salvador opened the gate. Men in yellow hard hats leapt across the yard. Curious neighbors snuck in behind them. They wore nightgowns and flip-flops and held toddlers, whose soft faces watched the fire like it was TV. One man shot a video with his phone. The firemen hustled out a sloppy hose. The chapel seemed bigger now that it was burning, its insides spewed on the lawn, a foul purging, a secret revealed. One by one, the walls fell, and when the belfry collapsed, the brass bell dropped like a severed head. Constance drank red wine straight from the bottle, rifle at her side, bony knees high in her slung-back chair. Two police officers questioned Salvador. Mexicans suspected Mexicans first. Chelo sat on the wall, rocking in the curl of the looter's arm. Anna remembered Thomas, but he had disappeared somewhere. Perhaps to the hospital.

"Where's Thomas?" she asked Salvador, who was clutching empty buckets, breathing hard.

"What?"

"Thomas." Anna pointed to where blood stained the grass. "Where *is* he?"

"*Ni idea.*"

Anna checked the house—the living room, the couches—and the ambulance, vacant but for two EMTs smoking, then circled back to Constance.

"He took off," Constance said, finger pointing to the woods.

"You didn't stop him?"

Constance answered slowly, her eyes fixed on Anna's throat. "I could never stop him."

"But by law . . ."

"The law?" Constance gave her a withering look. Her face was smudged with soot.

Anna gave up. Her eyes stung from the smoke. Her dress was stained, its hem ripped loose and sagging, but she was okay. Salvador was okay. So was her father.

"How did the fire start?" she asked, changing tack. "Do they know?"

"Eventually," Constance said, raising her wine bottle, "the small ones retaliate."

Down in the valley, a firecracker exploded. A sunflower of purple and gold blossomed, then trailed off in spermlike fizzles, some new kind of failure.

"They never stop with the damn *cohetes*. What time is it?" Anna checked her watch. Three a.m. She called out over the wall. "God is sleeping, people."

Constance raised a hand. "God was a collector. God was the *first* collector."

Anna whipped around. *"What?"*

Constance really did look crazy. Her pale eyes were remote and watery. Her painted toes curled into filthy terry-cloth mules. Her robe hung open and her nightgown dipped dangerously to one side. She gripped her weapon like an aging Amazon.

"The animals. The plants. The desert. *We* are his collection. This *was* his chapel." Constance swung her arm at the wrecked lawn, the crushed flowers, the oily puddles and embers, the hoses and fallen timbers, the charred chapel, a half-melted monster.

"And look what we've done with it," Anna said, assessing the apocalyptic vision.

Constance smiled darkly. "It's more fun to collect things than care for them. But I wouldn't worry too much about the mess."

The firefighters had the blaze under control. Salvador was on the phone again. Soledad was calming the dogs.

"You're right, we shouldn't worry," Anna agreed, her mood as black as her dress. "The Mexicans will clean it up."

Not long after, the police questioned Anna. She botched her grammar, but they didn't seem to care. The verb "shoot" was *disparar*, which always sounded like "disappear," which was the point of shooting something, or someone, after all, to make them disappear. Exhausted from inept conjugations and pantomime, Anna withdrew to a bench overlooking the pool, keeping an eye on Holly. Thomas had disappeared, but Anna was going to make damn sure the evidence did not. Her father joined her. He made a face at the skeleton and whistled.

"He's a real freak. Dressing the dead up like dolls. To think, all those afternoons, Daniel Ramsey sat on that patio, chattering away.

You know, I found my notes. Those Grasshopper masks, the Centurion, I'd bought them because—"

"Lorenzo Gonzáles told you to."

"How did you know?"

"Thomas made them. Gonzáles peddled them. Gonzáles probably tipped off the Met himself. He sells you junk, humiliates you, then offers to bring you back from the dead. *Daniel Ramsey will buy Montezuma's death mask.* You or Reyes. Only, his plan backfired: the death mask was real."

Her father pressed his temples. "Folk art used to be so innocent, but money ruined it. I ruined it. Thomas ruined it. Your mother always said I had an addictive personality."

"You do—"

"I prefer to call it 'passion.' But I had no business chasing masks when I hadn't taken care of the small decent thing."

"The ashes?"

"The ashes. You. Me. The house. Your mother would have been horrified by my drinking." He held up a hand to stop Anna from piling on. "I've been dry for six shaky days. Give me some credit, please. My head is killing me." He looked around, his righteousness collapsing. "You know, I've always pictured your mother resting under a tree."

Anna nodded. "A pine tree would be good."

The city lights pulsed beneath them. The cathedral glowed. Anna felt her mother was close. *I was seeing things through her eyes, as she had seen them. She had given me her eyes to see.* Rose's spirit had never left this proud, magical country, where the frogs yakked and the stars sighed, where tigers danced and the dead lingered, where each night the white lilies closed their petals against the dark. *Pobre México, tan lejos de Dios y tan cerca de los Estados Unidos.* Poor Mexico, so far from

God, so close to the United States. An old joke. Really, of course, it was the reverse.

Though she finally had the death mask, Anna didn't feel victorious. Here at the pool, as the Mendez children ran in circles, astounded at their luck to be out of bed, as the firefighters conferred, Anna watched the floating skeleton, keeping vigil. She felt the weight of objects, her obligation to the dead, to the past. *We destroy so many things with our touching, starting with the things we love most.*

Something shifted in the pool. The skeleton's foot dropped below the surface. Then a shin, then a knee. Holly was sinking. Weighed down by the legs, the pelvis hovered, then submerged, followed by the rib cage, until all that remained was the skull, two sockets, deep and black as life's unanswerable questions. Anna took her father's hand. He whispered something in her ear. She watched. She listened. For once, the dogs were silent.

twenty | SANTA MUERTE

No one ever asks me how I do what I do. My genius is another miracle people think they deserve. Like the miracle of a newborn child. Or the miracle of ocean tides. When people die, I put their bodies back together, sew them up, patch their wounds, paint them, polish them, pump their veins full of life until they are themselves again, dead but on their way to the village. That's all a saint can do. If I have time, I pack them a lunch.

I am an aesthetician, a seamstress, a coroner. I am the Frida Kahlo of the underworld. Coco Chanel with a golden sewing machine. I do more heavy lifting than the Virgin Mary, her royal chasteness, her hands idle and white. Once, I was a beautiful woman. Men got on their knees for me. They begged to slip their hands under my satin dress, snap my black garter, bury their faces in my breasts. I opened their presents, parakeets in tin cages, oleander soap, saffron.

Now there is nothing but the work.

I begin with the eyes. The embroidery is taxing and can't be rushed. It takes hundreds of silk stitches—brown, blue, emerald, overlapping— to make eyes that endure for eternity. They let you speak without saying a word. You could say "I love you" and you could say "Screw you" and you could say "Pass the *bolillos* and butter."

With a warm sponge, I wash limbs, scrub skin until it gleams like marble. At first, I dreaded the heavy ones, all that fat to work around, but I have become a person of greater sympathy, softening as I age. The children make quick work. So beautiful, so small.

After I drain the blood, I fill the body with an elixir of mint leaves and pomegranate, sprigs of basil, lemon juice, cinnamon, a dash of ouzo. The flesh regains its color, its heat and sensation. My hand pump keeps a steady pace. Each limb I massage in turn. I allow myself the occasional break. Smoke a cigarette. Why not? I am already dead.

The final touches—nails, lips, tongue. I sprinkle the hair with marigold oil and henna until it shines. The feet are often disastrous. I have seen toenails as gray and brittle as shale, and every kind of fungus. If it's bad enough, I pour myself a drink. I can work well high. I am the Pancho Villa of Purgatory. I am the Edith Piaf of Paradise. Some people do not recognize themselves. They say, "This isn't me at all. You have confused me with another." But death cannot remedy what life has spoiled. Each day, you make the face you live and die with. A saint is not a magician.

Go and live now. Use yourself up.

I'll be here waiting. The handmaiden of humanity. The auntie of the afterlife. The bitch of the great beyond. I will darn your eyes and scrub your teeth and water your mouth and hem your belly and perfume your earlobes with lilac.

Don't thank me. No one does. I am just a skeleton paying for her sins.

twenty-one | THE HOUSEKEEPER

Soledad found Hugo back at the cottage, shaking under a blanket, murmuring nonsense about an eighth omen, a burning temple, a fallen empire.

"Don't worry, my love," she whispered. "Tonight, we go."

She made a beeline to the Malones' pink house, ran up to her mistress's bedroom. She opened her jewelry box, lifting the gold to judge its heft. In Constance's underwear drawer, under push-up bras and silk slips, lay a stash of dollars bundled with a rubber band. Soledad had asked the Virgin Mary about the morality of stealing from the wife of the man who had shot her husband, and the Virgin told her to take enough to pay for medical bills, back wages, and a new dress. In the bottom drawer, she discovered pesos and a gun, and collected those, too, holding the gun at arm's length like a dead mouse. She raced back to the cottage and said good-bye to her kitchen, the curtains, the honeysuckle breeze.

At dawn, she and Hugo began the long journey north on a second-class bus. They nibbled pork sandwiches and shared a bag of Sabritas. They held hands.

They arrived in Real de Catorce late in the day. The two-and-a-half-kilometer tunnel into the city was closed to cars because of a festival, so they entered in a horse-drawn carriage, clutching their bags in the half-light. Every minute, a carriage approached from the other direction. The shadowed faces of passengers whisked past them, stirring up the manure-laced breeze. Nauseated, Soledad nibbled salty crackers.

When they emerged, the city lay wide and open and bright. The air was thin at 2,750 meters and they panted up the hill, past vendors selling mementos of San Francisco de Asís. In the Templo de la Purísima Concepción, they prayed. It was the first time they had been to church together since their wedding. Soledad thanked the Virgin and asked for forgiveness. (Perhaps she had taken sufficient money to buy several dresses.) When she finished praying, Hugo's head was still bowed. Soledad wished she could read his mind—*What does he believe? Whom does he love?*—but it was enough to have him at her side.

He is mine now.

I no longer have any need to learn English. I have always hated English. It is not a musical language. Maybe I will learn Italian instead.

twenty-two | ANNA

An odd group gathered on the morning after the fire. Anna, her father, Salvador, the looter, and Chelo clustered around a patio table at the Puesta del Sol. The looter looked like he'd slept in his clothes. Chelo's hand rested on her belly, protecting her baby from the next threat, though the patio was peaceful, bathed in sunshine, smelling like butter. Already the idea of a man in a tiger's mask seemed like a dream, a *pesadilla*, not quite credible, replaced by the much more palpable threat of the fire, which Anna could still smell on her fingertips and taste in her throat. She had barely slept, thoughts churning about this meeting, how to make everything come out right.

Salvador was sketching in a notebook, his face wan and depleted. Only Daniel Ramsey seemed bright-eyed, sipping coffee from a styrofoam cup, nibbling a mint toothpick, tap-tapping a tourist map on the table's edge, like he had places to go. Anna had two masks in her pack: the death mask of Montezuma and a fake fashioned by Emilio Luna's brother. The looter would fall for a lie. The truth would be harder to sell.

"Thanks for coming," Anna said. "I thought we should talk about what to do now." She gave the genuine death mask to her father. "You can confirm the mask for us?"

Her father's face softened as he ran his fingers over its bumpy surface. The looter snapped to his feet, lit a smoke, began pacing.

"An amazing piece of history," Daniel Ramsey marveled. "Stunning workmanship, a true piece of art, and then when you consider its role in history . . ." He dropped his head, suddenly shy. "But as I told Anna last night, I don't want it."

The looter stopped cold. Salvador did a double take. Anna had been just as stunned when her father had told her. At first, she'd been angry. Was he too proud to accept her gift? Was he collecting something new? Medieval sheet music? Fertility dolls?

"I don't want anything." Daniel had used these same words the night before. "Collecting made me happy once, but it doesn't anymore. For years, I was chasing something that was already gone. I wanted my wife back and—"

He looked away, shrugged. "Maybe, in a strange way, I was looking for myself. *This is me. This is what I love.* Anyway"—he gave the mask a brisk salute—"the mask is precious, priceless, but it isn't mine. Even if I bought it."

He handed it back to Anna.

"Then it's settled," the looter said. "I'll take it to Marisol."

"Mari?" Anna twisted her shoulders. "Actually, I've been thinking . . . this might sound crazy . . . but maybe we should just put the mask back."

The looter glared. "In the chapel?"

"No," Anna said. "In the ground."

The looter cinched down his cap. Chelo read his body language. Understood trouble. "And why would we do that?" he said. "We had an agreement."

"Right, we did, but I don't need the mask anymore, and you could give Mari this other one." She handed him the reproduction. "It's the copy we had made. Frankly, it just doesn't feel right, stealing from the dead. Mari wouldn't approve of grave robbing. Bad karma. *Mala onda.*"

Chelo flinched. She understood those two words.

"Mala onda," the looter scoffed. "Speak for yourself. Good things are happening to me. Don't you want the money?"

Anna stared at the door of her shitty hotel room. She was becoming rather fond of it. The ceiling fan, despite appearances, had not fallen, and she'd been messing around with the old typewriter.

"Not this way," she said. "Some other way, maybe."

The looter kicked a chair, stubborn, sullen. Anna imagined that different versions of this same thing had happened to Christopher Maddox before. He'd failed a test of courage or character, disappointing those he'd most hoped to impress. She remembered how he'd looked in Tepito. Crazy eyes. Pistol jerking. That addict was still inside him, a skeleton from his past.

Anna said softly, "You could bring Mari some other wonderful thing." She repeated herself in Spanish.

Chelo whispered. The looter shook his head. Before it was settled, Chelo piped up in Spanish. "He could give Mari my needlepoint. He helped make it."

The looter gazed at her with wonder. "You should see this thing. It started out just a bunch of holes, but she's colored in the whole Virgin Mary."

Chelo looked worried. *"¿No te gusta?"* The two of them bowed their heads, conferring, this time loud enough for Anna to hear.

"Of course I like it. But I couldn't ask you."

"You didn't ask. I offered."

"We could sell the mask. Buy a house for the baby. That's a lot of money to—"

"Not that way."

The looter swore, kicked the bricks, outvoted by the women he'd come to trust. "All right, then. Back it goes."

Anna lowered her shoulders. "You think you can find the cave?"

"You would hope. I spent two days down there."

"You'd have to seal it up somehow."

The looter perked up. "I could set an explosive and send a bunch of rock flying down. No one would ever find it."

Salvador winced. "How about a shovel?"

"That would work, too."

No one said anything. The mask had brought them together, but now nothing bound them, like a cast after its final performance. The looter, in particular, seemed reluctant to part. He put his arm awkwardly around Chelo. "I'm going to be a father."

"¿Sabes si es un niño o una niña?" Anna asked Chelo.

"I think it's a boy." The girl looked happy, proud.

When Anna presented the fake mask to Lorenzo Gonzáles, the dealer didn't even bother to pull out his magnifying glass. He was short with her. No pompous lectures about antiquities or the role of the collector.

"It's a cheap reproduction." He pushed the mask back at her. "I have no use for it."

Anna did her best to look shocked. "With all your connections, I'm sure you could find the right buyer."

Gonzáles leaned in, curious now. "And who is the right buyer for such a mask?"

"A collector with discriminating taste and unlimited funds. Someone who lost a precious mask and urgently wants it back for an upcoming show. In fact, if such a mask appeared in a rival's show, the dealer might be blamed for having, well, screwed things up."

Anna smiled sweetly.

Lorenzo Gonzáles gave her a look of pure hatred. He reached into a strongbox.

Anna couldn't resist one final jab. "I understand you've done a great job renovating your bathroom. Perhaps you'd give me a tour."

Gonzáles stiffened. "Tell me how much this treasure costs."

"It's very expensive," Anna said, cheerily. "But I'm sure you could resell it for a handsome profit."

"Yes, I suppose I could."

"You've heard the line '*Art is what you can get away with*'?"

The fat man brightened ever so slightly. "That's good. Who said it?"

"Another man who loved masks," Anna said. "Andy Warhol."

Anna fed a sheet of paper into the manual typewriter. She typed without thinking. She did not check her facts.

I've worn a mask most of my life. Most people do. As a little girl, I covered my face with my hands, figuring if I couldn't see my father, he couldn't see me. When this didn't work, I hid behind Halloween masks: clowns and witches and Ronald McDonald. Years later, when I went to Mexico, I understood just how far a mask can take you. In the dusty streets, villagers turned themselves into jaguars, hyenas, the devil himself. For years, I thought wearing a mask was a way to start over, become someone new. Now I know better. A mask doesn't change who you are; it lets you be the person you've always been, the person you paper over out of habit or timidity or fear. Some people—people like me—have to try on a lot of faces before they find one that fits.

She ripped out the sheet and placed it in a folder. *There. A start.* Salvador was right: she didn't hate masks, though she would never collect them. Instead, she would write a book, part history, part memoir. She would interview carvers—with Salvador's help, yes, she *did* need a guide, or better, a partner—and weave their tales together with the story of her own family: her parents' collection, the accident, the hunt for the death mask.

Anna lifted the mescal bottle. *Para todo mal, mezcal, y para todo bien también.* It was tempting. Tonight, maybe. Or tomorrow. But not alone anymore. Not every vice of her father's need be her own. She gazed out the window. Patio. Cherub. Pristine sky. She shuddered. Thomas Malone was out there. Somewhere. Everyone was somewhere, even when they were lost.

twenty-three | THE LOOTER

He had never been in a cave sober,
and in this old haunt, his craving for meth slammed against him, a flat
iron searing his heart. *I want you. You want me. Don't pretend otherwise.*
In his memory, he'd built the cave to be a magical place, but it was a
piss hole. Lighter, straws, tinfoil, razor blades. Artifacts of his mean
existence. He was a grave robber. His chest tightened at the thought.
What if, when he died, Chelo buried him with his dog or favorite boots,
and some cranked-up nobody stole his stuff? Sold it to a fucking
museum. Sold package deals to church groups. Who had that right?

He pulled out the mask, hunched down, back smarting. He'd lost
the flexibility for this sort of contortion. He stuck his trowel in the
ground. An amazing idea came to him. He was such an idiot. Montezuma wasn't buried with *just* a mask. A king would be buried with an
urn, jewelry, royal who-the-fuck-knew-what. Emperor shit. Loot. He'd

been so damn tweaked he'd run off without digging deeper. Once again, he'd stopped short.

It wasn't too late to say *Screw you, Anna.* Pawn the mask in Tepito, get high as a gargoyle. Come back. Dig this place dry. Who was this Anna to tell him what was right? Pico awaited. Pimply Pico and his brown bag of goodies. He could turn Chelo on. They could smoke ice and do needlepoint. Finish the Virgin in twenty-four hours.

The death mask wasn't the end; it was the beginning.

Shivering, he curled into a ball, held himself, hating himself, stopping himself from being himself, whimpering *nonononono.* How could one sweet Mexican girl save Colorado's trash? He was a looter. A walking corpse. Rocking now. Crying. Piece of shit that he was. Fucking baby. Baby. Baby. He was going to be a father. Baby. He was sobbing now. Baby. His heart shook. *Focus on the baby.* He didn't know shit about babies. Why would any baby love him? *Focus, asshole.* Okay, the Gerber baby. Fat cheeks. Mouth open. Goo-goo eyes. Baby. Applesauce. Pureed peaches. Steady. *Focus.* Your son. That was easier. *Your son.* Throwing a ball in the yard. Hamburger smell. Beer can. Cute kid. American Dream. Fatherhood. Dad. Daddy. Da-da. Da.

He could die here with the mask. Just let his heart explode.

He uncoiled, jammed the mask in the crevasse, let it go. Inching backward, he grabbed his shovel, hurled dirt, filling in the hole before he changed his mind. What was the opposite of looting? Burial. Consecration. Dedication. *Hallowed be Thy name.* He was going to have a son. Baby. You could sing to a baby. Baby. He sang now, the Grateful Dead. Jerry Garcia's honeycomb voice. *There is a road, no simple highway, between the dawn and the dark of night.*

The job got done. It was easier to bury things than reveal them. He'd known that ever since he'd had something to hide. He crawled into the sun, thinking, *Adiós, amigo.* Christopher Maddox, the college dropout from Divide, Colorado, was never climbing into another cave. He wasn't a looter anymore. He was Cruise Maddox, honest man, expectant father. That was something. Good enough for today. Tomorrow. Amen.

twenty-four | THE PAPERSHOP GIRL

On the eighteenth day, the papershop girl received his letter. She read it once, folded it into her diary, then went to the bathroom and looked in the mirror. A wavy line creased her forehead, a gentle but unmistakable groove, her first wrinkle. Timeline. Tightrope. Arrow. The girl studied it until she made up her mind.

That night, she tiptoed to her parents' bedroom. Her skin smelled like almonds and her heels were soft and her chest rose and fell as her heart beat like a blacksmith's anvil. She wore her lace gloves, and her nightgown was thin as a shadow; sparkling script stitched across the front read: *Salma Hayek Versión 4.* The girl went to the bed where her parents slept, and pressed a kitchen knife to her father's neck. He woke at the prick and gasped, *"Hija,"* and she hissed, *"No me toques. No me vuelvas a tocar."*

Don't touch me. Don't ever touch me again.

twenty-five | THE MEXICO CITY NEWS

OAXACA—For generations, art historians have disagreed over whether the Aztec Emperor Montezuma II was buried with a mask, and if so, if it would ever be found. The hunt now appears over.

The highlight of the Galería Xolotl's thrilling new show, "The Many Faces of Mexico," is a 16th century mosaic mask that scholars believe was the emperor's death mask. The turquoise mask has conch-shell teeth. Two intertwined snakes cross the forehead, the royal sign of Montezuma.

"This is an astounding discovery," said Lorenzo Gonzáles, retired director of the Anthropology Museum of Oaxaca. "As the mask has no eye openings for the wearer to see through, we know this is a funerary mask. I only wish we had it for the museum."

The show is the first public viewing of the collection of private businessman Óscar Reyes Carrillo. With works from all 31 states, the collection offers a colorful panorama of Mexican history, from antiquities to contemporary Carnival masks. Reyes said he purchased the Aztec mask from a Swiss collector, who wishes to remain anonymous.

"Everyone loves masks," said Reyes, who arrived at his opening wearing a Lucha Libre wrestling bodysuit, a face mask, and a pair of *chuntaro* cowboy boots with pointy foot-long toes. "Because everyone has something to hide."

A second mask collection, belonging to Thomas Malone, an American living in Oaxaca, was supposed to be shown at La Fábrica Gallery. The two rivals characterized the twin openings as an artistic duel and jousted openly in the press about whose collection would trump the other. But Malone abruptly canceled his show after a fire burned down the chapel where his masks were stored. Most of his collection was destroyed. Malone could not be reached for comment, but his wife, Constance Malone, said a falling candle ignited the blaze.

"The Malone affair is a tragedy," Reyes said. "But people who cannot safeguard art should stop collecting."

Montezuma II ruled his vast empire from Tenochtitlán when Spanish conquistador Hernán Cortés arrived from Spain in 1519. Montezuma lived in opulence, with a staff of cooks, wives, servants and concubines. Visitors to his chambers were required to wear simple robes and enter barefoot. They were not permitted to look the ruler in the eye. Indeed, one account maintains that no one had ever seen Montezuma's face.

twenty-six | ANNA

She dreamt she was riding a fast train, past olive trees and slate-blue hills. She sat alone. Without warning, the train shot under a tunnel and the car went dark. Pressure built in her ears. She yawned to release it. This first yawn led to a second, a third, to a yawn so wide her mouth got stuck, open, gaping. Her eyes watered. She screamed but no sound came out. And still the train went faster, rushing deeper and deeper underground.

Anna woke up with a cry. It took a minute to remember where she was. She shook Salvador. "I need to talk to you."

"Tell me in the morning." His voice was groggy. "It will be better then."

Anna said no. She needed to tell him now. He dragged himself up and they sat side by side and he listened as she told him about her days before David. How she followed a rock band and was passed among players. How she'd wander home barefoot from parties, still wearing a cocktail dress, having no memory of the night before. How later, in the city, she had met a married man and he kept an apartment for her. Nothing in it but a bed, two chairs, champagne and crackers. How he gave her money that she justified as gifts. How she stopped speaking to friends, filling the fridge from his charge account at the gourmet shop, little boxes of overpriced salads that she gobbled down with chopsticks, always hungry. She dropped to 105 pounds, worked as temp, fact-checking articles and books, losing herself in reference materials, the Web, the Library of Congress. She liked confirming information. Facts. The census. Anything undeniably true. That the sun had shone on a certain April morning in 1932. The chance one blue-eyed parent and one brown-eyed parent would create a child with blue eyes. The man never kissed her. He never spent the night.

"How did it end?"

Anna shut her eyes. "He arranged for me to meet his friend. I thought we were all having a dinner together, but when I got there, the friend invited me in and he had a bottle of wine and two glasses. Two hundred-dollar bills lay on top of the napkin. I told him there had been a mistake."

She released each word, a bird from a cage.

Salvador buried her head into his chest. "Is that it? Is that the worst?"

Anna said it was.

"Okay, then. It's my turn."

She checked his face to see if he was making fun of her, but he turned her head so he could whisper in her ear.

He told her all manner of things. And she listened.

twenty-seven | THE CARVER

Emilio Luna rose from bed and felt, though his furrowed hands attested otherwise, that he was still a young man. The mask carver made coffee, padded onto the concrete patio of his home in San Juan del Monte, a hill town outside Oaxaca. His tools lay strewn in yesterday's wood chips. The air smelled like cedar. He bent to touch his toes, came close, reached toward the sky, came close, hiked his pants, sat down on his tree stump, propping a pillow behind his back.

A familiar figure appeared, pushing open his gate with an air of entitlement. He was tall and lean. His eyes flickered, candle flames in the wind.

"Buenos días, Emilio Luna."

The carver greeted his guest cautiously. It was rare to see Thomas

Malone in the village. Emilio Luna did not like selling the American his masks, but what choice did he have? He had his pride, but he also had a belly. Every man, woman, and child came to him with a hand open wide. The old man stood. Compromise was its own sort of courage.

"*Buenos días, señor.* It gives me much happiness to see you in our village today. I have finished a mask that is perfect for you."

The collector looked older, his cheeks gaunt. He was using a cane. *Someone died, or he has suffered an illness or loss. His good faith has been shaken or his bad faith confirmed.*

"Have you been well?" The old carver had heard rumors, but wasn't sure what to believe. He showed Malone a chair.

The collector sat, rested his cane. "Give a man a mask and he will tell you the truth."

Emilio Luna passed him a tiger from the pile. With a weak smile, Malone took it and stared down the road, as if something better was waiting there, like he wanted to get it first. And Emilio Luna thought: *He would take the sun from the sky if he could reach it.*

The American said, "Even ugly things become beautiful after sixty years."

"That's good news for me."

"You can't tell people the truth all the time. It would crush them."

"Like medicine, you must serve only a spoonful."

"But every day you can start over. More directed. More precise."

"I carve a new tiger each morning."

Malone handed back the mask. "A collection begins with a single decision, one right choice. You find something you love. Set it apart. Say, *I will build a world around it.*"

A cool tremor passed through Emilio Luna's chest. He'd carved this man's face many times. Different versions of the same thing.

"*Señor,* you prefer the front room or the back today?"

The carver kept his voice neutral, as if he didn't know the answer already. The *señor* motioned down the steps. The two men crossed the patio. Emilio lifted the curtain door. It was dark inside, as always.

twenty-eight | CRUISE

Tickets in hand, they waited in the second-class bus station. It was an hour ride to the town where Mari lived. Chelo had to use the bathroom. She went all the time now, and Cruise kept expecting her to return with a baby nicely wrapped in a blanket.

"*¿Estás bien?*" he asked.

She licked her braces and smiled. It was getting like he needed to see that smile a couple of times an hour to feel right.

"*No te preocupes,*" she said, patting his shoulder. Don't worry.

She hoisted herself out of her plastic seat and waddled to the ladies' room. From the back, she didn't look pregnant. Cruise was pretty certain that baby was his even though he hadn't been there at the start. God would see to it. God would make sure the baby looked like him, because he was the one who'd stood by her. The asshole deserter didn't deserve to have his face plastered all over the place. Jesus looked like Joseph, not God. If Jesus looked like God, he would have been some fucked-up-looking dude no one would have trusted.

Cruise checked his dope, then stashed it away. He liked knowing it was there. Sometimes that was enough. He touched his skin. Even the raw parts had healed. He peeked at the needlepoint Chelo had wrapped in white tissue paper. The best presents were the ones you made yourself. His grandmother had taught him that.

Eleven minutes before the bus departed, three men in black burst through the terminal doors, guns drawn. Feo. Alfonso. Some other punk. Passengers dove under chairs, making animal noises. Cruise darted up, careened to the back exit, where the empty buses parked. Chelo came out of the restroom. She looked thin in her sundress and flip-flops. How could such skinny ankles support not one life, but two? He should have bought her decent shoes. He held up his hand to stop her.

The gunmen spread into a triangle. Cruise screamed for Chelo. She reached across the length of the bus station like she was the golden eagle of Mexico, who could pluck him in her beak and ferry him to safety.

A dispatcher with a microphone told people to stay down, then ducked under the counter. Gunfire erupted. Black guns. Black noise. Milky movement. Cruise felt a warm explosion in his belly. It spread to his heart. He saw the Virgin and knew she was kind.

twenty-nine | CHELO

After she'd kissed his cool forehead, collected his satchel, watched the police chalk the fallen silhouette on the tiles, after the crowd had pressed in, snapping pictures on their phones, and then, bored by the slowness of justice, dispersed, after his body had been draped in a stained sheet and carried outside, after the bus dispatcher had promised *normal service will resume,* after she'd returned to the bathroom to vomit, peed again, rinsed her mouth clean, wiped her shattered eyes, smoothed her face in the mirror—the woman staring back looked frightened, faint, as if she might dissolve in water— after she'd felt the baby kick and roll a warm turn in her womb, after she'd walked outside and seen the sun was still shining and cursed God for this indecency, after she'd climbed on the bus and secured an aisle seat, looking pregnant and irritable, so no one would sit next to her, after the driver had thrown the lumbering bus into reverse and merged into midday traffic and she'd slid over to the window and pinched her forearm in birdlike chirps—*You are still alive, both of you*—after she'd prayed to the Virgin for courage and told him, for the first time, that she loved him, dead or alive, she checked the needlepoint. It was safe.

The Virgin spoke softly. *"I will watch over you."*

She would bring their offering to Mari.

She would have their baby.

She would name their child after him.

Cruz.

thirty | ANNA

Anna sat at a wrought-iron table at the Puesta del Sol, studying the future tense. It was hard to conjugate but not impossible. Salvador drove up, parked his bike. Anna watched him from a distance, eager for him to come close.

"*¿Lista?*" He pointed back at his bike. "I brought apples and two beers."

Anna closed her book. "I brought you a present. Actually, both of us. Two masks."

"I thought we were done with masks."

"This is different."

Salvador opened the box, pulled back the newspaper, and laughed. "I am not sure the nose is big enough." He made a sad clown face. "All these years, I thought I was a handsome man." It was a mask of his face. "Let's see the other one."

Blond hair, green eyes, the impatient smile of a woman who wasn't sure where she was going but wanted to get there fast—indisputably Anna.

"Yours is good," Salvador said. "Put it on. We'll see if anyone recognizes us."

They tied on the masks, breathing in freshly cut cedar. The wood held no patina. No history. No dirt or sweat. Salvador climbed on the motorcycle. Anna slipped behind him. She tucked her yellow blouse into her jeans.

It didn't take long to reach the country. Wildflowers bent in the wind they made. The agave waved octopus arms. The road dropped into a canyon that smelled of mushrooms and moss. *There you'll find the place I love most in the world. The place where I grew thin from dreaming.* A sign warned CURVA PELIGROSA. Their bodies leaned together, riding the engine, achieving, as they rounded the bend, both speed and balance. They passed a shrine, a simple cross decorated with flowers. The wind made a wailing sound, like a call from the grave. Anna shivered, remembering Constance. *Death. Death everywhere. Who wants to think about it?* She touched her amulet of San Antonio. Patron saint of lost people and things. Patron saint of the traveler.

She gave thanks, gripped Salvador tighter.

When they rode out of the canyon into the sunlight, Anna lifted her mask and rested it on her head like a visor. The warm breeze touched her face. Above them, *todo azul.* They would find a strong tree and eat lunch under it. They would take a picture to be sure her father approved. Their masks had not been danced yet, but they would fix that tonight.

No hay mal que por bien no venga.

The good salvaged from the terrible.

ACKNOWLEDGMENTS

This is my first work of fiction, and I had a lot of help. Without Gail Greiner, there would be no book. Without Floating House, the book would still not be finished. My wonderful agent, Molly Friedrich, supported me at every juncture with her intelligence, wit, and affection. I am forever grateful to Marian Wood, editor supreme, who believed in the Tiger and fought for it, and Anna Jardine, the brilliant copy editor who saved me more than a thousand times.

Many friends read early drafts and provided advice and encouragement: Sarah McAdams, Greg Schwipps, Chris White, Dan Barden, Anastasia Wells, Susan Hahn, Gigi Fenlon, Barbara and Tony Graham, Dan Pool, Cindy O'Dell, Jonathan Coleman, Tom Chiarella, Claudia Mills, Alejandro Puga, Rebecca Schindler, and Eugene Pool. I am lucky to have such generous friends.

ACKNOWLEDGMENTS

I am indebted to Craig Childs for his book *Finders Keepers*, a fascinating investigation of the philosophical and practical controversies surrounding archaeological excavation. Several key lines of this novel come from his book, including the opening epigraph and "Even ugly things become beautiful after sixty years." Also this passage, which I slightly altered: "We threaten to devour the world with all our touching, starting with the things we adore most."

The *retablos* were adapted from the book *Infinitas Gracias* by Alfredo Vilchis Roque and Pierre Schwartz. Other books I used for reference include: *Folk Wisdom of Mexico* by Jeff M. Sellers; *Masks of Mexico* by Barbara Mauldin; *Mask Arts of Mexico* by Ruth D. Lechuga and Chloë Sayer; and *El Sicario: The Autobiography of a Mexican Assassin*, edited by Molly Molloy and Charles Bowden. The translation from the Huehuetlatolli comes from *Handbook to Life in the Aztec World*, by Manuel Aguilar-Moreno. The excerpts of *Pedro Páramo* are from the English translation by Margaret Sayers Peden.

Many thanks to the John and Janice Fisher Fund at DePauw University and to the Great Lakes Colleges Association's New Directions Initiative, funded by the Andrew W. Mellon Foundation.

Finally, I want to thank Peter, Madeline, and Lincoln, my dear family, my fellow travelers, who mean the world to me.